Lizzie's War

Rosie Clarke

W F HOWES LTD

This large print edition published in 2017 by
W F Howes Ltd
Unit 5, St George's House, Rearsby Business Park,
Gaddesby Lane, Rearsby, Leicester LE7 4YH

1 3 5 7 9 10 8 6 4 2

First published in the United Kingdom in 2016
by Aria

A CIP catalogue record for this book is available
from the British Library

ISBN 978 1 51005 174 4

Typeset by Palimpsest Book Production Limited,
Falkirk, Stirlingshire

Printed and bound by
Printforce Nederland b.v., Alphen aan den Rijn,
The Netherlands

PROLOGUE

'When shall I see you again?' Lizzie's throat was tight with tears as she looked at the man she loved. 'I know you can't tell me where you're going or what you'll be doing and I don't want to know – but you will come home again one day? Promise me!'

'Oh, Lizzie, Lizzie Larch,' Sebastian said and drew her to him in a loving embrace, kissing her mouth softly, tenderly, his fingers caressing her cheek as he gazed deep into her eyes. 'I love you, my darling, and one day I'll come home for longer and we'll marry . . . but don't expect it to be next week or next month or perhaps even next year. I may be away for months, even years. I simply can't tell you.'

'I know. I'm sorry,' Lizzie said. 'It's just that things have been so awful since Harry died – and I've never been so happy . . . this Christmas has been the best of my life . . .' Sebastian had insisted on buying a tree and lots of gifts for her and Betty, even though at only a few months old, Lizzie's darling daughter was much too young to appreciate them, but Lizzie had, and the way Sebastian

1

had behaved as though Betty was his own child; it was a promise he'd made her, unspoken but understood. Despite the few times they'd met over the last couple of years, mostly while she was working for Harry's uncle, for Lizzie it seemed as if she'd known him all her life. She instinctively knew that he was the man she should have married, if only she'd waited rather than let Harry rush her into marriage after her aunt died.

Sebastian drew the line of her cheek, his finger trailing down her white throat to the pulse spot at the base. 'Be brave for me, my Lizzie, and before you know it all this pain and horror will be over – tell me you understand that I have to do what I'm doing – please?'

Lizzie blinked away the tears and smiled. 'Of course I do and I'm being silly and stupid, Sebastian. Go, leave now, before I beg you to stay.'

Sebastian kissed her one last time on the mouth, all the passion he felt pouring into that embrace so that Lizzie felt his need and desire and wished with all her heart that they'd made love. Yet it was by mutual consent that they'd waited, because, as Sebastian said, they really hadn't ever had time to get to know one another, for him to court her – and he'd certainly done that these past few days, taking her everywhere, buying her presents of flowers and chocolates and a beautiful diamond and aquamarine ring.

It was too soon after her husband's death the previous September and the birth of Harry's daughter Betty, for Lizzie to marry again. Although Sebastian was instantly enchanted with the child when Lizzie showed him her beloved daughter, they'd decided not to rush into marriage, or even to bed, because Sebastian wanted Lizzie to get to know and trust him and to feel loved, so he hadn't even asked, but now she wished with all her heart that he had.

Lizzie watched as he went out into the dingy street outside the workshops and got into the sleek black car waiting to whisk him away. He was clearly important to the war effort; she'd realized that even though he'd been able to tell her absolutely nothing of his work – and yet the attitude of people they'd met at the theatre and when dining out told Lizzie all she needed to know. Men in expensive suits, and high-ranking officers' uniforms showed Sebastian the same respect. She'd felt a little shy, because they came from a different world, and yet with Sebastian at her side she'd held her head high and kept a smile on her face.

Perhaps Sebastian was right when he said she had to learn to trust him, because there was a wide gap between her life as a milliner making pretty hats in the East End of London and his as a gentleman and now an officer. Lizzie had dismissed Sebastian's pursuit of her as mere flirtation when they first met, because he liked to flirt with pretty women, and she couldn't accept that she meant more to him than all the others.

'Why?' she'd asked him once when they were

dining at the Mayfair Hotel. 'Why me, when there are so many beautiful women in the world, Sebastian? I'm not exceptional . . .'

'Maybe that's why,' he said, and she knew he was laughing at her. 'Maybe it's because you kept saying no . . .'

Glancing at the lovely diamond ring on the third finger of her left hand, from which she'd removed Harry's wedding ring, Lizzie shook her head. It would be ridiculous to let the doubts creep in, especially when she might not see Sebastian for months or even years. A swingeing pain caught at her heart as she faced the prospect of all those lonely days and nights without him, because if she'd ever doubted her own love for him, she didn't doubt it now. She knew she loved him with all her being, and she didn't know what she would do if he didn't return as he'd promised.

It was all very well for Sebastian to claim that bad pennies always turned up, as he had so often in the past when he'd visited Oliver's showroom, and the workshops where Lizzie had learned her trade as a milliner, but they both knew that during a war anything could happen . . . but then, Lizzie acknowledged, people were dying on the home front too. Only a few streets from here and, a few hundred yards from her friend Beth's mother's home, a young woman and her two small children had died in one of the first of the constant raids London was now enduring. Since then a great many people had met their end in the smouldering rubble left by Hitler's bombs, particularly in the industrial heart of the city. The destruction over the Christmas period had been so bad that every street seemed to have been hit and there were piles of rubble everywhere. Yet she couldn't allow herself to dwell on the fear that Sebastian would not return to her.

Lizzie knew that she had to get on with her life. Sebastian's love would help her to be brave and endure all the hardships as she waited for him to return. In the meantime, it was nearly the New Year, 1941, and Beth's family was expecting her to have dinner with them on New Year's Day, which was also Beth's brother's birthday and would be a double celebration, because he was home on leave from the Army. Ed, Lizzie's right-hand man in the new workshops she'd set up to design and make her beautiful hats, had been invited too and she knew he was looking forward to it, because he led a rather lonely life now that his wife Madge was dead; she'd been an invalid since the birth of her stillborn child, but he'd loved her and missed her . . .

For the sake of her friends, Lizzie must carry on and be cheerful, even if it did feel just at this moment as if her heart had been broken . . .

CHAPTER 1

'I like the look of that,' Beth said as she stopped by Lizzie's workbench, that morning, watching while she shaped her latest creation for *Lizzie Larch Hats*, the fledgling business she had begun some weeks after Harry's uncle had sacked her from his workshops. The straw boater was pale blue, a simple flat crown with a small brim; trimmed with a contrast ribbon and a large satin bow. 'It's just my colour too . . .'

'Yes, I know.' Lizzie smiled. She dearly loved Beth, who was like the sister she'd never had. They'd met when they'd both applied for a job at Bert Oliver's workshops and been fast friends ever since. 'I had you in mind when I started this, Beth – it would be nice as a going-away hat for your wedding . . .'

'If I ever decide to get married,' Beth said ruefully. 'Bernie asked me again last night, Lizzie. I don't know what to do.'

Beth's lover Mark had been in the merchant navy and died at the very beginning of the war. Ever since the twins were born, Bernie, her boss at the munitions factory, had been asking Beth to marry him, but she wasn't sure of her feelings.

'You're happy the way you are, living together at the house with the twins, and working here – aren't you?' Lizzie finished smoothing the bow and leaned forward to set the hat on Beth's head. 'Little present to cheer you up, love. Wedding or no wedding.'

Beth preened before the long cheval mirror. 'You always know what suits me, but you must let me pay something, Lizzie. You give me far too much as it is.'

'I like to give you presents. Until now I never had anybody to spoil and nothing to give,' Lizzie told her. 'It's nearly spring so think of it as an early Easter present. I wish I could tell you what to do for the best, love, but I don't honestly know. My marriage to Harry wasn't perfect . . .' She shook her head, remembering Harry's jealousy and the way he'd forced himself on her in anger during a drunken night, because he'd thought she was flirting with his friend Roger. Harry's behaviour had forged a wedge between them and things had gone downhill after that. For a while he'd stayed away, not coming home when he'd had leave from serving with the RAF and Lizzie had been glad of it, but then, just before their daughter was born, she'd wanted to try and make it up with him. Her letter had brought the desired response and he'd promised to come home on his next leave, but his car had left the road and hit a tree . . . and his death had brought back all the sorrow and waste of those months apart. Then Sebastian had come back into her life for a few glorious days at Christmas and she'd known what her heart had told her for months, that he was the man she loved but since then all she'd had was the occasional postcard from Scotland to say he was all right – but Lizzie knew he wasn't there. He was somewhere else doing secret work for the government. The postcards were just for reassurance; he'd told her to expect them, because while they kept coming it meant he was still alive.

'That was a big sigh,' Beth looked at her oddly. 'I know it's only a few months since Harry was killed, Lizzie, but you are all right – aren't you?'

'Yes, of course I am,' Lizzie assured her. Harry had been killed the previous September and she'd given birth to her daughter a few hours later in the midst of an air raid. Now it was almost April 1941 and her grief had become just a vague ache that lingered. 'Harry and I hadn't been close for a while, as you know. Besides, I'm lucky to have such good friends – you, Ed and your mum. She's so good to us, Beth, looking after the children so that we can both work. And there's Sebastian, of course . . .'

Beth understood that Sebastian was a special friend, but even she hadn't guessed how special. Lizzie hadn't wanted to talk about it too much, because it was all so new and she still couldn't

9

believe that it was real and that the ring Sebastian had given her was not just an illusion.

'He's never around though is he?' Beth frowned. 'I should've thought if he's in Scotland at one of those training places he could get down to London more. He isn't messing you around, is he?'

'No of course not,' Lizzie said turning away, because she couldn't tell anyone, even her best friend, that she knew Sebastian wasn't in Scotland. If he'd been in the regular forces, she could have shared her worries over his safety, but Sebastian's work was secret. He hadn't told her where he was going, though she had a feeling it might be behind enemy lines, but that was just instinct and something she must never discuss, even with Beth. 'Is your mum feeling better now? She looked so tired yesterday.'

'Mum loves all the kids, but that cold pulled her down last month,' Beth said looking thoughtful. 'She would always have them for us whenever she could . . .'

'It's nothing serious, I hope?' Lizzie was suddenly anxious. 'She isn't finding three babies too much?'

'No, of course not; she's in her element,' Beth hesitated, then, 'Dottie isn't always too pleased about it, though. She takes her Sheila round to Mum, but she won't ask her to babysit if she's looking after ours. She had a go at me about it the other day – and of course Mary is pregnant. Her baby is due any time now . . .'

'Is that what's worrying you? You feel as if you

ought to marry Bernie so that you could stay at home with the twins and your mother wouldn't be so tied and could help your sisters out?'

'Well, sort of,' Beth nodded. 'Bernie would be a good father to the twins. He would love them as if they were his – even now he acts as though he's their father. Sometimes when I get back from work he's sitting there with the kids and Mum, and he's forever bringing them presents; Mum and me get things too, a packet of tea or tinned food and sometimes flowers.'

These days, with so many shortages in the shops, a packet of tea or a tin of fruit was like gold dust, and Lizzie wondered how a man like Bernie Wright, the manager of a local munitions factory, was able to get such things – unless he just gave up his own rations for their sake.

'Bernie is all right,' Lizzie agreed. He'd stood by Beth all the way through her pregnancy, despite knowing she wasn't married. 'Would you give up your work here if you got married, Beth?'

'I should think he would expect it,' Beth sighed. 'I could have your little Betty sometimes and that would release Mum to look after Dottie's kids now and then.'

'You shouldn't get married just for that, Beth. We could afford to pay for someone to look after the children, and neither of us works the whole day.' After Lizzie inherited her uncle's house, they'd decided to live and work together, taking it in turns to go home and put the children to bed.

It was more often Beth who went early, and Lizzie sometimes regretted those moments she missed when Betty was warm, smelling of talcum and ready for a cuddle before bed.

'I'd better get off anyway. Mum will want to get on with the dinner for Dad, so I'll pick the children up and take them home. What time should I expect you this evening?'

'I'll close the showroom at six, as usual,' she said at last. 'I've got a few ideas for new hats, but I can work on them at home once the children are in bed.'

'Did you get that big order finished? Ed was telling me that it was the biggest order we'd had since you opened.'

Lizzie nodded, pleased with herself. 'Yes, it is. Mr Barton used to be one of Oliver's customers and he saw our window display by chance, came inside and liked what he saw. I think he owns three exclusive shops, one in London, another in Birmingham and also Manchester. It was a rush, but Jean's coming along very nicely, and soon I shall be able to leave her to finish the simple cloches herself.'

'What we need is another Tilly,' Beth said. 'She's clever and she's wasted at Oliver's workshops now that he doesn't make stylish hats. I saw her in the market on Saturday and she was moaning about how boring it is these days, just concentrating on Government contracts . . .'

'Yes, I'd love to have Tilly with us, she was always

12

the best of Oliver's girls at trimming the hats' Lizzie agreed wistfully, 'but I couldn't approach her. Her husband works for Harry's uncle and . . .'

'Not any more. Tilly said Oliver sacked him because he was a bit late with a delivery once. Their little girl was ill and he took her to the doctor and that made him late back . . .'

'Surely Oliver didn't sack him for that?' Lizzie was shocked despite the way he'd treated her. She'd liked Harry's uncle when she worked for him, and he'd been straight with her – until he started to blame Lizzie for Harry's death. And then she'd been sacked and had to start up her own business. Although daunting, it had turned out well, because now she could make the stylish hats she loved with no one to tell her it couldn't be done. Working for Harry's uncle had been a wonderful opportunity for her and she had been grateful to him, which made it feel worse when he'd turned against her.

'Tilly said he's dreadful to work for these days, snaps at her all the time. I think she would jump at the chance to come here, Lizzie. You'd need her in the showroom if I married Bernie . . .'

Lizzie was thoughtful; she didn't particularly want to do anything that would give Harry's uncle cause to dislike her more than he already did. Tilly was one of his best workers and he would have a right to be angry if Lizzie approached her.

'I know Harry's uncle has never forgiven me for his death.'

'That is so unfair,' Beth fired up instantly. 'His death was an accident; Sebastian told you it came out afterwards that there was something wrong with the car's brakes, and it was in a dangerous condition, not fit to be on the roads. At the time, some people thought it might be suicide, because Harry had been behaving oddly and they thought he was cracking under the pressure of flying dangerous missions, but you can't think he killed himself, Lizzie?'

'I never have. I tried to tell his uncle it was an accident, but he wouldn't speak to me. He thinks it was something I did that made Harry stay away . . . that I was going with other men . . . I couldn't approach Tilly if she's still working for Oliver – but if her husband is out of work perhaps I could find him a job here . . .'

'Oh, no, he's working at the munitions factory now,' Beth reassured her. 'He asked Bernie for a job and he was glad to take him on. That wonky leg of his kept him out of the Army, but he's strong and he can do the heavy lifting the girls at the factory can't manage.'

'Oh, that's good for Tilly.' Lizzie felt pleased that Tilly's husband had found another job. 'You'd better go. Beth, or your mum will think you've had an accident . . .'

Lizzie went through to the showroom as Beth left. Her friend kept it neat and was good at setting out the hats to make them look attractive. Beth loved hats almost as much as Lizzie did herself, but even so, she liked to keep an eye on the displays. Although they'd done well in the few months the showroom had been open, Lizzie knew they needed more new customers if the business was to grow.

Ed was a marvel. He'd taught Lizzie most of what she knew about making hats, when he'd been the chief cutter at Oliver's. He loved her flair for design and encouraged her to go for the more fanciful ideas that came to her at times, but without Ed's advice and help, Lizzie might never have learned how to make her creations take shape. He was the one who had taught her how to get those delightful curvy brims and how to make some of the bolder designs hold their shapes. Together they had been a successful team and Lizzie had invited him to be her partner in the new business when Harry's uncle threw her out, and though she hadn't thought so then, it was the best thing that could've happened. Forced to stand on her own feet, she'd invested every penny of her own money, but despite his offers to put money in, she'd told Ed to keep his money for the moment. Fortunately, at his age, Ed was unlikely to be called up for the Army, especially as he'd told her about his fallen arches, which had resulted from years of standing at his bench.

'If I need extra money I'll ask,' she'd promised when he'd offered to invest his life savings. 'I've got some money that was left to me by my uncle and it's enough for now.'

Lizzie frowned as she thought about the business. The little showroom had been busy almost from the day they'd opened just before the previous Christmas, and they'd begun to make a small profit almost immediately, but just recently that profit had dropped a little. Not enough to be worrying, but it made Lizzie wonder if she could afford to take on an experienced seamstress like Tilly even if she asked her for a job. The large order from Mr Barton would help them become established and if he kept his promise to tell his friends and colleagues about her showroom, the business could become successful overnight.

Lizzie's reverie was suspended as the door opened and a young woman entered. She smiled nervously as she saw Lizzie and then looked about her at the various hats.

'Is it all right if I try some on?' she asked. 'I know *Lizzie Larch Hats* is a wholesaler's, but I was told you sometimes make special hats for weddings and things?'

'Yes, the shop is mainly wholesale,' Lizzie gave her an encouraging look, 'but we also have our bespoke hats. Are you looking for something special?'

'Yes,' the woman giggled. 'I'm getting engaged to – well, Geoff is my boss actually. He's got pots of money and I don't want his family to look down on me when I go to meet them . . . but I can't afford some of the prices up West.'

'They can be expensive.' Lizzie was sympathetic. A lot of young women looked at the beautiful hats in West End shops and dreamed of owning one but couldn't afford the extortionate prices, which was why she served the few working women who ventured in, as well as her main customers. 'Did you want felt or a straw – or silk? A lot of ladies are going for softer designs now, because of the war. This is my new line for spring – it's velvet and fits on the back of the head . . . we may not be able to get velvet soon if stocks run out . . .'

'That's all we hear when we complain, isn't it?' the young woman said and laughed. 'When you ask if the shop has anything nicer they say, "You know there's a war on, don't you?" It gets so boring.'

'Utility fashions aren't wonderful, are they?' Lizzie agreed. 'I quite like the broader shoulders, but the material isn't as good as we could get before the war started – that's where a beautiful hat makes all the difference. We've been lucky because so far they haven't made women have coupons for hats.'

'That's exactly what I thought,' the young woman said eagerly. 'I have a blue suit; it's new but it looks a bit dull, cheap. I thought a special hat would cheer it up . . .'

'I'm sure it would,' Lizzie said. 'Pale blue is it?'

'Yes, sort of sky blue, and I've got a white silk blouse to wear under it, second-hand but all right . . .'

'The war has made it difficult to buy nice things,' Lizzie nodded as she thought about the hats she had in stock. 'I have a lovely white straw hat I've just made, but it's still in the workroom. If you'd like to try a few others on, I'll fetch it for you.'

'Thanks ever so . . .'

Lizzie left the young woman to try on the hats and popped through to the back room. She picked up the white hat she'd made that morning. It was a broad-brimmed white straw hat finished with a pretty navy blue ribbon and a silk rose. She thought the simple style would look very well on the young woman waiting in the shop. Picking it up, she heard the shop bell go and frowned. Had someone come in or had the young woman gone?

She saw the showroom was empty as she returned and frowned. Why hadn't the customer waited? She'd seemed happy to do so and Lizzie had only been gone a couple of minutes. Glancing round the room, she saw that a red cloche with a silk rose trim and a navy blue straw fedora were missing from their stands and she rushed to the door to look out, but the narrow street was empty, apart from the back of a shabby van just disappearing round the corner. It was a commercial area, not far from the Docks, populated by tradespeople who often lived over their workshops, and most of the buildings were old, but, unusually, there was no one around.

Lizzie felt sick and humiliated as she went back inside and closed the door, locking it after her. She'd been duped and robbed and wasn't sure which hurt most. It wasn't time to close up, but she felt too upset to serve any more customers that evening. What an idiot she'd been to leave the woman in the shop even for a moment!

'I've finished for the day,' Ed said, coming in from the stockroom. 'We need a few things ordering, Lizzie. I'll do it tomorrow . . .' He stopped as he saw her face. 'What's wrong?'

'I've been an idiot,' she said and explained what had happened. Ed shook his head, his kind, homely face concerned for her.

'It's a good lesson learned,' he said. 'You're too trusting.'

'Yes, I suppose I am,' Lizzie said ruefully. 'Well, I shan't make that mistake again, shall I?'

'It's all right if you know and trust a customer, but even then be careful,' Ed said. 'Oliver had a few bad debts in the early years, but after that he wouldn't give anyone credit unless he knew them well. Some folk will take advantage if they can, but I'm not sure the police would be interested.'

'She seemed so unsure of herself and I wanted to help.' Lizzie shook her head and changed the subject. Telling the police would be a waste of time when they had more important things to do. 'What are you doing this evening, Ed?'

'Oh, I'll walk down to the pub for a pie and a pint,' he said. 'Same as usual. I might listen to Dick Barton on the radio. My Madge used to like the concerts – Henry Hall and the like, but I don't bother much these days. Just the news now and then . . .'

Lizzie nodded, knowing that he still missed the

19

wife he'd loved terribly. Her death in a fire caused by a gas explosion had shattered him. He'd lost his home that day too and for a while it had seemed that he'd no longer had the will to live, but working here with Lizzie he had found himself again. Yet she knew he must be lonely and she tried to invite him round every now and then even though she knew he was still grieving for his wife and didn't feel like going out much.

'You know you're always welcome to come to us for a meal, Ed?'

'Yes, I shall one Sunday . . .'

'Make it this Sunday,' Lizzie said. Ed looked pleased as he nodded then turned and went up to his flat above the workrooms.

Lizzie locked up the workrooms. She was glad Ed had decided to come, because he spent too much time alone.

Lizzie understood his loneliness. Three months had passed since she'd last seen Sebastian . . . had those few days over Christmas been as wonderful as she remembered? Had he really held her close and told her she was the only woman he'd ever loved – and had he meant it? Would he come back to her when the war was over or would she wake up and discover it was a dream and he'd simply been flirting with her after all?

Sebastian Winters had always believed in Lizzie's talent. From the start he'd wanted her to work for him in his West End shop, to design beautiful hats for the wealthy clients he served, but she'd resisted.

She'd thought he was a womanizer and would let her down, but she'd been wrong to listen to gossip as he'd turned out to be a better man than Harry. It was Sebastian who'd given her the courage to become what she'd always wanted to be – a designer of beautiful hats.

Lizzie had known that Sebastian wanted her, but she hadn't been sure just what that meant. If she'd trusted him at the start, refused to listen to idle talk she might have been his wife and her unhappy marriage would never have happened. She'd thought Harry loved her and she'd been grateful, eager to get away from the aunt who hated her, but Harry had set her on a pedestal and when he'd discovered the secret of her past, he'd been bitter and cruel in his disappointment. Sebastian knew nothing about the rape and miscarriage that had robbed Lizzie of more than a year of her life when she was fourteen and still an innocent child, of the months when she'd lain in hospital not knowing who she was or what had happened to her – she still didn't remember the attack, though she now knew that she'd been beaten and abused. For years she'd been allowed to believe that it was merely an accident and that was Uncle Jack's fault; he'd thought he was protecting her, but in the end her ignorance of the facts had led to unhappiness for both her and Harry. He'd thought her a virgin and when he'd discovered the truth he'd been so hurt and angry that it had destroyed their chance of happiness.

She would have to tell Sebastian the truth one day, but somehow she didn't think he would react as Harry had when he learned the truth on their wedding night. Sebastian didn't see her as some kind of a Vestal virgin – he thought of her as a desirable, talented woman he loved and wanted. He'd encouraged her talent for designing beautiful hats, and asked her to work for him, but she'd thought he was merely flirting. How she wished she'd waited instead of rushing into marriage with Harry, out of gratitude and loneliness.

Oh, how she wished Sebastian would be waiting for her when she got home! She wanted to have him close, to make a warm comfortable nest for them, and her lovely Betty, where they could be happy together as a family and all the pain and fear of the war would go away.

Home to Lizzie and Beth was the good solid house that her uncle had left her in his will, as recompense she sometimes thought. Uncle Jack had blamed himself for her accident, as he termed it, and his gift had made his wife Jane furious. She'd turned her hatred on Lizzie, almost ruining her life with her nagging and cruel accusations, but she was dead now and Lizzie had forgiven her. Her aunt had been a sad bitter woman and Lizzie couldn't hate her – even though what she'd done had contributed to Harry's jealousy. If only Lizzie had been told the truth about what had happened to her when she was fourteen, perhaps she would have found the courage to tell Harry before they married and everything would have been different. Yet a little voice in her head told her that her marriage had been a mistake, because she'd given into Harry's urgings before she'd known her own mind. She *had* loved him, but perhaps not enough to be his wife.

She pushed the regrets from her mind. It was time to go home to her friend and the children. Lizzie had offered Beth the chance to live with her when Beth's father had made it clear he didn't want her and her children living under his roof.

Beth wasn't married and Mr Court had taken offence at his daughter's loose behaviour. He'd been hostile to her, forbidding her mother to have her at home at the start, though he'd got over that once the children were born. There was a sort of truce between the two now, because he was fond of the twins even though he didn't say much to Beth. Even so, she preferred to live with Lizzie, at least until she married and Lizzie was certain Beth would marry in time, if only for the sake of her twins . . . and it was hard bringing up children on just her wage, even though they shared the expenses.

Suddenly, becoming aware of something, Lizzie glanced over her shoulder and shivered, because she'd had the sensation that she was being followed. The street was well lit and she saw the man clearly. He was standing next to a red telephone kiosk wearing a greatcoat, the collar turned up about his neck and a trilby hat pulled down low over his face so that it was in shadow. A trickle of ice ran down her spine, because she was fairly certain he'd followed her all the way from the showrooms.

For a moment the old fear flared up in her, the fear of being attacked as she'd been that night when she was fourteen, the fear she thought she'd conquered since she'd learned the truth. As she saw the tram draw to a halt at the stop, she ran to join the others crowding on. She didn't want to miss it and have to wait for ages when someone was lurking in the shadows.

'Just caught it,' the tram conductor said and grinned at her. He was a friendly little man, in his seventies if he was a day, and enjoyed being called out to do essential work because the younger men had gone off to war. 'Your old man will think you're never comin' home, love. You want to get in afore they start up – if they do tonight. Safe and tight with your family that's where you ought to be.'

'I don't have a husband,' Lizzie said, glancing briefly over her shoulder but unable to see the man she was certain had followed her. 'Just a sweetheart – and he's away.'

'Well, poor devil, even if he's at the Front, he'd want you to be safe before those buggers get going . . .'

He was referring to the bombing, which had been horrific for months now. Sometimes the night sky would turn crimson with the glow of all the fires from incendiary bombs or the gas explosions they caused, and the emergency services were at full stretch, young women helping to drive the fire tenders and man the phones. You could never tell

24

when Hitler's Luftwaffe would pay another little visit; if it wasn't London's docklands and factories, or the rows of back-to-back houses in the East End, it would be somewhere on the coast or one of the other big cities. Even Buckingham Palace and the Houses of Parliament had been hit, though it was the docks and factories that were getting the worst of it. Parts of the East End had been reduced to piles of smouldering rubble, huge heaps of it where houses had stood, the families they sheltered left injured, dead or homeless. Some people camped out in the ruins, living like rats in the cellars, while others moved in with family elsewhere or wandered from shelter to shelter. Many others had simply deserted their lives and gone away, either to the country or, if they were young enough, to join the services and fight.

'Yes,' Lizzie agreed. 'I'm glad I did catch you. I think I was being followed . . .'

'Followed, were you?' He looked concerned. 'There's some funny types about these days . . . with the war an' all. He might 'ave been a spy. I'd give the so-and-so a good hiding if I got 'old of him. You be careful, love – and if you see him again shout for the police.'

'Yes,' Lizzie said, smiling. 'I shall.'

She felt better now she was on the tram and heading home. She was probably making something out of nothing, but she could never quite conquer the fear that what had happened to her when she was fourteen might happen again . . .

CHAPTER 2

'I'm worried about Mary,' Beth's mother said when they took the children to her first thing the next morning. 'She was round here last night, crying and carrying on – and if she doesn't pull herself together, she'll end up losing the baby.'

'Oh no,' Lizzie said, immediately concerned. 'What's wrong – is there anything I can do?'

'No, love, but it's good of you to ask,' Mrs Court said and smiled at her approvingly. 'Mary hasn't heard from Andy for weeks and she thinks something has happened to him. I keep telling her she will get a telegram if it has, but she says she can feel something is wrong inside. It's so bad for the baby . . .'

Lizzie nodded, understanding because both she and Beth had been in similar situations. Beth's Mark had promised to marry her on his next leave from the Merchant Navy, but he'd been killed and she'd discovered that she was carrying the twins; the children that had been born of a brief but sweet love affair right at the beginning of the war. Lizzie had lost her husband, and even though the love she'd first felt for him had faded, his death

26

had been hard to bear. He was young and vital and to think of a life wasted in that way was terrible. Harry was after all the father of Betty, the joy of her life, even if she had been conceived out of anger. She found it easy to understand that Mary was worried about her husband.

'Mary is missing her job,' Beth said, sounding a little harsh. 'She enjoyed nursing. She should go back to it once the child is born . . .'

'And how do you think she is going to manage that, miss? I shan't be able to have the child and she doesn't get on well with Andy's mother, as you very well know.'

Beth flushed as she heard the note of reprimand in her mother's voice. Obviously it would be too much to expect her to care for four children every day; three was quite enough and Beth had noticed that her mother was looking a bit tired again.

'Lizzie and me were talking. We might make other arrangements – for our children, at least sometimes . . . just to give you a rest.'

'Were you now?' Annoyance flickered in Mrs Court's eyes. 'And have I said it was too much for me, miss?'

'No, but perhaps it isn't fair to the others . . .'

'Mary and Dottie both have husbands and they don't need to work,' her mother reminded her. 'I don't mind having their children now and then, but yours and Lizzie's come first.'

'We're so grateful for it,' Lizzie said and kissed her daughter. She placed her in the playpen

27

Mr Court had made for the children. 'Be good for Nanny, Betty love.'

Mrs Court had asked Lizzie to call her Nanny for Betty's benefit and she was the closest thing to a mother that Lizzie had known since her own died. Her parents had both died of diphtheria when she was a small child and she'd been taken to live with her aunt and uncle. Lizzie's memories of her mother were still hazy, even though she'd found a picture of her parents in a box of items belonging to Aunt Jane. They'd been in the loft and discovered when there was a small leak in the water tank. Lizzie's aunt had put the things up in the attic years before and forgotten them, even though the photos and a few bits of old silver really belonged to Lizzie. Their discovery had been a joy to Lizzie and the photograph frame was now polished and stood in pride of place on her dressing table at home. It was wonderful to know that at last she had a few things that had belonged to her mother.

'You needn't worry, Lizzie,' Mrs Court assured her, taking Betty in her arms, 'your little love is never any trouble.'

It was a wrench leaving her daughter every day, but Lizzie knew she was lucky to have someone like Beth's mother to look after her.

'We'll get off then, Mum,' Beth said. 'I might be a bit later this evening. Lizzie was followed to the tram stop last night, so we shall come home together – you won't mind another half an hour?'

'No, of course not – but, Lizzie, that's awful; if it happens again you must go to the police,' Mrs Court looked anxious.

'I shall do,' Lizzie assured her. 'I could ask Ed to see me to the tram stop – but if he saw anyone following me, he would probably go after whoever it is and knock him down, and Beth offered to wait . . .'

'I'll keep them until you get here,' Beth's mother said. 'Get off and open that shop of yours up, Lizzie – but don't ignore this. If someone is threatening you, the sooner it's dealt with the better.'

'Yes . . .' Lizzie hesitated, not wanting to bother Mrs Court with her other worries, but Beth came straight out with it.

'A woman stole two hats from the showroom last night too. Lizzie went to fetch her a new one and when she came back the woman had run off with two hats.'

'What are we coming to?' Mrs Court exclaimed and shook her head. 'I blame the war, you know – the restrictions are making people depressed and some will do anything. All these black market people, selling stuff under the counter – and where is the good in that I ask you? It has to be stolen stuff and that's just not right. I don't mind an extra bit of sugar or meat if I can get it from my regular grocer, but I wouldn't buy pinched stuff.'

'Dad would have a fit,' Beth said. 'I'm sure he gets offered pinched stuff on his market stall, but I know he won't take it.'

'No, he won't, and you should hear him going on about those that do,' her mother said. 'He knew that butcher that got done for selling stolen meat last week. He said Alfie was a decent bloke before the war, but it's all the extra profit that has corrupted him.'

The girls knew that Mr Court took the war seriously; he'd been turned down when he offered his services to the Army, but he'd been accepted as an air raid warden and went out six nights a week wearing a tin hat with ARP on the front; it was one of his jobs to warn people about lights showing through the blackout curtains and he spent a lot of time helping to pull the injured from bombed buildings.

'We've got to go, Mum,' Beth said and kissed her cheek, then grabbed Lizzie by the arm and hurried her out. She grimaced when they were clear of the house. 'Once she gets on her high horse there's no stopping her. I know she's right, but it's so tempting and it's not like stealing hats, is it? I mean if you're offered a couple of sausages under the counter it seems like nothing. I used to go to Mr Henry and he was always slipping an extra chop in my bag – for the children he said, but they don't eat much meat yet, unless it's minced.'

'I think he fancied you,' Lizzie said and raised her brows teasingly.

'He's got a wife and two kids – poor woman,' Beth said. 'How must she feel, now that her husband has been given ten months in prison for receiving?'

'Awful, I should think. You know how people talk; it won't do his business any good, even though his wife has managed to keep it open . . .' Lizzie glanced over her shoulder as they climbed on board the tram. The conductor was a young woman with brassy blonde hair. She churned the tickets out without a smile and passed on.

Beth looked at Lizzie thoughtfully. 'You had a bad dream last night, didn't you? I heard you cry out but I didn't like to come in . . .'

'I wish you had,' Lizzie said and shuddered. 'It was the old one I used to have. I hadn't had it for ages, but after that incident last night . . . it got to me a bit. I woke up shivering and shaking . . . so ridiculous. It isn't going to happen again.'

'No, of course not, but it must have been horrid being followed,' Beth said sympathetically. 'You've had a lot to put up with, Lizzie. When I think about all you've been through, I consider myself lucky. I lost Mark but I have the twins – and Dad has almost forgiven me. I know he wishes I was married, but I'm still considering Bernie's proposal. I'm not in love with Bernie, but I suppose he's kind, and I know my family approve.'

Lizzie nodded and made an appropriate answer, but Beth had the feeling that she was preoccupied. It wasn't surprising really after what had happened the previous evening. It was bound to play on her mind even if she tried not to worry about it.

31

Lizzie didn't have a family to turn to. She treated Beth's family as her own, but it wasn't the same. It was rotten luck the way her parents had died when she was young, and then both her uncle and aunt had let her down – though her uncle had done what he could to make amends. Lizzie's Aunt Jane had been a misery and she'd revealed the shattering secret of Lizzie's past on the eve of her wedding. If she'd told her the truth years before perhaps Lizzie would have had time to tell Harry – and then he would not have discovered it on their wedding night . . .

Beth knew most of the story, though Lizzie had not told her everything about their quarrels. Yet she knew Harry had hurt Lizzie badly. He'd been jealous and cruelly suspicious of her. Lizzie hadn't complained at the time, but Beth reckoned it had been rotten for her back then.

'You're living your dream now, aren't you, Lizzie – you've got your chance to design beautiful hats like you always wanted?'

'Yes, I've got the shop, and I've got you and my lovely little Betty . . .' Lizzie hesitated for a moment, then smiled. 'It's what I wanted and I'm happy in my work, but . . .' she sighed and Beth guessed she was thinking about Sebastian Winters. Lizzie hadn't told her she was in love with him, but she'd seen it in her eyes when his name came up in conversation, as it did from time to time. Sebastian's manager was still one of their best customers, even though he hadn't heard from his boss for months.

'You don't know where Sebastian is, do you?' she asked and saw Lizzie frown. 'Is he in the Army – or what?'

'Sort of, I think,' Lizzie said softly. 'It's not something I can talk about, Beth – you know what they say about walls having ears.'

Beth looked at the woman in the hairnet and wool scarf sitting in front of them. She was clearly listening to their conversation and Beth made a face at her back.

'No, you can't be too careful,' she said and grinned at Lizzie. 'They say spies are everywhere. Did you hear about that woman who got sent to prison for helping one? All she did was give him a meal and a bath . . . I think they might hang her . . .'

The woman in front was sitting to attention now, straining to hear, but Lizzie gave Beth a poke in the ribs, because she knew she was taking the mickey out of their eavesdropper.

'You're a wretch, Beth,' Lizzie said when they got off the tram. 'That poor woman will be dying to know what that was all about and no one can tell her because you made it up.'

'Serves her right for listening to us,' Beth said. 'Did you mean it though – do you really think Sebastian may be caught up in something like that . . . spying – for us, of course.'

'I don't know, but it isn't regular Army,' Lizzie said. 'I know he was concerned before he went away last time, but I've no idea what he does.'

'He hasn't written to you?'

'Just postcards, and they don't say much. I'm sure he would have written, if he could . . .'

'Would you hear if . . .' Beth hesitated as they paused at the edge of the path, looking for a way through the rubble that had appeared overnight as the result of what might have been a gas explosion. Men were digging in the road, clearly trying to repair the damage. 'You know . . .'

'I'm not his next of kin, but I'm sure he has made some kind of arrangement . . .'

Beth nodded. 'What will happen when the war is over? Will you marry him if he asks?'

'I don't know,' Lizzie said honestly, because of late the doubts had crept in again. Those few days at Christmas seemed so far away now. 'I know I feel something for him, but until he comes back . . . I can't be sure if it's love.'

'What is love anyway?' Beth asked. 'I thought I was in love with Tony but we fell out and then Mark happened and it was like a thunderbolt; I didn't know what hit me until it was too late and they told me he'd died. Perhaps we expect too much of life, Lizzie. Mum seems content, but I'm not sure she was ever in love.'

'Oh, I'm sure she was and probably still is,' Lizzie said. 'I've seen the way she looks at your father now and then. I know they argue – but I think the love is there beneath the surface. I should like my marriage to be like theirs one day . . .'

They had reached her shop and Lizzie gave a

gasp of dismay as she saw that the large window at the front had been cracked, the glass falling inward amongst the display of hats; not as the result of an explosion, but from what looked like deliberate malice.

'I'm so sorry, Lizzie.' Ed came out to them, looking grim. 'Someone must have used a hammer on it. I found it when I came back from the pub last night; it was too late to telephone you, because there was nothing you could do. I've already made arrangements and they will put a new front in this morning – and this time we'll have stronger glass.'

'Who would want to do such a thing?' Beth demanded angrily.

'Perhaps the man who followed me last night,' Lizzie said and went white. 'Perhaps someone is trying to warn me . . .'

'What do you mean?' Ed asked anxiously as they all went inside.

Lizzie explained about the man following her to the tram. He listened, his expression becoming grimmer.

'I can only think of one person who would want to upset you, Lizzie. I knew he was mean and sharp-tempered, but I never thought Harry's uncle would stoop to this.'

'We don't know it was him,' Lizzie objected. 'You can't accuse him without proof, Ed.'

'Can't I?' Ed looked stubborn. 'I've got a gut feeling he's behind this – and if he is, he won't stop there . . .'

'Oh, don't let's talk about it,' Lizzie was close to tears. 'I'll put the kettle on. I could do with a cup of tea . . .'

Despite the upsetting start, the day began well for business because one of Lizzie's best customers came to see her and placed an order for six bespoke hats that she wanted for the spring. The window had been swiftly repaired and it didn't seem worth worrying about what might just have been someone's spite.

'I haven't been in for a while,' Mabel Carmichael said with a faint smile. 'I wasn't well after I had the baby and didn't feel like going out much.'

'I'm sorry you weren't well,' Lizzie sympathized. 'I hope you're feeling better now?'

'Much better, and my husband says I need a whole new wardrobe, though I told him the clothes available now are awful, but I thought if I could get some lovely new hats the dresses I had before the utility look came in would do. I've put on a little weight, but I can get someone to remodel them for me.'

'Do you have a good seamstress?'

'Yes, I do actually. I've known her for ages – but no one makes hats like you do, Lizzie.'

'Thank you,' Lizzie laughed at her enthusiasm, because Mabel had been the first customer to order her hats straight from the drawing pad. 'I've got a few new designs in my sketchbook and one or two hats I'm working on – why don't you come through to the workshop and have a look?'

'Oh, I'd love to,' Mabel agreed. 'I haven't seen where you work since you started up on your own, have I?'

'No, probably not,' Lizzie said and smiled at Beth who was serving one of their regular customers with hats at wholesale prices. Mabel paid more for hers, but still found them much cheaper than buying from the West End stores.

Mabel spent an hour looking through the new designs and then purchased three hats that Lizzie was working on and ordered another four from the drawing pad.

'When will they be ready?' she asked as she prepared to leave.

'On Monday I should think. Yes, Monday,' Lizzie said after consulting her order book. 'I'll make sure they're ready for you.'

Just as Mabel was leaving, the door opened and Beth's elderly grandmother entered looking very upset. She'd been very ill the previous year and they'd wondered if she would pull through, but she'd recovered and now lived with Beth's parents though she spent most mornings in bed. Seeing her looking so anxious and upset made them realize that something was very wrong.

'You've got to come home, Beth,' she said. 'Mary's been taken bad and your mother is in a state. She needs to go to the hospital to see your sister and she can't leave the children.'

'Yes, you must go straight away,' Lizzie said, immediately concerned, especially when she saw the old lady's hands shaking. 'I'm so sorry you've had to come all this way.'

'Bless you lovey; Beth's mother said we should telephone from the box on the corner, but I took a cab and it's waiting outside to take us back. I'd have looked out for the babies, but your mum said Betty and Jenny would probably sleep through until their feed, but Matt has been playing up all day again, and he would be too much for me.'

'It isn't fair my going off and leaving you in the lurch,' Beth said but Lizzie gave her a little push towards the back room.

'Get your things and go. Your mum needs to get to the hospital, I can see to things here.'

'All right, thanks, Lizzie. I'm sorry . . .'

Beth had grabbed her coat and she went out, throwing Lizzie a look of apology mixed with distress. Lizzie knew that Beth wasn't on the best of terms with Mary, but she still cared for her and none of them would want Mary to lose her baby.

Lizzie took over the order Beth had been preparing. The customer looked at her hesitantly, and then decided to speak.

'I was in two minds whether to order from you today, Mrs Oliver,' he said. 'I've been warned that you might be closing down soon . . .'

'I don't know who told you that, but it isn't true.' Lizzie frowned 'If someone has been trying to stop

38

you coming to me it is for the wrong reasons, Mr Harris. I've no intention of closing.'

'I'm glad about that, because Oliver told me he wouldn't serve me if I continued to buy from you. However, he doesn't sell what I need these days, I'm afraid. I should be very sorry if you let me down too.'

'Oh . . .' Lizzie bit back the angry retort that sprang to her lips. 'That is rather unfair of him – but I know he is angry with me.'

'He tried to tell me some cock and bull story,' Mr Harris said, 'but I don't hold with that kind of thing – and a person's private life is their own – but some folk wouldn't think that way. I'm afraid you might lose some of your customers if he continues . . .'

Lizzie felt a sinking sensation inside. She had half a dozen good clients who had been regulars with Harry's uncle until he cut back on everything but his Government orders and she'd started up her business. They'd come to her and been pleasantly surprised to see her stylish hats, transferring their custom immediately.

'I hope you're wrong, Mr Harris. I couldn't afford to lose too many customers.'

'Well, I hope so too,' he said and took his wallet out to pay her. 'As I said, I don't take notice of nasty talk like that, but some will. Thank you – I'll call again next month. You've got some nice new lines in and if they go well in the shop, I'll be ordering more.'

Lizzie thanked him and watched as he left the showroom. He'd been honest enough to tell her that Bert Oliver was trying to put some of her customers off buying from her. She'd known Harry's uncle was angry with her. He'd jumped to conclusions and blamed her for making Harry miserable and causing him to take his own life, which some people had suspected at the time – until the car was discovered to have been faulty.

'You're a whore and I'll ruin you,' he'd shouted at her when he'd believed that Harry had killed himself out of desperation over his marriage. Obviously he still blamed Lizzie, even though he must know the car had been the cause of the accident. She could only hope that most of the customers wouldn't believe his lies.

Lizzie spent a couple of hours working on her new designs, and then went into the showroom once more when one of their regular customers came in. He'd ordered fifteen special hats the previous week and his order was ready waiting and boxed.

She smiled at him, 'I'll fetch your order, Mr Jenkins.'

'Thank you, Mrs Oliver . . .' He looked her straight in the eyes as he said, 'I'm a man of my word, and I'll pay for this order – but I'm afraid it's the last I shall be buying from you . . .'

Lizzie swallowed hard, her mouth suddenly dry. 'Would you mind telling me why please? Have we let you down in any way?'

'No, your designs and your work are as good as ever, but I'm afraid I don't do business with persons of your sort, Mrs Oliver.' He sighed heavily. 'Oliver is an old friend and after what he told me . . . women who cheat on men who are risking their lives for this country sicken me.'

'Would it change your mind if I told you that Mr Oliver had made a terrible mistake?'

'No, I'm afraid it wouldn't,' he replied and shook his head sorrowfully. 'There's no smoke without fire – and my customers . . . well, they are decent ladies and if they thought their hats came from . . .'

'Very well, if you prefer to believe lies,' Lizzie said, pride making her cold. 'I shall fetch your order.' She was tempted to tell him she wouldn't deal with someone who couldn't tell the truth from a scurrilous lie, but couldn't afford to take the risk. Fifteen special hats were a lot and she might be losing a few more customers judging from what the previous two customers had told her.

Lizzie fetched the order and accepted payment.

'We shall be sorry to lose you, Mr Jenkins,' she said politely as he picked up his order and went to the door. 'Perhaps one day you will discover your mistake in believing malicious lies.'

He went out without another word and Lizzie returned to the workshop. She sat staring into space, on the verge of tears but refusing to give in to the anger and despair inside her.

41

'What is it, Lizzie?' Ed's voice brought her head up sharply.

'Mr Jenkins has been told something about me – and he won't be ordering from us again . . . and Mr Harris had heard the same, but he doesn't believe in listening to tales . . .'

'Damn Jenkins for hurting you!' Ed said and looked furious. 'Oliver is behind this, mark my words. He told me he intended to ruin you if he could and he's a mean vindictive old devil.'

'Harry's death hurt him,' Lizzie said and sighed. 'I expect he misses him, and Betty too, and I imagine Aunt Miriam is lonely. I haven't dared to call on her because he wouldn't like it, but I feel uneasy about it, after all she has a right to see Betty. Harry's uncle wasn't always like this, Ed – he was difficult and he expected a good day's work, but I liked him. I'm sorry he thinks so badly of me now – but what can I do? Even if I tried talking to him, he wouldn't listen . . .'

'He'll listen to me all right,' Ed said and clenched his fists.

'No, I don't want you to quarrel with him, Ed,' Lizzie touched his arm. 'Let's just wait and see what happens. He's an old man and my husband was his only nephew, like his son really. He's hurting and he's angry . . .'

'Yes, but he has no right to blame you, Lizzie.'

'No, he doesn't,' she agreed. 'But I don't want you to go round there, Ed. It would cause trouble for you – and if I have to, I'll sort him out myself. I can if I want . . .'

Ed looked at her for several minutes. 'Yes, I know, Lizzie. It just makes me spitting mad that Bert wants to hurt you like this. It's vindictive, telling lies to ruin your reputation and your business. What would Harry think? He's harming Betty too, because if this destroys the business, what would happen to Harry's daughter then?'

'He thinks he has reason,' Lizzie said sadly, 'and there's no changing his mind. He's too stubborn for that.'

Ed listened to Lizzie and conceded it might be best to wait before charging off to confront Bert Oliver, but he insisted on walking to the tram stop with Lizzie that evening.

'Thanks, Ed,' she said and squeezed his arm. 'I'll be all right now – I just hope the news about Mary isn't too bad when I get home . . .'

Ed waited until she was on the tram and then walked away. Lizzie looked out of the window and then noticed the man walking away. The shock of recognition spiralled through her, because he'd been there watching her; the man who'd followed her before. He was dressed as before in an overcoat and trilby pulled low over his face, but for a moment she saw him in the light of a street lamp – thin-faced, pale skin and a scar on his cheek. Was it the same man? She couldn't be sure, but she was relieved that Ed had insisted on walking her to the tram.

Lizzie didn't feel like shopping and Beth would have taken the children home. They were already fed, washed and in bed when Lizzie walked in and Beth was preparing some chips to go with the thinly sliced corned beef they'd purchased the previous day for their meal.

'That smells good,' Lizzie sniffed appreciatively. 'How is Mary? Have you heard?'

'Dad came round a few minutes ago to tell me the news,' Beth said. 'He'd been to visit Mary at the hospital but she was still in labour so he didn't wait. He says Granny is cooking his tea and Mum is stopping at the hospital until Mary has had the child.'

'Your granny has had a big day,' Lizzie said. 'Won't she find it a bit much cooking tea for her son-in-law?'

'She seems to be enjoying herself,' Beth laughed. 'When she moved in with Mum she seemed poorly, but she hadn't been eating properly, now she's fine again and happy to do her bit.'

'She's a marvellous lady,' Lizzie said as she washed her hands. 'I'll just pop up to see Betty and then make a pot of tea . . .'

Lizzie left her to the cooking and went into the children's room, bending over Betty's cot to make sure she was all right. Her cheeks looked rosy and she was sleeping peacefully, so she went back down and filled the kettle.

Beth turned the chips in the frying pan. 'I hope these will be all right. I've done them in olive oil

I bought from that grocer's on the corner. It's supposed to be for putting on your salads, but it says you can cook in it . . .'

'Yes, you can. I've used it a couple of times before,' Lizzie said. 'I put it in sponges too – I think it comes from Italy or somewhere like that . . .'

'We shouldn't be buying from the enemy . . .'

'It doesn't say that's where it came from on the bottle, though the shop used to be Italian. The owner packed up and left when the war started, and I'll bet this is old stock – it's perfectly all right though.'

'It smells all right. Besides, we've run out of lard.' Beth ladled out the chips and they sat down to their meal of corned beef, chips and some red beet out of a pickle jar.

'I like red beet with corned beef,' Lizzie said. 'I'd rather have ham of course . . .'

'What's that?' Beth quipped and they smiled at each other, because it was almost impossible to buy ham these days. Rationing and shortages had made things they'd always taken for granted a rarity and both girls ate hungrily, knowing they were lucky to have a decent meal to come home to. A lot of families sent their kids to school with nothing but a bit of bread and dripping to tide them over until their tea, which was likely to be more of the same unless their mothers were lucky enough to get a bit of scrag end or offal from the butcher to make a filling pie. There were all kinds of recipes these days for making pies out of grated

45

vegetables and they all tasted awful, at least in Lizzie's opinion. The days of tasty pork chops or sausages for tea were a distant memory.

'Are you going up the hospital when we've eaten?' Lizzie asked.

'Would you mind?'

'No, of course not. I'll be here to look after the children tonight, and I can do a few sketches. You go and see how your sister is. Persuade your mother to go home and rest for a while, tell her you'll be there for Mary – and don't even think about coming to work tomorrow.'

'Thanks,' Beth smiled at her. 'I don't know what I should have done if we'd never met, Lizzie. You're the best friend I've ever had . . .'

They had finished their meal and were clearing the table when someone knocked at the door. It was Bernie; he'd heard about Beth's sister.

'I'll take you to the hospital in the car,' he offered. 'If you walk you might get caught in a raid.'

'Yes, you get off now,' Lizzie urged, thinking they were fortunate that the siren hadn't yet sounded that evening. 'Go on, Beth. You must be worried to death . . .'

Beth nodded gratefully and went with him. Lizzie washed the plates and frying pan and put them all away. She was also feeling a bit tired because it had been a long day, but at least she hadn't had time to fret about the man following her or the problems at the showroom.

When she allowed herself to remember that

unpleasant interview with Mr Jenkins, she felt like weeping. It was so unfair after all her hard work setting up the business. She'd noticed that after a good start the profits hadn't been so positive recently, and now she understood why she hadn't seen one or two of her customers. They must have listened to the spiteful gossip. Why did Harry's uncle hate her so much? Because he'd seen her with Roger and then with Sebastian, he'd jumped to conclusions, and if he was telling her customers that she was a loose woman she knew they wouldn't trade with her. If he understood the real reason Harry hadn't come home for months, perhaps he'd change his mind – and yet Lizzie was reluctant to tell him. He would probably think she was lying anyway.

Was he also responsible for the smashed window? Lizzie couldn't bring herself to believe that he would do such a thing, or even pay someone to do it. He might be angry and he might think Lizzie had cheated on Harry – but surely he wouldn't go that far?

Worrying about it wasn't going to solve anything. Lizzie got out her sketchbook and began to design some new hats for her spring and summer range. In the distance she could hear the sound of muffled explosions and thought perhaps the Docks were catching it again. Nothing showed through the blackout curtains, but she knew the sky would be lit up over there. She just prayed that Beth wasn't caught up in it and that she wouldn't have to fetch the children down to the Morrison shelter on her own.

After a while, Lizzie went upstairs to look at the children. All three of them were sleeping peacefully and she bent to kiss their soft cheeks, feeling protective of their sweet innocence and whispering a prayer that they would all come through this terrible war safely.

By ten o'clock Beth hadn't come home, but the all-clear had sounded so she accepted that her friend had decided to stay at the hospital and she went up to bed; the door was locked but she hadn't put the chain on, because Beth would need to be able to use her key if she came back in the early hours. It felt odd knowing that she was alone with the three children, and she could only be grateful that Hitler's bombers hadn't visited her district of Spitalfields that night.

CHAPTER 3

Beth's bed hadn't been slept in all night. Lizzie frowned when she looked in and saw it was untouched. Was Beth still at the hospital? She hoped everything was all right. The children were waking up; Beth's twins taking it in turns to scream for attention. Betty was grizzling when Lizzie went into their bedroom. All three children slept in the same room in their separate cots, which often meant that if one started crying they all set off. Matt was yelling the loudest, so Lizzie picked him up and rocked him for a moment, but he just yelled all the louder. He was obviously hungry. Lizzie put him back in his cot, bent over Jenny and stroked her forehead and then picked up her own little Betty and kissed her damp cheeks.

'It's all right, Mummy is going to make the bottles and then you'll all be fine,' Lizzie said.

She took Betty down to the kitchen with her and started to make up three bottles with the special powdered milk they got from the chemist. Her daughter had settled down in the old armchair and was smiling, happy now that she wasn't

49

disturbed by the twins' crying. Lizzie made Betty's bottle first and fed her; she changed her daughter's nappy and then left her on a blanket gurgling and smiling in the playpen, while she went up to feed and change Beth's twins.

Jenny was wet but her tears stopped as soon as Lizzie fed her and she was able to turn her attention to Matt. He was red in the face from screaming for attention, and, discovering his nappy was heavy, Lizzie changed him. She threw the spoiled napkin into a bucket and wiped his little bottom clean, noticing that he had quite a nasty rash. She found the cream and smoothed it over his now clean flesh, soothing him as she rocked him in her arms.

'No wonder you were in such distress,' she said and then began to feed him. 'I thought it was just temper . . . I'm sorry I left you to the last.'

Beth always said that Matt had a terrible temper and Lizzie had thought he had been screaming and crying so loudly just to grab the attention from his sister but now realized that he must have a tummy upset. A visit to the doctor or at least the nurse's clinic for babies might be in order, and she made up her mind to take him herself if Beth didn't get back. She would have to telephone Ed and ask him to look after the showroom. The orders would have to wait. However, just as she was getting ready to ask the next door neighbour if she would have Jenny and Betty, Beth turned up looking dreadful.

'Thank goodness you're back. I was beginning

to worry you'd been caught in the raid. I've got the kettle on,' Lizzie said and put Jenny and Matt into the playpen with Betty. 'Matt has a sore bottom and judging by that nappy in the bucket he has a tummy upset. Would you like me to take him to the doctor while you rest and keep an eye on the other two?'

'What about the shop?'

'Ed will manage,' Lizzie said. 'I just rang him. Your mother thought the telephone an expensive luxury, but I was glad of it this morning.'

'I'm shattered,' Beth said. 'I persuaded Mum to go home for a few hours, but only when Dad turned up and nearly dragged her away – but then Mary had the baby about twenty minutes later.' A little sob escaped her. 'Poor little mite, her skin is yellow and the doctors took her away. They told me the child has some kind of liver infection.'

'Poor Mary,' Lizzie said and her eyes stung with tears. 'To go through all that pain and then to have your baby so ill . . .'

'I went in to see her for a while, but she wouldn't talk to me, even though the doctor says she's all right now.' Beth choked on the tears she was holding back. 'She turned her face to the wall and didn't answer when I tried to tell her things would be all right. She just muttered something about it being all right for me . . .'

'Oh, Beth, I'm sure she didn't mean it. She was just exhausted and miserable.'

'Yes, I know, but she does resent me – both Mary

51

and Dottie think I'm the favourite and have things easy . . .'

'They're just being silly. Your mother was right when she said they both have husbands and don't have to work. Besides, I'm sure she would have their children sometimes. She doesn't babysit for us at weekends.'

'No, but they don't see it like that,' Beth said and glanced nervously at Matt, who was banging his rattle on the chair. 'It was awful seeing Mary's little girl like that, Lizzie. It made me realize how lucky we both are to have happy healthy children. At least they are most of the time . . . do you think Matt is really poorly?'

'His bottom is sore.' Lizzie pushed a hot sweet cup of tea in front of Beth and a piece of toast with strawberry jam. 'Drink your tea, love. I'm going to take Matt to the doctor's surgery and ask for someone to take a look at him. I'll bring him home as soon as I've been seen and then I'll go into work – but your mum won't come today so you'll be here with the children. Hopefully, we'll have something to settle Matt's tummy by then.'

Beth nodded and kissed her son before Lizzie whisked him off. Going out into a morning that for almost the first time that year had a hint of spring about it, Lizzie nursed the child who was beginning to whimper again.

She walked the two streets to the doctor's surgery, noticing the gaps where houses had once been, feeling sympathy for the people who had lost their homes and blessing her lucky star for keeping her family safe.

Though the doctor himself was too busy to see her, the nurse invited Lizzie in and took a look at Matt. He'd already filled his nappy again and the smell was sour.

'He's given us another nice surprise,' Nurse Henderson said and laughed. The mother of four herself, and in her fifties, she was a dependable woman who dealt with the situation deftly, wrapping Matt's bottom in a soft wad of cotton wool and pulling the rubber pants on over it. 'He has a nasty tummy infection. I'm glad you brought him in, Mrs Oliver, because you need to be careful it isn't passed on to the others – be scrupulous about washing his nappies separately for a while and keep all the bottles sterile. I'm sure you know, but just to remind you. I'll give you something for his sore bottom and we'll make up a mixture for his tummy.'

'Thank you. I was a little worried, because he was screaming so much. I thought it was temper, but then when I saw his bottom – and the nappy.'

'Yes, that smell gives it away,' the nurse said. 'I'll wrap this soiled one in some newspaper for you – but remember what I said. Give it a good soak in cold water and a drop of disinfectant.'

Lizzie thanked her again and left the surgery, carrying the soiled nappy in her string shopping bag. She hurried home and gave Beth the welcome news that it wasn't serious but they had to be careful about not passing it on to the other two.

'The nurse said it was a good thing I took Matt, because it might have been serious if we hadn't realised he was unwell.'

'Matt is always the one that screams the loudest,' Beth said looking concerned. 'It's a lot for Mum to cope with – the three of them – and I suppose she didn't realize he was ill.'

'I wasn't sure which of them to see to first this morning, and I thought Matt was just having a tantrum. I expect that's why your mum hadn't noticed he wasn't quite right.'

'We'll have to think hard about the future,' Beth said. 'Mrs Jones from down the road popped in a few minutes ago. She'd heard about Mary and said she would look after the children for a few hours if I wanted to go up the hospital. I think she might help out on a regular basis if we paid her. She told me she'd had to give up her job at the jam factory because it was too hard on her feet.'

'What a shame for her. It was good of her to offer,' Lizzie said. She didn't tell Beth that she considered Mrs Jones a well-meaning woman, but a bit slapdash. Although she'd only been to her house once, that had been enough for Lizzie; everywhere had been in need of a clean, and the kitchen smelled of old greens. 'We shall have to think about it for a while. Now, I must get off – remember what the nurse said about keeping Matt's nappies separate.'

'I'll do them later,' Beth yawned. 'I'm going to have a rest in here with the kids, catch up a bit on the sleep I lost. Mum said she would come round when she could, but it depends on how bad Mary's baby is and if she's perked up at all . . .'

Lizzie nodded. The children were in the playpen, Jenny and Betty curled up together like a pair of little kittens, while Matt rocked himself and grizzled but less loudly than before. It seemed that the first dose of his medicine had done some good, and Lizzie hoped Beth would get some rest before he started to scream again.

She ran for a bus and arrived at the showroom at half past ten. Ed was serving a customer and greeted her with a smile.

'Everything under control at home now?'

'Yes, I think so,' Lizzie said and went into the workroom. She filled the kettle, made tea and took one to Ed as he finished with the customer.

'He's a new customer and he bought ten of the new lines,' Ed said. 'Sebastian Winters' manager told him about us and I think he will be a regular from now on.'

'Thank you so much for holding the fort, Ed. I don't know what I'd do without you.'

'Bless you, Lizzie,' he looked pleased with her praise. 'I don't know what I'd have done if you hadn't given me this partnership. I think I'd have been down the boot factory hating my work and life . . .'

'Well, you're here with us,' Lizzie said. 'I'd better get busy. I promised Mabel her order would be ready by Monday and I need to get started . . .'

It was mid-afternoon when the telephone rang in Lizzie's office. She answered it and heard a sob at the other end, and then Beth crying.

'What's wrong, love?' Her heart caught with fright. 'Matt isn't worse, is he?'

'No, it's Mary's baby . . .' another sob of grief broke from Beth. 'The child died a couple of hours ago. Mum was with Mary when they told her and she went mad, screamed at them and tried to get out of bed. She was shouting that they'd killed her baby, fighting everyone that came near her. Mum tried to calm her and she punched her in the face. She's got a black eye . . .'

'That is terrible, Beth. Is your mother very upset?'

'Yes, she is – but about the baby and the way it will affect Mary rather than her own injury. She says that is nothing. She offered to look after the children while I came into work, but I'm not going to, Lizzie. She needs company and to be looked after herself for a few days.'

'Yes, of course she does and we can manage here. We've only had two customers in this morning – so don't you worry about me. I'll be home at the usual time and do what I can. Shall you visit your sister this evening?'

'I'll go to the hospital and ask how she is, but I don't think she'll want to see me. She's going to resent me more than ever.'

'No, Beth, you mustn't feel like that,' Lizzie said. 'It isn't your fault that Mary lost her baby. Your

56

mum has been telling her for weeks that she should take more care of herself.'

'Yes, I know, but Mary has always been stubborn. She thinks she knows best because she is a qualified nurse. When we were all at home she never took much notice of me. I think she was jealous when I was born . . .'

'Oh, Beth,' Lizzie sighed, feeling for her. 'I always wanted brothers and sisters, but it seems that isn't always as good as it might be.'

'You've been better to me than either of my sisters,' Beth asserted. 'I don't want to let you down, but especially with Matt unwell, I feel I shouldn't leave Mum alone. I can't leave her to cope by herself . . .'

'Yes, of course I understand.'

They talked some more and then Beth rang off. Lizzie went back to her work, packing Mabel's hats in tissue as she finished them. She only had one to complete now and then she could start on some new ideas for stock . . . but she felt a little bit unsure of the future. If Beth had to stop coming in she would need to find another assistant but supposing the orders dried up and she couldn't afford to pay her? The girl she really wanted was Tilly, but she couldn't entice her away from Harry's uncle – especially if her own business was in danger of going down . . .

Even as she sat in gloomy contemplation of the future the doorbell went and Lizzie saw two young women enter the showroom. They reminded her a little of the girl who had stolen from her, but she refused to let that unpleasant incident ruin her pleasure in dealing with new customers who wanted a pretty hat.

'Can I help you?' she asked and one of them blushed shyly.

'I'm getting married and I want a pretty hat to go on honeymoon and my friend Sheila wants a hat for the wedding, don't you, Sheil?'

'Yeah, if yer got anythin' we can afford . . . it's a bit posh in 'ere, ain't it?'

'I like it to be nice for my customers,' Lizzie said. 'I've got hats you can buy from thirty shillings upwards – if that isn't too expensive?'

'No, I can afford a bit more than that,' the prospective bride said. 'How much do you want to pay, Sheil?'

'As little as possible. 'Ave yer got any cheap in the sale?'

'I haven't had a sale yet,' Lizzie replied, frowning. 'It would be old lines or shop-soiled goods, but I'm not ready for anything like that yet.'

'We was told yer were havin' a closin' down sale soon, so we thought we would get in first.'

'That's a silly rumour. I'm not closing down – and thirty shillings is my lowest price, other than a simple cloche or a beret.'

'Show us what yer've got then,' Sheila said grudgingly. 'We see a nice white straw in the winder didn't we, Mave?'

'Yes – a cloche with a navy ribbon and a silk rose . . .' the girl looked hopefully at Lizzie.

'I'm afraid that one is silk and it costs three pounds,' Lizzie said. 'Look, why don't I show you some that range from thirty shillings to two pounds ten and see if there is anything you like.'

'Go on then,' Sheila said. 'It's a bit of a lark any road – can we try 'em on?'

'Yes, of course you can.' Lizzie opened the cupboards and took out three cloche-style hats, one in white felt, one in navy felt and one in yellow straw. They all had price tags of thirty-five shillings. She took two other hats from the stands, which were a similar shape, but a little softer and made of silk velvet; these were priced at two pounds and two guineas. Lizzie knew she had more in their price range in the back room but wasn't inclined to fetch them after her previous unpleasant experience.

She showed the girls the hats they could afford, including some smart berets at twelve shillings and a brown cloche with a cream ribbon at the same price, but they didn't seem interested in them, because they were after the more stylish hats. Mave wanted a special hat and tried on three of the more expensive ones. She hovered between the white felt and one of the silk velvets and sighed as she preened before the mirror.

'I love them both,' she said. 'I've got three pounds and that isn't enough to buy them both, is it?'

Lizzie did a calculation in her head. She would be making just three shillings on the sale, but she was tempted to give in and agree to sell both for the price, but then Sheila spoke up.

'This navy one is all right, but I've only got twenty-seven and sixpence ter spend. Can't yer let me 'ave it fer that?'

Lizzie would still make five shillings on the hat. She took a deep breath and then inclined her head. 'I'll let you have that one for twenty-seven shillings and sixpence, but I need three pounds and five shillings for the other two – and that's a special price for you, Mave, because it's your wedding. I don't usually discount my hats, but you were misinformed about a sale so I'll offer them for what I've suggested.'

Mave's face fell. 'I ain't got no more . . .' she hesitated, then, 'I'll bring yer five bob when I get back from me honeymoon. Bobby is taking me to Southend for a week . . .'

Lizzie hesitated, knowing that she could quite easily end up losing the five shillings, but for once she was willing to take a chance. 'All right, just this once,' she agreed, 'but don't tell your friends, because I shan't make a habit of it.'

'Thanks,' Mave said and her thin, pretty face lit up. 'I shan't let yer down, miss. I promise. I'll 'ave both them hats please.'

'Yeah and I'll 'ave this un an' all.' Sheila grinned. 'You're all right – Lizzie, ain't it, same as the name over the shop?'

'Yes, Lizzie Larch,' Lizzie said, using her professional name. She packed the hats carefully in tissue and a box, just as she would for customers who bought large orders from her. 'I hope you'll be happy, Mave – and enjoy the wedding, both of you.'

They thanked her and went out, giggling and looking at each other as they walked off down the road. Lizzie wondered what Ed or Harry's uncle would say if they knew what she'd done. They would probably think she'd gone soft, but Lizzie hadn't forgotten what it felt like to spend almost the whole of your wages on a hat. Somehow she didn't mind whether she got her five bob or not, because those hats had suited Mave, and after all wasn't that what making pretty hats was all about . . .?

CHAPTER 4

Matt was sleeping peacefully when Lizzie got home that evening. His tummy trouble had passed and neither of the others had caught the bug. Beth had fed the children and put them to bed, and her mother had gone back to the hospital to visit Mary.

'Dad's gone with her so I decided I'd stay home and look after the kids,' Beth said. 'I gave Matt some more of that medicine the nurse made up for you and he seems much better. I didn't want to leave him with anyone, though, just in case.'

'Very sensible,' Lizzie said and hugged her. 'He's your priority for the moment, Beth. Mary will have your mum and dad, and I expect Dottie will call and see her too. You can go tomorrow if you feel like it.'

'Bernie said he would sit with them for a few hours if I wanted.' Beth looked at her oddly. 'Would you mind if he did that, Lizzie? I trust him to look after the twins, but it would mean leaving Betty as well . . .'

'Perhaps I could take her in with me,' Lizzie said. 'It wouldn't be so much for you to manage

– and I'm sure the twins would be enough for Bernie, and it isn't fair to ask him to have Betty as well.'

Lizzie wasn't sure why she didn't like the idea of Bernie looking after the children, but something niggled at her. She couldn't tell Beth what to do, but she would prefer Betty to be where she could keep an eye on her rather than leaving her with a stranger. Bernie seemed perfectly respectable, but Lizzie had her reservations, even though she couldn't have said why she didn't quite like the man. It was just something about him that made her distrust him, but she hadn't voiced her feelings aloud, for Beth's sake.

Beth frowned for a moment. 'Well, that's up to you – but won't she be in the way when you want to work?'

'I'm sure we can fix up a makeshift playpen for her,' Lizzie said. 'Ed loves her – he loves your two as well, Beth, but three might be too many. Yes, I think I'll try it and see how we get on. I may need to do it in the future sometimes, because I can't expect your mum to be responsible for my daughter all the time . . .'

'Well, if you want to,' Beth looked at her oddly. 'Bernie could put their carrycots in the car and drive me to the hospital.'

'It's a good idea to see how he copes with the twins,' Lizzie said. 'If you do marry him, he'll have to help out a bit with them, won't he?'

Beth nodded but turned away to take the pie

out of the oven. She'd made a fish pie with mashed potato on top and sliced carrots and chopped cabbage to go with it.

'Gosh that smells good,' Lizzie said. 'A lot of people don't like fish, but I think it's nice like this with a tasty sauce. I'm getting spoiled with you staying home, Beth.'

'Mum showed me how to make it,' Beth said, looking pleased. 'I'm quite a good cook, according to Mum.'

'Yes, you are,' Lizzie agreed. 'I think you're better than me, Beth. I've no idea what I shall do if you get married. It will be awful coming back here alone . . .'

'Don't talk about me getting married,' Beth snapped. 'You're as bad as my mother. That's all I've had from her today. Bernie popped over in his lunch hour and wanted to fuss round me, telling me that he'll have a girl in to help me with the twins when we're married so I'm not tied all the time – taking it for granted that I'm going to say yes eventually . . . you'd think it was all cut and dried the way he and mum went on about it.'

Lizzie looked at her and saw that she was really upset and shook her head. 'I'm sorry, love. I didn't know how you felt . . .'

Beth stared at her for a moment and then gave a strangled sob. 'It's what both my parents want, Lizzie but – I sometimes feel as if I'm being trapped into something . . .'

'Yes, I know,' Lizzie gave her an understanding look. 'People can be very thoughtless – me included. I was being selfish, thinking of how much I should hate living here alone.'

'That isn't selfish,' Beth said. 'You've stood by me all this time and I don't want to fall out with you. I'm just tired and upset after sitting up the hospital all the time last night on those hard chairs – and Mary can't stand the sight of me. I think she hates me now, Lizzie.'

'Of course she doesn't hate you. She's just very sensitive right now because you've got two lovely children and she's lost her baby, but she doesn't hate you.'

'Yes, I expect that's it. It's awful for her and I'm being unfair.' Beth sighed. 'Eat your supper and forget my silliness. I know you've got your own worries. How did you get on today?'

'I had a couple of girls from the munitions factory in today,' Lizzie told her. 'One of them is getting married and she wanted two hats, and her friend bought one.'

'Could they afford your prices?'

'I gave them a bit of a discount,' Lizzie said, 'but I told them not to tell their friends.'

'They will,' said the practical Beth. 'They'll soon get told what's what if I'm in the showroom. I'm not as soft as you are, Lizzie.'

'You've proved my point – I can't do without you.'

Beth nodded her head and they both started

laughing. 'Yeah, that's what I'll tell Bernie when he next asks. I'll say Lizzie can't manage without me . . .'

'Right, I'll get off then,' Lizzie said one evening a week or so later. 'I'll leave you to lock up the workrooms when you've finished, Ed. I promised Beth I'd be home a bit earlier so that she could go to the hospital to visit her sister.'

'How is the poor lass?' Ed said sympathetically. 'That was a terrible thing to happen to her . . . I remember how my Madge felt when we lost our son.'

'Yes, of course you do,' Lizzie said and felt the tears sting her eyes. She'd been very fond of Madge and she still got emotional when she thought about her loss. 'Mary must feel awful. She's lost her baby and she hasn't heard from her husband for ages.'

'It's worrying for her but the post from over there can be dreadful,' Ed said. 'A lot of letters go astray for months, sometimes they just get lost altogether.'

'Yes, I expect that is what has happened, but Mary thinks the worst, of course. Oh well, I'd better go . . .'

'Are you sure you don't want me to walk you to the tram stop?'

'No, I'm all right. I haven't seen anyone lurking about for a while now, so I should think whoever was following me has given up.'

'Well, if you're sure. I need to finish this cutting if we're to get Mr Johnson's order out on time and we don't want to let him down.'

'No,' Lizzie understood his meaning. Two of their regular customers hadn't been in this month and she suspected it was due to Harry's uncle meddling. They really couldn't afford to upset the regulars who remained loyal. 'Don't work too late, Ed. Goodnight.'

'Night, Lizzie.'

Ed bent over his work and Lizzie left him to it. He often worked late, perhaps because there was no one waiting for him upstairs in his flat. In his late forties, he was surely young enough to find someone else if he wished, but he was the faithful sort and he wouldn't rush into things. She could only hope he'd find happiness again one day.

Outside, it was chilly again even though it was officially spring, and Lizzie hugged her scarf tight round her neck, feeling the cold nip at her nose. Oh, she would be so glad when they got some sunshine!

She was almost at the tram stop when the back of her neck started to prickle. Turning, she saw him following – the man in the overcoat with the trilby pulled low over his face. He was back; she'd seen him three times now, he had to be following her! Lizzie sensed the menace in him and shivered. Her tram was just coming down the road and she hastened her step, but the man was quicker. He grabbed her arm just as the tram pulled to a halt.

'Got you, you little bitch,' he hissed. 'Think yourself clever, don't you – but I'll always be there waiting and when I get the chance – you'll be sorry . . .'

Lizzie didn't answer, because she was too scared. She pulled away from him, kicking out at his shins in desperation and he cursed her. His hand released her as swiftly as it had grabbed her and Lizzie rushed for her tram as it was about to leave the stop, managing to jump on board as it began to move.

'Careful there, lady,' the conductor said and grabbed her arm to steady her. 'Left it a bit fine, did we?'

'That man . . .' Lizzie was still shaking as she sat down. 'He grabbed me and threatened me . . .'

The conductor peered at her and shook his head; then memory dawned. 'I recall you tellin' me the other week, miss. You want to go to the coppers. He sounds a nasty piece of work – did you know him?'

'No. This is the third time I've noticed him following me, but this time he threatened me . . .'

'Take my advice and go to the police,' he advised, issuing her ticket and moving on as the tram slowed down for the next stop.

Lizzie drew a deep breath and tried to stop herself shaking. What would've happened if she hadn't managed to get away from him? It was like being back in her nightmare and she felt sick. She was going to have to speak to someone about it – either the police or Ed. Ed thought Harry's uncle was behind it, and she supposed he was the most likely person to want to upset Lizzie – but it just didn't seem Bert Oliver's style. He could be mean and he had a sharp temper – but was he the sort to hire someone to frighten her? That spoke of a truly vindictive nature and she just couldn't see him going to those extremes. Telling lies about her was one thing, but paying someone to threaten and frighten her was quite another – and why else would a stranger follow her and make threats? Who would dislike her that much? Lizzie didn't think she had enemies, but someone must hate her. Could it really be Harry's uncle behind it all?

Somehow it didn't fit in Lizzie's mind, but she decided to go round at the weekend and speak to him. She couldn't just let things drift the way they had, and she was pretty sure the police couldn't do much to help her. It would need someone to keep watch over her wherever she went and the police didn't have time for such things. These days it took all their time to keep up with the looters and rescuing people from bombed-out areas. No, she was going to have to sort this out for herself . . .

Lizzie had calmed down by the time she got home and felt it would be wrong to distress her friend by telling her what had happened. Beth had more than enough on her shoulders as it was.

'Mum says Mary won't stop crying,' Beth

announced as soon as Lizzie walked into the kitchen. 'They need her bed at the hospital and the doctors are talking about sending her some- where – somewhere they treat mental patients – if she doesn't calm down and stop accusing them of murdering her baby.'

'Oh, Beth,' Lizzie sympathized. 'You'll have to talk to her, shake her out of it somehow. A mental institution is the last place she wants to go. Once you're in there it isn't easy to get out . . .'

'You went somewhere a bit like that when you had that trouble as a young girl, didn't you?'

'Yes, and what I remember of it – and that isn't much, because they had me drugged most of the time – was horrible. Tell Mary that she wouldn't like it in one of those places, Beth. She has to come home. Losing a baby is bad enough; she doesn't want to lose her freedom or her sanity too. If Uncle Jack hadn't used all his savings to help me to move me to the private sanatorium, I might still have been a prisoner in that place. Even though I'd been raped, I was treated as if I was a bad girl just because I'd miscarried a child and I was only fourteen. It's all still hazy, but since Aunt Jane told me, I've half remembered things about that time . . .' A shudder went through Lizzie. 'But it's too horrid to want to remember it properly . . .'

'Oh, Lizzie, I'm sorry. I shouldn't have reminded you,' Beth apologized. 'It's just that Mum is so worried about Mary.'

'Of course she is,' Lizzie said. 'Speak to Mary tonight, Beth, and if she won't listen to you I'll visit her and tell her where she's headed if she doesn't attempt to get better.'

'Mum says she can't do anything with her. She thinks the doctor is right and Mary might be better off somewhere like that for a while . . .'

'No, she wouldn't,' Lizzie corrected instantly. 'Tell your mum, and tell Mary, what it was like for me. If that doesn't make her stop nothing will . . .'

'I'll try.' Beth sighed. 'So what sort of a day did you have today?'

'Pretty quiet,' Lizzie said, not wanting to worry her about her narrow escape at the bus stop. She would tell Ed the next morning, but Beth had enough on her shoulders just now. 'Only a couple of customers and Ed finished the order for Mr Johnson. The order book is almost empty after that, Beth. Unless things change . . .' She sighed and took the cup of tea Beth offered. 'I've done some new designs for the window. I can only hope that will bring some customers in . . .'

'Right,' Ed said when she told him the next day. 'I'll go round this evening and sort things out with Oliver, Lizzie – and I'll be walking you to the stop every night now.'

'That man warned me that he'd always be there, waiting for me,' Lizzie said. 'Do you think I should go to the police?'

'It's disgusting, threatening a decent girl like you – and you a widow . . .' Ed said. 'I can't see that going to the police would do a lot of good, Lizzie. They might come round, take a statement and keep watch for a few nights – but that sort knows to stay in the shadows when coppers are about. He would wait until they gave up and then come after you again. If we want protection we'll have to pay for it – and once *that type* get their claws into you, you might find yourself in a worse place.' Lizzie knew he meant the criminal types who would offer protection to a business for payment. 'It might be that someone is trying to put the squeeze on you – a protection racket . . .'

'Oh no, not that,' Lizzie groaned. 'Surely they wouldn't bother with us – we've only just started to trade. We don't earn enough to make it worth their while – do we?'

She knew that some businesses in London did pay protection money to racketeers, but they usually went after club owners and successful restaurants and pubs. As yet she was only a small wholesaler and if she had to pay protection money she might as well close her doors. Lizzie didn't feel that it was a petty criminal threatening her – but someone with a personal grudge, and the only person she could think of was Harry's uncle.

'Who knows?' Ed shrugged. 'First off I'll pay Oliver a visit and warn him to leave you alone and then we'll see. I could ask around a bit. I've kept out of their way, but there was a time when

I knew people – the wrong sort of people, Lizzie. I could see if some of my old contacts have heard anything . . .'

'Just talk to Harry's uncle,' Lizzie said, 'and then we'll see . . .' She wasn't sure it would do much good, but as long as Ed kept his temper and didn't hit him it surely couldn't make things worse. Ed wasn't usually a bad-tempered man, but she knew he felt protective of her and it had upset him to hear that she was being threatened.

Ed met her the next morning as she arrived at her premises and told her about the row he'd had with his former employer, Lizzie was speechless and then she started to laugh when he told her the reason for their quarrel.

'Oh, Ed, that is just so ridiculous that it would be funny – if it weren't so serious. He must be losing his mind . . . to accuse us of having an affair!'

'He means it, Lizzie, and he's tellin' everyone who will listen that we're lovers . . .'

'How could he be so unfair?' Lizzie asked. 'I do love you as a friend and I respect you as a colleague, Ed – but I'm not in love with you and you aren't with me either. It would be an insult to Madge's memory to think you would do something like that so soon after . . .'

'That's what I told him, Lizzie,' Ed said, a tiny pulse throbbing in his neck. 'To say such a thing about you . . . I'd have thumped him, but to tell you the truth he looks ill. I think he's taken on too much and he can't cope – and he's let Harry's death fester inside him until he's so bitter he can't see the truth even if it's in front of him.'

'Yes, I think that must be his problem,' Lizzie said. 'He's working too hard, worried about his business and grieving all at the same time. I understand the bitterness, but sending someone to threaten me . . .'

'No, I don't think that was Oliver,' Ed said and looked thoughtful. 'I asked him straight out and said we were going to the police and he looked shocked. Told me he would ruin your business if he could by blackening your reputation, but he swore he hadn't sent someone to break your shop window or threaten you . . .'

'Did you think he was telling the truth?'

'Yes, I did think so . . .' Ed hesitated, then, 'He almost looked upset at the thought. Told me I should go to the police because there were some nasty types about . . .'

'What did he mean by that? Lizzie wondered aloud. 'I think I shall have to talk to the police – and perhaps you should ask people you know, see if anyone has been noticed hanging around . . .'

CHAPTER 5

'Mary has gone home with Mum,' Beth greeted Lizzie with the news when she walked in that evening. 'The hospital let her go because she promised to stay with Mum for a while, until she feels better again.'

'I'm glad she's out of the hospital. If they'd decided she needed treatment at a mental institution . . .' Lizzie shuddered at the idea. 'Thank goodness for that, Beth.'

'Mum said she'll have the children again as soon as she can – but we could leave them with a neighbour for a while if you need me back in the showroom.'

'I'm not sure,' Lizzie said. 'What do you feel, Beth? Perhaps we should interview a few people or look for a nursery?'

'Mum will have them again soon. I just thought you might feel I was letting you down?'

'I want you back at work, of course I do,' Lizzie said. 'But I'd rather you stayed here to look after the children until your mum can take over again, love. I don't trust other people with our babies . . .'

'All right then,' Beth said. 'You're the boss . . .'

'We do everything together,' Lizzie said. 'I was thinking we ought to have them all christened soon, ask the vicar if he will do it all on one day. Perhaps the twins' birthday in June . . .'

'Lovely idea,' Beth said. 'It would cheer us all up to have something nice to think about . . .' She yawned and stretched. 'Do you think Hitler's lot will let us have a bit of rest tonight?'

'God knows what will happen if they don't soon let up,' Lizzie said. 'Did you hear the news? Half of London was on fire this morning, one of the worst raids we've had since the Blitz started.'

'The papers say Hitler's claiming it's in reprisal for us bombing their towns. I don't know who's to blame, I just wish it would stop . . .'

Lizzie shook her head and went upstairs because she could hear one of the children crying. Betty was sleeping peacefully and Lizzie resisted the urge to pick her up and cuddle her. Jenny was fretful and when Lizzie touched her forehead, she discovered she felt a bit hot so she picked her up and took her downstairs.

'She's awake again then,' Beth frowned as she saw that Lizzie had brought her daughter down. 'It took me ages to get her off and . . .' she broke off as the doorbell rang. 'I'll go – it might be Bernie . . .'

Lizzie was sitting nursing the baby when Mary walked in. Her eyes went to Jenny, who had quietened, her eyes closed and for a moment a look of sheer envy showed on her pale face, but in an instant it had gone.

'I came round because Mum said you were staying off work to look after the children,' she said. 'I wanted to tell you there's no need. Mum can come round here or have them at home. I'm going back to my house tomorrow.'

'But the hospital let you go because you promised to stay with Mum . . .'

'Who cares what they said,' Mary shrugged. 'I'm fine now, Beth. Can I hold Jenny for a bit?'

Beth hesitated and Lizzie knew she wanted to refuse, but she met Lizzie's eyes and then nodded. 'All right, but Lizzie has just got her to stop crying. Please don't upset her.'

'She's hot, probably teething,' Mary said and there was resentment in her eyes as she looked at her sister. 'I do know a bit about children. I was on the children's ward until I got pregnant.'

'I'm so sorry for your dreadful loss,' Lizzie said as she handed over the baby. 'It's very hard for you . . . if there's anything we can do . . .'

'Oh, well, I suppose it happens,' Mary said carelessly, but she looked down at the baby with such intensity that Lizzie felt a jolt of fear. It just wasn't natural that she should look at her sister's child that way.

'Come up with me and we'll put her back in her cot,' Beth said. 'Come on, Mary. She needs her sleep . . .'

The two sisters went up the stairs together. Lizzie made a fresh pot of tea but Mary refused the offer when she came down. 'No thanks, I've been drinking tea all day. Remember what I said, I'm going home so you can bring them round to Mum and go to work – it's quite safe . . .'

Lizzie and Beth looked at each other as she left. It was obvious to both of them that Mary still wasn't right, even though she was pretending she was over the worst.

Beth washed her hair before she went to bed that evening. She hadn't much time to look after it lately, because of all the visits to the hospital and having three young children to care for. She was in two minds about leaving the children with her mother, because something kept niggling at the back of her mind – something in the way Mary had looked at Jenny.

She knew that Lizzie had noticed it too, but being Lizzie she hadn't said anything. Beth didn't want to worry her, because Lizzie had enough to cope with. Beth was well aware that the business wasn't doing as well as it had at the start – and she knew her friend was hiding something, even though Lizzie wouldn't say what. Once things were back to normal she'd get it out of her – but was it too soon to return to work? Yet no one could force Mary to stay at home and be fussed over if she didn't want it.

Beth was thoughtful as she sat drying her hair. It had got a bit long recently and she ought to have it trimmed; it was less trouble when it was shorter, but she'd let it grow because Bernie liked it long and shiny – like spun gold, he said when

78

he'd come round a few weeks earlier and found her just after she'd washed it.

Bernie was pressing hard for marriage. Beth couldn't blame him, because he'd been patient for a long time, but she still didn't feel like giving him an answer. The truth was that he was good to her and she found it useful when he ran her about in his car – but did she want to be his wife?

Beth knew she would have to give him an answer soon. It would make sense to say yes, because she wasn't likely to find anyone else to take her on with another man's children. The man she'd once believed she was in love with certainly wasn't interested; he'd been angry because she'd fallen for Mark and had his twins. Tony had told her bluntly when she was pregnant that he wouldn't be such a fool. Beth sighed and a sharp surge of regret went through her. Tony had been so impatient because she wouldn't go to bed with him; they'd quarrelled, and he'd stopped coming round, and that was when she'd gone to the party at Mr Winters' house and met Mark. Sometimes she wished she'd never met Mark, never fallen in love with him – and if she could go back, she certainly wouldn't be as careless again. She had loved Mark but she'd been too reckless and it had been a heavy price to pay, losing him too soon and having to bear the shame of her condition. Yet she loved the twins and wouldn't be without them, which was a complete contradiction and made her laugh and throw off her reflective mood.

She had time enough to make up her mind, and she wasn't sure what she was waiting for; it was just something inside her that held her back every time she was on the verge of telling Bernie that she would marry him. Perhaps she was a fool to hesitate; her parents had made it clear they thought she should marry him for the sake of her children.

They would be a year old in June and were already difficult to control. When they started running around and getting into mischief they would be a handful and she wasn't sure whether her mother would cope, which would make it difficult for Beth to work. Perhaps they did need a father and at least Bernie was prepared to take them on, which a lot of men wouldn't.

'You told me you'd soon have her in the palm of your hand,' the man in a suit said glaring at the thin man with the scar on his cheek. His light topaz eyes glittered with anger. 'I haven't seen any signs that she's running scared. In fact, I've reason to believe that she intends to carry on regardless of your efforts . . .'

'I smashed her winder, got a floosy of mine to steal from her – and I give her a warning the other night afore she caught the tram. If yer give me the word, I'll mark her,' Norm muttered and fingered the knife he always wore strapped to his arm inside his left sleeve. 'One word and she's dead.'

'If you so much as touch her with that knife, I'll make sure the cops know where to find you,' Norm's employer muttered. 'I want her scared. I want her out of business – but I want her alive and unmarked. Is that clear?'

'Yeah,' Norm scowled, annoyed because he wanted to do more than throw a scare into that defiant little bitch. He could just imagine her struggling, clawing at him with her nails while he thrust into her and then . . .' Norm licked his lips, because he knew the pleasure it would give him to cut her – tiny cuts that went on and on for a long time and in the end one swift sharp one across her throat. Just the way he'd done for the lying whore Nancy after she'd run to the police with her tales of a beating. Nancy was at the bottom of the river now, good riddance. The police were looking for Norm but they hadn't cottoned on that Nancy was missing. Who would miss one more little bitch? Once he'd got the money this devil had promised him, he would be off to another big city where he could start over . . .

'Do some more damage to the shop,' his employer instructed. 'I want her out of business and I'm running out of patience.'

Norm regarded him curiously. No one who didn't know the secret side of this man would guess at what he did in the shadows. Openly respectable, he was a cruel devil and Norm respected him because he knew what he was capable of if pushed to take action himself. He liked to keep his hands clean and paid others to do his dirty work, but Norm had seen him in action once with the girls that worked for him, and he'd never forgotten it. It was at one of his houses that Norm had first met Nancy, the pretty little whore who had thought she could make a fool of him, and if this man knew what he'd done to her, he'd slit his throat soon as look at him, because the bitch was a good earner on her back for her master. If truth were told, there was something about him that sent the shivers down Norm's spine. He wasn't afraid of much, but he'd take care to stay on the safe side of this one and not just because he hadn't been paid yet.

'What did the bitch do to you then?' Norm growled.

'That ain't your concern.' His employer's face twisted, a flicker of hatred in his eyes. 'Keep your nose out of my business, your trap shut and do as I tell you – or you might get a visit from a certain Inspector Martin . . .'

Norm clenched his fists, wanting to give the bastard what he deserved for threatening him with the rope, because that was what waited for him if the cops caught up with him.

'I'd take you with me,' he muttered beneath his breath, adding aloud, 'I'll give 'er such a scare she'll shut up the place termorra . . .'

'Good. Here's what I owe you for now, but if the shop closes down you'll get the rest and there will be a bonus.'

Norm pocketed the wad of notes. The money was useful, because London was getting to be an uncomfortable place. He would need to make a run for it before much longer because he was going to have his fun once he'd finished his business. Oh yes, Norm didn't intend to let that little bitch get off with a few warnings, because she'd defied him – if he hadn't succeeded in scaring her yet, she would never sleep again after he'd finished with her.

Lizzie cried out and woke with a start, sitting bolt upright in bed. It was still dark and she sat staring into the blackness, shivering with fear and feeling the trickle of sweat between her breasts and under her hair at her nape. Had the siren gone? She listened for a while but it was quiet. They'd had a raid earlier in the evening, but then the all-clear had gone. No, it wasn't a bomb that had woken her. She'd had an awful dream . . . but it wasn't the old dream. It wasn't like a dream at all. No, it was very different. Her mind was still filled with vivid pictures and she could see the man lying injured on the ground – it was a scene of chaos and carnage: it was war and the man was badly hurt – and the man was Sebastian.

Lizzie felt the tears on her cheeks as she whispered his name, 'Sebastian . . . Oh my love, I wish you were here with me. I don't know where you are or if you're hurt . . . but I feel you with me and I feel your pain.'

Lizzie had the strongest sensation that Sebastian needed her – that he'd called to her over and over in his anguish. It was as if her dream was replaying in her mind now that she was awake. Sebastian was hurt and he wanted her, needed her – but she couldn't go to him, because she didn't know where he was.

Lizzie tried not to worry about Sebastian's whereabouts when she was awake. She knew that he wouldn't write to her often. She had a few letters saved in her drawers but her instinct had told her he was safe – perhaps in a dangerous situation, but safe. Now she was worried and all her other worries seemed to fade into the background.

'Come back to me, Sebastian,' she murmured and dashed the tears from her cheeks. There was no point in crying. He would come to her when he could, because his letter had promised it and she could only cling to the belief that he would keep his word – but tonight she felt so vulnerable and so unutterably lonely.

Lizzie was never going to sleep again that night. She got up and went into the children's bedroom, checking on them all to make sure they were sleeping peacefully, lingering to kiss Betty softly, and then she walked down to the kitchen, closing the door before she switched on the light and filled the kettle. A cup of tea would help to relax her and then she would start work on some new designs for the summer and autumn collections.

She'd been feeling upset over Ed's row with

Harry's uncle, because it was so unfair that he should start scurrilous rumours about them – unfair to Ed as well as Lizzie.

She was just pouring a cup of tea when the kitchen door opened and Beth entered. Yawning, she gave Lizzie an odd look as she fetched a cup for herself.

'Did you have one of your bad dreams?'

'Yes, did I wake you?' Lizzie grimaced. 'I knew I wouldn't sleep again so I came down to make a pot of tea – and then I think I'll do some work.'

'The children didn't wake, so you couldn't have made much noise. I couldn't sleep either so I heard you get up . . .'

'It wasn't the same dream, Beth, just a silly nightmare.' She didn't want to talk about the horrific dream because then that would be like making it come true.

'It's all this bother with Mary and the shop, and the rest of it,' Beth said. 'Things play on your mind and then you make all sorts of things happen in your dreams.'

'Yes, I expect you're right,' Lizzie agreed, though her dream had had nothing to do with her life. It was definitely a war scene, men lying on the ground injured and blood everywhere . . .

Something inside her was telling her that Sebastian had been injured, but there was no one she could ask for news. She just had to hope it was a dream . . .

CHAPTER 6

Lizzie gave a cry of distress when they arrived at the showroom the next morning. Once again her window had been broken, though because they'd had stronger glass, it had merely cracked and no fragments had fallen on the display. It still meant the expense of a new pane of glass, but that wasn't the worst of it. What upset Lizzie the most was the red paint sloshed on the walls and shop door – the word WHORE written in bold letters.

'Oh no,' Beth said and put an arm about Lizzie's waist. 'That is disgusting. You will have to tell the police now, Lizzie.'

'Yes, I shall. I don't have a choice,' Lizzie said. Ed had just come out with a bucket of hot water and a brush. He sent her a grim look and started scrubbing at the offending word.

'I hoped I'd have this done before you got here,' Ed told her, 'but the police sent someone out and I had to stop and talk to them. One of the neighbours reported it, but I was going to myself – this can't go on, Lizzie.'

'No, I realize that,' she said and shivered. 'I

thought it might all just go away – but now I know it won't. Whoever hates me is determined to put me out of business.'

'I can't understand it,' Ed said. 'Why should anyone hate you, Lizzie? You've never done anyone a spot of harm – and I told the police so. I told them everything, Lizzie, so Oliver will be getting a visit from them – and serve him right.'

'But you didn't think he was involved in trying to frighten me?'

'No, but this has made me think again. Who else would call you that filthy name, Lizzie? You've never given anyone any cause . . .' Ed broke off as one of their neighbours came to join them. He was carrying a bucket and brush and offered to give Ed a hand.

'I'm sorry about this, Mrs Oliver,' he apologized to Lizzie. 'I didn't hear a thing last night or I'd have called the police then – but as soon as I saw it I gave them a call. It's bad enough what we have to put up with from the Germans without this. A nice lady like you . . . well, the least I can do is to help clean it up for you. I've got some stuff here to get the paint off, Ed, and then you can wash it away.'

Lizzie thanked her kindly neighbour and left the men to get on with their task. Ed had abandoned the order he was working on to clean up, so Lizzie took over and cut some of the basic shapes needed, moulded them into the simple cloche that their customer had ordered and gave them to Jean, her trainee seamstress, to finish. Work helped her to calm down and there was nothing she could do, except carry on. The order was for six basic hats trimmed with ribbons, bows or a flower and not the kind of hat Lizzie preferred to spend her time on, but at the moment it was the only order they had. Unless she had some more orders in soon she would have to start thinking of how she was going to make ends meet. She didn't want to ask Ed for some of his savings, though she knew he'd be happy to give them to her.

There must be a way to find new customers, despite the war and the spiteful attacks on her property. Lizzie knew that before the conflict there had been trade fairs, where firms like Oliver's had taken their stock to show off and make new contacts. Since the war had started all that had been put on the back-burner . . . but perhaps she could put on something at the local church hall. She might make a range of inexpensive hats; like the ones she'd sold to Mave for her wedding. Perhaps she could encourage more working women into the shop, sell direct to the public rather than wholesale or bespoke hats for her wealthy clients. The trouble with that was that she might lose some of the clients who wanted an exclusive line if they thought she was selling cheap copies. Besides, she hadn't had even one inquiry from the public since Mave had been in. Everyone was feeling down because of the constant bombing. There wasn't much point in buying new clothes, when everything you owned might be lost in a raid. She would be better concentrating on her wholesale business, because the shops she sold to had customers that were always able to afford new hats, and the West End didn't catch it as much as they did here, where all the manufacturers and the Docks took a pounding most nights.

Everywhere you looked in Bethnal Green there was evidence of the terrible damage; the City of London Chest Hospital had recently received a direct hit, destroying the nurses' home, the chapel and the wards. The Approach Tavern was hit the same night and several people living in Approach Road were killed in the raid.

It was no use she couldn't get the horrid incident out of her mind. Feeling restless, she went outside to discover the men had managed to scrub off the nasty word and were now trying to get rid of a red smudge on the walls.

'Oh, that's so much better,' Lizzie said. 'Thank you, Mr Jacobs. May I get you a cup of tea or coffee?'

'No, thank you, Mrs Oliver. I'll get back to my shop now.'

'Well, thank you for your kindness . . .'

Lizzie sighed as she saw that although the door was looking much better the wall was never going to be properly clean again. They could always paint the door over with a coat of gloss paint, if they could get any – but the wall would have to bear the stain until the weather wore it away.

89

'Come in now, Ed. You've done all you can. Jean has put the kettle on and I've rung about a new pane of glass.'

'She's a good girl, I like her.' Ed gave a grim nod of assent and followed her into the office. 'It's a nasty piece of work, Lizzie. I'd like to know who's behind it . . .'

'We'd best leave that to the police,' Lizzie said. 'I don't want you getting hurt, Ed. It was a shock, but nothing really matters but people. I can buy a new window and you've washed away the slander – we'll just have to carry on for as long as we can . . .'

'You're not thinking of giving up?' Ed frowned. 'It's what he wants, whoever he is – he's trying to upset you so much that you shut down.'

'But why?' Lizzie asked. 'We're not treading on anyone's toes, surely – and this was always a workshop for fine hats. So who doesn't want me to be in business? It just doesn't make sense.'

'Well, you know who I blame . . .'

'But you said he was shocked about the broken window and the threats. This was much worse,' Lizzie was thoughtful. 'I can't honestly think that Harry's uncle would do this . . .'

'He can't forgive you for Harry's death – and I think he misses you in the business. Your leaving has hurt him in his pocket and that's half of the problem. He's finding it a bit too much.'

'It was his decision to sack me and not give me a reference,' Lizzie said.

'Perhaps he regrets that . . .'

'Then why try to ruin me?'

'Because he wants you to run back to him and beg him for a job?'

'No! He couldn't think this would bring me running back to him? Oh, Ed, surely he wouldn't try to put me out of business for that reason?'

'Well, I can't think of another,' Ed said and took the mug of tea she handed him. 'You've been followed and threatened – and they've made life thoroughly uncomfortable for you – what other reason makes sense?'

'None of it makes sense to me,' Lizzie said. 'Surely he must know that I wouldn't go back to him after this?'

'Maybe he's not thinkin' properly.'

'I know he's under a strain,' Lizzie said. 'But he has no right to hurt me just because he was hurt by Harry's death – I felt it too.'

'He's a silly man,' Ed said. 'As if we haven't all of us got enough to do with worrying about where the next bomb will fall . . . Several houses were damaged again last night and only two streets from here. I keep wondering how long we'll escape.'

'Oh don't,' Lizzie begged.

'If the worst happens we'll just have to start again somewhere else,' Ed said. 'But I feel for those who've lost their homes and their livelihoods. If you lose everything there's no compensation, business and homes gone in a night. I sometimes wonder how much we can take as a nation, Lizzie.'

'But without our boys in blue it would have been so much worse. I think London might have been razed to the ground – the way they say some German cities have been since it started. I know they're the enemy but . . .' she sighed. Ed knew well enough how bad things were, because he was out on fire watch several nights a week.

'It's war, Lizzie,' Ed said and looked grave. 'We can't let ourselves feel sorry for the enemy. We might feel it's wrong to kill so many people, but we have to win and if that means bombing German towns and cities it has to happen.'

'Yes, I know,' she said. 'But it makes my problems look insignificant, doesn't it? What are a cracked window and some red paint when we're in the middle of a blitz?'

'We're catching it every single night here in the East End,' Ed said grimly. 'We lost three shops in the next road last week and a whole row of houses two streets away, and the Falcon pub in Victoria Park Square was demolished. Honestly, I sometimes think we have a guardian angel looking after us.'

'It wasn't just us in the East End last night; Westminster Hall caught it and the House of Commons was reduced to rubble. Big Ben was hit and the British Museum and St Paul's . . .'

'Well, as I said, I think we've got someone up there looking out for us . . .'

'I could do with his help now,' Lizzie said but she laughed. Sometimes she tended to forget the war when she got wrapped up in her own problems, and talking about it, remembering, and thinking of the men who were out there risking their lives, well, it did make her troubles seem almost trivial . . . A broken window was nothing compared with what many people had lost.

'We'll ask one of our constables to walk past a couple of times on his beat,' the police sergeant told Lizzie when he came to interview her later that day. 'But I'm afraid we haven't time to do more than that, madam. With the war on, we're at full stretch. All the best men are at the front and we have to make do with special constables, grandfathers what ought to be sittin' by their fires of an evenin'. We're supposed to be a reserved occupation. They don't 'ave to go, but there's no stoppin' them when they get the urge. Half strength that's what we've been for months.'

'Yes, of course I understand and thank you for coming to see me,' Lizzie said. 'I wouldn't have troubled you, but it isn't the first time.'

'I dare say one of your competitors has it in for you,' the constable said. 'We'll have a word with Bert Oliver – hear what he has to say . . .'

'I don't think he did this. He's not really well. I'd rather you didn't upset him too much . . .'

'We shan't do that, Mrs Oliver, but it sounds to me that he might have a grudge. A word to the wise could be all that's needed here . . .'

'Yes, perhaps.'

Lizzie sighed as he left. She wished it hadn't been necessary to call the police. It was just too unpleasant and she didn't hate Harry's uncle – in fact she felt sorry for him.

Beth came through from the showroom that afternoon. From the look on her face, Lizzie knew something was wrong and her heart sank. Not another cancelled order!

'It's Harry's Aunt Miriam. She is demanding to see you, Lizzie.'

'Ask her to come through,' Lizzie said, wondering why Harry's aunt had decided to visit her. Surely she hadn't come to quarrel as well? She hoped not, because she'd had enough of it. 'I'll talk to her in private.'

'She's upset and angry,' Beth warned as she went back through to the showroom.

Lizzie prepared herself for the worst. Aunt Miriam's face looked pale, but there were red circles under her eyes and Lizzie knew she'd been crying. She'd hardly seen her since Harry's funeral and felt upset to see the woman she was quite fond of looking so distressed.

'Come and sit down, Aunt Miriam. Jean, go and put the kettle on please – and knock before you bring the tea into the office.' She took the older woman's arm and led her through. 'We can be private in here . . .'

'Oh, Lizzie,' Aunt Miriam said and sat down in the comfortable old wing chair that Lizzie kept for visitors. 'I thought you would be so angry, but I had to come. It wasn't Bertie that did all those things. I give you my word. I know he's put a few customers off recently by telling them things he shouldn't – but he was shocked and hurt when the police came. He would never do such a thing, Lizzie. He gets angry and says things he ought not, but he wouldn't harm you. I was upset when he sent you away. You know I think of you as family – and I love little Betty . . .'

'Yes, I know you do,' Lizzie said and smiled at her. 'I wish you could see her more often, but I didn't like to bring her round, because Bert would be angry. I didn't think Bertie was to blame for the red paint and the smashed windows, but really they aren't the worst of it – it's the customers leaving me because of his lies . . .'

'I know and I'm sorry.' Aunt Miriam dabbed at her eyes with a large handkerchief. 'It's very bad of him and I've told him not to do it. I'll make him stop, Lizzie – and I'll make him tell those customers that he was mistaken.'

'I don't think he will listen,' Lizzie said, 'and although I don't think he did this, others do. He seems to be the obvious one, because who else would want to ruin me?'

'I don't know, Lizzie. You don't deserve it, no matter what anyone says – I know it wasn't your fault that Harry was killed, though I did blame you at the time, because he stopped coming home on leave. Why didn't he want to come home, Lizzie?'

'It wasn't my fault,' Lizzie said. 'If I told you the truth about why he didn't come, it would be a betrayal of Harry's memory. Please believe me when I say that it hurt me as much as it hurt him – or you.'

'Well, it isn't my place to pry,' the older woman said and blew her nose on a large handkerchief. 'I know you're busy, Lizzie, but I was wondering if you could spare one evening a week to help us out at the canteen – well, it's more of a social club, as you know. You could serve or just help make sandwiches if you wanted . . .' Lizzie had gone to help at the social club for servicemen regularly before she had Betty, but since then and the quarrel with Uncle Bertie, she'd stayed away, partly because she didn't have much time, and partly because she hadn't been sure she would be welcome.

'I'll have to talk to Beth about it,' Lizzie said. 'I can't expect her to look after Betty – but I should like to help. I enjoyed it before.'

'Well, I was thinking about things . . .' Aunt Miriam's eyes were filled with longing. 'I could come round and babysit for you both – and you two could have a night at the club. It would make a change for you, Lizzie – and I'd get to see you and Betty sometimes.'

'What would Uncle Bert say?'

'He won't have to know,' Aunt Miriam looked guilty but determined. 'He'll think I've gone to the club – I've kept it up all this time, twice a

96

week. Please say yes. It's tearing me apart, Lizzie, never getting to see you and the child. You're all I've got you know . . .'

The handkerchief came out again as Jean knocked and then brought in a tray of tea and some biscuits. The short interval gave Lizzie time to think; she and Beth could do with a change, and one night a week at the servicemen's social club would do them both good.

'Yes, all right, I'll ask Beth. I think she will be pleased. We never get out because her Mum looks after the children most days so we can't ask her at night or the weekends. I know I can trust you with the children – they will sleep most of the time anyway.'

'Yes, but I'll get to see Betty in the bath and if she wakes up I can nurse her, can't I? Just for a while . . .'

'Yes, of course.' Lizzie made a mental note to find a way of seeing more of Harry's aunt. Because she had no family of her own, it was important that Betty should have a few people she could count as her own when she grew up.

Beth came in for her lunchbreak after Harry's aunt had gone. She was surprised when Lizzie told her about the offer she'd made.

'Are you sure you can trust her?'

'Oh yes,' Lizzie smiled. 'She's all right really, a bit of a fusspot sometimes, but she would never harm the children – and she wouldn't neglect them either.'

'What will her husband say?'

'She isn't going to tell him,' Lizzie said. 'What do you think – shall we take her up on it? It's nice at the club, Beth. The young soldiers are so grateful for all we do – and you might get asked to dance. You might meet someone, fall in love and get married . . .'

'I doubt it, when they know I've got twins at home,' Beth laughed harshly. 'But it would be fun – it's ages since we had a night out together, Lizzie.'

'Well, we have to help out with making the sandwiches and serving the men, but we shan't be working all the time and it is a way of getting out . . .'

'We'll do it,' Beth said and laughed in relief. 'I thought she'd come to have a row with you – she looked so angry.'

'Angry with her husband, not me,' Lizzie said. 'Perhaps things will start to get better now. She said Bert Oliver had a shock when the police went there so perhaps he might stop telling lies about me . . .'

'It will do the pair of you the world of good,' Beth's mother said when they told her about Aunt Miriam coming to babysit one evening a week. 'You know I'd have done it if I could, Beth, but I couldn't manage evenings or weekends.'

'We wouldn't dream of asking,' Lizzie told her. 'We are so grateful for all you do, and I know I would prefer you to anyone else – but Aunt Miriam is to be trusted. She wanted children but couldn't have them and she adores Betty – she's more likely to spoil them than neglect them.'

'Well, that would be easy enough to do,' Mrs Court said and smiled at her. 'I popped in with the children to see Mary this afternoon. She was just sitting there staring at the wall, but she cheered up when she saw the children.'

'That must have been hard work for you – pushing all three in the pram together?' Beth said and frowned.

'I used to have three of mine in together when the twins were babies.'

'You were younger then,' Beth objected. 'You shouldn't wear yourself out like that, Mum.'

'Well Mary carried Matt home in her arms because he was screaming,' her mother said, 'it wasn't so bad – and it cheered your sister up a bit. You mustn't grudge her a little happiness, Beth.'

'I don't,' Beth replied but she was uneasy.

Lizzie looked at her anxiously as they fed the children and then popped them into the bath before taking them up to bed.

'You're worried about Mary, aren't you?' Lizzie asked.

'Yes, because . . . she's not right,' Beth said and shook her head. 'I don't mind her helping Mum with the children sometimes, but I'm nervous of what she might do if she was alone with them. She's so intense, Lizzie.'

'Beth! You can't think she would hurt your babies? She's grieving because she lost hers, but that doesn't make her a monster.'

Beth nodded but she turned away and didn't answer.

Later, when she was in bed she dwelled on the answers both Lizzie and her mother had given her. They both seemed to think she was being unfair to Mary, even though Lizzie had understood how she felt. Beth's mum was bound to feel for Mary, because she'd lost her baby – Beth was sorry for her too, but she didn't quite trust her sister. She couldn't have said why, but when Aunt Miriam came to babysit for the evening, she would make certain she knew never to leave Mary alone with them. If her sister called round on some pretext, she wasn't to be left with the children . . .

'Why don't we ask Mary if she'd like to come to the social club too?' Lizzie said as they travelled to work the next morning, after a night that had been remarkably quiet. The sirens had gone but they hadn't heard any bombing and then the all-clear had sounded. No one believed it meant the blitz was over, but perhaps they were going to get a bit of a rest; it was certainly needed, because the fires were still burning from one of the worst nights London had ever seen. 'It might take her mind off her loss and perhaps she would enjoy it . . . it could be her salvation, being around men who've endured hell . . .'

'We could ask her I suppose,' Beth said, still feeling a little dubious. 'She's not easy to understand. Mary's always gone her own way in the past . . .'

'Yes, I know you don't always get on with her, Beth, but she must be going through her own private hell. If it helps a bit, perhaps she'll come out of her misery . . . I know you're worried about her, but giving her some help might be better than treating her like a leper.'

'I haven't! I don't . . .' Beth was indignant, but she knew Lizzie's words carried some truth. She would have much preferred it if she didn't have to ask her sister to go with them, but she couldn't refuse because Lizzie would think she was being mean.

Mary shook her head when Beth told her about the club and asked if she'd like to help out. 'You'd be with us and I'm sure they would be glad of the help, Mary.'

'What would my husband think if he came home and heard I was out at some club? I've just lost his child – do you think I want to go dancing and drinking?'

'You don't need to do any of that,' Beth said. 'You could help with the food and perhaps serve if you wanted. There may be music and dancing, but you can just listen and watch.'

'It's all right for you,' Mary said, her mouth twisting with scorn. 'You've no husband to worry about. It's just like you to carry on with men you don't even know. Everything goes right for you, doesn't it? Dad thought you were a little tart when you got pregnant by that toff – but you soon got round him and Mum. Now you're living in a posh house with that friend of yours – and she's making lots of money with her hats . . .'

'Lizzie works hard for what she gets and it isn't easy. She makes a living but she isn't rich . . .'

'No?' Mary looked at her with dislike. 'Who else do you know who could afford to give you presents like she does? You're getting above your stations, Beth. One of these days you'll take a tumble . . .'

'Oh, Mary . . .' Beth sighed, holding on to her temper. 'I don't know why you've taken against me. I'm sorry you lost the baby. I know what it is like to lose someone you love, but you're so bitter and jealous—'

'I'd like you to leave,' Mary said. 'And don't bother me again. I've got more to do with my time than run after servicemen . . .'

Beth left her to it. She was angry that she'd wasted precious time, time she might have had with her children. Weekends were very precious for both Beth and Lizzie, because it was the one chance they got to take the children to the park or out for an ice cream at Lyons. They were all a bit young to appreciate the treat yet, but they loved being all together with their mums and Beth loved it too.

It was one of the reasons she'd kept refusing Bernie. It was comfortable living with Lizzie, sharing the bills and their rations, and she knew that if she'd been managing in one little room in a lodging house she would probably have taken him long before this, but she'd been lucky, just as Mary claimed. Her father had disowned her for a while, but he'd come round after the twins were born, and she was lucky to live in Lizzie's house. Lizzie's uncle had been well off in his own way, even though his wife had behaved as if she hadn't a penny to her name, but after her death Lizzie had come into quite a bit of money as well as the house – and she'd shared her good fortune with Beth – just as Beth helped her when she'd been more or less thrown out by her aunt. And it was better for both of them to share pool their resources.

Beth's conscience wouldn't let her rest after her meeting with Mary. She told Lizzie that she'd come close to hitting her sister and they'd parted with harsh words, but Lizzie only laughed and shook her head.

'You've got a temper too, love,' she said. 'I tell you what, I'll pop round there and talk to her. We'll give her another chance, because she needs our help and support, Beth.'

'Yes, I know,' Beth said and felt a bit ashamed. 'I suppose sisters do quarrel a lot and there's always a certain rivalry – but she's right, I did land on my feet, and most of it is down to you, Lizzie.'

'We're closer than sisters,' Lizzie placed an arm about her shoulders. 'Whatever I've given you, you've given back, Beth. I couldn't manage without you. I mean that.'

Beth nodded and sighed. 'Bernie wants to take me out shopping next Saturday. He wants to buy me a new coat and things for the kids – and he says we'll have something to eat. Would you mind if I went . . .? I know it lands you with the kids all day . . .?'

'Ed asked if he could take us out. He'll come here and we can take the children to the park and feed them ice creams and then we'll have fish and chips and mushy peas. He's like an uncle to them and Matt loves him . . .'

'I think I'd rather be with you,' Beth said and laughed. 'But Bernie is so insistent and I don't feel I can say no again.'

CHAPTER 7

Lizzie had better luck with Beth's sister than she'd had. Mary seemed a bit shamefaced and subdued as she invited Lizzie into her home. The sitting room looked almost as bad as if a bomb had hit it, clothes and shoes all over the settee and the floor.

'I'm having a sort out,' Mary explained. 'I can't afford much new, so I'm going to see what I can make out of my old clothes, because some of the material is still good . . .'

'I think a lot of people are doing that now,' Lizzie said ruefully. 'There isn't much in the shops these days, and what is available has no style. If you need help with anything, Mary, you could bring it round to us and I'm sure Jean would help. She's our seamstress and a lovely girl, though still learning herself.'

'You're always so generous,' Mary said but there was a hint of resentment in her face.

'I like to help friends where I can.' Lizzie hesitated, then, 'That's why I wanted to see if I could persuade you to come to the social club with us. The men are grateful for what we offer them, some nice food, a cup of tea and the piano. Usually they have a sing-song and sometimes they dance . . . it's all very informal. I used to go twice a week then stopped after I had Betty, but I'm pleased to be doing something useful again.'

'I'll think about it,' Mary said. 'Beth asked me but I got cross with her. She seems to think all she has to do is wave her finger and we all come running . . .'

'That isn't very fair, is it, Mary?'

'No, not fair at all,' Mary laughed harshly. 'Beth always brings out the worst in me. I've never known why. I loved Dottie and my brother, but I never could take to her – perhaps because she was the baby and they all made so much fuss of her.'

Mary really was jealous of her sister and nothing Lizzie could do or say would change that.

'Well, the offer is there and you would be welcome if you turned up, Mary.'

'I'll think about it – but thanks for asking.'

Lizzie put Mary and her problems out of her head and went to work. She'd thought Mary might have been drinking sherry when she called, because she could smell it and there had been an empty bottle on the table with a used glass. Lizzie knew that drinking alcohol wouldn't ease Mary's pain, but she wouldn't listen to wise advice, from her mother or anyone else. There certainly wasn't anything more that Lizzie could do to help her.

She was surprised but pleased when one of her

old customers came through to the workrooms that morning.

'Mr Carter,' she said. 'How nice to see you. I wondered why you hadn't been to order for – it must be two months now . . .'

'Beth told me I could come through,' he said a little pink in the cheeks. 'Truth is I've had a lot on my plate recently, Mrs Oliver – but things are sorted now and I'd like to place an order with you please.'

'I have several new lines for spring and summer. If you would like to look at these examples Ed has been working on. We have a range of silk hats . . . well, it's artificial silk actually, because we can't get anything from Italy these days, and you know we used to buy a lot of our best materials from there. However, this is produced in England and it is such nice quality that only a true connoisseur would know. Besides, it's cheaper and that means more women can afford it . . . I can sell you all these lines at just twenty-two shillings each.'

'Ah yes, price always helps,' John Carter said and smiled at her. 'Well, you've been busy – and I like all of what I've seen. I'm going to take three of each of those new styles, one in each of the colours you have on show – and I like the velvet bonnets too. No one else is producing anything like these.' He picked one up to admire it, because it was so unusual. There was a little poke brim, which gave it the style of a bonnet, but the rest was soft and squashy and sat on the back of the head like a little cap rather than an old-fashioned bonnet. 'I'll try the red and the mauve in this one, just to see how it goes . . .'

'Thirty-two hats?' Lizzie asked, a little surprised because his order was usually no more than ten or twelve at a time.

The colour rose up his neck and he couldn't quite look at her as he said, 'Well, I've neglected my stock for a while and my manager bought some rubbish while I was out – we've still got it on the shelves after two months and its likely to be there next year unless I have a sale and get rid of it . . .'

Lizzie smiled but didn't comment, though she was fairly sure that Mr Carter had tried another supplier after listening to Bert Oliver's tales and discovered that he couldn't sell the stock the way he could sell the stylish hats he bought from her.

'Well, I'm delighted to have you back,' Lizzie said. 'I shall give your order priority and it will be ready by next Monday – will that suit you?'

'Wonderful,' he said. 'If you continue to design such lovely things I'm sure you will soon be a huge success.' He tipped his hat to her and went back through the showroom.

Ed came over to her when they heard the shop bell go and knew Mr Carter had left. He scratched his head and looked at her with respect.

'That was masterful, Lizzie. I thought we were selling them for twenty-one shillings each?'

'A little lesson for him,' Lizzie said and gave him

a wicked look. 'He left us in the lurch, Ed, and he's realized that a hat priced at around a pound or so here is a lot better than he will get from most places for that price. It seems that he has overcome his moral objections in favour of his pocket.'

'Perhaps Oliver has relented and told him the truth. John Carter is one of Oliver's oldest customers and if he believed what he'd been told – well, I was surprised when he walked in.'

'I'm just glad he did,' Lizzie said. 'But we'll keep the price at twenty-two shillings now, for a while anyway.'

'You know what Sebastian Winters used to say – he told you not to sell your work too cheaply. If he had his way, he'd be selling your lines at ten guineas a go in his West End store.'

The mention caused Lizzie a pang of grief, because it seemed so long since she'd seen Sebastian, and she hadn't forgotten that awful dream when he seemed to cry out for her, but she kept her smile in place as she said, 'That reminds me; isn't it time his manager came for an order? I hope we aren't going to lose him too . . .'

'Oh, no, that would be more than his job is worth,' Ed said with a knowing look. 'Mr Winters would have something to say when he got back, and no mistake.'

Lizzie agreed and they began to plan the order for Mr Carter.

The mystery of why he'd come back to them

was solved the next evening when Aunt Miriam came to their house armed with a bag of sweets and some cake she'd made for the children. She was obviously looking forward to having the care of them for the first time, and it wasn't until Betty was bathed and in her cot that she remembered to tell Lizzie.

'I happened to see Mr Carter on Monday,' she said as Lizzie and Beth were putting on their coats. 'I told him the truth – that Ed was just working for you and living in the flat because his house was burned down. And that you lived here with Beth and your children, and I hinted that Bert was overworking and might say things he didn't mean . . . did I do right, Lizzie?'

'Aunt Miriam, you're a darling,' Lizzie said and gave her a big hug. 'Mr Carter came and placed a huge order yesterday – the biggest he'd ever given me.'

'Well, I never,' Aunt Miriam said and glowed with pleasure. 'I shall have to see if I can happen on a few more of the old customers, Lizzie. Now off you go, and enjoy yourselves. The children will be fine with me, and you've shown me where the shelter is in case we get a raid.'

They thanked her and left, feeling excited and laughing over what Aunt Miriam had done.

'I'm sure she waylaid him after he'd been visiting with Harry's uncle,' Lizzie said and hugged Beth's arm. 'She did us a good turn, Beth. That order was the only one on our books when he placed it, though two smaller ones came in later – just repeat orders by the phone, but it means we shall keep going for another week or two.'

'Was it getting that bad, Lizzie?'

'Not quite,' Lizzie said ruefully, 'but if more customers stop coming it could be soon. Ed would put money in if I asked, but that could go the same way if things didn't pick up.'

'Oh, Lizzie, all your bright dreams – smashed by a vindictive old man . . .'

'No, you mustn't call him that,' Lizzie said. 'He's hurt and he's lonely – and probably frightened. He's finding it difficult to cope these days. He took on all those Government contracts, but so many of his staff have left for one reason or another – and he couldn't find anyone as skilled at cutting as Ed. Aunt Miriam said he's gone back to cutting himself, which means he'll have to work longer hours to get the paperwork done. I imagine he was bitter about that and he took out his anger and frustration on me.'

'Well, I still think it was mean of him – but good for Aunt Miriam; if she has her way we'll get most of the customers back again . . .'

'Let's forget our troubles for now,' Lizzie suggested. 'The men we're going to be looking after tonight have suffered more than we can even guess, Beth. We've had bombs, rubble and dirt everywhere, but some of these men have been to hell and back. We've got to be bright and cheerful and make them feel relaxed. At least the constant raids have stopped now, so we shan't have to make a dash for the shelters . . .'

Lizzie looked round the crowded room. There were far more servicemen here than there had been when she'd come the first time, but that was more than a year ago and the war had only just started. Everyone had been optimistic then about the outcome, but recently the news in the papers hadn't been good. The Allies were fighting on several fronts and if something went well in one area, it was sure that somewhere else there would be nothing but bad news.

'Hello, darlin',' a soldier with a cheeky grin came up to Lizzie as she took her place behind the serving counter. 'I'll 'ave a cup of rosy lee and one of them sausage rolls . . .'

'All right.' Lizzie smiled back. 'Do you like milk and sugar in your tea, sir?'

'As much sugar as you can spare,' he replied, giving her a wink. 'Afore the bleedin' war I had four teaspoons in a mug like that, but now I 'ave to make do with one if I'm lucky.'

'Well, tonight you can have two,' Lizzie said and poured two heaped spoons of sugar into his mug and then passed it to him with a plate and a sausage roll.

'Cor lovely,' he said as he took a sip and then arched his brows at her. 'This is me lucky night – don't suppose you'd make it even better and let me walk you home?'

'No, I'm afraid not,' Lizzie said but laughed softly to show she wasn't offended. 'Enjoy your tea, soldier.'

'Me name is Alfie, darlin',' he winked and went off chuckling.

Lizzie was amused, because she knew that wouldn't be the last time she was chatted up that evening, but it went with the job and she could handle cheeky but friendly young men like Alfie.

It was getting on for nine thirty when Mary walked in. Lizzie saw her first and was surprised when she walked up to one of the airmen at the piano and spoke to him. He nodded and started to play an American jazz number. Almost immediately three airmen got up and started to jitterbug with one of the girls who had come with them.

'What does she think she's doing?' Beth hissed to Lizzie as she brought a fresh pot of tea through from the kitchen. 'She was asked to help out not to be in charge of the entertainment.'

'Leave her alone,' Lizzie murmured. 'At least she's here.'

'Wonder where she got that outfit . . .'

'I think she remodelled it from old clothes,' Lizzie said, eyeing the bolero and skirt with appreciation. Mary had added a strip of contrast material to the flowered skirt to give it length and bound the short sleeves of the bolero with the same contrast braid. 'She obviously has some talent with her needle . . .'

Beth sniffed and went off to pour tea for three

young sailors who had entered together. Lizzie smiled as Mary came up to her.

'I'm glad you came, Mary. Do you want to take over from me and I'll go to the kitchen and help out? We need more sandwiches. You'd think some of this lot hadn't eaten in a month.'

'They eat better than we do most of the time,' Mary said, eyeing the food caustically. 'Yes, all right. All I have to do is pour tea and hand out the food, isn't it? Is it rationed?'

'Only the sausage rolls – we give one per person, otherwise there won't be enough to go round, but there are plenty of corned beef and pickle sandwiches. We had some large tins donated to the club . . .'

Mary came round the counter and started to serve almost straight away. Lizzie went into the kitchen where she discovered a huge pile of washing up. Janet, who was the only one working in there, shot her a grateful look as she started on the washing up.

'Thanks for that, Lizzie. No one likes doing it and I usually get stuck with the lot when we've finished.'

'That's a bit unfair on you,' Lizzie said. 'I don't mind giving you a hand when I come in, Janet.'

'Most of the girls think they're here to flirt with the men and they take the first opportunity to go off with whoever takes their fancy.' Janet sniffed in disapproval. 'Some of them have got husbands or boyfriends serving – and I can't stand that. Our

114

men have enough to cope with; they don't want one of those *Dear John* letters.'

'No, that must be terrible when they're out there in the thick of it. Have you got someone over there, Janet?'

'My husband and two brothers,' Janet said. 'We don't know where any of them are, because they can't tell us. Me and Jim arranged a bit of a code before he left, so I know when he talks about a seaside holiday that he's somewhere nice and warm.'

'The censor doesn't blue-pencil that then?'

'No . . .' Janet laughed. 'We've got several code words that we recognize but no one else would. I think Jim is with the Desert Rats, because he talked about the nuisance in the attic and we had rats once.'

'I think that's a brilliant idea,' Lizzie said amused by their ingenuity. 'Do you fancy a cup of tea? We should both have a sit-down for a moment, and then I'll take those sandwiches through.' Just then they heard the wail of a siren and automatically looked up at the ceiling, but neither of them made a move to evacuate the building. There was a cellar that some people used during an air raid, but a lot of the men and girls simply chose to ignore the warning.

'I'd like that,' Janet said a little shyly and pulled a chair out. The music was still playing in the front room so obviously their guests had carried on in spite of the siren. 'You make hats, don't you?'

'Yes, I do,' Lizzie said and explained where the showroom was. 'Why don't you pop round and see me?'

'I should love to, but I think your hats would be too expensive for me. I usually get all my clothes from the market, you see. It's all I can afford. Jim and me have got three kids. Mum looks after them one night a week to let me come here and I work a few hours while they're at school – but Jim wouldn't like it if he knew. His Army pay doesn't cover all we need these days. I don't tell him, because it would hurt his pride.'

'What sort of work do you do?' Lizzie asked.

'I do a bit of housework for someone,' Janet said. 'It's just a few hours in the middle of the day, but the six shillings a week I get helps to buy the kids things they wouldn't otherwise get.'

Lizzie was thoughtful, then, 'Come and see me, Janet. I might be able to find you something that pays more than six shillings . . . if you ever decide to make a change.'

'That's very kind,' Janet said. 'But I couldn't leave poor old Mrs Jones in the lurch. I do a bit of shoppin' for her and give her house a tidy up – and I see to the laundry for her.'

'I wouldn't dream of asking you to leave her,' Lizzie said. 'I think that's really nice of you, Janet.'

They heard the all-clear sound. It seemed the warning had been a false alarm again. Her tea drunk, Lizzie took the fresh sandwiches and went back to the room where the soldiers, airmen and a sprinkling of Navy men were enjoying themselves. Beth threw her a look of relief when she arrived.

'Thank goodness! I want to pop to the toilet, but I couldn't get away. Take over for me, please, Lizzie.'

'Where is Mary?'

'She went off with a solider just after the siren went,' Beth scowled. 'She wasn't interested in helping, just in having some fun. I thought she was supposed to be grieving for her baby – and worried about her husband! The first chance she got she was off!'

Beth hurried away and Lizzie was kept busy serving tea and offering the sandwiches. Most of them went in a few minutes and all the sausage rolls had gone. There wasn't much left in the kitchen and they would be down to toast and margarine soon, perhaps with a smear of jam if the men were lucky. When she glanced at her watch she saw it was nearly ten o'clock and the club was due to close in another quarter of an hour. Lizzie decided not to offer toast, because the club was gradually emptying. The men knew that ten o'clock was their time and the doors would be locked at ten fifteen.

'Night, miss,' Alfie said as he pulled on his cap and headed for the door. 'Sure I can't see you safely home?'

'My friend and I will be safe enough,' Lizzie replied. 'Thanks all the same.'

'See you tomorrow then . . .'

'I only come once a week. Perhaps next week?'

His face fell and he shook his head. 'I'll be back on holiday then,' he quipped and she knew that he meant he was returning to the fighting.

'Oh, well good luck then,' Lizzie said and he offered a hollow grin, looking a bit scared.

By the time Beth returned the club was empty, the last servicemen going out of the door.

'Janet says she'll lock up,' Beth told her. 'I offered to help clear up, but she said you'd done most of the washing up and the rest could be left until the morning, when the next shift comes on.'

'We'd better get our coats then,' Lizzie suggested. 'We don't want to miss the last bus home . . .'

'No, Aunt Miriam might not want to come again if we're too late back.' Beth hugged her arm. 'I really enjoyed this evening, Lizzie. It was nice just being out of the house and talking to different people.'

'Yes, I enjoyed it too. Janet is lovely, isn't she? She never asks to come out and serve, just gets on with the work in the kitchen.'

'I wish Mary was a bit more like her.'

'You shouldn't be annoyed with her, Beth. She came for a while and that must have taken some courage.'

'Huh. If you ask me she just came to flirt and enjoy herself.'

'Is that so bad? Isn't it better than her sitting at home feeling miserable?'

118

'Not when she still has her husband. . . .' Beth sighed. 'Take no notice of me, Lizzie. I'm not a big fan of Mary, even if she is my sister.'

Lizzie shook her head but didn't argue. Mary envied Beth her children, and Beth didn't trust her sister. It was an unhappy state of affairs for a family, but Lizzie knew better than to interfere.

They'd just reached the house when they heard the siren go again, and this time it was for real, almost before they could fetch the children down to the Morrison they could hear the loud explosions and whooshing noises that told them the bombs weren't far away. Most of them would be falling in the docklands, but as one tremendous explosion seemed to shake the house they knew that it must have been in the next street.

Aunt Miriam scrambled into the shelter with them, which made it a tight fit, but Lizzie had refused to let her leave once they'd realized that the raid was genuine.

'Bert will be worried half to death,' she said as the hours ticked by before the all-clear sounded. 'He'll think something's happened to me . . .'

'What will you tell him?' Lizzie asked. 'He won't like it if he knows you were here with us . . .'

'I'll tell him I was on my way home and went down the Underground,' Aunt Miriam said. 'I don't like lying to him, Lizzie, but I'm not giving up coming here, and he's brought it on himself . . .'

It was light when Miriam was eventually able to

leave and walk home. Lizzie and Beth put the children back in their cots and put a kettle on the range to boil. Lizzie had kept it for heating the water and some cooking even after she'd bought a gas cooker, and now she was glad of it, because the thing you wanted most after a raid was a cup of tea, and the last thing you dared do was light the gas.

'What a night,' Beth said after they'd drunk their tea. 'I don't know about you, Lizzie, but I'm going to get half an hour's shut-eye.'

Lizzie nodded but she made no move to follow her friend upstairs. It had been a close thing, the nearest they'd come to being on the wrong end of one of Hitler's bombs. For several minutes she just sat staring into space, tears on her cheeks.

'Where are you, Sebastian?' she asked of the empty room. 'I need you so much . . .'

CHAPTER 8

Lizzie popped round to see Tilly at her home on that Sunday afternoon. She took some fairy cakes she'd made as a present for Tilly's daughter Sally and a pretty dress that she'd run up in the workrooms from a few odd pieces of velvet.

'Oh, Lizzie, it's so lovely to see you,' Tilly greeted her with a kiss and a big smile. 'I really miss you at work – and I've been meaning to come and see you about something . . .'

'It's lovely to see you too,' Lizzie said. 'I knew it was your little Sally's birthday soon – I hope I've judged the size of the dress right?'

Tilly ripped the paper off and exclaimed in delight. 'I know this will fit her and she'll love it,' she said and hugged Lizzie impulsively. 'Her granny has taken her to the park to see the ducks this afternoon or I'd have tried it on her. It was so kind of you to make this for her.'

'I enjoyed doing it,' Lizzie said. 'I had some pink velvet left over that I bought from Arthur Stockton and a few bits of lace – and it's difficult to buy anything new for children in the shops.'

'My Sally has never had a new dress from the shops,' Tilly said. 'It's second-hand from the market, unless I have time to make something myself – and it isn't easy to find material like this now.'

Lizzie had made the bodice and skirt of pink velvet, added a wide white waistband and little white sleeves and a lace collar. It would suit Sally's colouring, because she was darker than her mother and took after her father.

They talked for a while about the war and how difficult it was to find anything, and then, after Lizzie had drunk two cups of tea and eaten a piece of fatless sponge filled with strawberry jam, she prepared to leave.

'I wanted to tell you . . .' Tilly said, blushing. 'I think I may be pregnant at last.'

'You must be over the moon,' Lizzie hugged her. 'I'm thrilled for you . . .'

'Yes . . .' Tilly hesitated, then, 'I think Mr Oliver may sack me when he knows, because he won't want me taking time off, and I'm not sure how many hours I'll be able to work in future.'

'Surely he'll let you stay until you have the baby?'

'He might – but I was wondering . . .' Tilly looked awkward. 'If I only wanted a few hours a week afterwards . . . would you take me on?'

'I would've offered you a job ages ago, Tilly, but I didn't think it was fair to Harry's uncle – and I'm not sure I could afford to offer you a full-time position, but a few hours a week would be ideal.'

'Don't be surprised if I turn up one of these days,' Tilly grinned at her. 'Knowing me, I'll be as sick as a dog for weeks and Oliver is sure to kick me out if I take days off.'

'He doesn't know what it's like,' Lizzie said. 'I remember all too well and it wasn't great, but you know where to come if you want me.'

She left Tilly and walked home. It was a pleasant early summer evening and it felt good to be alive, even though the evidence of war was all around her. Some of the bombed-out houses had been pulled right down and most of the rubble cleared; it wouldn't be long before weeds started to grow between the broken concrete. So many people had lost their homes, but there wasn't the manpower or the resources to rebuild houses, especially as they might get blown up again very soon.

The sound of a siren close by made Lizzie start, because it was still daylight and though there had been occasional daylight raids it was rare. She looked about her, wondering what best to do. Some distance from her home, Lizzie knew she might not have time to get back before the raid started, if it did – but perhaps it was simply a false alarm.

Rather than spend hours down the underground, waiting for the all-clear, she decided to ignore the warning and get home as quickly as she could. Beth was looking after the children to give Lizzie the chance to visit Tilly and she would take them under the Morrison if necessary.

She walked swiftly through almost empty streets as people rushed to take shelter wherever they could. Some of the larger shops had cellars they'd strengthened so that their staff and customers could seek refuge if an air raid should come during working hours, but there were none around here that Lizzie knew of and the shops were shut as it was Sunday. She quickened her pace, wanting to be home.

Lizzie had almost reached her street when she heard the noise overhead and looked up to see the planes swooping over the river and the Docks. She shivered as she heard the sudden explosion as the bombs began to drop and saw flames shoot into the air. It looked as if that one was much closer, in the next street . . . her street . . .

A scream building inside her, Lizzie started to run. She saw the damage as soon as she entered the street; it was at the far end, not near her home, although it had looked to be nearer. Appearances were deceiving, but as Lizzie saw the flames leaping up, she kept running towards the scene of the disaster.

The house that had taken a direct hit was beyond help, because it was on fire, but several other houses had been affected by the blast, tiles lying shattered in the street, glass everywhere and a great hole in the side of a house two doors down. Lizzie saw a woman staggering out and a man carrying a child emerging from the damaged building and went up to them.

'Is there anyone else inside?'

The woman was too shocked to answer, but the man shook his head. 'It's just us . . .' He was looking at his neighbour's home. 'Oh my God, there was five of them in there – grandmother, mother and three kids . . .' He thrust his child at Lizzie. 'Here, take him. I'm going to see if I can get in . . .'

'It's impossible,' Lizzie told him but she held the small boy in her arms as he cried and shouted for his father. The woman screamed her husband's name as he disappeared into the burning building.

'Johnnie . . . No . . . don't . . .'

'You can't do anything,' Lizzie said as the woman tried to follow her husband. 'Here, hold your son . . .' She went to the gaping hole in the wall, which was where the man had burst in through the flames and saw him coming back with a child in his arms. He thrust the little girl at her and went back into the flames. 'Be careful . . .' Lizzie cried, but she knew it was useless, his jacket was already smouldering and she could see that the fire had blistered his skin, but he was driven by his mission and when he stumbled out some seconds later with a baby in his arms, she saw that he was overcome with smoke and the pain of his injuries.

Lizzie took the bundle he was still holding as he collapsed, but his wife was kneeling beside him, tears falling as she begged him to speak to her. Lizzie stood with the two rescued children and watched as the house seemed to impound and collapse.

Only the man's quick actions had saved their lives, but perhaps at the cost of his own.

An ambulance came screaming up to them, and the fire engine followed. Lizzie stood back, comforting the whimpering children as best she could as the firemen started pumping water into the house, but she knew it was too late for those still inside.

'Are these your children, madam? Was it your house?'

'No, I just came to see if I could help, I live the other end of the street . . .' Lizzie said. 'That man saved these children – but the rest of the family didn't get out . . .'

'No one else is alive in there,' the ambulance driver, who Lizzie now saw was a woman, said. 'I'll take the children, madam – do you need hospital treatment?'

'No, look after that poor man and his wife. She's having hysterics . . .'

'My colleague will sort her out,' the woman said grimly. 'It's a bloody business, isn't it?'

'Yes, yes, it is,' Lizzie said and watched as the capable woman loaded her ambulance and drove off.

She felt sick and shaken as she walked home. Of course she'd known that the bombs were causing damage everywhere, but to see it – to watch as that brave man risked his life twice for the sake of his neighbour's children brought home the war in a way she'd never experienced before. It made her feel proud of the camaraderie, the spirit of the East End that triumphed at times like these. However little they had they were willing to share, and do what they could to help those in trouble . . .

Beth rushed at her as she walked into the kitchen a few minutes later. 'You're shaking,' she said. 'Were you caught in the raid, Lizzie? By the sound of it, it was pretty close this time.'

'Yes, just up the street . . .' Lizzie was trembling as she told her tale. 'All I could do was to hold the children. I felt so useless, Beth . . . that man was badly burned and overcome by the smoke – but somehow he got two children out.'

'It was a miracle that he managed it,' Beth pushed a cup of tea in front of her. 'I've put extra sugar in; you need it, love.'

'Oh, Beth, why – why is it happening?' Lizzie felt the tears trickling down her cheeks. 'I've just accepted it, felt it was a nuisance we have to cope with – but it's so terrible when you see something like that . . . I feel as if I should be doing something to help.'

'We do what we can,' Beth said. 'Dad's an ARP; we help out at the club for servicemen and we carry on with our lives. Hitler is trying to break us – and if you give up then he succeeds. You make people happy with your hats, Lizzie – and what else can you do? You're not a nurse and you can't drive an ambulance . . . and you can't join the services, because you have a child.'

'I know . . .' Lizzie drank her tea. 'It's stupid – but I felt so useless. I know I can't do much but I shall think of something . . . something that will help even if only a little . . .'

Lizzie inquired after the children from the burned out house at the hospital the next day. She had to phone several before she got the right one, but the news was better than she'd hoped. Mr and Mrs Barton were in hospital and their son was being cared for by its grandmother; Mr Barton had severe burns but would recover eventually. The two children he'd rescued were doing well and it had transpired that the mother had taken one of the children to visit a friend, and it was just her mother who had died in the fire. Like so many others, they were being cared for until they could be rehoused, either with friends or in the country.

The news helped Lizzie to recover from the trauma and guilt she'd felt at being so helpless, but she knew she had to do something more for the war effort, though at the moment she wasn't sure what she could do – she had a business to run, a child to care for, and little time to spare, but the horror she'd witnessed had made her more aware and she was determined to help.

Janet came to see them at the workshops three days later. She'd obviously been to the market and had taken a detour on impulse on her way home. Beth was in the showroom and called Lizzie through to see her.

'How lovely of you to come and visit us,' Lizzie greeted her with a smile. 'Come through and I'll show you where we work and what we do. I was just about to make a cup of coffee . . . are you ready for yours, Beth?'

Beth shook her head as one of their regular customers entered the showroom. 'I'll have it later, Lizzie.'

Lizzie greeted their customer and then took Janet through to the back room. She spent some minutes showing her the cutting table, the steamer and the boxes of trimmings, and then some of the hats in various stages.

'We don't make many fancy hats these days, because some of the more expensive materials are difficult to get now. In fact, most of our hats are felt these days, but we still try to make them look stylish and pretty.'

'I like these softer hats,' Janet said and looked at a cherry red velvet beret with undisguised longing in her eyes. 'How much would something like that be?'

'Oh, they vary,' Lizzie said. 'They start at ten shillings for the very plain ones and go up to twenty-one shillings for these . . .' She showed Janet the floppy range that she'd just started to make for spring and summer. 'Try it on and look at yourself in the mirror.'

Janet laughed and shook her head, but Lizzie arranged the hat over her short curly hair and stood back. 'Yes, that is just you, Janet.'

Her new friend glanced in the mirror, her face a picture of wonder as she saw how attractive it made her look. 'Oh, that's too good for me,' she said regretfully and took it off. 'I could buy my son the new coat he needs for twenty-one shillings. Not a new one, but a decent coat off the market that hasn't had much wear.'

Lizzie was very tempted to give the hat to her as a present, but her instinct told her that Janet might be embarrassed or even offended. She was a decent hard-working woman and she wouldn't accept charity.

'Of course,' Lizzie said easily. 'This one belongs to a customer anyway, but perhaps one day, when the war is over, you'll want a nice hat to welcome your husband home.'

'I'll save up when I can,' Janet said and smiled. Lizzie made a cup of coffee for them. It was only the chicory stuff in the bottle, but she heated some milk on the gas ring in her office and it tasted nice.

Beth came through from the front with the order book as they were finishing.

'I sold six ready-made hats to Mr Bracks,' she said, showing her the order book, 'and he's ordered others Lizzie. I told him next week. He said he would call in on Thursday.'

Lizzie looked through the order and nodded. 'Yes, this is brilliant, Beth. Ten good hats and the six you sold him today. Things are looking better.'

'I've put the latch on the door, Lizzie. I've got

a bit of a stomach ache and it is almost time to close anyway . . .'

'Come and sit down, Beth. I'll put the kettle on, love. If you're not feeling well, you should go home. I can manage . . .'

'I'd offer to stay and help,' Janet said, 'but I shouldn't know the prices or how to talk to your customers. I might be able to help in the work-rooms, though – just for a couple of hours if you need me. The old lady I look after has gone into hospital and I don't think she will ever come home again; it's all the bombs and the upset these days. She ought to have gone to the country, but now it's too late.'

'I'm so sorry,' Lizzie said. 'I could give you a few hours each week, Janet, if you'd like. Jean will show you what we need from you.'

'Thanks ever so,' Janet's face lit up. 'You didn't mind my saying?'

'No, of course not,' Lizzie said. 'And don't worry about the showroom, Jean will go in for a while if Beth decides to go home.'

'I'll be going then,' Janet said. 'Can I get out without leaving your door unlocked?'

'Why don't you go the back way?' Lizzie said. 'You just walk down the alley to the main street and you can catch a tram or a bus there.'

'I'll get a tram,' Janet said as Lizzie opened the door for her. 'It was nice spending some time here, Lizzie – and I shall enjoy helping you.'

'I'm glad you came round,' Lizzie said and

closed the door after her. She returned to Beth and looked at her in concern. 'Is your tummy really bad, love?'

'It's my period and rather unpleasant this month.'

She broke off as the telephone shrilled and Lizzie picked it up.

'Is Beth there?' Mrs Court asked, sounding strange. 'Will you ask her to come home as soon as she can please?'

'Is something wrong with one of her children . . .?'

Mrs Court gave a strangled sob. 'I had such a headache, Lizzie. It isn't like me to take a nap in the afternoon, but I was feeling a bit down. I left them in their cots, because they were all sleepy. When I woke up quite suddenly I felt something was wrong and I went straight to the bedroom – the twins have gone. Betty was all right but crying, but the twins' cots were empty.'

'No! Are you sure you didn't leave them in the playpen or in their pram?' Lizzie knew she was clutching at straws. Mrs Court was crying and telling her that she was sure she'd left all the children sleeping. Beth had been listening to Lizzie's side of the conversation and now she grabbed the phone.

'What's happened, Mum?' Her eyes widened with fear as her mother told her the twins were missing. 'I'm coming home right now . . .'

'Beth, don't jump to conclusions,' Lizzie said as she slammed down the receiver. 'They will be somewhere in the house – they couldn't have got out. I know Matt can toddle about, but he couldn't open the front door.'

'Mum always leaves it unlocked. If one of her neighbours came in and couldn't find her – they might have gone out again and left the door open.'

'What about your gran? Wouldn't she have known if someone entered the house while your mum was lying down?'

'She isn't there today. It's her afternoon at the Women's Institute.'

Beth had grabbed her coat and bag and left hurriedly. Ed looked anxious as he came in to see Lizzie.

'Something about the children?'

'Mrs Court was in a panic. She can't find the twins and asked for Beth to go home at once.'

'Your little Betty?' he asked looking worried.

'She's all right, just crying. I wonder . . .' she hesitated uncertainly.

'What are you thinking?'

'Mary has been acting oddly since she lost the baby. Could she have taken them?'

'Surely not?' Ed looked disturbed. 'Why don't you run and catch Beth up, Lizzie? I can look after things here and Jean can manage if we have more customers – but it's unlikely at this hour.'

'All right, I will,' Lizzie said. She grabbed her coat and bag and ran after Beth. She caught up with her just as the bus drew up and they both got on. Beth looked at her gratefully.

'I couldn't ask, but I'm glad you came. I think it's Mary . . .'

'The thought occurred to me too,' Lizzie said. 'She won't hurt them, Beth. She's just being silly, jealous of what she thinks you've got and she hasn't . . .'

Beth shook her head impatiently. 'I have to go home and make sure they haven't turned up – but then I'm going to Mary's house.'

'Yes, all right,' Lizzie said. 'Your mum may have found them. I saw Matt trying to climb out of his cot the other day. He might have found a way to escape; they could be hiding somewhere . . .'

Lizzie didn't really think the twins were old enough to try something like that; Matt was the strongest and could toddle about, even if he took a tumble sometimes, and Jenny scooted about on her bottom, and they would both be into everything if not secure in their cots or playpen, but Matt usually just screamed until someone came and let him out. She was simply trying to reassure her friend, but Beth would know, as she did, that it wasn't possible.

She felt just as anxious as Beth. She'd always felt that the children were safe with Beth's mother, but now she wasn't sure. If it was too much for Mrs Court to have all three children she might have to make other arrangements.

The bus journey took so long because there were so many repairs going on and congested roads because of all the bomb damage, and Beth jumped off before it had hardly stopped, running up the road to her mother's home and pushing open the front door. Lizzie followed, feeling apprehensive and upset, because if anything had happened to the twins, Beth would be distraught – but it would be all right. Mary wouldn't hurt them . . . would she?

Lizzie entered the house and heard Beth's raised voice. Mrs Court was crying and blaming herself, and Beth was saying it had to be her sister. Her mother was denying it, claiming it was all her fault for leaving them while she had a nap.

'They must have got out of their cots,' she said when Beth let her get a word in. 'We need to call the police, Beth – and go looking for them.'

'I know where they'll be,' Beth said bitterly. 'Mary should have gone to the mental institution. She's just not right in the head, Mum.'

'Mary is upset but she wouldn't do something like this – worrying us all.'

'She doesn't care two hoots what she does to me,' Beth said. 'I'm going round there now . . .'

'What's all this then?' Beth's father walked in, staring at his wife and daughter.

'The twins have disappeared,' Mrs Court said. 'I put them in their cots and went for a lie down. When I woke up a couple of hours later they'd gone – and Beth thinks Mary has taken them, but she hasn't been here . . .'

'When did she leave this then?' Mr Court picked

up a scarf that was lying on the kitchen floor. 'This is Mary's, isn't it?'

'Yes, but she could have left that at any time . . .' his wife stared at it as if she hadn't seen it before.

'Not on the floor,' he said. 'You would have seen it and picked it up this morning. I think Beth is right. You're upset and I don't like to admit it, love, but Mary's been acting strangely since she came out of hospital.'

'I'm going round to get them,' Beth said and turned towards the door, but her father caught her arm.

'No, Beth, leave it to me please. Lizzie can come if she wants, but you'll just get angry and make things worse. I'll bring the twins back if they're there – and if not, I'll get up a search party. Someone came into this house and went upstairs and took those babies from their cots. I doubt if it was a stranger.'

Beth stared at him rebelliously. 'They are my children, Dad. She had no right to take them.'

'Not without your agreement,' he confirmed, 'but Mary is your sister. She isn't evil, even if she is unwell. I'll talk to her and I'll make sure she won't do it again – and in future, your mother can lock the door if she wants a rest.'

'It's my fault . . .' his wife wailed her remorse. 'I'll never forgive myself if . . .'

'If you'll come with me, Lizzie. We'll see if the twins are with Mary,' Mr Court said.

'Yes, of course.' Lizzie met Beth's anxious gaze.

'Stay with your mum and make her a cup of tea. I'll just take a quick look at Betty and then I'll go with your father. We shan't be long, I promise you.'

Beth looked angry but then inclined her head. 'Yes, all right, Lizzie, I'll stay here and see Betty is looked after, but be as quick as you can . . .'

'Thank you for that, Lizzie,' Mr Court said when Lizzie came back down the stairs. 'Is Betty all right?'

'Sound asleep, so I didn't disturb her.'

'Good. I'm sure the twins are fine too, but it's as well to make sure.' They went out to the shabby but serviceable van he used for his work as a market trader. 'Beth is in too much of a state and Mary needs understanding, not a blazing row.'

'She isn't well,' Lizzie told him. 'No one wanted her to go to that mental institution the hospital suggested, but she does need help.'

'And she'll get it from me,' he replied firmly. 'Mary just needs a strong hand to guide her. She ought to have her husband with her and that's a part of the trouble. Because she hasn't had a letter in months, she thinks he's dead and she hasn't got much else to live for.'

Lizzie nodded but made no reply. Mary had been through an awful lot but what had made her behave in such a reckless fashion? She must know how much it would upset both Beth and her mother?

It seemed to take ages to reach Mary's house but was in fact only a few minutes. Lizzie sighed with relief as she followed Mr Court into Mary's kitchen. It was strewn with bits of dresses and skirts she'd cut up, but otherwise it looked clean enough, and she was sitting in an old rocking chair, nursing Beth's little girl, and Matt was sitting on a cushion at her feet, chewing on a biscuit she'd given him and knocking down some brightly coloured bricks.

'Hello, Dad,' she said, looking up at him. 'Have you come for the twins? Mum was asleep and she looked so tired, so when Matt started grizzling, I brought the twins back here. I've fed them, so Beth won't have to when she gets back from work.'

'That was good of you, Mary,' her father said in a gentle voice. 'Gave them egg and soldiers, did you? I remember you liked that when you were little – but you should have left a note, you know. Your mum and Beth were worried.'

'They didn't need to be,' Mary said. 'Beth never did like sharing her toys.'

'Babies are not toys,' he said. 'You mustn't ever do that again, Mary. If it does happen, I might have to make sure you can't do it anymore, love. I don't want to do that, but you know I can – and what would Andy say if he knew?'

'Andy won't say anything, he's dead,' Mary sounded calm, almost disinterested, as she glanced at the mantelshelf. 'I got one of those things the day I went to the social club It says he's missing

138

presumed dead . . . I told Mum I knew he was dead weeks ago but she didn't believe me.'

'Oh Mary, love,' her father said. 'I'm so sorry. Why didn't you tell us it had come?'

'It doesn't matter.' Mary's eyes were dark with grief now. 'Nothing matters – so I'm going back to nursing. I'm going to ask if they will send me overseas. I want to do something useful . . .'

'Lizzie, take the twins to the van,' he said, sending her an urgent message with his eyes. 'I shan't be long.'

'Certainly,' Lizzie said and lifted the little girl from Mary's arms. She held on for a moment but then let go. Lizzie hoisted her in one arm and then took hold of Matt's hand. He toddled confidently by her side as she took him out to the van.

'Mum, mum?' he said and rubbed at his dirty face.

'Soon. We'll be back with Mummy soon,' Lizzie said.

Mr Court was about ten minutes before he came out. Lizzie didn't ask questions; he looked grim and she didn't really want to know what he'd said to his daughter in private. The children were unharmed and that was all that mattered to Lizzie.

She couldn't wait to get all the children home and bathed and in their own cots. Beth was going to need time to come to terms with what her sister had done and they would have to discuss what to do about the children in future. Mrs Court had looked tired and it was obvious that having all three children was too much for her.

Lizzie wondered if she could find someone trustworthy to look after them for part of the day at least, though she wouldn't want to offend Beth's mum by taking them away from her completely.

It was a difficult decision to make.

CHAPTER 9

'I never want to go through that again,' Beth said after the children were clean and settled in their own room for the night. 'I was terrified that Mary might have run off with them – or worse . . .'

'She was nursing Jenny,' Lizzie reminded her. 'The telegram about Andy being missing was too much for her – and explains the way she behaved at the serving men's club. I think she just went wild, didn't truly know what she was doing.'

'Yes, I can see that,' Beth agreed. 'But how can I be sure she won't do it again?'

'Your father told her what he would do if she did,' Lizzie said.

'What did Dad say to her?'

'I didn't hear all of it – but I think he was telling her that as her father he could ask for her to be committed to one of those places for wayward girls if she did anything like that again.'

'Oh, poor Mary,' Beth said. 'She thinks the world of Dad, so coming from him that would upset her. I don't want her shut up in a place like that, Lizzie. I just want to make sure she keeps away from my children.'

'Well, she's had a warning and if she goes back to nursing, as she plans, that should be the end of it. You have to feel for her, Beth. The baby dying was terrible enough to make anyone nearly lose their mind and then to get one of those telegrams . . . it must be awful.'

'I know it hasn't been easy for her, but I can't risk it happening again.'

'I know . . .'

'Mum is feeling tired, so I'm taking a week or so off work, Lizzie. I shall stay with the children until we can find a way to lighten the load. Dad says it's too much for Mum to have all three of them every day. We have to find someone else we can trust.'

Lizzie started in alarm as the front door bell rang. 'It's half past nine – who could that be?'

'We'll both go,' Beth said and grabbed a poker, holding it menacingly as the bell rang again.

Lizzie went ahead of her to open the door. She felt nervous because whoever was there was determined that she would answer, knocking continuously.

'All right, please don't wake the . . .' she began as she opened the door and then the words died in her throat and she felt a rush of emotion. Her eyes stung with tears as she moved towards him, and all the emotions of the last few days welled up and spilled over. 'Sebastian . . . Oh, Sebastian – I never thought . . .'

'May I come in, Lizzie?'

'Please do,' she said. 'We were just sitting talking and we couldn't think who could be at the door . . .'

'I'm sorry it's so late, but they only let me go this afternoon and I've had a long train journey.'

As he stepped into the light, Lizzie could see that he looked tired and pale; there was a red mark at his temple and another scar near the corner of his eye. Both had healed, but she sensed that his injuries had taken their toll, because there was a change in him; he seemed weary, almost vulnerable, and that wasn't like Sebastian. He'd always been so strong, invincible.

'Come in and sit by the fire,' she invited. 'We can make coffee or tea – and we have a bottle of sherry . . . oh it's so good to have you back . . .' Emotion caught at her throat as her eyes went over him, taking in every beloved detail.

'Just coffee,' Sebastian said. 'They've given me some pills that might not take kindly to alcohol. I'm sorry for arriving out of the blue, I ought to have waited until tomorrow. Shall I leave and visit you again at the showroom in the morning?'

'No, stay here and rest please,' Lizzie insisted, reluctant to let him leave even for an instant, 'I'll make some coffee – we've got some decent stuff in the cupboard that we keep for special occasions.'

'I'll go up and check on the children,' Beth said. 'Nice to see you, Mr Winters. Goodnight . . .'

She closed the door behind her. Beth had been

understanding leaving them together and Lizzie was grateful. She gazed into Sebastian's eyes and then moved towards him, putting her arms about his waist. She rested her head against his chest and he touched his chin to her head. She felt the tremor that ran through him and held him closer.

'I've missed you,' she said, breathing deeply. 'When were you hurt?'

'Some weeks ago. I was unconscious for a while and then too ill to know what was going on. It was some time before I was sent home – and I wouldn't let them send you a telegram when I was in hospital, because I didn't want you upset.'

'How were you hurt?' Lizzie asked wonderingly, touching his cheek with her fingertips as he drew back to look at her. 'Are you better now?'

Sebastian laughed softly. 'One question at a time. I have some of my own – have you missed me?'

'I've missed you so very much, Sebastian.'

'I've been longing for this and now . . . I'm just too tired to say all things I want to say, my darling.'

'You don't have to say anything. Just being here is enough.'

'Is it?' He looked long and hard into her face. 'Last time I was here – I wondered if I'd dreamed it. Did you really tell me you loved me, Lizzie?'

'It has seemed like a dream to me too,' she murmured softly. 'I wasted so much time denying you, Sebastian. I should have taken your offer to work for you when you first asked . . .'

'No, I don't think so. I might have taken advantage and ruined things between us then,' Sebastian said. 'You've become so much more, Lizzie. You've grown up and made your dreams come true – and you've learned what life is all about. I hope you will be my wife one day soon and that we'll carry those dreams to a higher plane. You've suffered, but you've become a woman, Lizzie, a very beautiful woman.'

'Oh, Sebastian,' Lizzie said and lifted her face to his. 'Sometimes I wondered if I would ever see you again . . .'

'Didn't I tell you that bad pennies always turn up?'

Lizzie shook her head. 'You've always been good to me, Sebastian.'

His head bowed and he kissed her, softly at first and then with increasing passion. This is what she had longed for, dreamed of, ever since he left her after their blissful Christmas together. Lizzie melted into him, her body soft and pliant as she gave herself to him and the kiss. When he let her go at last, she was breathless but reeling from the pleasure. She wanted to know him in the fullest sense and felt bereft when he stopped kissing her.

'I need that coffee, Lizzie,' he murmured softly. 'And I don't want our first time to be on a kitchen mat with your friend and the children upstairs. Besides, I'm too damned weary to do you justice, my love.'

'Beth wouldn't take any notice . . . but you need to rest and I want us to be alone together somewhere nice . . .'

'Can you come away with me please? Just for a couple of days?'

'I'm not sure.' Lizzie hesitated. 'Beth was speaking of taking a week off to be with the children – and if I go too . . .'

'I know you're thinking of the business but I only have ten days, Lizzie. I love you and I want to spend them with you.'

'All right,' she said. 'I'll tell Ed to shut the showroom for a few days. If anyone really needs us they can ring the bell and he or Jean will see to things.'

'You need more staff,' Sebastian said. 'You can borrow some of my salespeople from the shop. I'll make a few calls and fix it up – and then we'll go away for a day or so.'

It was two in the morning when Lizzie finally went to bed. Sebastian had gone to stay with a friend at his London apartment. He'd made a couple of calls and his manager was sending along an experienced salesperson to take Lizzie's place at the workshop for a few days.

'Ed can brief Paula on whatever she needs to know,' he'd told Lizzie after he'd made his call. 'You've told me about the trouble with Bert Oliver. I'll sort him out for you – and we'll see about the rest later. I shall be here at eleven tomorrow morning, Lizzie – will you be ready to leave?'

'Yes, please,' she said. 'Where shall we go?'

'You'll have to wait and see,' he said and kissed her nose. 'I love you, my darling. I want to spend as much time as I can with you before I have to leave – and perhaps persuade you to marry me . . .?'

'Oh, Sebastian, I do love you so very much . . .'

It had been a long day and Lizzie fell asleep soon after her head touched the pillow. Beth woke her in the morning, opening the curtains and offering a cup of tea.

'What time did you get to bed last night?'

'It was this morning,' Lizzie said and laughed. 'I'm going away for a couple of days, Beth – and Sebastian mentioned marriage. . . .'

'Are you going to say yes?'

'I think so,' Lizzie replied and stretched. 'I need a little time alone with him, but I'm pretty sure that I'm in love with him, Beth.'

'Then you should grab him with both hands.'

Lizzie woke, stretched and wondered why she felt so marvellous and then became aware of the warmth of the man lying beside her and smiled, turning to snuggle into his body. She was in bed with Sebastian and he'd spent most of the previous night making love to her, and it had been wonderful. In the arms of the man she was now sure she loved, Lizzie had discovered a pleasure she'd never even guessed she could experience until the previous night and now she felt like a lazy kitten, curled up in luxurious warmth. For once she didn't have to get up or go to work or even look after her darling daughter; Betty was being lovingly cared for by Beth at home for a couple of days, and they'd spoken briefly on the phone the previous evening, because Lizzie had never been away from Betty like this before, but Beth had assured her she was fine.

'You're awake then?' Sebastian's voice was soft but deep with passion and she looked up and saw a reflection of the happiness she was feeling in his eyes. 'You've been sleeping for ages, darling.'

'What time is it?' she asked and reached out to touch his cheek.

'Ten thirty or thereabouts,' he murmured. 'I've been watching you for the past hour. You looked so lovely and so peaceful. I want to drink you in so that the memory of these few days stays with me forever.'

'You should have woken me,' Lizzie said and reached up to kiss him.

'You obviously needed the sleep.'

'I don't always sleep this well. It must be because you're here with me.'

'Worries about the business?' Sebastian eased himself up against the pillows, reaching for a cigarette. He offered her the pack but she shook her head. He took one out but then replaced it and drew her close to him. 'If something bothers you, tell me. Harry's uncle won't trouble you again, believe me – but when I spoke to him yesterday, he swore he didn't order someone to break your windows or paint foul words all over your walls and I believe him.'

'He told Ed the same thing.' Lizzie sighed. She didn't want her problems to intrude on their time together. 'It doesn't matter.'

'It matters to me if someone is trying to harm you.' Sebastian frowned at her. 'If it's not your business that's worrying you – what is it?'

'It's shocking and goes back to when I was fourteen . . . you might not like it, Sebastian.'

He bent over her, gazing deeply into her eyes. 'I love you, Lizzie, and if something hurts you I need to know.'

Lizzie took a deep breath and told him from the start. She told him what had happened when she went to fetch her uncle some cigarettes, how she'd been beaten, raped and left for dead.

'I miscarried a child in the infirmary and I was ill for months, and afterwards I couldn't remember anything that had happened to me . . . I couldn't even remember my own name, until my uncle paid for me to go to a private sanatorium . . .'

'Lizzie darling,' he said and wrapped his arms about her holding her close, his mouth against her hair, his body firm and strong against hers. 'I'm sorry, my love, so sorry for what happened to you. I had no idea how much you'd been hurt . . .'

'It doesn't make you feel disgust of me?'

'It makes me want to kill whoever hurt you,' he said fiercely. 'Why should you think it might disgust me?'

'Harry felt like that . . .' Lizzie's voice broke. 'He left me on our honeymoon and I came back to the flat alone . . . he could never forgive me . . .'

'Forgive *you?* The bloody fool!' Sebastian reacted so angrily that Lizzie's eyes filled with tears. 'Didn't he understand what it had done to you? My poor little love, what a thing to happen on your wedding night . . .'

'It was because I didn't tell him before we married . . .'

Lizzie explained how she'd been told on the morning of her wedding, how she'd not known what to do and Sebastian drew her into his arms as the tears came. He stroked her hair, holding her and kissing her until she'd finished her story, finishing with Bert Oliver's accusations and the way he'd told her he wanted nothing more to do with her.

Lizzie smiled up at him, relief washing through her as she saw nothing but love and concern for her in his eyes. 'It hasn't changed how you feel?'

'I just want to love and protect you for the rest of our lives, my darling. I wish I could take all the pain away . . .'

Lizzie pressed closer. 'You already have,' she whispered, breathing in the scent of him so that he would always be imprinted into her senses.

'I wish I never had to leave you again, my love . . .' He held her tightly. 'But you know I must go . . .'

'I know . . .' she whispered against his chest.

'For a long time I had nightmares but they've almost gone – but I did have a dream about you. I saw you lying hurt, Sebastian, and I felt you called to me.'

'I did, over and over again,' he admitted and drew her closer. 'I hated the thought of dying and never having had you in my arms like this, never having had the chance to show you how much I love you.' He held her closer, his lips against her brow. 'You don't know how much I love you – how much I need you in my life.'

Lizzie looked at him, because there was underlying pain in his voice Was there something he hadn't told her? She would wait until he was ready to share it with her, because he would when he was ready, and for now all she wanted was to be held like this and to know she was loved.

'Marry me, Lizzie? Marry me now . . .'

'Oh yes, my darling. Just as soon as we can . . .'

'We only have a few days before I leave . . .'

'Then we shall just have to make the most of what we have, shan't we?' She lifted her face for his kiss. His lips set her tingling and she felt the slow burn of desire spreading up from deep down inside her and laughed up at him as he rolled her back in the bed and set to work with his lips and tongue to bring her to a state of perfect bliss.

They moved in harmony, their bodies fitting together as if they were two halves of the same being, rising and falling as they sought to please and be pleased. Lizzie panted and moaned as

151

the glorious feeling surged inside her, pooling low in her belly and sending heat all over her, making her feel as if she were dissolving with ecstasy and dispersing like spray on the seashore. She felt so light, so free, and so much in love, as Sebastian lavished her body with caresses and kisses. It was heaven as she let herself give everything, holding nothing back and screaming with her release as he came in her.

Afterwards, bathed in their own sweat, they lay side by side, just holding each other as if they would never let go, but in the end they decided they must bathe, dress and find some breakfast – and then start to plan the rest of their lives.

They were going straight back to London to arrange things, because it would have to be a quick modest affair with only a few friends invited. In times like these, there was no point in waiting, even though Lizzie knew that she was risking more heartbreak. Sebastian's work was dangerous and she might be a widow again before she'd got used to being a wife, but there was something precious in knowing you belonged to someone and she was willing to take that risk.

Sebastian had told her that he was going to make a will that would leave his house and business to her and when she shook her head, a little embarrassed, he smiled.

'What else would I do with it, Lizzie? You and Betty are my family now, and the children I hope we'll have one day, my love.'

'Oh yes, I want several children,' Lizzie said . . . perhaps even now she was carrying Sebastian's child. The thought made her mouth curve in a smile and she looked up into those wonderful blue eyes. He was so attractive, the little forest of silver hairs at his temples making him even more distinguished and handsome. She loved him far more than she'd loved Harry, with a deep needing, aching wanting that would leave her empty when he left.

'I know you may not want to live at my house, especially if I don't come back. If you hate the idea when it comes to it, we'll find somewhere else, perhaps nearer to where you work, Lizzie. I've held on to the house because it belonged to my family, but I can live anywhere.'

'Let's leave that until the time comes,' Lizzie said and kissed him, wanting to block out the possibility that he might not return. 'I don't want to think about the future – I just want to enjoy what we have now, Sebastian.'

She was greedy for every minute with him, savouring every second they spent together, walking, dancing, sitting in the theatre laughing at one of the comedians who were doing their best to lighten the atmosphere of war-torn Britain, because she knew that all too soon Sebastian would have to leave, and this time he would leave a huge hole in her life.

'You spoil me,' Lizzie said as he slipped the beautiful sapphire and diamond ring on her finger, it was not new but an antique, something that had been in his family for generations. 'I've never seen anything so beautiful. I'm not sure I shall dare to wear it.'

'You mustn't worry, it will be insured,' Sebastian laughed and swept Betty up from her playpen to show her Mummy's ring. The child laughed with delight and patted his face. 'You've had to struggle for years, Lizzie. You see, I know more about your family than you realize, my love. Now you are mine, I want to spoil you and this little lady – give you both all the things you've never had. There are other pieces in the bank that match the ring, and they belong to you now, but I know you won't wear them, because they're old-fashioned and ostentatious. One day we'll have them reset in a simpler fashion just for you.' He shifted Betty into one arm and touched the end of Lizzie's nose with one finger. 'You're a special woman, Lizzie Larch. I'm not sure you realize it yet, but you have it in you to be successful and to be much admired – and you'll do it alone, whether I'm there to cheer you on or not, but remember, even if you can't see or touch me, I'll always be there for you, my darling.'

'Oh, Sebastian, don't. I need you so much.'

'I need you more. You may not believe that, Lizzie, because you don't know your own strength yet – but I want you to love me and I promise I'll never stop loving you. Now, I've got another surprise for you . . .'

'Not more presents, Sebastian. I don't need them – all I want is you.'

'Ah, but this is something for Betty – a pretty doll with a china face, the sort you can't buy these days. It's not new, of course, but I think she will like it.' He kissed the child and put her back in her playpen as she struggled to be free.

'I'm sure she will. How could I say no to a gift for her?' Lizzie kissed him and felt the passion of his embrace in return.

Lizzie smiled, because it was nice being spoiled. From somewhere Sebastian had obtained several extra clothing coupons, which she was able to use to buy a nice suit for her wedding and she'd bought some pretty summer dresses and sun bonnets for Betty too. This spring of 1941 was Betty's first taste of the sunshine, the second spring of the war that was still making itself known across the country.

Lizzie asked if the coupons were black market, but Sebastian shook his head.

'Don't worry, they're legal. I was owed them,' he told her with a grin that set her heart racing. Lizzie suspected a ruthless streak in him, but something told her she could trust him and she did, because she knew that without him life would seem dull, almost pointless.

'That's all right then,' she said and smiled at him as he leaned down and kissed her. 'I love you so much, Sebastian.'

'Good, because I'm crazy about you, Lizzie. I

can't wait to get my wedding ring on your finger
– and I want to get to know Betty too. She's your
daughter and she'll be mine too. This time we'll
take her to the sea with us, because you can't
be parted from her again . . . and I want you to be
happy, darling. You mean the world to me . . .'

'Thank you for caring for her too, Sebastian – I
love you more than I ever thought possible . . .'
Lizzie felt the ache of desire inside as he kissed
her and held her tight. What was she going to do
when he left her, as she knew he must?

No, she wasn't going to think about that; she
would think about the wedding and the happiness
yet to come.

CHAPTER 10

'I 'm so glad for you, Lizzie,' Beth said as she looked at her, dressed for her wedding to Sebastian. 'It's time you were looked after and I know he cares for you – you can see it in the way his eyes follow you wherever you go.'

'And you're sure you can manage at the show-room until I come back? We're only having four days away and this time we're taking Betty with us. Sebastian says he's looking forward to discovering what family life is like, but he's told me I should employ a housekeeper or a nurse to look after her when we're back to normal.'

'Are you going to live in his house?'

'No, not until he comes home,' Lizzie said. 'He's let it out for the time being as some sort of private office for a member of the War Department, a friend of his I understand. I shall continue to live here for the time being – but I shall take his advice and look for a housekeeper to care for the children and keep things straight here. After all, we couldn't expect your mum to do it for ever.'

'No – and I shan't be here much once you're back to work . . .' Beth drew a deep breath as Lizzie stared. 'I'm going to marry Bernie. I shall stay on for a while and give you time to replace me, Lizzie – and I'll visit often, but it's best this way.'

'Are you sure, Beth?' Lizzie asked.

'I made up my mind while you were away,' Beth said. 'I've told Bernie I'll be his wife, so I can't change my mind – and I'm fed up with trying to manage on my own. I know you let me live here and share everything, but I feel I shouldn't let you give me so much – especially now . . .' She stopped short of saying that she felt in the way now that Sebastian was sharing Lizzie's bedroom. 'We'll always be best friends – but I think this is the right thing.'

Beth had felt she was contributing when Lizzie was in the same boat as her, but now it would be different. Lizzie was marrying a wealthy man. Even if he didn't come back, she would be taken care of for the rest of her life; Beth would have felt like a hanger-on and she would rather marry again. Bernie seemed generous and kind and she believed that he sincerely loved her and the twins. It made sense to marry him – didn't it?

'Well, if you're certain,' Lizzie said. She was tempted to change her mind, to tell Lizzie that she didn't really want to be Bernie's wife, but then her mother entered the room to tell them the taxi was waiting and the moment was lost.

After that it was all excitement and laughter as they piled into the cars that took them to the Registry Office where the marriage was to take place. Lizzie was wearing a pale blue suit that she'd managed to buy with Sebastian's coupons; it was the regulation style with an almost straight skirt and a fitted waist to the jacket, but although it wasn't what Lizzie would have chosen for her wedding if there were more choice in the shops; it looked wonderful over a lovely French white silk blouse Sebastian had given her and teamed with the stylish hat she'd made herself, she looked beautiful.

Sebastian certainly thought so. Standing beside Lizzie as they were showered with confetti after the short service, he looked very handsome, much like one of the Hollywood stars they liked to watch at the flicks. Beth felt a twist of envy as she looked at Bernie. He was as tall as Sebastian but thicker set and his face was very . . . well, ordinary, she thought. Bernie wasn't good-looking, neither was he ugly – just boring: the traitorous thought shocked Beth, because she realized it was wrong to feel that way about the man she'd promised to wed. It wasn't fair to Bernie, but she just didn't fancy him – she didn't feel anything much for him, except gratitude. He'd been so good to her. She would try to be a good wife to him. She had to, because she didn't know what else she could do.

Beth had given her heart twice now and in both cases she'd been hurt – Tony had seemed to be more interested in setting up his shop than courting her; they'd quarrelled and stopped seeing each other and then she'd fallen for Mark, her handsome Merchant Navy officer. Beth knew that if he'd lived, Mark would have married her – even if his family disapproved and she was sure they would have – but they never got the chance.

No one but Lizzie knew that she'd written to Mark Allen's parents after his death. She'd received no reply to her letter and guessed that they either thought she was lying about having Mark's children or didn't want to know her. Marrying Bernie was the way forward. It might not be what she truly wanted, but at least the twins would have a father and a home of their own.

'They're leaving now, Beth,' her mother gave her a little nudge after the cake had been cut and everyone had drunk a toast to the bride and groom. Despite the rationing, Sebastian had somehow managed to provide an excellent buffet lunch and a cake that was a huge delicious sponge filled with jam and fresh cream, and dusted with icing sugar and the traditional figures on top. 'Give Lizzie the horseshoe for good luck, love.'

Brought back to herself, Beth rushed to give Lizzie the horseshoe they'd got for her; it was tied up with blue ribbons and rosettes. They kissed and embraced and then everyone went outside, and all at once Lizzie was getting into the back of the large sleek car with Betty's carrycot beside her and then Sebastian was following her.

Beth waved like mad as the car drove off, feeling empty as it disappeared round the corner. She felt as if she'd lost something precious, as if a part of her life was over, and she was unsure about the years to come . . .

'Come on, Beth love, I'll take you home.' Bernie's hand on her arm made Beth jump. She felt coldness at her nape, and for a moment she wanted to pull away; she wanted to tell him she couldn't marry him, but when she looked at him and saw the way he was smiling at her she couldn't say the words. He'd been patient and it would be unfair to let him down now.

'Lizzie looked lovely, didn't she?'

'Very nice,' Bernie said. 'It's a good thing she's married. She doesn't need you now, Beth. You can start making plans for our wedding. We shall be married in church and you'll have a white dress. I'm proud of my Beth and I'll make things proper for you.'

'Bernie . . .' the words of denial hovered on Beth's tongue but she couldn't say them. 'Are you sure – I mean won't people say I shouldn't marry in white?'

'I don't mind what they say. Besides, they won't say it to us,' Bernie said and something glittered in his eyes like ice 'You'll be my wife, Beth. No one will say anything nasty to you or they'll answer to me.'

For a moment there was something different about him. A little shiver went down her spine. Beth looked round for her parents but they were talking to Miriam Oliver, who had come to

161

the wedding, although her husband had chosen to stay at home.

'I'll just say goodbye to Mum,' she said, but Bernie's fingers pressed into her arm and he steered her towards his car.

'I've told her I'm taking you somewhere,' he said. 'Come on, Beth – I'm going to show you our house and you can choose our room and where the children will sleep . . .'

Beth let him ease her into the front seat. She had the sense that her life was no longer in her control and felt a moment of panic. She wished that things were the way they always had been, with her and Lizzie living together and Mum looking after the kids – but Lizzie was married and things would never be the same. Beth knew she couldn't go back, she just had to make the most of the future . . .

Beth knew as soon as Bernie showed her the house that she'd made a mistake. It was old and dark, with heavy ugly furniture and dark cream paint with old-fashioned paper on the walls; it looked as if it belonged to the Victorian era and she guessed he hadn't touched a thing since his father had left it to him. She hated the musty smell and felt defeated, even though she tried her best to seem pleased and picked the largest and lightest room for their bedroom.

'Good choice,' Bernie approved. 'This was my mother's room. She slept here alone after she became an invalid – but I'll have all this stuff cleared out and you can pick your own furniture, Beth. I shouldn't want to sleep in my mother's bed.'

'Thank you,' Beth said, though she could hardly form the words. 'We can make things brighter and nicer everywhere – if you'd like that, Bernie?'

'You must have things as you want them,' he said, looking at her oddly. I shall give you an allowance and you can spend it as you wish – on the house or yourself and the twins. You know I want you to be happy, love . . .'

'Thank you,' Beth said, and since he seemed to expect it, she kissed him on the lips. They felt dry and his arms about her were loose. She drew back, feeling relieved. Perhaps all Bernie really wanted from her was compliance and someone to look after his house . . . a sort of housekeeper. 'You've been so kind and good to me, Bernie.'

'I care for you, Beth,' he said. 'As long as you're a good wife to me, I'll make sure you have all you need.'

Beth nodded, glancing once more at the house before Bernie locked up. Perhaps it wasn't so awful after all. She might be able to turn it into a home with some new curtains, a bit of polish and the smell of good cooking.

CHAPTER 11

'I wish you didn't have to go,' Lizzie said and clung to her husband, lifting her face for his kiss. Their honeymoon had been a perfect interlude, but now it was over and they had to face reality. They'd had just ten days of married life, and now he was leaving again on a mission he couldn't tell her anything about, but which she knew would be dangerous. 'I love you so much, Sebastian.'

'I love you more than life,' he said and kissed her deeply with such need and longing that she knew this parting was costing him every bit as much as it was her. 'Take care of yourself, my love, and believe that I shall return to you. I promise I'll come back and next time I'll settle for a nice safe desk job.'

'Promise?' she said on a laugh that was more a sob.

'Cross my heart,' he said and smiled down at her. 'I've left money available for you should you need anything – and I've done what I can to mend fences with Oliver. Hopefully, you won't get any more trouble, but if you do – go to this address and ask for Jack. Tell him what's been going on. I've spoken to him and he'll help if necessary.'

'What do you mean help – and who is Jack?'

'Just a useful man I know,' Sebastian said. 'Jack is what they call a caretaker and if you're bothered again, tell him at once. Promise me, Lizzie. I don't like the sound of whoever was hanging around your place, so don't delay if you get more trouble – and make sure you're not out late at night on your own. Remember that you're important to me.'

'All right, I promise,' Lizzie said. She drew a deep breath, knowing that she had to say goodbye with a smile on her face. 'I'm fine now – go on, I know you have to leave.'

He kissed her briefly once more and left. Lizzie gulped the tears back. She wasn't going to cry. The few days she'd had with Sebastian had been the happiest of her life and she would cling to the memory and the promise he'd made to return. In the meantime, she had Betty – and the business, which she'd neglected for the past two weeks or so.

Ed had kept the orders going, but she needed to work on the summer and autumn lines for the showroom, and she wanted to pop into the news-agent and advertise for a housekeeper. It would be best if the person she chose could live in, because otherwise she'd be alone here after next week. Beth's wedding banns were being be called in church and she was getting married the Saturday of the first week in June, which was a good thing for her, Lizzie supposed. She'd been staying with her mother for the past few days, but was coming back to stay with Lizzie that night.

Lizzie wondered what to give her friend as a wedding gift. There wasn't much new to buy in the shops these days, though it was possible to buy a few pretty bits in junk shops, and Lizzie had discovered a silver coffee pot, with some other bits and pieces in the attic, together with some old photos and trinkets that had belonged to Lizzie's parents. Her aunt had put them up there and forgotten about them.

Lizzie considered giving Beth the coffee pot, but somehow a piece of antique silver didn't seem of much use to Beth. Besides, Bernie had a house filled with furniture and most things she would need and Lizzie suspected that her friend preferred modern things if they could be found.

Lizzie already planned to make her a pretty hat, but she wanted something better for her. She would have liked to give Beth a share in the business or something substantial, as she'd intended to do when things picked up, but something held her back – a vague unease concerning Bernie Wright. If Beth had asked Lizzie she would have told her about the feeling she'd recently had concerning her husband-to-be, but she seemed to know what she wanted and so Lizzie kept her thoughts to herself. She suspected he resented her influence with Beth and had a feeling that if she gave Beth a substantial gift Bernie wouldn't like it . . . but that was silly, of course he wouldn't mind.

It was time she went to work, but first she had to feed Betty and dress her. Her daughter had just started whimpering. Lizzie hoped she wouldn't miss her Daddy too much. Sebastian had fallen completely under her spell and had been trying to teach her to say Daddy but more in hope than expectation. Betty wasn't advanced enough to speak or walk yet, though she was like lightning on her bottom and could be across the room if you turned your back for a second. She had laughed and clapped her hands and seemed delighted when Sebastian made a fuss of her, and she made unintelligible sounds that he fondly supposed were his name. Beth's twins were that bit older, approaching their first birthday in the second week of June, and were already making sounds that did resemble Mumma and Lizzie, though Matt was far ahead of his sister who tried to walk but fell down at every other step.

Lizzie realized that she was going to miss living with Beth and the twins when she married; seeing her just on visits wasn't the same, and Bernie didn't even have the telephone connected. Lizzie wasn't sure Beth would be happy with him but her friend knew what was best for her and it wouldn't be right for her to interfere. She had a new life of her own and it was right that Beth should have the same.

*   *   *

167

'So Sebastian went this morning then?' Beth said when they met at Mrs Court's house and left the children with her. She'd told them she was quite happy to carry on babysitting for the time being, offering to have Betty if Lizzie wanted her to, even though Beth would be looking after her twins herself when she was married. 'I'll be coming back with you this evening, just until the wedding – but you'll have to get that housekeeper soon, Lizzie. You don't want to be on your own there . . .'

'No, I don't,' Lizzie agreed. 'It's a bit lonely in that big house on my own. If we hadn't agreed to live together after Harry died I should probably have sold it before this.'

'There are plenty of people looking for somewhere to live,' Beth's mother said, 'especially after all the terrible bombing recently, but you wouldn't want to live in a couple of rooms, Lizzie.'

'No, I've been spoiled,' Lizzie admitted, feeling lucky. 'I'll be fine once I get a housekeeper.'

She'd spent the night before with Sebastian at home. The siren had gone early in the evening, and the resulting raid had been a terrible one. Sebastian had gone outside at one point and told her it looked as if most of London was on fire. The sound of ambulances and fire engines screaming through the streets had kept Lizzie's nerves on edge all night as she huddled in the Morrison with Betty, and yet she hadn't been frightened, perhaps because Sebastian was with them.

Mrs Court broke into her thoughts. 'Well, I've enjoyed having the children, even if they are getting to be a handful – especially Matt. You'll have to take a firm hand with him, Beth. He has a mind of his own.'

Beth nodded but said little as they left. Lizzie looked at her sideways as they boarded the bus and sat down. 'Something up, love?'

Beth grimaced. 'I'm glad I'm coming back with you this evening. Mum is good with the children, but she thinks she knows best all the time and I get a bit fed up with being told how to look after them.'

'I'll bet mothers are all like that,' Lizzie said and laughed. She had a feeling there was something Beth wasn't telling her but she didn't want to pry. Beth would say if she wanted her to know. 'What is the situation with Mary?'

'She's gone back to nursing and they've sent her to a military hospital in Cambridge – well, it's part of Addenbrooks, I think. They've put up a lot of prefabs in the grounds for the wounded. She seemed better in herself when she came to tell us she was off – more like she used to be and yet . . .' Beth shook her head. 'Dad says he's sorted her out, but I'm glad she's going away. I still wouldn't trust her around the twins.'

'Oh, Beth . . .' Lizzie felt sorry for Mary, because she couldn't imagine what it would be like to lose both her daughter and Sebastian; she didn't think she would want to go on living. 'It's so hard for her . . .'

'She isn't the only one to lose everything,' Beth said and looked grim as the bus had to take a detour round a huge crater in the road. On either side of the road they could see piles of rubble where a house had once stood, and those that were still standing had tape criss-crossed over the windows to stop them shattering in the event of a nearby blast. The air smelled of smoke and an acrid odour that made their nostrils tingle. 'Everyone is losing something – look at that house, completely gone. It makes you wonder if the people got out or if they died in there.'

'Mrs Jones two doors down was telling me that her sister-in-law lost her father, mother and aunt in one night's raid. They went to a shelter but it took a direct hit and collapsed.'

'Dad built the Anderson in the garden for Mum. He reckons it's safer than a lot of the shelters.'

'I know, but I don't like the Andersons,' Lizzie said. 'We've been in the one your Dad built and its cold and cramped and smells – the Underground is the best, but it takes several minutes to get there and I feel safer in the house than on the streets.'

'We've been lucky so far,' Beth nodded her agreement. 'The Underground is all right, but as you say, we have to run for it in the dark and I'd rather just get under the Morrison and pray.'

'I've noticed that in houses that are hit the stairs nearly always stay standing. It might be as safe under them as anywhere – but surely the Germans are going to get fed up soon and go elsewhere?'

Their bus had ground to a halt and looking out they saw it was impossible to go any further. Devastation was all round them and a factory building was still smouldering, even though the fire brigade had obviously drenched it thoroughly. Getting down with the rest of the passengers, Lizzie and Beth picked their way through the debris of broken bits of charred wood and brick. They had only one street to go and Lizzie's heart sank as she saw smoke coming from near her showroom. Had her luck run out? If the showroom and stock had gone she would have to think about what she did next.

As they turned the corner, Lizzie saw that the shop three doors from hers had been reduced to a pile of rubble, but her own was still standing. She looked at the blackened ruins and her eyes stung with tears as she thought of all the hard work that had gone on in the small tailor's shop that had stood there for three generations. Most of the street had received some damage, windows blown out, roofs with gaping holes in them, but the tailor's shop had taken the brunt of it.

She saw Mr Jacobs standing looking at the devastation, his face blackened and his grey hair streaked with smoke. He was Jewish and lived alone since his son joined the Army and his wife had died of a fever.

'I'm so sorry,' she told him. 'Will you come to us and have something to drink?' She knew that he must have lost everything in the blast: business, home, personal belongings. 'I'm sure we can find somewhere for you to sleep if you need to rest.'

He looked at her blankly for a moment, and then shook his head. 'Thank you, Lizzie, but I have friends who will give me a home – it's just that everything has gone . . . the business my father and grandfather built . . . all gone.'

She saw tears slipping through the smoke trails on his face and her heart caught with pity. He wasn't young and now he had nothing but the hope that his son might one day return.

'If you have orders for customers, we could find you a bench to work at and you can borrow our sewing machines,' she offered, but he shook his head sadly.

'Thank you, no. I shall find work elsewhere – but you are very kind . . .'

Beth pulled at her arm and she walked on. Once inside the workrooms, she saw that her own premises hadn't completely escaped. Some of the back windows had shattered and would need replacing and there was a hole in the kitchen roof. Ed was up a ladder repairing it with a piece of corrugated iron and some wood.

'We were lucky,' he said grimly. 'It was bad here last night, Lizzie, and even worse down the Docks. I was down the Underground and when I came back I thought we'd been hit, but this was just the fallout from the blast. I think a gas main went at the end of the road and those nearest got the worst of it.'

'Yes, I saw what happened to Mr Jacob's property. It's so sad for him, because it's harder to start again at his age.'

'He'll go to friends and in time he'll find a new place to work.'

'It won't be quite the same for him, though,' Lizzie said.

'I'll put the kettle on,' Beth said, 'if we've got any gas in the emergency cylinder.'

'I think we're all right,' Ed answered. 'But wait for the moment, just until I check everything and make sure there are no leaks from the mains. We don't want an explosion.'

'All right,' Beth said and took her kettle through to the back scullery to fill it with water. She was longing for a cup of tea, but you had to be careful after a bombing raid; even if your home was still standing there might be problems with water, gas and electric supplies. Fortunately, they still had running water and she hadn't smelled gas, but she daren't switch the electric on just in case.

The walls were thin, just a wooden partition between this tiny scullery and the kitchen, and she could hear Lizzie and Ed talking in the next room. Jean hadn't turned up for work; she was always reliable, so it made them wonder if something had happened to her or her family.

'Tilly came round last night after you'd left,' Ed was telling Lizzie. 'She has left Oliver's, because she says he's impossible to work for. I told her I

173

thought you might have a place for her and she's coming back later this morning.'

'Oh, that's brilliant,' Lizzie cried. 'I would have asked before but I didn't want to take his best girl from him – but if she's left there's no problem. I may take on another part-time girl as well once Beth has left us, because trade is picking up again . . .'

Beth felt awful hearing herself spoken of in that way – as if a tie with her past had been cut. If she had a choice, she would still come to the show-room part-time, but she knew Bernie wouldn't agree. He'd promised her all kinds of things, but he'd made it clear that he didn't intend her to work. She was his wife and it would shame him to let her work. He had no objection to her visiting her family, but he thought a wife and mother's place was in the home.

Beth had wanted security, but sometimes she felt as if she were falling into a trap, even though she knew she had no real choice. Since she'd seen Bernie's house and instantly disliked it, she'd wished that she was marrying someone who didn't already have everything. She would have liked to choose where she lived and what she lived with. His house was big and filled with dreary brown furniture that looked donkey's years old – and the carpets were old-fashioned, as were the curtains, the colours faded to a sludgy shade that she hated.

Smothering a sigh, Beth went through to the showroom just as Jean turned up for work. She had her right arm in a sling and a bruise on the side of her face, her eyes dark shadowed.

'We were up all night helping people,' Jean said. 'So many of our neighbours lost their homes, though we were luckier and all we got was a hole in the scullery roof and some broken windows. It was the worst night I remember. I helped pull some children from the rubble of a house and fell over and sprained my wrist. The first-aid people made me wear a sling, but I'm sure I can use it to machine.'

'You mustn't dream of trying,' Lizzie said as she came in from the back scullery. 'It was a terrible night for London, Jean. I doubt we'll have many customers today. You can help me do the stock-taking until your wrist is better – Ed is going to double tape our window today. We didn't want to do it, but after last night I think we should.'

They all sat and drank their tea. Jean told them about a stray puppy she'd found in the ruins of a house, apparently abandoned. Everyone had been advised to get rid of pets before the war started, but of course some people couldn't bear to part with the animals they loved, but the poor things got very frightened in a raid and often ran away and got lost.

'I was going to take him home,' she said, 'but a little boy turned up crying and claimed he belonged to him so I gave it to him. He said they'd looked for the pup but couldn't find it when the siren went and his mum dragged him off down the shelter.'

'Lucky you found it for him,' Beth said, 'though most people have got rid of their pets now, because they can't get enough food to spare for animals. I know some friends of ours took their cats to the vets just before it all started; they told their children their pets had run away, but they'd had them put down.'

'Oh, that's awful,' Jean said. 'Mum kept our old cat until it disappeared in one of the raids. We used to feed it leftovers, particularly mum's rice pudding that no one likes, but old Ginger caught mice for herself.'

The shop bell went, surprising them all, and Beth went through to serve their intrepid customer. She was gone for almost an hour, because he was a regular and had decided to take an extra-large order just in case anything happened to their workrooms and he couldn't get his usual supply.

'That was Mr Henry and would you believe it, he's taken almost everything we had in the show-room. All he left were a couple of plain cloche styles, Lizzie. He paid me in cash – look.'

'Good gracious,' Lizzie said as she took a small wad of crisp five pound notes and tucked it in her till. 'Do you think he sat up last night making them?'

Everyone burst into laughter. The joke wasn't

that funny, even though the thought of Mr Henry forging banknotes was amusing, but it helped to clear the tension everyone had been feeling.

'What have you got ready that isn't someone's order?' Beth asked, looking round.

'Well, there are those soft silk berets – and a few basic hats, but nothing fancy. I shall have to get busy,' Lizzie said. 'I think Mr Henry may be our only customer, Beth, so I'll work and leave you and Jean to stocktake.'

However, in thinking that the terrible night that had just passed would deter her customers from coming out, Lizzie was far from the truth. They had a stream of customers, because, they all said they were determined that Hitler wasn't going to make them hide at home in fear; it was business as usual in London, even though transport was almost non-existent in some parts of the city. Some customers were content to order from the styles on show or Lizzie's design book, but several were disappointed she had so little ready-made stock to offer. It was a relief when Tilly walked in halfway through the morning.

'Thank goodness you're here,' Lizzie cried and gave her an overall. 'You can start right now – if it suits you?'

'Yes, my neighbour is looking after my daughter so there's nothing to stop me,' Tilly said and looked delighted as Lizzie dumped a pile of basic shapes in front of her and told her to make them look special. 'I'm going to enjoy this . . . I wish I'd come before.'

'You've chosen just the right moment,' Lizzie said and went back to cutting some of her more elegant shapes.

As she worked, she heard the showroom bell going several times and the sound of Beth's voice. Tilly had finished ten stylish hats and Lizzie took them through herself. To her surprise she saw a queue of three customers, none of whom were known to her.

'May I help you?' she asked one gentleman.

'Yes, please,' he said and looked at the hats she'd brought in with interest. 'I haven't been here before, but I'm impressed . . . and I should like to buy from you.'

'We're always happy to welcome new customers. How did you hear of us?'

'My regular supplier was bombed last night. He's lost his workroom and most of his stock, though he has some materials at a different location – but he told me to try here. Joseph Wainwright Milliner, don't know if you've heard of him?' Lizzie shook her head. 'Well, he says he's had enough and he's getting out of London, retiring. I shouldn't be surprised if he offers his remaining stock to you, Miss Larch.'

'I should be interested in looking at it,' Lizzie said. 'I'm grateful to him for sending me his customers . . . Mr . . .?'

'Ralph Stevens,' he said. 'I own and run a

department store in the West End. Hats are only a small part of my fashion business, but they are more readily available than clothing these days.'

'Well, I'm afraid we don't have as many styles to show you as usual. We seem to have had a run on our stock today. I thought after last night we should be slow, but it's exactly the opposite.'

'Everyone is determined to show they haven't been beaten,' Ralph Stevens said. 'I think a night like last night just brings out our fighting spirit as a nation.'

'Yes, I believe you're right,' Lizzie agreed. She looked round as Tilly brought another four hats through. 'Ah yes, now this is one of my more expensive styles – I could make up a special order for you in a day or so.'

'This is exactly what my customers are looking for,' he said pouncing on the white straw with lots of ribbon and a huge silk bow. 'There just aren't many people making these now, Miss Larch.'

'No, I think we've all been trying to be sensible with softer styles or something more suited to these times of austerity. Utility hats almost – felt fedoras with just a bow or a stylish feather.'

He nodded agreement. 'Yes, and those styles appeal to the younger client, but my older ladies do like their pretty hats . . .'

Lizzie served him with six more hats and took an order for another twelve of her fancier styles. She was thoughtful as he took his leave, because while she needed her business to grow she hated to think that she was profiting from another's misfortune.

However, when Joseph Wainwright called to see her that afternoon with an offer for her to buy his remaining stock, she didn't feel so bad; he was well into his seventies with a shock of white hair and faded blue eyes.

'I've been sending all my customers your way, Miss Larch,' he told her. 'I've admired your work from a distance and I thought you might like to purchase my stock. I still have some good silk, tulle and quite a few boxes of trimmings, which I kept separate from the workrooms just in case.'

'I should like to see them,' Lizzie said and made arrangements to meet him at the small lock-up later that evening.

After he'd left, Lizzie remembered what Sebastian had said about not being out late at night by herself and asked Ed if he would like to go with her.

'Certainly I will, Lizzie,' he said. 'It was good of Joseph to give you the offer. He was known for the quality of his stock, so it ought to be decent stuff.'

'Well, if he really has some nice silk trimmings I'll be very interested in buying them.' She smiled at him. 'It's turned out to be a good day for us after all, Ed . . .'

Lizzie was delighted with the rolls of materials and at least a dozen boxes of ribbons, lace and silk flowers she was able to purchase at a price that was fair to both her and Mr Wainwright. He promised to deliver them to the showroom the next day and they parted company on good terms.

Ed congratulated her on making another friend in the business. 'You could have knocked him down, but you gave him what he asked and he appreciated it, Lizzie. He'll send more of his regular customers your way. It's always good to have friends in the business.'

'Yes; besides, I liked him and I thought he offered a fair price. I don't want to cheat anyone, Ed – and especially not someone who has lost so much.'

He laughed and shook his head at her. 'Oliver would say you were too soft, but I like the way you are, Lizzie – and you deserve all the success that comes your way, despite the efforts of someone who wanted to hurt you.'

'After last night my little troubles seem as nothing,' Lizzie said and pulled her collar tight around her neck as she felt suddenly cold. 'We haven't had a warning yet tonight. Do you think the Germans are giving us a rest?'

'They're probably just letting us think that and then they'll come back again with a vengeance,' Ed said. 'We didn't think it could get any worse than it was last year in October, but last night . . . I pray I don't ever see that again. So many old buildings have gone, Lizzie; they really had it in for us. It's a miracle St Paul's is still standing. I heard it was hit, together with the British Museum, Westminster Hall and the Lords . . .'

Ed saw her to her door and waited until she was

inside. She asked him in for a cup of cocoa but he refused. Beth was sitting listening to music on the radio but she turned it off as Lizzie entered and smiled.

'Was it worth the bother?'

'Yes, I bought enough stock to keep us going for some weeks,' Lizzie said. 'I don't know about you, but I'm going to bed. I'm worn out after today. It's ages since we've sold hats we've only just finished.'

'I'll make the cocoa,' Beth said. 'It was lucky Tilly turned up. She's going to make a difference to your business, Lizzie – you won't miss me.'

Lizzie yawned and then looked at her askance. 'You know that's rubbish, Beth. You're my special friend. I shall miss seeing you every day. We've shared everything these past few months and it won't be the same without you. Besides, Tilly won't be there all the time; she's having another baby and I'm not sure what will happen when she has two little ones to look after.'

'I shall miss coming in to work,' Beth admitted but walked through to the kitchen. After a pause Lizzie followed her.

'Is something wrong? Are you upset or worried?'

Beth hesitated, then, 'A bit nervous. Have I done the right thing, Lizzie?'

Lizzie looked at her thoughtfully. 'Only you can answer that, Beth. If you've changed your mind you can stay here with me until you're sure of what you want.'

'Yes, I know.' Beth sighed and then laughed. 'I expect I'm just being silly. No, I can't change my mind now. Bernie is a good man and I can't let him down . . .'

Lizzie yawned and left her to it and went upstairs to look in on the children, because she knew Beth was too stubborn to change her mind. If she'd made a mistake she wouldn't admit it. She could only hope that her friend would not regret her decision.

CHAPTER 12

'You look really lovely,' Lizzie said as she saw Beth dressed in the white gown and pretty lace veil that she'd managed to buy with the extra coupons Bernie had got for her. He'd told her that some were his own and some from a friend, but Lizzie suspected they were bought on the black market. However, she didn't voice her suspicions, because she knew Beth wouldn't have used them if she'd guessed.

'Thank you,' Beth said, 'and thank you for all your presents, Lizzie. The money will come in useful . . . give me a bit of independence.'

Lizzie hadn't been able to think of a suitable gift for Beth so she'd given her two pretty hats, the silver coffee pot and some money. It was enough so that Beth could pay for things she wanted without having to ask her husband for every penny, and for a girl who had been used to having her own wages that was important.

'I'd hoped you would become a partner one of these days, as we expanded,' Lizzie said, 'but Bernie wouldn't allow that, so I wanted you to have something.'

'It's more than I've ever had in my life before,' Beth said. 'I shall put it in the Post Office and save it until I need it.'

Lizzie nodded but didn't answer, because Mrs Court entered with a lovely bouquet of lilies, roses and ferns that Bernie had sent for Beth. After that, Lizzie was kept busy greeting friends and helping Beth's family with organizing the cars and the guests leaving from their house. Dottie was there minus her children, whom she'd left with her mother-in-law for once, but Mary had telephoned to say she was on duty at the hospital and couldn't make it. Beth's granny, mother and some distant cousins were amongst those crowding into the cars. Lizzie and Dottie were Beth's maids of honour and Lizzie had left Betty with Aunt Miriam who adored the beautiful little girl and insisted on coming over to Lizzie's house to look after her, despite any grumbles she might have from her husband.

At the church everyone clustered round the bride as they waited to go in, and then it was just Beth, her father and the maids of honour. Lizzie and Dottie walked behind Beth as she drifted down the church aisle on her father's arm and the organ played the wedding march. Beth's parents were smiling, happy that their daughter was getting married and would be respectable, no longer an unmarried mother but the wife of a man with an important job at the munitions factory.

Beth handed the bouquet to Lizzie when she

took her place at Bernie's side. For a moment Lizzie thought she saw distress in her friend's eyes, but dismissed it as fanciful nonsense. Beth wouldn't marry a man she didn't really like or respect – would she?

Once the ceremony was over, the bride and groom emerged into the sunshine of a late May morning. A small crowd had gathered outside and Beth was showered with homemade confetti.

A fairly lavish reception followed. Mrs Court whispered to Lizzie that Bernie had provided all the tinned ham and also the tinned fruit for the trifles – and he'd sent the pork for the sausage rolls, but even he hadn't been able to produce a proper iced fruit cake and they'd settled for two tiers of fatless sponges iced with jam and some whipped fresh cream, which their milkman had wangled for them.

'I don't know where Mr Wright got it all,' Mrs Court said, a little frown creasing her brow, because she didn't approve of black market goods and even she had started to wonder. 'If it wasn't Beth's wedding I'd have sent it back, but she deserves a nice do.'

'Yes, she does,' Lizzie said. 'Perhaps we shouldn't inquire too deeply just this once.'

'Well, just this once,' Mrs Court agreed but she was still looking doubtful. 'I didn't think Mr Wright was that sort of man . . .'

'Well, he probably did it because he's so fond of Beth and wanted her to have the best – and we don't know where it came from, do we? He might have friends who obliged him.'

Beth's mother nodded, but she wasn't convinced. Lizzie knew that you couldn't provide this kind of meal on the sort of rations they all had to manage with. Most people had friends who helped out for weddings and special parties, but she was certain Bernie had got his supplies on the black market . . .

Beth asked Lizzie to go upstairs with her when she went home to change for her honeymoon. Lizzie helped her out of her dress and stood watching as she put on her new suit and one of the hats Lizzie had made for her. She looked pale and nervous and Lizzie was suddenly anxious for her.

'You are all right with this, Beth?'

'It's too late now if I'm not,' the practical side of Beth came out and she gave Lizzie a lopsided grin. 'Just nerves about tonight, Lizzie. I know I'm being silly – it isn't as if I'm a shy virgin, is it?'

'No – but he isn't Mark,' Lizzie said and squeezed her hand impulsively. 'If ever things go wrong, you know you're welcome at my house, Beth.'

'You're not going to live in Sebastian's house then?'

'Not until he comes home for good anyway.'

'I thought it might be safer there than in the East End,' Beth said, 'but they seem to be leaving us alone since that awful night. Bernie says they've turned their attention elsewhere for the moment.'

'Yes, thank God. I'm not sure we could've taken

many more nights like that last one. People were weeping on the streets – yet they carried on as best they could as if nothing had happened.'

'Fighting spirit,' Beth said and lifted her chin. 'That's what we Brits are best at – and I'm a Brit . . .'

'Of course you are and braver than most,' Lizzie said. 'It may not be as bad as you think, love – and remember what I said, you can come to me if you need to . . .'

'Ah, there you are, Beth,' her mother said, entering the bedroom. 'Bernie is ready to leave when you are and the car is here.'

'Yes, I'm ready now.'

'Good luck,' Lizzie said and squeezed her hand.

She hung back at the top of the stairs as Beth went down to be greeted by more home-made confetti and the congratulations of her friends and family. Bernie smiled at her as she reached him, and then, just for one second, he glanced up at Lizzie. The expression in his eyes was so strange at that moment that it made her shiver. In an instant it had gone and he was smiling at Beth, fussing over as she kissed the twins goodbye and left them in her mother's care for the next week. Matt screamed and punched as Beth handed him back to her mother, but Bernie touched his bare leg with one finger and the child turned to look, his screams ceasing abruptly.

Lizzie had an awful foreboding. She wanted to call out to Beth, to warn her to come back, but

Beth didn't catch her eye and then they had gone out to the waiting car. It was too late now. She was Bernie's wife and he wouldn't just let her walk off.

No, she was being silly. Bernie was in love with Beth and he was probably just a bit nervous on his wedding day. She hadn't seen dislike in his eyes when he looked at her. Lizzie must have mistaken it – or it was a trick of the light, and yet Bernie seemed to be telling her that he'd got Beth now and she'd better keep her distance or else . . .

Beth woke to hear the sounds coming from the adjoining bathroom and a feeling of distaste crept over her. Bernie was washing, cleaning his teeth to be more precise, and the noise of his gargling and spitting irritated her. She closed her eyes as she tried to shut out the previous night, when he'd spent nearly half an hour in the bathroom before coming to her. She hadn't found the sound of his ablutions particularly romantic and when he finally climbed into bed beside her, she'd wanted to push him away – but of course she couldn't. It was what being married was all about as far as Bernie was concerned. He'd promised her so many things and Beth knew she had to keep her side of the bargain.

It was bearable after the first couple of minutes when he climbed on top of her, and after a quick fumble at her breasts he'd parted her legs and

189

thrust into her. Had she been a virgin it would have been unbearably painful, but because she'd had the twins she hardly felt anything. It crossed her mind that Bernie was much smaller down there than Mark had been, and he was certainly no great lover. Half a dozen thrusts and it was over, leaving Beth feeling empty but relieved. After a moment, he rolled off her, pecked at her cheek and then closed his eyes.

Within minutes Bernie was snoring. Beth knew he'd drunk quite a bit that evening after they arrived at the hotel in Brighton. It was a lovely place, what Beth would call posh, and they'd had a nice meal of roast chicken with potatoes and beans, accompanied by some lovely wine. Beth had drunk two glasses, because it helped to ease her nerves, but Bernie had finished the bottle.

His efforts at making love had been pitiful, but at least it had been over quickly, Beth thought. Maybe she could bear it, if only he wouldn't spend so much time making those revolting noises in the bathroom! She'd been a fool to sacrifice personal happiness for security, but she'd made her decision and she must live with it.

Beth sat up cautiously, keeping the sheets up to her breasts as Bernie came back into the bedroom. He hardly glanced at her as he said, 'You can use the bathroom now. You were sleeping so I went first. You need to be quick, because breakfast will be over in half an hour – and we want our money's worth, because they know how to charge here.'

'It's a nice place,' she said, pulling her dressing gown round her as she got out of bed. 'It was kind of you to bring me here, Bernie.'

'I'd do anything for you, love,' he said, but his eyes gleamed. 'I expect value for my money though – always have, always will.'

Beth wasn't sure he was talking just about the hotel. Had he noticed that she wasn't very responsive to him the previous night? Beth hadn't refused him, but she hadn't exactly welcomed him with any degree of warmth. She wasn't sure now why she'd been so nervous, but she would try to do better in future. After all, Bernie had given her a lovely wedding, as well as presents for herself and the children. He would expect something in return and it probably wasn't enough to keep his house nice and cook a decent meal in the evenings.

Her practical side had reasserted itself. She'd chosen this path and there was no going back. It was only right to show him a bit of affection now and then. Walking over to where he stood before the mirror, Beth put her arms about him and kissed his neck.

'You're a lovely man, Bernie, and I'm lucky to have you.'

To her surprise he shrugged her off, moving away from her sharply. 'That's enough of that, Beth. I don't hold with silly stuff at this hour of the day. You just be ready for me at night and we shall suit all right.'

Beth felt as if he'd thrown cold water over her, but something switched off inside her. If that was what he wanted it was all right with her. She'd lie there and let him have his own way and she would never try to show affection again. She should have cancelled the wedding. She'd been afraid of her father's disappointment and hadn't had the courage to cancel things at the last minute – but she'd thought Bernie really loved her and she didn't want to hurt him. If he called a quick fumble in bed loving, he wasn't the man Beth had expected, but if it was what he wanted she couldn't object because she'd married him for what he could give her and this was the price she must pay.

She turned away and went into the bedroom, wishing that she'd thought things out for longer and then told him no – but he'd always been there when she needed help and the children seemed to get on with him; he could make them stop screaming with a touch of his fingers and Matt needed a firm hand or he would get out of control. Her parents had seemed to want to see her settled – and Beth had felt awkward when Sebastian came back and married Lizzie, and it had scared her thinking that she might have to manage alone. She'd known she couldn't go on living in Lizzie's home forever and it'd seemed that her best option was to marry Bernie. Now she'd realized she'd made a terrible mistake . . .

★　　★　　★

The next day, Beth got up and went to the bathroom as Bernie lay snoring beside her. She stood looking at her white face in the mirror and then ran the taps in the bath, needing to scrub the touch of her husband's body from her flesh. Bernie hadn't been drunk that evening and he'd certainly had his money's worth from her, suggesting things she found disgusting and forcing her to take him in her mouth when she said she didn't want to. He'd come in her mouth and then, when she'd spat out his semen, he'd slapped her face.

'Don't treat me as if I'm scum,' he threatened. 'You're my wife now and you'll do whatever I tell you.'

And then he'd turned her over and taken her in a way that made Beth want to vomit. Why couldn't he be tender and loving as Mark had been she'd wondered bitterly as she felt the pain of his entry and had to bite her lip to stop herself screaming.

'You're no good to me the other way,' he muttered as he drew away afterwards. 'It's those bloody kids. I'll have you this way when I want you, but don't think you're getting out of havin' my kids, because I'll have you the other way when I want an' all.'

Beth could only lie there like a log and let him satisfy himself. If her wedding night had been disappointing, the second night was hell. She wished that she could just disappear into the floor and for a moment contemplated cutting her wrists in the bath and letting all the blood seep from her body, but the mother in her wouldn't let her do that – she had her twins to look after. They were her reason to live and she'd brought this on herself; they didn't deserve to be punished just because she'd done something stupid.

After she'd rinsed her mouth and cleaned her teeth she felt a bit better. She'd cleansed all trace of him from her body but she would never get this night out of her mind, and it made her wonder how much of this she could take. Wild thoughts of running away went through her head, but all the fear of telling her parents came rushing back and she knew she wouldn't do it. Somehow she would have to bear whatever Bernie did.

Besides, where could she go? If she went to Lizzie or her parents, he would fetch her back – and her father would tell her she should stay with her husband. Rebellion flared in Beth and she planned what she would do if he attacked her like that again – because she was not going to let him treat her like a slut again, even if he hit her.

However, when he woke, Bernie seemed subdued, even regretful, and after she'd dressed, he touched her hand, looking at her oddly.

'I'm sorry about last night,' he apologized. 'It made me angry because I knew you didn't want me – and I was jealous of the children's father. If you'll stay with me, Beth, I promise I shan't behave like that again. I knew you didn't love me when you agreed to marry me – but I thought you might like me a bit.'

'I did . . .' Beth said and saw the glint in his eyes. 'I still do, Bernie – but I shan't if you hurt and humiliate me like that again.'

'I know. It was bad – I shouldn't have treated you like a whore,' he said. 'You're my wife and I love you – even if it didn't seem like it last night. Please say you'll forgive me.'

'I will try,' Beth replied but didn't smile. 'I didn't deserve what you did to me last night, Bernie, and I shan't put up with it.' She took a deep breath. 'Lizzie told me I can go back there if I want – and if you ever do things like that again I shall.'

'Just try going there . . .' For a moment there was such anger in his eyes that she didn't recognize him, but then in another moment, he had it under control. 'You won't have the need to leave me, Beth – and if you do, you and that bitch will be sorry. I'll be good to you and I shan't hurt or humiliate you again, but you have to be a good wife to me.'

'I'll do all the things a wife should,' Beth replied coldly. 'But if you want affection you must remember your promise to me.'

'I'll remember,' he said. 'Just remember you are mine, Beth. You belong to me and I would make anyone who stood in my way very sorry . . .'

Beth managed to keep her inner shudders from showing. She was such a fool to have been taken in by his meek, kind and generous manner. Bernie wasn't really like that at all – underneath the charm and caring manner there was a different kind of man altogether: a man who frightened her.

Beth looked at the suitcases waiting to be unpacked, and turned away. After that awful night when he'd done those unspeakable things to her, Bernie had been kind to her, taking her to all the best shops, buying her whatever she saw that took her fancy. There wasn't really much to buy, but he'd bought her an antique silver bangle and some Victorian diamond earrings. She hadn't really wanted them, but it would be stupid to refuse and make him angry again. After his buying spree, he took her to the theatre and on another occasion to the flicks, and then back to the hotel both times. She'd waited in trepidation but he hadn't come to bed until the early hours and he'd fallen asleep without touching her.

He'd made love to her once more but he'd been drinking and it was rather like the first time. Beth felt nothing, but it was better than the humiliation that she'd felt the night he'd abused her.

Now they were back home and Bernie had gone to work. Beth knew she should unpack her things and then go shopping for food. Her husband would expect a decent meal when he got home, and she'd decided that she would try to give him value for money, at least through his stomach and by keeping his house clean and his clothes nicely washed and pressed.

She longed to visit Lizzie; it would in any other circumstances be the first thing she did on getting home, but something held her back. She'd managed to convince her mother everything was all right when they'd collected the twins the previous night, but Lizzie would know how bad things were immediately and Beth couldn't tell her the truth. It was just too humiliating, too horrible to confide to anyone – even her best friend.

CHAPTER 13

Lizzie consulted her order book. She'd never been this busy and she knew she had several people to thank for her new success. Aunt Miriam had stopped her husband telling slanderous lies, and he had done so, because now that she was married no one would believe them anyway. She sighed as she thought how good it would have been to talk to Beth about the way things were going now, but her friend had been back from her honeymoon for three weeks and she hadn't been in touch.

Lizzie thought it strange, but perhaps Beth was caught up in the excitement of being married and having a husband and a home to care for, as well as looking after her children She hadn't seen Mrs Court either, even though she'd called round one Sunday with a gift for the twins' birthday. She'd gone there after trying Beth's home unsuccessfully on two occasions. No one had been in there either and Lizzie had left the present with a neighbour. Perhaps she ought to try and visit Beth again, but she had a feeling that Bernie wouldn't welcome her in his house, and she'd been expecting

Beth to bring the twins to see her, even if just to say thank you for their presents.

It was almost as if she'd been cast adrift by the family and Lizzie felt a bit hurt, but scolded herself for being silly as she worked on her orders. Having Tilly work for her was wonderful, because she could trust her to trim the best hats, which gave her more time to design, and some of her customers were keen to buy her special creations; it seemed that Sebastian wasn't the only one to recognize Lizzie's talents. Ralph Stevens was becoming a frequent visitor and his order was never less than twelve of her best hats. It meant that she had very little time for anything but work these days.

Thankfully, Lizzie had found her housekeeper two days after Beth's wedding. She'd offered interviews to the four women who rang in answer to her advertisement and three of them were hopeless; two were such sour-faced creatures that Lizzie couldn't have left her darling daughter with them to save her life; the third was a pleasant enough woman but older than Lizzie had envisaged and although she felt sympathy for her because she was a widow and lonely, she didn't seem right. The fourth candidate told her that her name was Hatty Simpson; she was a widow with three sons, all of whom were serving either in the Army or the RAF.

'I've been privileged to know happiness, Mrs Winters,' she said when Lizzie asked her how she felt about living in. 'I've had my own home and enjoyed it, but my sons have wives and homes of their own – and while I'm fit enough I would prefer the kind of job where I live in as part of the family. I don't like living alone, though I'm not averse to my own company sometimes.'

'You would have two rooms of your own,' Lizzie said, 'but I would prefer it if we had our meals together – what I'm really looking for is a friend, Mrs Simpson. Betty needs a family and I don't have any of my own – Aunt Miriam is her great-aunt by marriage but that's all we have. My second husband doesn't have much family either as far as I'm aware.' They certainly hadn't come to the wedding, though Sebastian had invited several friends. 'I want someone who is happy to look after my daughter and keep the house tidy, wash a few delicate bits and send the sheets to the laundry, perhaps some shopping – though I can do that on my way home. I have a window cleaner and we can have someone in to do heavy work. Oh, and I like to work at the serviceman's social club one or two nights a week – Aunt Miriam comes round to sit with Betty then.'

'That's fine for me, but I shall be here if I'm needed,' Hatty said and smiled. 'I kept house, cleaned for my husband and three sons and nursed him until he died of lung cancer . . .' Lizzie caught her breath. 'Oh, don't be sorry for me, I know people don't talk about that awful disease, but it's been with us for centuries, a dark shadow lurking that people fear and don't mention . . .'

200

'Yes, we don't talk about these things enough, do we?'

'I've learned to live with my memories and – I shall be happy to do all you need, Mrs Winters, and pleased to live as one of the family.'

'Then all I have to say is when can you start?'

'Tomorrow, if that is all right with you. I'll be here at seven in the morning and bring some of my things. The rest can come later. I've given a month's notice on my house and I'll have anything I can't bring either stored or sold down the market.'

'That sounds wonderful, Hatty,' Lizzie said and smiled in relief. She'd taken to the friendly woman instantly and knew she would fit in with her ways. 'But if there are any bits of furniture you'd like to bring, I'm sure we can make room for them. I didn't over furnish the spare rooms when I moved in – so bring whatever you want with you.'

'In that case I'll bring my bedroom stuff and some comfortable chairs for my sitting room,' Hatty looked pleased. 'I haven't got much I want, because I was bombed out last year and only a few bits survived the blast – so I shall be quite content to sell most of it, because it was second-hand and all I could get.'

Lizzie offered her a cup of tea, but Hatty said she had things to do and went off, promising to be on time in the morning.

She'd been as good as her word and was nicely settled in. Betty had taken to her and now that she was not disturbed by Matt's screaming she'd become the peaceable child she'd been at the start. Hatty had not had to get up to her once in the weeks since and nor had Lizzie, and even better, her bad dreams had gone.

Lizzie walked to her bus alone now, because no one had followed or threatened her since before Beth's wedding. She'd begun to relax and enjoy her life again – but she did miss Beth, despite having Tilly and Hatty, as well as Ed, Jean, Janet and Aunt Miriam. Beth had been special to her and she couldn't understand why she hadn't wheeled the twins round to the showroom to see her. Lizzie made up her mind that she would make time to call on her friend on her way home later.

It was two o'clock that afternoon when someone came into the showroom as Lizzie was rearranging the window with some fresh stock. She smiled as she saw it was Mrs Court, pleased that she'd come to see her.

'How lovely to see you! I've been thinking I would come round soon, but I've been busy . . . and you weren't in when I called with a present for the twins' birthdays.'

'Yes, I should've thanked you but . . . Lizzie, have you seen Beth recently?' Mrs Court's anxiety made her almost abrupt.

'No, I haven't; I went round there a couple of times but she must have been out, because she didn't answer the door,' Lizzie felt coldness at her nape as she saw Mrs Court's worried look. 'Is something the matter?'

'I was hoping you would know,' Beth's mother said and sighed. 'She never comes to see me. I went round this morning; she let me in and she's got that place like a new pin, but something wasn't right, Lizzie – I could see it in her face, though she kept saying she was fine. I'm sure she isn't happy, but she won't talk to me about it. I thought she might have said something to you?'

'I haven't seen Beth once since the wedding,' Lizzie said. 'I waited for a while, because I didn't want to intrude . . . I don't think her husband likes me.'

'What makes you say that?'

'I don't know – just the way he looked at me once. I had the feeling that he resented my friendship with Beth . . .'

'Her father and I thought he would be good to her – but if we were wrong . . . we pushed Beth into getting married, Lizzie. I kept telling her he was a good man and her father said she would be respectable if she got married, but if he's making her unhappy . . .'

'You don't know that,' Lizzie said. 'We can't be sure he isn't everything he seemed – kind and generous . . .'

'Beth had a bruise on her cheek this morning,' Mrs Court said and looked grim. 'She said she caught herself when she was running after Matt, but I'm sure she was lying . . .' A sob caught in her throat. 'I couldn't bear it if I thought he was hitting her, Lizzie . . .'

'Oh God, no,' Lizzie said, feeling sick at the thought. 'I know Beth wasn't sure she was doing the right thing. I think she would've liked to change her mind right at the last minute but she was afraid of upsetting everyone. If he knows that she doesn't love him. . . .'

Mrs Court looked pale and worried. 'If my husband knew he was hurting her, he'd kill him. He thinks the world of Beth, even though you might not think it after the way he behaved when she got pregnant – he was just so disappointed that his precious girl had let him down . . .'

'I know. He came to the hospital the night she gave birth and I saw his face when the doctor said she was all right. You mustn't tell him – not yet anyway. I'll pop round there on my way home this evening, before Bernie gets back . . .'

'Oh, Lizzie, you think he's a bad person, don't you?'

'I don't know for sure,' Lizzie said. 'Yet there was something at the wedding – and a couple of times before, if I think about it. I don't know what we can do if Beth is being ill-treated, but I won't let it go on if I can help it.'

'Thank you, Lizzie.' Mrs Court dabbed at her eyes with her handkerchief. 'I'm glad I came. Her father would sort him out, but I really believe he would kill him if he thought Beth was being ill-treated – and there are the twins to think of, too. Bernie might take it out on them if we meddled . . .'

'No, we don't want that,' Lizzie said anxiously. 'If I'm right, Beth may be in a lot of trouble and we have to be very careful we don't make things worse.' She hesitated, then, 'I'll see what she has to say later . . .'

Lizzie left work at half past three that afternoon. Jean had gone into the showroom to take her place and she couldn't wait any longer because she needed to see Beth for herself.

She found the house, an old-fashioned Victorian villa in one of the better areas overlooking what would have been a nice green before the war but which now had marks where the wheels of heavy vehicles had run over it and one tree had been so badly damaged in a bombing raid that it was only a blackened stump There were spotless lace curtains at the bow windows of Bernie's house and the doorstep had been freshly scrubbed, gleaming white in the July sunshine. There was no answer when Lizzie knocked, so she knocked again louder and went on doing so until the door was opened. Beth stared at her but didn't smile in welcome or ask her in.

'I wasn't expecting you. I've just got Matt to sleep. He's teething again and kept us awake last night. Bernie wasn't too pleased about it.'

'No, I don't expect anyone would be if they

couldn't sleep,' Lizzie said. 'May I come in just for a few minutes please, Beth?'

'I'm sorry, Lizzie. I can't ask you in. Bernie wouldn't like it – please go away. When I'm ready I'll come and see you . . .' She made to shut the door, but Lizzie moved to stick her foot in the way. 'Lizzie, I can't talk to you. Please – he'll be home soon and if he sees you he'll go mad again . . .'

'Did he hurt you, Beth?' Lizzie said, looking her straight in the eyes. Beth's gaze fell, and even though she shook her head, Lizzie knew she was lying. 'You mustn't put up with it, love. Leave him and come to me. He doesn't deserve you, Beth, and he shouldn't hit you.'

'He didn't exactly hit me – he just pushed me against the door,' Beth said and her head went up, eyes cold and proud. 'All right, I'll tell you. He's a brute and I hate him, but I'm afraid of him, Lizzie. If I leave him he'll come after me and he'll hurt us all – me, the twins and you. He doesn't like you at all, Lizzie. He doesn't want me to see you . . . you mustn't come here again.'

Beth pushed Lizzie out of the door and slammed it tight. Lizzie stared at it in frustration. She wanted to hammer on it and shout until Beth was forced to answer, but if she did that people would hear – and then Bernie would know too and Beth would suffer for it.

Lizzie walked away in distress. She must go to Mrs Court and tell her the truth, but there was little Beth's mother could do to help her daughter. Beth's father could give Bernie a good hiding, but Lizzie suspected Bernie might be a dangerous man and unless Mr Court killed him he would simply take his fury out on her – and on others. And the last thing any of them wanted was Beth's father to be hung for murder.

'Oh, Sebastian,' Lizzie sighed. 'I do wish you were here. She was sure that Sebastian would know what to do against a bully, but she had no idea how to contact him. He was busy with his work, whatever that was – and yet she knew if he were here he would help her.

She thought about the card he'd given her with a name – the mysterious Jack who Sebastian told Lizzie to go to if she were in trouble. She wasn't sure that she could ask him for help in Beth's case. The police would say it was a domestic affair and best left to husband and wife to sort out – but it couldn't be right that a man could get away with hitting his wife.

The look in Beth's eyes had cut Lizzie to the quick. She looked defeated, as if she'd given up hope – and that just wasn't the Beth Lizzie knew. What had Bernie done to her?

Beth stood with her back to the door and let the tears roll unchecked down her cheeks. She felt so low that if it hadn't been for the twins she might have killed herself. Bernie hadn't kept his promise; he alternated between sweet words and gifts and blows to her face and body, but he'd stopped coming to her bed after Beth threw a bowl of cold water over him. She'd been driven too far when he once more raped her from behind in the manner she found so disgusting, and when he'd fallen asleep, snoring like a pig, she filled a bowl from the washstand and poured it over him in the bed.

Of course she'd paid for it. He'd hit her until she fell to the ground half-unconscious and then he'd knelt by her side and started to weep and blubber as if he were a child, begging her to forgive him. At least, she thought he'd been begging her, though a couple of times he'd called her Mother. The feeling had grown in Beth's mind that her husband was either evil or not right in his head – and yet when anyone came to the house that he wanted her to be nice to he played the loving husband to perfection. It made her feel sick and she wanted to stand in the street and scream the truth, tell everyone what a bastard he was, but of course she didn't – she had to think about the twins.

Bernie had a habit of picking them up, particularly Matt, and dangling him under the arms until Matt started to scream and then he shook him until he stopped. Afterwards he would put the child back in his cot and look at Beth and she knew what he was telling her – he could kill her children whenever it suited him.

She'd thought she was giving them a home and a father but she'd brought them into danger, and she wasn't sure what she could do about it. Lizzie was still her friend and she wouldn't give up on her, even though Beth had tried to keep her at arm's length so that she wouldn't guess what a bully Bernie had turned out to be – but had she the right to take the children and go home to Lizzie? Bernie would punish them all if she did . . . and Beth had heard him whispering with some of the men who came at night. She didn't know why they came or what hold Bernie had over them, but most of them seemed scared of him – and one of the men had a scar on his face. Beth remembered something about a man with a scar on his face but couldn't place it. The look that man had given Beth as he followed Bernie to his study had made her shake with fear. She had the feeling that he would kill her as easily as he might swat a fly and smile as he did it.

If Bernie wanted to harm her or her family, he wouldn't even have to do it himself, because he had people who would oblige him for money. If her dead body turned up in the canal, he would play the broken-hearted husband to perfection.

She wiped a hand over her eyes and went to wash her face. She didn't want Bernie to see she'd been crying. If he thought she was cowed, he would treat her worse than ever; it was only the way she'd stood up to him that had saved her from worse. He'd known that if she could throw cold water over him as he slept it could as easily be acid or a knife plunged into his neck, and because of that he slept in his own room with the door locked.

For a moment as she took out the carving knife and began to chop the rabbit for the stew that evening, she thought about using it to cut his throat as he lay sleeping . . . but the idea terrified her. Murder wasn't the answer for Beth. She didn't want to go to prison or hang, she wanted to live – and she would think of a way to turn the tables on him, because she knew Bernie had secrets.

If she could find something – something that the law might want to know . . . perhaps she could force him to let her go . . .

Bernie stood on the corner of the street and watched the woman walk away. He'd known it was only a matter of time before that nosy bitch came poking her oar into his business. She was just like his sodding mother! He'd noticed that bossy manner the first time he'd met her. Bernie had hated and feared his formidable mother in equal amounts. She tyrannized him until he was old enough and big enough to teach her a lesson, beating him with a cane, forcing him to go hungry if he'd wet his bed and making him look a fool when he cried and begged for love. Once he was sure of his own strength, he'd turned on her like a cornered rat. She'd learned what it was like to be shut in a cold dark cellar with things crawling over her in the blackness, to be left until the hunger gnawed at your belly and your tongue stuck to the roof of your mouth because you were so thirsty you thought you would die. Oh yes, she'd learned, his sainted mother, with her prim mouth and her black clothes, and she'd never recovered from the shock, dying of the resulting pneumonia that developed once he'd carried her back to her room after she'd fallen unconscious.

And that snooty bitch who wanted to take his wife away from him would learn too! Norm had promised to scare her, but she was made of sterner stuff. She'd got friends and they'd protected her and she was doing better than ever. Once Beth promised to marry him, he'd told Norm not to bother with the bitch anymore, but now she was round here making trouble for him – and he'd bet she'd been trying to get Beth to leave him. Well, he'd make sure she had too much to worry about to poke her snout in where it wasn't needed in future.

He hesitated and then turned away. He'd been intending to get home early and take Beth out to the theatre or the flicks for a treat, because he knew he'd treated her badly. It wasn't that he planned to hurt her, but she made him lose his temper – it was the defiant way she looked at him, as if warning him that she wasn't broken yet. And throwing that water over him had made him see red.

What had made her do it? She must have known he would punish her – she knew the routine now. If she pleased him he gave her presents and if she didn't – he took a present for himself. An unpleasant smile curled over his thick lips. Bernie knew he wasn't handsome, but he wasn't ugly either – a lot of women would lick his arse if he gave them what he gave Beth, but she hated the things he wanted her to do. He'd thought she would learn after the first time, but she still looked at him in that defiant way, and he knew that although she was frightened of his brutality at times, she was still herself inside. It was as if she had armour round her inner being and he couldn't touch her.

He wanted to go back and teach her a lesson, but then he remembered it was the other one he had to see to – if she were out of the way, Beth would have nowhere to run. Bernie had his wife's parents eating out of his hand and he knew her father thought he was a decent bloke – which left only that snooty bitch. Yeah, if she was out of the way there would be nothing left for Beth but blind obedience and that was how he liked his women.

There were a few whores around who could've told Beth it was best to take everything he handed out and keep quiet, but she was different – strangely enough it was the difference, her pride, that had drawn him to her, but after all she was just another whore when it came down to it. A decent woman would never have given birth to twins out of wedlock and kept them with her the way Beth had – most girls who got caught had the kid adopted and tried to keep it a secret, but not Beth. She'd flaunted it, almost as if she were proud of being an unmarried mother.

Bernie wanted a son of his own; it was the only reason he'd married. One of these days Beth would give him one – and then he'd get rid of her other brats. A few more months and she wouldn't dare to do anything but obey him . . . and in the meantime he'd tell Norm to have a little fun with the other one.

Norm loved his knife. He'd been itching to use it on that snooty bitch, but Bernie hadn't wanted her dead then. Now he'd tell Norm he could do whatever he liked . . .

CHAPTER 14

Lizzie thought long and hard before she went to the address on the card Sebastian had given her. It was meant to be used for her protection but Beth was in trouble and Lizzie didn't know who else to turn to for help. She chose to visit as she went into work the next morning, but her first attempt brought no answer. She looked at the card again and decided to come back on her way home that evening.

As she left the bus later that evening on her way back to the address, for the first time in weeks, Lizzie felt she was being watched. She glanced round once but saw nothing, and because there were several people in the street she wasn't unduly worried, and yet just as the bus drew away she thought she glimpsed him in the shadows – the man in the overcoat and trilby hat.

A little shiver went through her. Why had it started up again? Lizzie was sure she hadn't been followed for weeks – since just before Beth got married. It took a few minutes for the significance of that to sink in and at first she just refused to believe it. Bernie couldn't have had anything to do with all that . . . the attacks on the shop, the broken window and the red paint – the threats. Why would he?

An explanation presented itself, but she dismissed it as being too fanciful. Surely Beth's husband wasn't the kind of man who would do something like that just because he thought Lizzie might encourage Beth to stand up for herself – and yet who would have suspected that he would hit Beth?

A horrid suspicion entered Lizzie's mind. If Bernie was behind the attacks and they'd started again, he must have reason to believe that Beth was thinking of leaving him and running to Lizzie for help. For months Beth had told him she couldn't marry because Lizzie needed her. Was that the reason he'd arranged to have her threatened and caused trouble for her at the workshops? Surely not, yet it fitted neatly enough, if you accepted that Bernie Wright – a seemingly meek-mannered man who worked hard for the war effort – was actually a mean and vindictive bully. A man moreover, who had access to violent criminals . . .

No, it wasn't possible. Lizzie dismissed the idea as ridiculous, but then little things began to make sense. Bernie always seemed to have money to spend, far more than most men who worked in a factory, even as the manager. He always had petrol to run Beth wherever she wanted to go . . . and there was the strange look in his eyes when he'd stared at Lizzie on the day of the wedding.

It wasn't much to make a case against him, but

added to the bruise on Beth's cheek and the change in her, Lizzie felt it meant something – and if she were being followed again, it was a good thing she'd decided to ask Sebastian's friend for help.

She hurriedly walked to the house, knocking firmly this time. It was opened by a young woman dressed in slacks and a man's sweater, her hair cut short and swept back behind her ears. She was wearing spectacles with thick rims but took them off to peer at Lizzie.

'Yes?'

'I was told I could find Jack here if I needed help.'

'Who are you?'

'My name is Lizzie and I was given this address by Sebastian.'

'You'd better come in,' the woman said and invited her into the hall. She led her through into the kitchen where something that smelled delicious was cooking. There was no sign of anyone else and Lizzie frowned as the woman invited her to tell her story.

'Is Jack here? I would rather speak to him.'

'I'm Jack,' the woman said and laughed as she saw Lizzie's face fall. 'Don't worry, there are others – we're all Jack. It's safer that way. You can tell me what's wrong and leave it with me.'

'What do you mean?'

Jack stirred her stewpot. 'We'll take care of things but you won't see or hear from us – and you never come here again. This is an emergency address. I'll give you a number to ring if you need us again – but I doubt you will.'

Lizzie felt coldness at her nape. Something about this woman unnerved her and she almost wished she hadn't come, but Sebastian had told her to if she needed help and she was pretty certain she did.

It took a few minutes to tell her story, because Jack kept asking her to explain various details over and over again and she made notes on a pad in squiggles that Lizzie didn't understand but thought must be some kind of code.

'Is that it?' Jack asked at last. Lizzie nodded. 'OK, time to go – and remember don't ever come here again. In fact, give me that card please.'

'What if I need you?'

Jack wrote a telephone number on a scrap of paper and Lizzie tucked it into her coat pocket. 'Thank you,' she said and was shown to the door without another word. Jack – whoever she really was – didn't have a lot to say and she wasn't in the least comforting or friendly. Lizzie could only hope she really would be able to help her.

She left the house and saw a tram standing just down the street. Jumping on it, she discovered that she was shaking. Lizzie wasn't sure why the encounter with Jack had upset her, but perhaps it was just the whole business – which seemed sordid and unpleasant.

It was comforting to enter her house and be

greeted by warmth and the smell of baking. Hatty had fresh scones and her delicious fatless Victoria sponge on the side cooling, and there was the smell of a pie baking in the oven.

'It's rabbit pie again,' she said. 'I'm afraid it was all I could get – but I'm sure it will be delicious and I've got some fresh runner beans and jacket potatoes to go with it.'

'How lovely,' Lizzie said. 'Did you have to queue for long to get them?'

'As a matter of fact Mr Court brought them round earlier. He wanted to see you – about Beth, I understand . . .'

'Ah yes, I see,' Lizzie said. 'Has Betty been good today?'

'She always is,' Hatty replied and smiled. 'I don't think I've ever known such a contented baby, Lizzie. She took her first steps today. It only lasted a moment because she sat down again almost at once, but by the weekend she'll manage a few more, I should think.'

'It's the one thing I regret about working,' Lizzie felt a flicker of disappointment. 'I am going to miss those first moments – but at least she is safe and happy with you and that's what matters.'

'She'll be running around and talking before you know it,' Hatty said and then gave her a long look. 'You look tired, Lizzie?'

'Yes, I am a little. We're busy at work, but it isn't that – just a little problem I need to take care of.'

Sebastian had told her she could rely on Jack,

but from what she'd seen the woman hadn't seemed interested.

Lizzie sighed. Perhaps she ought to give Beth's father just a hint of what she suspected if he returned that evening.

Mr Court did not return that evening and it was not until the following day that Lizzie learned why. Janet came rushing into the showroom and asked to see her. Lizzie was smiling as she went to greet Janet, thinking she'd come to tell her some news about the social club, but one glance at her face warned her that it was serious.

'I don't usually gossip,' she told Lizzie, looking grave, 'but I wanted to tell you what I've just heard – it concerns that friend of yours that came to the club with you a few times.'

'Beth,' Lizzie said.

Janet nodded. 'Well, I've just heard some terrible news. A man down the market said that Beth's sister had died – the one who is a nurse . . .'

'Mary is dead?' Lizzie stared at her in shock. 'I don't understand. Do you know how it happened?'

'That's what upset me,' Janet said. 'I'd been to the undertaker's; the old lady I used to look after has died and I had to arrange things for her funeral because her nephew is away fighting – and it was while I was there that I heard him say the funeral he was arranging was for Derek Court's daughter Mary. They were discussing the arrangements and I heard the undertaker's assistant say that if the coroner decided it was suicide it would be better to have a cremation, because they wouldn't let him bury her in the churchyard . . .'

'Oh, Janet, that's terrible,' Lizzie said and shook her head in disbelief. 'I knew Mary was desperately unhappy – but suicide . . .?'

'Well, I don't know for sure, but I'm sure that's what I heard the assistant say . . .'

'I shall have to go and see the family,' Lizzie said. 'I don't suppose you could give us a hand for an hour or so, Janet? Tilly will tell you want she wants you to do and Jean will go in the show-room – we're working on a big order but I ought to go round at once.'

'Of course I will, if you think I can do it.'

'Tilly will help you. It's just the same as usual, but I can do with extra help today.'

She left Janet to take her hat and coat off and then set off to catch her bus in a hurry. It was broad daylight, a pleasant summer day, and Lizzie didn't even bother to glance over her shoulder. Her shadow only came out at night.

She was feeling tense and upset as she paid her fare and looked out of the window at the busy streets. Things were getting back to a kind of normality since the heavy bombing had stopped back at the end of May, but the scars of the Blitz were everywhere. Large gaps where shops and houses had been; the rubble had been cleared in some cases, but the gaps were a reminder of all the horror. Lizzie sometimes wondered why she had been so lucky, both her home and her business had survived – as had Beth's home. Yet perhaps both she and Beth had had more than enough tragedy in their lives without being bombed . . . She pushed the thoughts from her mind as she saw they were coming to the stop she needed.

A short time later, she stood outside Mrs Court's house and hesitated, knowing how devastated the family must be, and then knocked the door. Dottie answered and looked relieved to see her.

'Thank goodness you've come, Lizzie. Dad has gone to fetch Beth and Mum is in a bit of a state, crying and saying it's her fault – and my two have been screaming their heads off. If you could perhaps stay with Mum while I take these two home, please? I need to get them fed and in their beds and then I'll come back if I can get my neighbour to sit with them.'

'Yes, of course I will be only too happy to sit with your mum, Dottie. I'm so sorry about Mary.'

Dottie's face crumpled; Mary was her twin and special to her. 'It's rotten luck. They tell us she'd been out drinking and fell into the river – at first there was some story of suicide, but the police have since told us it was an accident. She was with some students; they were all drunk and several fell in, but Mary drowned.'

'That is so distressing for all of you.'

'Mary has a habit of upsetting people,' Dottie said and looked both upset and angry. 'Dad should be back soon. I went to Beth's and told her but she wouldn't come for me so Dad said he would fetch her.'

'It's the best thing he could do . . .'

'What do you mean?'

Lizzie hesitated, then, 'Didn't you think Beth seemed different?'

'A bit, but I didn't notice much – I was too upset about Mary to notice. What do you mean, different?'

'It's not for me to say . . .' Lizzie hesitated uncertainly, but she was saved from replying when Mrs Court came through from the kitchen to ask who had called. She looked pale and her eyes were red from crying, but she managed a wan smile when she saw Lizzie.

'Thank you for coming. We were going to let you know, but there's so much to think about . . .'

'Yes, I know. It isn't easy arranging things when you lose someone you love.'

'I'm going now that Lizzie is here,' Dottie said. 'I've got to look after the kids, Mum – but I'll come back later if I can.'

'No, Dottie; you look after your children. I'll be all right when your Dad and Beth get back . . .'

'Right, I'm off then – thanks, Lizzie.'

As Beth's sister departed to collect her children, Lizzie followed Mrs Court into the warm kitchen. It was as clean and tidy as ever, the smell of a casserole coming from the oven.

'Dottie made that for me,' she told Lizzie. 'She's not a bad little cook – both she and Beth make a good pie, but Mary . . .' a little sob escaped her.

'Mary never took to cooking much. She preferred to sew . . .'

Sitting down at the table, she bent her head and covered her face with her hands, the sobs breaking from her. Lizzie hovered awkwardly, not knowing whether to put an arm about her or not.

'I'll put the kettle on,' she said in a practical tone and set about filling the kettle and getting the tray ready with Mrs Court's blue and white china.

'There are some biscuits I made in the tin,' Mrs Court had recovered herself by the time she had everything prepared. 'Help yourself, Lizzie. I might eat one. I haven't had anything since a slice of toast this morning and I couldn't eat most of that . . .'

'It is a terrible time for all of you, but I know you loved Mary.'

'Not as much as I do Beth and her twins,' Mrs Court said, surprising her. 'I think that's why I feel so guilty. 'Perhaps if I'd looked after her better instead of telling her to pull herself together when she lost the baby . . .'

'You were right. Left to sink into herself, Mary might have ended in a mental institution. None of you would have wanted that.'

'I thought she was doing so well. She said she'd made friends – her last letter sounded almost cheerful . . . and now she's gone.'

'Perhaps it was just an accident,' Lizzie suggested. 'She was out with friends and they were all drunk – she didn't take her life on purpose . . .'

'Didn't she?' Mrs Court asked unhappily. 'What was she doing with those girls in that boat?'

'I suppose she wanted some fun . . .'

'Mary was a nurse. She should have been behaving herself– not out getting drunk with friends on the river, whoever they were. She told me the wards were overflowing with wounded . . .'

'Perhaps that's why she needed to let off steam,' Lizzie suggested. 'She would have seen some terrible things, men badly wounded – and it must have made her think of her husband. Was she with a man or girlfriends?'

'Both I think,' Mrs Court said and took one of the biscuits that Lizzie had pushed in front of her. 'I believe the man was a soldier on leave after being wounded, but the girls were students. I'm not sure how it happened – whether there were two boats or one.'

'I expect it will all come out at the inquest,' Lizzie said. 'I am so sorry, Mrs Court – I wish it hadn't happened . . .'

'Yes, but it has and I blame myself,' she said and then a little wistfully, 'I wish you'd call me Mum as you used to, Lizzie.'

'I wasn't sure you wanted me to anymore,' Lizzie said. 'We don't see each other much these days . . .'

'No, we don't and perhaps that's my fault too, but after Beth got married you seemed self-sufficient and I wasn't sure if you wanted me to come round . . . you've got your housekeeper now . . .'

'I've taken Hatty into my family because I hated the idea of living alone and I knew looking after three children was too much for you,' Lizzie said. 'I hoped that Beth might come back to the workshops at least part-time after a while, though I should've known Bernie wouldn't let her . . .'

Mrs Court stared at her. 'I've never known anyone stop Beth doing what she wanted before. She'd argue with me and her Dad until we ran out of breath – but she seems quiet and withdrawn and she hasn't been here for weeks. When I went round last time, she didn't seem to want to ask me in.'

'She wouldn't have me in at all, but she did tell me her husband was a bully,' Lizzie said and hesitated, then, 'If I'm wrong I'm sorry – but I think Bernie is hurting her . . .'

'Oh no!' Mrs Court drew a sobbing breath. 'So I was right – he did hit her. She denied it to me, but she didn't look me in the eyes – my poor little girl . . .'

'We've got to help her,' Lizzie said. 'If her father gets her here you should tell her you can't manage without her and perhaps she'll stay here for a few days, at least until after . . .'

'The funeral?' Mrs Court nodded, making an effort to be brave. 'Yes, I'll try, Lizzie. Perhaps one of us can get her to tell us what's going on.'

'It might be best not to ask, just let her tell you when she's ready. You know Beth – she can't bear fussing . . .'

'I'll try not to ask her, but I can't help being

upset, Lizzie. I kept telling her to marry that beast and her father thought it was a good idea too.'

'I'm going to try to help her,' she said and as Mrs Court looked at her hopefully, she shook her head. 'I'm not sure if there's anything I can do except listen if she decides to talk to me and then ask her to come back to live with me. There will always be a room for her is still empty and she's always welcome.'

'But will he let her leave him?' Beth's mother asked. 'I knew someone like that years ago – he was married to a friend of mine. Shirley was such a bright pretty girl until she married Fred Benson, but after a few years of his bullying she let herself go and her children were neglected. In the end she died of some fever or other – at least that's what the doctors said, but I think her heart was broken.' She gave a little cry of despair. 'I asked her once why she stayed with him and she just shook her head and looked miserable – I don't want that to happen to my Beth . . .'

'It won't,' Lizzie said fiercely. 'I promise you we'll get her away from him somehow, Mum. Beth is my friend – my sister – and I don't want her to spend the rest of her life with a bully.'

Mrs Court got up to look at the casserole in the oven. Lizzie washed the cups up and was looking round for something more she could do when the door opened and Mr Court entered carrying the twins. Beth followed behind with some bags bulging with their things.

'Bernie was home and he told me to bring Beth round for a few days,' he said, looking at his daughter oddly. 'Beth kept saying she couldn't come but Bernie soon set her right – told her it was her duty, so here she is.'

Matt scampered off to explore as soon as he was set down and grabbed his granny by the legs. She bent down to tousle his hair and then picked him up as he clamoured for more attention.

Beth wasn't looking at anyone. She just left the kitchen and took her bags and the children's things upstairs. Lizzie hesitated for a moment and then went after her. Beth was unpacking and didn't look round until Lizzie spoke.

'What's wrong, Beth?' she asked softly. 'This isn't like you, love.'

'You have no idea what you're talking about,' Beth said without looking at her. 'Don't feel sorry for me, Lizzie. I don't need it.'

Beth was hurting inside and she was striking out in defence. Lizzie took a deep breath then, 'I know you well enough to know something is very wrong. If you don't want to tell me, you don't have to – but if you decide you do need to talk, I'm always here for you, Beth.'

Beth didn't answer and Lizzie walked away. She didn't want to quarrel with Beth, who was clearly uptight and unwilling to talk about what was upsetting her. Until she was ready to do so there was nothing anyone could do.

CHAPTER 15

Lizzie sensed that someone was following her that evening the instant she left work. It was the first time she'd left work at night since her visit to Jack, but obviously no one had done anything about her shadow, because he was still there. Her heart was racing and she felt a prickling sensation at the nape of her neck, but controlled the need to look round. If someone was trying to scare her, the worst thing she could do was to show fear. Even when she heard the footsteps behind her, she forced herself not to quicken her pace, but she couldn't help but cry out when someone caught her arm and a voice hissed in her ear.

'I'm going to teach you a lesson, you little bitch. You've upset someone and he wants you dealt with . . .'

Lizzie gave a scream of fear despite her determination to remain calm. The man was trying to drag her into a dark alley and she knew if he succeeded he would certainly carry out his threats. She had to fight back or she was in terrible trouble. Kicking out at his shins, she made contact and heard him swear, but he circled her throat with his arm, pressing back so hard that she almost choked and her scream was hardly a whisper. With all her strength she struggled and kicked, managing to wrench free and stumbling away from him, gasping for breath.

He lunged at her again and then suddenly she heard a shout and pounding feet and a large body dressed in khaki threw himself at her attacker. Lizzie drew back, watching the struggle, which was short-lived as the soldier who'd come to her rescue found himself lying on his back on the ground. From somewhere near at hand came the sound of a police whistle. The would-be assassin sent Lizzie a look that warned he wasn't finished with her before scrambling to his feet and disappearing into the alley into which he'd tried to drag her moments earlier.

Lizzie moved towards the young soldier, giving a little cry of distress as she saw that there was blood on his hand, dripping down from a wound to his arm. For a moment she thought it might be a fatal wound but he muttered a curse and struggled to his feet. She moved towards him, feeling anxious.

'He hurt you,' she said. 'I'm so sorry. I can't thank you enough for what you did for me, sir.'

'Sergeant Jones – Bryan,' he said and gave her a lopsided grin. 'The bastard had a knife or I'd have got him for you . . .' He looked towards the alley down which her attacker had fled. 'I thought I heard a police whistle?'

'So did I but there doesn't seem to be a police officer to go with it.'

'Never is when you need one,' the soldier said with a grin and then grunted and clutched at his arm in pain.

'Let me help you,' Lizzie said, more concerned for him than herself at that moment. 'I can take you back to the office and bind it up for you or help you get to the nearest hospital?'

'No hospitals,' he said. 'I've seen enough of them recently to last me a lifetime, miss . . .'

'I'm Lizzie Winters,' she said. 'Let me take you back to where I work and we'll have a look at your arm.'

'Thanks,' he said. 'I don't want to go home with blood drippin' or me Ma will have a fit. I've only been out of hospital a few days.'

'It's my fault,' Lizzie said. 'I should've been more careful . . .'

'After your bag, was he?'

Lizzie nodded. The soldier had his own problems and couldn't be caught up in hers. If the knife had struck his chest instead of his arm, he could have died and Lizzie would hate anyone else to suffer because of her. Ed was about to lock up when Lizzie led the young soldier inside and told him to sit down in the kitchen while she went for her first aid kit. Her friend followed her to the office as she took the box from the drawer of her desk.

'What happened, Lizzie?'

'My shadow came out of the shadows and tried to drag me into an alley. Sergeant Jones stopped him and got a knife in his arm as thanks for his gallantry. He didn't want a doctor, so I brought him back to patch him up.

'Give me that,' Ed grunted angrily and took the first aid kit from her.

Lizzie gave it to him without a struggle and went to fetch cold water in a bowl. She helped the soldier out of his battledress jacket and saw the blood had soaked through his shirt. Ed took over and washed away the blood, revealing a nasty cut that was bleeding a lot but didn't go too deep. He shook his head as he pressed a cold damp pad of linen to the wound and held it for a moment or two, and then looked again. The blood had slowed to a trickle and he applied a pad of fresh linen and bound the soldier's arm tightly.

'I think it ought to have a stitch,' he said. 'Have you got a GP, Sergeant?'

'Yes,' the soldier squinted at his arm. 'I suppose I'd better go round and let him take a look – but it feels fine now.'

'It might be all right, the cut wasn't really deep, but just check in case the blade was infected,' Ed said. 'You were lucky. If the knife had struck your heart you might not have got away with it – but I have to thank you, because if you hadn't been so brave, Lizzie might have been murdered.'

'I was glad to help,' he said and gave Lizzie that shy grin again. 'Damsel in distress and all that – I

231

should have liked to give that bastard a good pasting. If you know who he is, I'll take some mates with me and make him wish he'd never been born.'

'I've no idea who he is,' Lizzie said, thankful that she could give a truthful answer that would stop him putting himself and others at risk.

'Pity. Scum like that don't deserve to get away with it.'

'Shall I call a taxi for you?' Lizzie asked. 'We've got a phone here and I'm not sure you should travel on the bus alone.'

'I'll be fine,' he replied. 'Will you be all right, miss?'

'I'll be seeing Lizzie to her bus,' Ed said grimly, then turned to Lizzie. 'This has to stop, Lizzie. We have to tell the police what has been going on . . .'

'Tomorrow,' Lizzie said. 'We'll talk about it tomorrow.'

'I'll lock up then, and I'll walk you both to the bus stop,' Ed said severely. 'But this has to be sorted once and for all.'

'I thought it was' she said but shook her head when he questioned with a lift of his brows.

She took Sergeant Ryan's uninjured arm, looking at him in concern. 'You look a bit pale,' she said. 'Are you sure you don't want one of us to come to the doctor with you?'

'I'll be fine,' he reassured her. 'It's just a scratch – but I'll go to my doc and ask him to put a stitch in it for me . . .'

Lizzie chewed at her bottom lip as she thought about what had happened. There was no doubt in her mind that she would have been badly hurt if the young soldier hadn't turned up when he did.

So much for Jack! Sebastian had believed that he'd protected her by giving her that address but the help she'd been promised hadn't materialized and if it hadn't been for Sergeant Jones she might have been lying in the alley with her throat cut.

Lizzie shuddered as she realized how much danger she'd been in. Ed was right; she was going to have to go to the police . . .

Hatty was waiting for her when she got in. The motherly woman took one look at her face and put a hand on her arm.

'What happened, Lizzie?'

'Oh . . . nothing much to me,' Lizzie said, 'but it might have done . . .'

She explained to a horrified Hatty who stood staring in dismay until Lizzie had finished speaking and then pushed her into a chair and handed her a hot sweet cup of tea.

'You must go to the police,' she said. 'I think you need protection, Lizzie. I can't imagine who would want to hurt you, but . . .' she got no further because Lizzie's phone rang. 'Sit there and I'll answer it . . .'

Hatty went into the hall but in a moment she was back, looking puzzled. 'It's a man for you – he says he must speak to you and he insists it is important . . .'

'I'll take it,' Lizzie said and stood up. 'I'm all right, don't worry.'

She picked up the receiver and held it to her ear. 'This is Lizzie Winters.'

'Mrs Winters – that little matter you were worried about has been resolved. I'm sorry about this evening; we were late on the scene, but you won't be bothered again.'

'Who is this?' Lizzie demanded but the call had been ended. She stared at the receiver for a moment before replacing it, feeling shocked and disbelieving. What had she just been told? Lizzie shuddered as an icy shiver went down her spine. She was sure no one else had been there when she was struggling for her life. At least she hadn't seen anyone. Sergeant Jones was just a young soldier on leave – she was pretty sure he wasn't Jack . . . he couldn't have been. So how did Jack know and what did he mean by saying she wouldn't be bothered again?

She went back into the kitchen. Hatty turned from the oven with a sizzling hot pie dish held in two tea towels. 'Who was it, Lizzie?'

'I've no idea,' Lizzie said bending the truth. 'He hung up before I got there.'

'It couldn't have been important then,' Hatty shook her head. 'Some people . . .'

Lizzie smiled, feeling glad that she had Hatty living with her. Just at this moment she wouldn't have liked being alone much.

She made an effort to put her unpleasant

encounter out of her mind and talk to Hatty about the shop and about Beth, telling her that she was staying with her parents until after Mary's funeral.

'I feel for them, I really do,' Hatty said, her eyes sad. 'We're all going through a tough time at the moment. None of us know when we'll get one of those wretched telegrams – but to lose a daughter like that, well it's hard . . .'

Lizzie agreed. Hatty was in the mood to talk and told her about her sons and their wives and families. She had two grandsons and another child was on the way. Although, she hadn't wanted to live with any of her daughters-in-law, she was fond of them and visited one of them every week, taking it in turns to spend Christmas with them.

Lizzie let her talk, feeling glad that she didn't have to make the effort. She went up to visit Betty while Hatty made their bedtime drinks and saw she was sleeping soundly. Bending down to touch her cheek, Lizzie caught the warm sweet smell of her and felt tears on her cheeks. If Sergeant Jones hadn't come when he did, Betty might not have had a mother by morning – and yet perhaps someone else was there waiting in the shadows. Someone who had since made sure it couldn't happen again . . .

Lizzie made herself think of other things. She didn't want to know what the voice on the phone had meant when he said her little problem was solved. She hoped that it really was over, but as for details – the less she knew the better.

Beth looked so pale as she stood with her mother, father, sister and granny. Lizzie had followed them from the church and stood just a little apart, feeling their grief but unable to offer comfort to the stricken family. She knew only too well how it felt to watch the coffin of a loved one being lowered into the ground. Lizzie might not have been madly in love with Harry, but she'd cared for him and it had hurt, just as it had hurt when she'd lost her uncle – and it hurt Beth to lose her sister, even though she'd quarrelled with Mary, perhaps more so because of that . . .

Bernie hadn't turned up for the service so Lizzie went to stand by Beth as Mr and Mrs Court moved away to talk to friends and relatives who had come to share this sad time with them. Beth seemed tense and when she turned to look at her Lizzie saw the anguish in her eyes.

'Is it my fault?' she whispered. 'If I'd let her share the twins . . . trusted her to look after them some- times, she might not have gone away.'

Lizzie put an arm about her shoulders and Beth turned her face into her, grief breaking from her in heavy sobs. 'It wasn't your fault, love,' Lizzie whispered and kissed her forehead. 'Mary just couldn't cope with losing the baby and her husband all at once. Even if you'd let her take care of the twins, she might have been just the same.'

'I think I must be a bad person . . .'

'No, of course you aren't. That's nonsense, Beth . . . why would you say that?'

'I'm being punished for something . . .'

Lizzie looked into her face. 'It's him, isn't it? He's the one that has made you feel like this . . .' It wasn't a question; they both knew who she meant. Beth was going to deny it, but then she nodded her head. 'We have to talk, love. You know we do. Whatever is upsetting you – maybe I can help.'

'I don't think anyone can,' Beth said and for a moment her eyes were bleak. 'But I want to talk soon, Lizzie – not now. He's here now . . .'

Lizzie glanced towards the church and saw Bernie walking towards them. He was frowning, a thoughtful look in his eyes. Beth moved away from Lizzie, and understanding why, Lizzie made no attempt to bring her closer.

Bernie had stopped to speak to Mr Court. His deep voice carried easily to them as they stood a short distance away. 'I'm sorry I'm late,' he said. 'I was delayed. The police were round – someone I knew was found in the canal. Apparently, he hit his head and fell in – probably drunk they say . . .'

'Why did they want to see you?' Beth's father looked unimpressed by the excuse. 'I should have thought the funeral of your wife's sister was more important than answering their questions.'

'That's what I told them – but the man was once an employee at the factory and they thought I might know something about him; I told them I'd dismissed him because he drank too much and we can't have that when there's dangerous materials around.'

Lizzie sensed his eyes dwell on her for a moment but refused to look at him. She turned her back on him and mouthed to Beth, 'Come to the show-room,' then aloud, 'I have to go, Beth. I've got a rush order on . . .'

'Yes, of course you go,' Beth said, and added in a whisper, 'I'll come . . . promise.'

Lizzie nodded and turned to say goodbye to Beth's parents. 'I'll visit on Saturday,' she said. 'If I can do anything . . .'

'We know, Lizzie dear,' Mrs Court said and kissed her. She whispered in Lizzie's ear, 'Beth seems a little better – don't you think?'

'Yes, she does,' Lizzie whispered back. She smiled at Beth's father, nodded to Bernie and walked away, conscious that his eyes stabbed her in the back.

She didn't know for sure that the man the police had found in the river was the one that had tried to abduct her, but something in Bernie's gaze made her suspect it might be. Lizzie wasn't sure how she felt about that, because she would be relieved to think that the man couldn't harm her again – and yet it wasn't pleasant to wonder if she might have been responsible for a man's death.

She comforted herself with the thought that she hadn't asked for anything that drastic. All she'd hoped for was that her attacker might be warned off, but perhaps she was naïve. Perhaps with that sort only drastic action worked.

It was unlikely she would ever know the truth. The sooner she could put all this behind her, the better.

It was that same evening that Sergeant Bryan Jones turned up at the workrooms just as Lizzie was about to lock up. He looked at her a little bashfully, his cap in his hands.

'Came to see if I could walk you to the bus stop,' he said. 'Have you had any more trouble since the other night?'

'No,' Lizzie said. According to the cryptic phone message from Jack he'd made sure it couldn't happen again, but she couldn't tell this nice young man something like that.

'Hopefully, you frightened him off and it won't happen again. How is your arm?'

'My doc put a couple of stitches in and it's fine,' he said. 'The Army medics have given me a couple of extra weeks off, said I should take a little time to recover – and told me no more heroics because I'm needed out there . . .'

'Yes, of course you are,' Lizzie agreed. 'I'm glad you're better, Sergeant Jones; it was very brave of you to charge in like that . . .'

'Acted without thinking,' he said dismissively but his neck was red. 'I wondered if you would come out with me – to the flicks or for a drink perhaps.'

'I don't think I should,' Lizzie said and smiled to soften the blow. 'My husband might not like that very much – but you're welcome to come back and have supper with my housekeeper and me. She looks after my little girl . . .'

'Oh, I see,' he said, looking disappointed. They had reached her bus stop just as the bus was pulling in. 'Well – why not?' He hopped on the bus after her and went to sit next to her, pulling out his money as the conductor came to take their fares. 'I don't have anywhere else to go – my girl got bored and found someone else while I was out there . . .'

'I'm so sorry.' Lizzie touched his arm. They were drawing to a stop and she didn't notice the man in the seat behind her as he got up and walked to the door. Nor did she notice the way his cold eyes stared at her.

CHAPTER 16

It was the evening after the day of Mary's funeral and Beth had returned home with her husband after the service. He'd hardly spoken to her since, having left the house before she was up that morning, and she thought he was brooding over something; she could only be glad of the respite. She held her breath as she listened at the door of Bernie's study. He had a visitor in there and one he didn't want her to see, because he'd told her to go upstairs and stay there if she knew what was good for her.

They'd left the door into the hall open a crack and Beth could hear what they were saying if she tried very hard. Not every word was distinguishable, but she could get the gist of most of it.

'Who killed Norm that's what I want to know,' Bernie's visitor demanded 'It would have had to be a professional – someone who knew what they were doin'. He ain't easy to fool . . .'

'The bloody police say he was drunk,' Bernie answered. 'He didn't often drink that much – it wasn't the way he got his kicks . . .'

'No, we all know what Norm liked,' the other

man muttered. 'Did he get out of line? If he talked to someone it could mean trouble for us all . . .'

'Norm wouldn't talk.' He hadn't been tortured or the cops would've said – No, it was a neat job . . . someone wanted him out of the way. I thought you . . .'

'It wasn't me. I thought he might have upset you?' the visitor questioned.

'No!' Bernie's denial was sharp. 'He was too useful for the moment. I need to know if we've been rumbled – if so I'll have to close the houses . . .'

'You don't want to do that . . .'

'Then find out who is responsible . . .' Bernie's voice was threatening. 'And now get out – don't come here again unless you've got something important to tell me . . .'

Beth fled upstairs as the door handle was grasped. She was trembling and she felt sick with fear, because she'd never suspected that her husband could be involved in something involving shady business that might come to the attention of the police.

What was he talking about when he spoke of closing the houses? The only thought that came to mind was that he might mean brothels – a tide of vomit rose up her throat and she made a dash for the bathroom to be sick. If the man she'd married was mixed up in something so awful . . . her thoughts were suspended as the door was thrust open and Bernie walked in.

'What's wrong with you?' he asked, glaring at her.

'I was being sick,' Beth said. 'It must have been something I ate.'

'You hardly ate anything from what I saw,' Bernie said, his frown intensifying. 'Maybe you're pregnant . . .'

Beth hesitated before answering. He hadn't been near her for some weeks now but if she denied it he might start at her again.

'I might be,' she said.

'Go to the doctor tomorrow,' he said. 'If you're having my kid I want you to take care of yourself – don't lose it . . .'

'All right . . .' Beth drew a sigh of relief. He was turning away, going to his own room. He wasn't going to force himself on her and he didn't suspect that she'd overheard him talking to that man in his study.

Beth washed her face, then went through and locked her door before getting undressed. She didn't want Bernie walking in on her in her petticoat, because he might change his mind.

As she lay wakeful, Beth thought about what the two men had been saying in the study. If Bernie was involved in something illegal and worried that the law might catch up with him, he was vulnerable. If Beth could discover what his secret was she might convince him that if he ever tried to hurt her again, she would send her evidence to the police – but where would she get hold of any evidence? Would Bernie keep anything in the house that could incriminate him?

It was very unlikely but Beth was going to have a good look round when he was out. She'd had enough of her bully of a husband and she didn't intend to let him carry on dictating her life a minute longer than she had to . . .

Beth glanced round the study. She'd tried the desk drawers, one of which was locked. The ones she'd searched had nothing of any importance other than a few bills and a cash tin, which she hadn't bothered to open. Bernie gave her enough money for the housekeeping and she didn't need anything else – though she wouldn't hesitate to take his money if she decided to leave.

Hearing the clock in the hall strike the hour, she decided to leave her search for now. Matt and Jenny were dressed and playing in the pen Bernie had bought for them. It was time she got them into the pram if she wanted to see Lizzie – and she did need to talk; though she wasn't sure how much she dared to tell her best friend . . . and she would have to be careful, because there would be a big row if Bernie discovered she'd been to see her friend. He'd had no choice but to let her go to her parents after Mary's sudden death, but he'd warned her not to make a habit of it.

'Why don't you leave him?' Lizzie asked as Beth finished her recital later that morning. 'You should have walked out the first time he hurt you . . .'

'He threatened the children,' Beth said, because she hadn't told Lizzie all the sordid details. She couldn't tell even Lizzie how humiliated she'd felt. 'You probably wouldn't risk it if you had Betty to think of – and how could I explain to my father? If I'd told him what Bernie did – Dad would have gone after him and . . . he's dangerous, Lizzie. He frightens me.'

'Your father is a strong man. I think he could handle Bernie Wright . . .' Lizzie said but Beth shook her head.

'It wouldn't be like that, Lizzie. Bernie wouldn't try anything himself – he knows people. People who might kill Dad . . . stick a knife in his back or something.'

'What makes you say that?' Lizzie asked.

'I've heard him talking – to men, secretly,' Beth said and wrinkled her brow. 'I think Bernie is mixed up in something nasty . . .'

'Like what?'

'Maybe brothels . . .' Beth nodded as she saw Lizzie blench. 'Yes, it made me feel sick too, but I don't know anything for certain. I need to find some proof – something that would send him to prison . . .'

'And what then – shall you turn him in?'

'Yes, if he threatens the twins . . .' Beth said. 'But, I'll use whatever I find to blackmail him if I can . . .'

'That's dangerous . . .'

'It's the only way I can live with him, Lizzie. I'm on thorns all the time in case he takes it into his head to attack me again. If I can get some evidence that would incriminate him . . . I can force him to leave me and the twins alone.'

'Why not just leave him?'

'Because my parents would feel bad about it if I told them why I'd walked out on him. They were both so set on my getting married, Lizzie. I was uneasy from the start, but I let myself be pushed into a situation and then I didn't know how to stop it.'

'You wanted to stop it on your wedding day,' Lizzie said. 'Why didn't you tell me you were worried?'

'You've had so much worry over things and you went through too much when Harry was killed – I couldn't talk to you . . .'

'I know I was partly to blame, Beth,' Lizzie said, nodding her head regretfully. 'I realized that on your wedding day, but it was too late by then – I'm so sorry for all that's happened to you.'

'It isn't your fault; it isn't my parents' fault either. I should have seen what he was, Lizzie – but he kept his true nature so well hidden. I glimpsed it once and should've been warned, but I felt in the way at your house after you married and I didn't want to live with my parents again.'

'I'm sure your parents would listen if you talked to them; besides, I would never have asked you to leave – and you know Sebastian isn't here often. I may not see him for months or even years. You're welcome to come home to me whenever you wish.'

'I think Bernie would put up with anything but that,' Beth said. 'I don't know why he hates you, but he does . . .'

'I don't know what I've done – unless it was to give you a home and a job . . .'

'Well, I'm going to go home and find that evidence if I can,' Beth said and sighed. 'I can't leave him yet, Lizzie. Mum and Dad are devastated by Mary's death. If they thought, I was so unhappy it would hurt them . . .'

'But why should you have to bear the brunt of Bernie's meanness? I'll take the risk of whatever he wants to try if you will.'

Beth smiled. 'I know what a good friend you are, Lizzie – but I'll manage for a while longer.'

'Be careful, Beth,' Lizzie said. 'I think you're right – and I believe Bernie might have tried to have me roughed up, even killed . . .'

'By someone called Norm?' Beth asked. 'That's the name of the man the police found in the river . . . Bernie says it must have been a professional killer, because he, and the man who came to see him, said Norm was too clever for most to get near him.'

'Oh, that's frightening . . .' Lizzie felt chilly, because she felt responsible if Jack had killed for her sake. 'Someone did try to kill me one night, Beth – I was saved by a young soldier who ran at him and got a knife in his arm as a reward, but he scared him. I don't think Sergeant Jones would have killed this Norm – if it was him – and put his body in the river. It must have been someone who could get close to him, surely?'

'Bernie and his friend seemed to know all about things like that – I think Bernie is afraid someone may be out to move in on his territory – I'm not sure what it's all about but it's nasty . . .'

'It sounds like it,' Lizzie said with a frown. 'But Bernie works in the munitions factory and he looks as if wouldn't say boo to a goose . . .'

'Not when he's angry,' Beth reminded her. 'I would never have believed it either – but he's not what he pretends to be. As for his job, well, it's the perfect cover, isn't it? He's doing a patriotic and worthwhile job for his country – and no one would suspect him of being involved with the underworld.'

'I suppose he might have been called up if he wasn't in charge at the factory,' Lizzie agreed. 'It's a good cover and allows him to go on with whatever he's mixed up in . . .'

'Yes, it does,' Beth said and then as Matt let out a yell of anger. 'I'd better go. Bernie thinks I've gone to the doctor, so I need to make an appointment.' She pulled a face as Lizzie questioned with her eyes. 'He thinks I might be pregnant . . .'

'Are you?'

'No – but he caught me being sick after I'd heard what he was saying last night and it was all I could think of . . .'

'Go on then,' Lizzie picked Matt up and sat him

in the pram despite his yells of protest. 'You are getting a big boy . . .'

'He'll soon be too heavy for me to carry far,' Beth said and smiled at her son. 'Matt looks more like his father every day. He reminds me of Mark and what might have been . . .'

'He's a lovely bonny boy,' Lizzie said and kissed the little boy's forehead.

Beth picked up his twin. 'Jenny isn't anywhere near so heavy. I sometimes wonder if anything is wrong . . . they're so different . . .'

'Perhaps it's because she's a girl,' Lizzie suggested. 'Why not take her to the doctor and let him check her out?'

'Yes, I will,' Beth said. 'I hadn't thought much about it until you mentioned how heavy Matt is getting – I'll make an appointment for her and tell Bernie I'm waiting for my tests. Hopefully, I'll have found something that I can use against him by then . . . Bye for now, Lizzie.'

'I'm so glad you came round. Whatever Bernie says or does, Beth, don't let him make you think less of yourself – he's at fault not you. You've done nothing wrong. You'll recover from this and be stronger for it. I know, because it happened to me.'

Beth nodded but she was thoughtful as she left Lizzie. Lizzie had been attacked and hurt and she had been deserted by her husband – but she didn't remember the attack when she was fourteen and Beth was willing to bet Harry hadn't done to Lizzie what Bernie had done to her. Beth had been terrified of Bernie for a while, but now her fighting spirit was back and she was angry – angry with him for using her and angry with herself for falling into his trap. How on earth could she have thought him a meek, kind man? One way or another she would free herself from his petty tyranny.

Lizzie was thoughtful after Beth left. She prayed Beth would be careful in her search of the house. If Bernie caught her, he might decide to teach her a lesson – or he might take his meanness out on the twins.

Lizzie would've liked to go to the police with her own suspicions but she knew they wouldn't help – and she'd need proof or she would be accused of slandering a good man and dragging Beth's name through the mud. Bernie cleverly hid his true nature in public. Lizzie had glimpsed malice in his eyes a few times and Beth had experienced his cruelty, but Lizzie couldn't prove anything . . . and Beth wouldn't be pleased if she interfered with her plans.

If Mr Court knew what his son-in-law was really like, he'd go round there and fetch his daughter home instantly. Lizzie toyed with telling him, but it could have unfortunate repercussions and it wasn't her decision. For as long as Beth chose to keep her problems from her parents, Lizzie must do the same . . .

'Lizzie, how many of the specials does Mr Jenkins want?' Ed said, coming into the office with the order sheet. 'It looks like twelve, but then down here it says sixteen . . .'

'Yes, but it's two different hats,' Lizzie said. 'This is the straw with silk trimmings and this one is the grosgrain but in the same broad-brimmed style. He wants four of each colour we have on show, which is three in the straw and four in the grosgrain . . .'

'Ah yes, I couldn't read it,' Ed said and shook his head. 'Tilly is a brilliant seamstress, but her writing is shocking.'

'I know,' Lizzie laughed as she handed him the order sheet back. 'I might not have known if I hadn't heard him give her the order – it's a big one again this time. I think he's stocking up in case we run out of materials . . .'

'We shan't be able to get any more of that Italian silk once it's finished,' Ed said, 'but that new source of English materials will be just fine. It's different, but it's lovely quality, and once you decide how best to use it I think it will be just as popular.'

'Yes, I agree,' Lizzie said. 'I think the Italian silk was softer but this new stuff is good. It should retain its shape well . . . and the artificial silk makes good trimmings for the lower end of the trade.'

'We haven't got much left of that silk velvet you bought from Arthur Stockton last year.'

'No, I noticed that,' Lizzie said and sighed. The war was making it difficult to find so many things. Naturally, the Merchant Navy was too busy to import things like fine straw or silks for making hats, because they needed to bring in many other more important things. However, so far they were managing to buy most of what they needed from various sources, in England, Scotland and Wales. Because they could come by rail or the rivers, there was no restriction on what could be bought – and a lot of the manufacturers in the district had either been bombed or moved out into the country recently. That meant the manufacturers were keen to find new buyers for their products and Lizzie had made several useful contacts recently. 'We'll find something to keep us going, Ed – I've got a young woman coming to see me next week. Her family's firm produce materials we can use and she thinks we can do business, so let's hope she's right.'

'How did you hear about her?'

'She heard about me,' Lizzie said. 'Some friends of hers bought hats that I designed and made – and so she wondered if I would be interested in buying some of their more expensive ranges. I jumped at the chance naturally.'

Ed nodded and smiled. 'You're a good business-woman, Lizzie, always were . . .' He broke off as they heard a commotion in the showroom and went through in time to hear a woman shouting at Tilly.

'What's wrong, Tilly?' Lizzie asked, puzzled because the customer was red in the face.

'So you're the one that runs this place,' the woman said bitterly. 'I've heard what sort you are – married and taking soldiers home with you . . .'

Lizzie gasped. 'If I chose to do so that is my business and I fail to see what it has to do with you . . .'

'We don't want people like you round here,' the woman said. 'You should take yourself off where you came from – and take your rubbish with you an' all . . .'

'Take no notice, Lizzie,' Tilly said. 'She started being abusive when I caught her trying to sneak out with one of our best hats. She thought I hadn't seen her slip it under her coat while I was serving another customer – but I wasn't born yesterday.'

'You're no better than 'er,' the woman snarled. 'You're cheats, the lot of you . . . charging folk too much fer rubbish . . .'

She went out as Ed moved towards her, throwing a malicious glance at Tilly before slamming the door.

'I thought we'd finished with all that nonsense . . .' Lizzie said anxiously.

'If Oliver has been up to his tricks again I'll sort him out . . .'

'No, Ed,' Lizzie placed a hand on his arm. 'I think it's time I went round to talk to Harry's uncle myself . . .'

Lizzie took a deep breath before she opened the door to the workroom where she'd begun her training as a milliner and met her first husband; it was sure to bring back memories and she half wished she'd let Ed come in her place.

The workroom was busy, bits of material strewn all over the floor. Lizzie's first job had been to keep the scraps tidy and she frowned because it didn't look the way it had back then. There was an air of neglect about the place, as if no one really cared about what they were doing, and she saw one of the girls chewing as she worked, a half-eaten sandwich on her counter. Bert Oliver wouldn't have put up with that when she worked here.

One of the girls looked up. 'If yer hopin' fer a job, yer out of luck. We ain't got none.'

'I'd like to see Mr Oliver please.'

'In his office,' the man cutting shapes jerked his head. 'I should warn you, he's in a right mood.'

Lizzie nodded and made her way towards the office she knew so well. When she'd worked here, a trip to the office usually resulted in a telling off – well, this time it was going to be her who was doing the telling off . . .

She tapped the door but walked in without waiting for an invitation. Harry's uncle was staring at a pile of papers on the desk in front of him and frowning over something. He looked up and she saw the colour drain from his face. For a moment he stared at her in silence, then, 'What do you want?'

'When are you going to stop this senseless quarrel?' Lizzie asked. 'I thought we'd got over it, but now I have a woman screaming abuse at me because I took a soldier back to have supper with me, because he saved my life and I wanted to show my gratitude. I don't know how you even knew about it, because it was only once and my house-keeper was with us all the time. I'm not having an affair with anyone and I was never unfaithful to Harry . . . and it's not fair to blame me for his death . . .'

'I didn't know about the soldier until you told me – but I believe you . . .'

'What did you just say?' she asked, taken aback.

'I believe you, Lizzie. I know you didn't have an affair when you were married to him. Sebastian Winters told me I'd made a mistake . . .' Bert Oliver met her angry eyes and she noticed with a shock how ill he looked. 'I'm sorry I started those rumours, Lizzie – but I was angry because you were doing so well and I blamed you for Harry's death . . . but I know now that it was an accident.'

'You do?'

'Yes. I was angry because I thought my boy had killed himself over you . . .'

'You weren't the only one who thought he'd done it on purpose,' Lizzie said. 'That's why Harry's best friend came round after Harry died to tell me not to believe it if I heard he'd committed suicide. He didn't believe Harry would deliberately drive off the road into a tree, even if he was terri-fied of getting killed on their low-flying missions. I never believed it either. Why would he take his own life when he so much wanted to live?' Lizzie's throat was tight. 'We weren't as happy as we might have been, but we were trying to sort it out . . .'

'Harry was jealous though, wasn't he, Lizzie? I know he was upset about something. He didn't tell me, but I knew when I saw him the last time.'

Lizzie was silent for a moment, then, 'Do you want the truth – even though you won't like it?'

'Yes, please,' he said. 'I'd like to understand, Lizzie.'

Drawing a deep breath, Lizzie started where it really began and told him about the way Harry had gone off alone on their wedding night when she'd told him the truth about being attacked, raped and left for dead as a young girl – and how Harry come back to her a few days later and they'd been happy for a while.

'I should've told Harry before, given him a chance to call off the wedding, but I didn't know what to do . . .' Lizzie faltered, then, 'Harry said he believed me, but he could never get it out of his head that I wasn't a virgin when we married – and when his friend Roger flirted with me that Christmas, Harry drank too much . . . and, later, at home, he forced me. He hurt me and humiliated me and, afterwards, when he apologized, I told him it would take a while to forgive him. Even though I tried, it didn't work and so he stayed away . . . but I'd written to him just before he died and asked him to come home, I'd told him I wanted to try again . . .'

'Oh my God,' Bert Oliver's face went a shade

greyer when she finished, and he sat down heavily in his chair, breathing hard. 'No wonder he didn't come home – he was ashamed of himself . . . I'm so sorry, Lizzie . . .' He clutched at his arm and gave a little moan. 'My pills . . .'

Lizzie saw him pull frantically at his desk drawer. She realized that something was wrong and went round, jerking the drawer back as his face contorted with pain and his eyes rolled. He pointed to a little pillbox and she opened it, tipping one of the pills onto the palm of her hand and offering it to him, but even as he reached for it, he gave a cry and keeled over, tipping his chair and falling to the ground. He was jerking, obviously in pain. Lizzie cried out for help and then bent down to try to open his tie and top button.

Someone entered the office and she told them to send for an ambulance. A man's shape appeared beside her; then he grabbed the phone and asked the operator for a number. Lizzie tried putting the pill on Bert's tongue in the hope that it might pull him round, but it just fell out of his mouth as his tongue lopped to one side and saliva dribbled down his chin.

'It's his heart,' the man told her. 'He should've packed up after he had the first attack, but he's a stubborn old fool. He was going to sell years ago and then he saw your talent and how his business could grow and he kept it on . . .'

'He isn't really old,' Lizzie said, tears stinging

her eyes. 'Only around sixty. It's just that he's had too much work and worry of late . . .'

She stroked his hair back from his forehead, wishing that she hadn't come. She shouldn't have told him what Harry had done. It had upset him too much and this was the result.

If Harry's uncle died, Lizzie would feel like a murderer.

It seemed ages before the ambulance arrived. The driver told her they were rushed off their feet and apologized, but Lizzie hardly heard him. Harry's uncle had lapsed into a coma and she felt like weeping, because this was the last thing she'd wanted or expected. He might be a silly old fool who had done his best to ruin her business, but she didn't hate him and she didn't want him to die.

'May I go with him?' she asked and was told she could if she was family.

'I'm his niece,' Lizzie said though it wasn't quite true. She looked at the man who had called the ambulance. 'Go round and tell his wife – and tell her I'm going to the hospital with him. The rest of you should carry on with whatever work you're doing, please. Mr Oliver would expect it.'

'Yes, Mrs Winters.'

Lizzie climbed into the ambulance and sat on the bench provided, leaning forward to hold the sick man's hand as it bumped and jolted its way to the hospital. She prayed that he would recover, because otherwise she was going to feel so guilty . . .

CHAPTER 17

Beth looked around Bernie's study, her gaze lingering here and there as she tried to discover the most likely hiding place, but she'd searched everywhere and she was beginning to think there was nothing to hide. The only place she hadn't managed to look was in locked drawer of her husband's desk. She hadn't found the key, so Bernie probably kept it in his pocket, perhaps on his watch chain.

Beth decided to try forcing the drawer open. Perhaps she could break the lock carefully so that he wouldn't notice. She picked up the strong paperknife and wedged it into the crack above the drawer, pressing against the metal lock with all her strength. When it wouldn't give, she looked round for something heavy and then banged the knife into the opening as hard as she could. The old wood split, making a crack through the drawer, and Beth gasped in horror because she would never be able to hide that. It made it all the more imperative that she found something to use against him – and soon. She thrust the spike at the end of the knife into the lock itself and turned and heard it crack and finally she was in.

Tentatively opening the drawer, Beth saw some notebooks lying on top of a bulky envelope. She took the books out and opened them, running her finger down columns of figures in the first book and then a list of girls' names in the second. Beth wasn't quite sure if this proved her theory about the brothels, but when she opened the large envelope and saw that it was stuffed with five pound notes, she knew that she'd discovered Bernie's secret hoard of ill-gotten gains. Whatever he was doing, he would never keep so much cash in the desk if it was legally earned. It had to have come from whatever nasty little business he was running on the side.

Beth took everything out and put it on the desk. She had to think fast, because Bernie would be back in an hour or so – and when he saw his desk he was going to be very angry. She came to a hasty decision and stuffed the books and money into the large envelope and wrote her name care of Lizzie's home address. Then she went round the study like a whirlwind, pulling down things from the shelf so that vases smashed and books and papers were strewn everywhere. She did the same in her bedroom and the sitting room, then she grabbed the twins and the money and left the house, swiftly wheeling the pram down the path.

Beth stopped at the post office and sent the letter

to Lizzie's house. Her nape tingled with fear. If she wasn't home when Bernie returned, he might just believe that an intruder had broken into the house and taken what was in his desk – and the best way to convince him was to visit her mother and ask her father to take her home later after she'd eaten with her family.

Beth was shaking inside, but she was glad she'd done it. She would let Lizzie know to hold on to the packet for her until she was ready and when she was sure just what it all meant, she might have a hold over Bernie that would force him to let her go . . .

Beth's father drove her home that evening. He'd been surprised but pleased to see her sitting feeding the twins scrambled egg and bread and butter when he got in. He insisted that he would take her home when she pretended she hadn't realized the time and Beth was comforted by his solid bulk beside her on the journey back to her husband's house.

The lights were on in every room as they pulled up and Beth trembled inside. Her father looked at her as he helped her get the children from the van and she opened the front door. He entered with her, gazing about him in a puzzled way as Bernie came charging into the hall, clearly furious.

'Where the hell have you been?' he demanded and then halted as he saw her father.

261

'I went to visit Mum and forgot the time,' Beth said. 'What's the matter – why are all the lights on?'

'We've been burgled,' Bernie said grimly. 'They've made a mess in most of the rooms – and my desk has been ransacked . . .'

'You'd better take the children up, love,' Beth's father said, handing the little girl to Beth. 'I'll help Bernie have a look round and see what damage has been done.'

'Did they take anything important?' Beth had to ask, though she trembled inside, but her husband seemed to have accepted her excuse.

'Something important to me,' he said. 'Money I was puttin' by for a nice holiday for you and the kids – and a few other bits . . .'

Beth nodded, her heart beating so fast she hardly dared to look at him for fear he should see through her act. Escaping upstairs while her father and Bernie continued to search the house, Beth wondered how long she would get away with her crime and what he would do if he ever discovered what she'd done.

Bernie was sullen all evening. He started grumbling at her the minute her father left, accusing her of going out and leaving a window open upstairs. Beth had opened it a crack deliberately, because the thief had to have a way of getting in, and it was better to let him think she'd been careless that have him know that she'd stolen from him. Her husband continued to blame her as he ate the spam fritters and chips with tinned peas that she gave him for his supper; of course that wasn't right either, and Beth expected his temper to get worse as the evening went on, but at nine o'clock he told her he was going out.

'I'll be late back. I'll take my key, so don't put the bolts on the front door. Don't worry if you don't hear me come in.'

Beth nodded. She wouldn't worry if he never came back, but she did wonder where he was going, though she knew better than to ask. Was he going to visit one of his houses? She felt a little sick at the thought but pleased that she'd outwitted him so far. He might work it out in the end, but that would be her chance to tell him that she wouldn't put up with his temper anymore . . .

Beth didn't hear her husband return, and in the morning when she got up to make breakfast he wasn't in the kitchen getting ready for work; his bed hadn't been slept in either.

Beth fed the children, washed and dressed them and left them in the playpen while she tidied the house. When she had everything looking spick and span, she put the twins in their pram and went off, making sure everywhere was locked. The pram was heavy to push and she wouldn't be able to take the children out like this much longer. She would have to ask Bernie to buy her a pushchair – if he'd got any money to spend now that she'd taken his secret hoard.

She walked round to Lizzie's but discovered her friend wasn't at work. Ed told her that Lizzie was with Aunt Miriam.

'Harry's uncle had a heart attack yesterday when Lizzie went round there,' he said. 'He collapsed and Lizzie went to hospital with him and she's been looking after Miriam, because otherwise she'd be on her own and she's very upset.'

'Yes, of course. If Lizzie comes in, can you give her a message – tell her to hang on to the package I sent to her house . . . and not to tell Bernie or my mother.'

'Right, I'll remember.' Ed gave her a puzzled look. 'Is something the matter, Beth – anything I can do to help?'

'No, thanks all the same,' Beth said. 'I'll come round again, but it's best if Lizzie doesn't come to me.'

Ed's puzzled look deepened but Beth didn't dare to tell him anything more. The less her friends knew, the better. She hadn't wanted to involve Lizzie at all, but there was nowhere in the house she could hide anything from Bernie. If he thought she'd got those notebooks, he would tear the place apart. She would have to think of a safer place to hide them, because if Bernie suspected Beth had stolen them he might go after Lizzie and make her give them up – no, Beth would find somewhere else, and in the meantime, she needed to get home so that she had Bernie's tea ready when he came in.

Bernie was home at his usual time that evening. He seemed subdued and thoughtful as he ate the beef and kidney pie she'd made for their meal.

'This is good,' he said and wiped his mouth on the napkin she'd put out for him. Bernie liked things nice and she'd found the set in one of his mother's drawers when she first got married.

'Yes, I was lucky,' Beth said. 'I was first in the queue this morning and got a little piece of kidney to make it tasty, but I used most of the meat coupons, I'm afraid.'

'You don't want to worry about that – I'll be gettin' a chicken and some ham at the weekend.'

Beth often wondered how he managed to get extra rations, because he certainly didn't use the books she'd had stamped that morning by her local butcher. Bernie seemed to think the rules about rationing were there to be broken and she wondered if he ever thought that he was robbing other people of a chance to buy something nice by buying pinched meat – because it had to be stolen, didn't it?

'Where have you been today then?' he asked, catching her wrist as she walked past him with their used dishes. 'Not to visit your family . . .'

'Just shopping . . .'

'You hadn't heard about Bert Oliver then?'

'No, Beth lied. 'What's wrong?'

'He had a heart attack – been unwell for a while now.'

'I wasn't aware you knew him . . .?' Beth questioned.

'He let me down over a business deal once . . .'

'You mean your black market stuff?'

'Bernie glared at her. 'Mebbe. Keep your nose out of my business if you know what's good for you.'

'I heard they sent a butcher to prison for buying and selling stolen meat.'

'He was a fool to get caught,' Bernie said. 'Besides, I'm doing an important job and no one is going to suspect me . . . unless whoever took my stuff tries to get clever and go to the cops.'

'What stuff. I don't know what you're talking about.' Beth tried to walk on, but his fingers tightened on her wrist.

'I think you do,' he said and his eyes glittered like ice. 'If I find out it was you that broke into my desk, I'll make you wish you'd never been born . . .'

Beth pulled clear of him and sent a blue and white dish flying; it fell to the floor and smashed. 'I don't know what you mean, but if I did know it would be daft of you to upset me, wouldn't it?'

'Just be careful, very careful,' Bernie said. 'You know what I'm capable of – and if I thought it was you I would make you regret it. What I've done up to now is nothing to what I can do if you make me angry . . .'

'What the hell are you talking about? I don't even know what you've lost.'

'Maybe not,' Bernie grunted. 'But someone did it and I'll find out who and make them sorry.'

Beth bent to pick up the broken china but didn't answer him. He was suspicious but still inclined to believe her.

She'd thought that once she had the proof of his secret activities she could control him, but now she wasn't sure. He was much stronger than she was and he might hurt her so much that she was forced to blurt out the truth. He wouldn't be easy to intimidate and she was beginning to think she'd made a mistake to break into that locked drawer . . .

Her hands in hot water, Beth thought furiously about her precarious situation. If she went to Lizzie she would put her in danger . . . but if she went home her father would protect her and the children. She knew her father's opinion of men who dealt in stolen goods – and if she was right about the brothels her father wouldn't ever let her go back to Bernie again. If he went to the police it would be a good option, but supposing he decided to go after Bernie himself?

Beth was calmer but still uncertain what to do for the best when she took the tea through to the sitting room. Bernie was reading a paper and didn't even notice her.

'I've got a headache and I'm going to bed,' she said. 'I'm going to lock my door and if I have any more of your temper I'm going home to my parents.'

She walked out on him and didn't look back, but he hadn't answered her back and she knew she'd taken him by surprise

She could only hope his uncertainty would keep him in restraint for a while, because if he started to abuse her again she would have to carry out her plan and send those books to the police – and Beth knew that if she ever got that desperate she would have to make sure her children were out of his way and safe first . . .

CHAPTER 18

'Oh, Lizzie, I don't know what I'm going to do if anything happens to my Bert,' Aunt Miriam said, her eyes red from weeping. 'He's all I've got and I'll never manage the business without him, let alone anything else.'

Lizzie reached for her hand and squeezed it. 'You're not alone, Aunt Miriam. You've got me and I promise that I'll help you sort things out – but he isn't gone. He might get better . . .'

'Yes, perhaps,' she agreed but sniffed and dabbed at her eyes. 'The doctors told him he should cut down at work months ago, even before Harry was killed . . .'

'Mrs Oliver?' the doctor asked. 'I wanted to let you know that your husband has stabilized for the moment. We have given him some sedatives, so you won't be able to visit him this evening – why don't you both go home and rest? We can call you if there is any change.'

'You're coming home with me tonight,' Lizzie said. 'Hatty will be putting Betty to bed soon and you can help bathe her. I don't think you should be on your own this evening.'

'Oh, Lizzie, thank you.' Aunt Miriam sniffed. 'I don't know what I should have done without you.'

'Well, we'll make sure we see more of each other in future whatever happens,' Lizzie said and smiled at her

'I should like that.' Aunt Miriam blinked rapidly to hold back the tears. 'You've been like a daughter to me, Lizzie – the daughter we never could have . . .'

'Well, you've got Betty to love and fuss over now,' Lizzie smiled and took her arm as they left the hospital and summoned a taxicab from just outside. They got in and Lizzie gave them her home address. Taking Aunt Miriam home with her was the least she could do. Even though the doctors had told Lizzie that this latest attack was only to be expected because Bert had refused to slow down and be sensible, she was still feeling guilty . . .

Bernie glowered as he watched Lizzie get out of the taxi with Miriam Oliver. Damn the bitch! She was too well protected and he couldn't get near enough to frighten her. He'd trusted that fool Norm to do it, but Norm had let him down. They'd had a bitter row when the idiot let that soldier knock him down. Norm had stabbed the soldier, but hadn't killed him; if he went to the police with a description and they traced the culprit, Norm would've split on him; he'd tell all he knew, about Bernie's secret business as well as his feud against Lizzie Larch. Bernie was in no doubt that Norm would've made sure he went down with him – and he knew too much. Besides, he'd been running scared. Norm had been warned off by someone who had managed to throw a fright into him, someone who worried him more than his boss did; he'd told Bernie he was finished with him and was getting out of London for a while, but Bernie couldn't let him do that. So he'd done what he had to – struck him from behind . . . struck him such a blow that he'd fallen into the river and drowned. If he wasn't already dead when he went into the water. Bernie had been shaking with fright as he walked home, needing time to pull himself together. He had done many things, but that was the first time he'd killed . . .

It had put the wind up Bernie when the police came to the house asking questions. Fortunately, they'd believed his story about Norm having been a disgruntled employee that he'd had to dismiss from the munitions factory.

A scowl settled on Bernie's face now as he watched the bitch go inside her house and lock the door. He should've let Norm have his fun with her at the start, because for as long as she lived, Beth had somewhere to run. Oh, she'd said she would go back to her family if she left him, but he knew she'd creep back with the bitch as soon as she could. She was a lying whore and he'd decided it was time he taught her who was the master once and for all. She had no right to shut him out of her bedroom – and if she'd taken his stuff he was going to make her very sorry. He wanted that money back, and more particularly the notebooks.

'She'll find out, Ma, just the way you did . . .' he muttered feverishly, the light of near madness in his topaz eyes. 'I made you sorry and she'll be begging to die by the time I've finished with her.'

He'd been a fool to leave important business materials in a drawer an amateur could break into. He should have locked them in a safe, built one into the wall, but he'd never thought she would have the guts to break open a locked drawer. If it was Beth of course. Bernie couldn't be sure, but there had been something in her eyes when she'd challenged him at supper.

Sometimes he thought it would be better just to let that lying whore of a wife of his leave him, but he'd married her because he'd wanted what other men had – a wife to cook and clean for him, and to give him children. He should have been gentler with her, because he had plenty of whores who would let him do whatever he wanted and he should have remembered that Beth wasn't used to that sort of treatment. She'd made him angry and he'd lashed out in temper; afterwards, he'd been sorry and tried to make it up to her with presents, but the scorn in her eyes – and lately hatred – had cut him like a knife . . .

A little smile touched his mouth at the thought of a knife. Norm always thought his knife would protect him, but he hadn't been expecting that blow to the back of his head. Bernie had been scared by what he'd done at first, but now he liked the thought that he'd killed and got away with it. The feeling of power was exciting and it made him want to kill again . . . the bitch that stood in his way.

Well, he'd get to this other bitch first. He would teach her to interfere in his business. Bert Oliver had been all ready to sell him the premises in Bethnal Green until she started working for him. It had taken ages to negotiate what would've been a good deal, because Bernie knew what Oliver didn't, that the whole area was due for slum clearance. Oh, the clearance had been put off for the duration of the war, but afterwards the scheme would come up again, and Bernie wanted to own the land; he had quite a few properties in the area already and would've had the controlling interest, if the deal hadn't fallen through. He'd thought Oliver might come back to him after his nephew died and he'd turned against Lizzie, and he'd done his best to harbour lies about her, feeding the gullible fool titbits, but despite his bitterness, Oliver had hung on to the end – probably hoping she'd go back to him.

The bitch had cost Bernie a lot of money, and she'd always come between him and Beth. She was just like that she-devil who had terrorized him for years. He'd seen scorn in her eyes and known she didn't like or trust him, and he knew she'd tried to put Beth off marrying him. Bernie never forgot a slight, as Norm had just found out. If Lizzie Larch didn't get her oar out of his business, she'd find herself in a watery grave one of these days . . .

Lizzie was at work a couple of days later when Beth came into the workshop with the twins. She looked tired and anxious and Lizzie drew her into the office where they could be private.

'What's wrong? Have you had another quarrel with Bernie?'

'Not exactly, but he's been in a foul mood since his desk was broken into and some things stolen . . .'

'You were burgled? Oh, I didn't know, Beth. I haven't seen your mum because I've been busy, up at the hospital and talking to Aunt Miriam, so I hadn't heard from anyone. She's in a bit of a state over Bert.'

'Yes, I heard about him having a heart attack. I'm sorry for her – but he hasn't treated you right, Lizzie.'

'I went round to make him stop causing trouble for me and he asked me for the truth about Harry – and that brought on his attack, so I feel responsible in a way . . .'

Beth shook her head. 'It's too easy to blame yourself when someone else is at fault – I should never have married Bernie, but I couldn't know what he was really like.' She took a deep breath.

274

'We weren't burgled. It was me that broke into his desk and took some things – as insurance in case he gets rough with the children or me. I sent it to myself at your house but I'm going to collect it, because if Bernie knew he would come after you . . .'

'It hadn't come when I left this morning. When it does, I'll bring it in with me and put in my safe for you.'

'OK, I'll fetch the parcel and put it in a luggage locker at the railway station . . .'

'What about the key? What if he finds that?'

'I'm going to give the key to Dad and tell him to keep it for me.'

'Do you think that's wise?'

'If you have it, he might come after you . . . I don't want you to be hurt because of me, Lizzie.'

Lizzie thought for a moment, then, 'What if we ask Ed to look after it for you? Bernie wouldn't think of that.'

Beth hesitated and then nodded. 'Yes, that's a good idea – if he doesn't mind.'

'We'll ask him . . .' Lizzie went to the door of the office and called her partner in. She explained that Beth had an important package she needed to keep secret and asked if he would keep the parcel for her.

Ed frowned, then looked at Beth. 'Are you in trouble, lass? I didn't want to say before but I've heard some things that husband of yours – things I didn't like to repeat.'

'What kind of things?' Lizzie asked.

'He's not the generous man he tries to make out, but it isn't my business to tie labels on him – I'd just be a bit careful if I were you, Beth.'

'Why can't you tell us?' Lizzie persisted.'

'My mate wouldn't like it if he knew I'd told you what he told me in confidence . . .'

'It's all right, I think I've guessed what he told you,' Beth said and swallowed hard. 'It's best you keep it to yourself, Ed. Bernie might threaten you if he knew you were telling me about him.'

'He'd regret it if he did,' Ed told her with a smile. 'I'm still a bit handy with my fists if I've a mind to it. If Lizzie gives me your parcel, I'll put it somewhere no one will find it, unless you ask for it. Then neither of you knows and you can say in all innocence you have no idea where it went . . .'

'Yes, please,' Beth agreed at once. 'I may never have to use it – but if anything happens to me or my children, Ed, I want the police to have it.'

'I doubt Bernie would risk really harming you or the children; he knows you've got family and friends – he might threaten and bluster, but if he does, you tell him that you've got the evidence and if anything happens it will go straight to the police,' Ed told her solemnly.

'Yes, all right,' Beth agreed, though Lizzie thought she looked unconvinced. 'I'd better go, Lizzie. I hope Mr Oliver gets better . . . give my best wishes to Miriam.'

'Yes, of course,' Lizzie said. 'I'm going to the hospital with her this afternoon. She is staying with me for a few days – until she feels calmer.

'You take care, Lizzie,' Beth said. 'It sounds daft, but I think Bernie was behind those threats you had. I don't know why he wanted to harm you, but I can't help feeling he was the one who started it.'

Lizzie nodded, because she too suspected that her friend's husband had set that thug on to menacing her, and she was worried for Beth.

Ed looked at her oddly after Beth had left. 'Do you think it was Bernie Wright that organized all that business with the paint and the smashed windows?'

'I think it very likely.'

'I'll talk to my mate and see what I can find out.'

'Be careful, Ed. If Bernie did do these things, he's a dangerous man.'

'Don't worry, Lizzie. He won't get to hear that I've been asking questions. If I'm right, there are a few people who dislike him . . .'

'Please, don't do anything silly.

'Don't you worry, Lizzie,' Ed said. 'Nothing will happen to me and I'm going to do my best to make sure that both you and Beth are safe too . . .'

Lizzie nodded, but made no answer. She could only hope that Ed's friends wouldn't take the law into their own hands . . . A sigh broke from her as her partner went back to his workbench.

If only Sebastian was here. She missed him so much and she hated the dreadful war that kept them apart.

Where was Sebastian now – and was he thinking about her?

CHAPTER 19

'Oh, Lizzie,' Aunt Miriam sobbed against her shoulder. 'He was a little better yesterday. He spoke to me when I sat with him and told me . . . where to find things, his will and various papers . . .'

'I'm so very sorry,' Lizzie felt a lump in her throat. Despite their disagreements, she still retained some liking for her former boss. Harry's uncle had taken her on at his workshops and let Ed train her. He'd allowed her to have hats she'd designed made up and shown them to Sebastian. In a way she owed her present success to him, and over the course of the past week she'd prayed and hoped that he would recover, but unfortunately he'd had another sudden heart attack and died during the night. 'I wish it hadn't happened – but if the hospital couldn't save him no one could.'

'He should've done as he was told and cut down his work,' Aunt Miriam said and drew a deep breath. 'Well, it's over now and we can't bring him back – so there's no more to be done.'

'Would you like me to help you with the arrangements?'

'Yes, please,' Aunt Miriam looked at her gratefully. 'Bert always looked after everything. I've never had to do any of the legal stuff. He just gave me my housekeeping money and paid all the bills himself . . .' She made a helpless gesture. 'I feel so useless. I should've asked about the business but he never wanted to talk about things like that, especially since Harry died – I've no idea how things stand.'

'His lawyer will have some idea,' Lizzie reassured her. 'I'll sort things out for you at the workshops, at least until you get used to the idea . . .'

'Oh, but . . .' Aunt Miriam hesitated. 'I suppose I should wait until the lawyer reads the will – but Bert told me. He's left the house to me and everything else to you, with the proviso that you pay me the same allowance every month and pay all the bills from the profits the way he did . . .'

'But that isn't fair or right,' Lizzie cried in dismay. 'You're his wife; it should all be yours.'

'Bert felt he owed you something, Lizzie – besides, it was always his intention to leave the business to Harry, and you, when you showed such promise at the workshops. He'd spoken of selling up years ago but when you married Harry, he decided against it. He changed his will after Harry died and took you out of it but then, recently, he changed it back again. He wanted you to take over – and it's what I want too. I have some money of my own, Lizzie – and I could never manage the business. It would soon end up in debt.'

'I don't deserve it,' Lizzie said feeling tearful. 'If I hadn't quarrelled with him . . .'

'Another attack was on the cards. Besides, you're my friend and the nearest I have to a daughter. I don't want the worry of it, Lizzie, and that's the truth. All I need is my money each month and my house – and when I die that will be Betty's.'

'I don't know what to say . . .'

'Don't say anything. Bert knew what he was doing. You'll keep things ticking over for the duration and afterwards you can expand to become the successful woman Bert knew you to be. He was angry with you and he spoke against you – but he didn't do any of that other nasty stuff at your workshops, though he told me once he might know who did . . .'

'I believe I know who was behind all that horrid business, but I'm glad to know it wasn't Harry's uncle. As for the business, I'll gladly run it and when I've had time to discover how much profit it's making I shall be able to settle things. You should have your fair share, Aunt Miriam, and at the very least I shall try to give you more money than you've had previously.'

'What a lovely girl you are,' Miriam said and pressed her hand affectionately. 'It was a lucky day for us when Harry brought you into the family – and now, my love, I'm going to go home.'

'Are you sure? Why don't you stay at mine until it's all over?'

Aunt Miriam shook her head. 'The worst has

281

happened now, Lizzie. Nothing more can hurt me, and I like my own home. I'll get used to being alone – and I know I can visit you and Betty whenever I want.'

'I'll come with you and see you settled,' Lizzie said. 'We'll talk to the undertaker and make all the arrangements – and then I expect you'll have a few visitors, people wanting to pay their respects. It's Betty's birthday next week and I'm having a little party on Sunday, just Ed, Jean and her children, and Tilly and her daughter. Beth can't come, which is a shame because Betty misses the twins; she thinks of them as a brother and sister.'

'Of course I'll come,' Aunt Miriam said. 'It's after the funeral and I'll feel better when it's over. We'll have the tea at home, but we shall need a caterer because I think there will be quite a few at his funeral.'

'Yes, I expect so. He knew a lot of people.' Lizzie thought quickly, then, 'I'm going to take a week off work. Ed can manage the orders with Tilly to help him. I can work on my designs wherever I am and I want to make sure everything is as it should be for you. I'll pop into the workshops – but I think we'll close on the day to show respect and allow everyone to attend if they want to.'

'Good.' Aunt Miriam signalled her approval. 'I knew you would do things properly, Lizzie – and so did he. That's why he left things the way he did . . .'

★   ★   ★

'I don't know if I shall be able to get to the funeral,' Beth said when Lizzie told her the details. She'd popped into the workshops to give Lizzie a little present for Betty's birthday. 'Mum will probably have the kids if I ask, but Matt has been unwell, tummy trouble again – and Jenny is teething, though she's putting on a bit of weight now, thank goodness.'

Her friend looked pale and tired and she could see a slight bruise on her cheek. 'What's wrong?' Lizzie asked. 'Has Bernie hit you again?'

'We had a row,' Beth said. 'Somehow, he knew I'd been to see you, though I don't know how, and he was so nasty – tried to tell me you were a controlling bitch and said all sorts of things. I told him he was mad and he lunged at me . . .' her hands clenched at her sides. 'I warned him that if he hurt either me or the twins he'd be in trouble with the police. That stopped him but he's been looking at Matt so viciously and hinting what he'll do if I defy him. I don't want to worry you, but be careful not to be out alone at night, Lizzie – I think Bernie might harm you if he got the chance.'

'Why should he?'

'I don't understand it, Lizzie – but I'm sure he hates you. I thought it was because he was jealous that I took too much notice of you, but surely there must be something more? You don't have any idea I suppose?'

'None, I'm afraid.'

'It might be anything, he's so vindictive.'

'I'm not afraid of him,' Lizzie said, though she knew that perhaps she ought to be. 'I worry about what he might do to you or the children.'

Beth shrugged her shoulders. 'I think he's done his worst, for the moment at least. For some reason he's letting me escape lightly – because he still thinks I may be having his child . . .'

'You're not, are you?'

'No, but I haven't told him,' Beth admitted. 'When we married I was prepared to be a good wife in every way – but after the way he treated me I've told him to leave me alone. I cook and clean, but that's all . . .'

'He won't put up with that forever.'

'No, I'm sure he won't,' Beth agreed. 'He seems amused about something – I've caught him smiling to himself in a horrible way. Sort of smug and malicious. I think he's planning something unpleasant, but I have no idea what.'

'Well, take care.' Lizzie leaned forward and kissed her cheek. 'I wish I'd told you not to marry him, Beth – I know you should only marry for love.'

'Oh Lizzie . . .' Beth said tight with emotion. 'Have you heard from Sebastian?'

'No, not one letter. He used to send post-cards when he went away, but I knew he hadn't posted them and I told him I only wanted genuine news. He'll be in touch as soon as he can. I know what he's doing is important and I have to be patient.'

'Mum told me that Tony went round hers the

other day and asked about me. She said he was disappointed when she told him I'd married . . .'

Lizzie's gazed narrowed. 'Do you still care about him?'

'I don't know . . .' Beth's eyes mirrored her despair. 'I'm not sure I could ever trust a man again. Even if I were free . . .'

'Oh, Beth, I'm so sorry,' Lizzie said. 'I felt a bit that way once – but I think you've suffered more than I did . . . Harry forced me but he didn't mean to hurt me, not like Bernie does you.'

Beth swallowed hard. 'I think I'd kill him if he ever tried to rape me again,' she said, and met Lizzie's sorrowful eyes. 'Yes, it was rape, but I know things can be different. I've known love with Mark and whatever foul things Bernie does to me I keep that thought inside . . .'

Lizzie moved forward to take her in her arms, but Beth stepped back, shaking her head. 'Don't, Lizzie. If you make me cry, I don't think I shall stop. I'm going home, but remember – if I don't come to the funeral it's because I can't . . .'

'Yes, all right.'

Lizzie made no further attempt to comfort her friend, but she was thoughtful after she'd left. Beth's warning lingered at the back of her mind, but even if Bernie was planning more of his nasty little tricks there was nothing she could do. She just wished that Sebastian was home, because it would be good to have someone she could really talk to about things. Ed was a good friend and she knew he was concerned for both her and Beth, but she needed Sebastian. She needed his arms about her and the warmth of his body beside her. She needed to be loved and protected.

Beth was upstairs changing Matt's nappy when she heard someone knock at the door and the sound of Bernie's voice as he asked whoever it was through to his study. Matt's bottom was red and sore and she remembered that she had a new pot of cream that the nurse had given her in her shopping bag downstairs – and that would give her an excuse to hear what was going on.

She went softly down the stairs and paused outside her husband's study when she saw the door had been left slightly ajar. It was eavesdropping and she would normally never have thought of spying on anyone, but Bernie needed watching.

'If you want us to do the job, you'll have to pay us more.'

'I've already paid you a hundred quid . . .' Bernie growled.

'Murder is dangerous work. We want more . . .'

Beth gasped, putting her hand over her mouth to stop herself betraying herself. Murder was a terrible crime and she could scarcely believe what she was hearing.

'How much?'

'Three hundred more.'

'That's too much!'

'If you don't pay up, the job is off . . . you can do your own dirty work.'

'See to her first and then I'll give you the extra.'

'Think I was born yesterday? It's up to you – give me the money now or it's off . . .'

Bernie muttered something Beth couldn't catch it but she'd heard more than enough and it made her feel sick; she moved away quickly, fetching the cream for her son's sore bottom. As she passed the study on her way back she saw the door had been shut.

Up in her room, she heard the back door open and shut and then the heavy tread of Bernie's feet on the stairs. Tensing, Beth waited for the tirade of anger from her husband but it didn't come.

'I'm going out and I'll be late,' he said. 'I'll lock the doors and take my key. Don't go to the door to anyone, Beth.'

'Why not?'

'Because I told you not to,' he said, and then, 'There are a few people who don't much like me. One of them might decide to pay me a visit, so it's best you don't let anyone in – especially at night.'

'What have you been doing, Bernie?'

'Nothing. Keep your mouth shut and you won't come to harm.' He glared at her. 'You can go to Oliver's funeral if you want – I might come myself if I get the chance.'

Beth didn't answer, just inclined her head. She

felt surprised and relieved as he left her and went downstairs, hearing the door shut behind him. She tried to make sense of what she'd heard . . . had Bernie really been paying someone to commit murder? And what could she do about it if he was?

CHAPTER 20

Lizzie woke with a start. She felt cold as she struggled out of the dream that had held her. For a moment she'd thought it was the old dream, but then she realized that it hadn't been the nightmare that had haunted her for years. Her dream had been of Sebastian and he was in danger.

'Sebastian . . . where are you?' Lizzie spoke his name aloud. She felt uneasy and anxious, because the dream had been so very real, and yet she couldn't recall the details.

Glancing at the clock on her bedside, she saw that it was six o'clock in the morning. There was no point in trying to go back to sleep, because she would only toss and turn and think about Sebastian. She'd had a dream but it didn't mean anything, and yet Lizzie couldn't shake off the idea that something bad had happened.

It was the day of Bert Oliver's funeral. Lizzie threw back the covers and pulled on her dressing robe. She would go down and make herself a cup of tea; it would be a busy day . . .

She filled the kettle and set the table for

breakfast. Lizzie wished that Beth was still living with her, because she needed to talk and Hatty would only think she was being fanciful. Beth might have understood but her housekeeper was kind, helpful and down to earth and would tell Lizzie it was just a bad dream. Perhaps it was, but Lizzie couldn't help feeling that sense of unease – as if something bad had happened.

'Please don't let anything happen to Sebastian,' she whispered. 'Please let him come home to me.'

Lizzie felt as if she wanted to cry but she blinked back the stupid tears. It was just that so much had been going on – things that worried and distressed her – and she needed Sebastian to come back to her. It was such a desperate need at that moment that she hardly knew how to contain her fear and emotion. The war had robbed her of one husband; it mustn't happen again. Yes, she had her daughter and she was doing the work she'd dreamed of, designing beautiful hats. Her money worries were a thing of the past, because with the two showrooms she would have a large and varied business – but what Lizzie had realized lately was that none of it meant anything without love.

'Oh, Sebastian,' she said, tears stinging her eyes. 'Please come back to me, my darling. I can't do it without you . . .'

It was Sebastian who had encouraged her to trust her talent; he'd had so much faith in her and he'd helped her as often as he could. Now she was gaining a reputation for quality and style and he would be proud of her . . . but she needed him to be here to share her success.

'Couldn't you sleep?' Hatty asked sympathetically as she came in wearing her comfortable dressing robe. 'I checked on Betty and she's sleeping soundly – unlike her mother.'

'It's a big day,' Lizzie said, making the funeral her excuse. 'I just hope I haven't forgotten anything – or anyone.'

'I'm sure you haven't,' Hatty reassured her. 'As you've made a pot of tea, why don't we share it – and then you should go back to bed for an hour or so? No point in tiring yourself out before it starts . . .'

Beth came to the house nice and early so she could accompany them to the church. Lizzie was surprised but pleased to see her and she sat on Lizzie's left side and Aunt Miriam's niece took the seat next to Beth. Lizzie remembered the young woman from her wedding and Harry's funeral and sent her a sad smile. Aunt Miriam was crying silently, but Lizzie had no tears to cry for the man who had once been her boss. Lizzie felt regret and sorrow, but mainly for the woman sitting beside her. Miriam Oliver was going to find things difficult without her husband. Lizzie squeezed her hand, reassuring her, because whatever happened she was going to help take care of her daughter's great-aunt.

After the service they all went back to Miriam's house. It had two large reception rooms and they were crowded with mourners, most of whom were her husband's business friends – some of them former customers of Lizzie's, also Aunt Miriam's niece, her fiancé and other relations. One or two of them looked at her oddly at first, but when they saw the way his widow clung to her they seemed to accept it and came over to speak to Lizzie.

'I hear Oliver left his workshop to you,' one man said, looking curious. 'I thought he'd cut off all relations with you after Harry died.'

'He did for a while,' Lizzie said. 'But he wanted me to look after things for Aunt Miriam – and of course Betty is his great-niece.'

'Ah well, yes, I see,' he said. 'I heard you had some stylish hats for the spring, Mrs Winters – perhaps I'll call in and have a look one day.'

'I'm sure we'll manage to fit an order in for you if you do,' Lizzie replied. 'I expect to be very busy this autumn and winter . . .'

He nodded and moved on to talk to Aunt Miriam, glancing Lizzie's way several times and listening intently to what Bert's widow had to say. Lizzie was talking to Beth but still conscious she was being discussed. Aunt Miriam came over to her soon after he left.

'Mr Knight was asking all sorts of questions, Lizzie. He seemed to think it odd that Bertie had left the workshops to you, but I told him I couldn't manage them and if they'd been left to me I should have begged you to look after them for me.'

'They will be good for all of us,' Lizzie said. 'I meant what I said, Miriam – whatever the will states, I'm giving you a share of the profits.'

'Well, the solicitor has just arrived so we'll hear what he has to say very shortly, but I'm sure I'm right, because Bertie told me that last day when he seemed better.'

Lizzie nodded, because if Harry's uncle had left her with the responsibility it was going to be hard work, but she would have helped his widow anyway, and perhaps he'd known that . . . and admitted to himself that he hadn't treated Lizzie fairly.

They gathered in the smaller parlour after the guests had gone; the will was very brief and clear. Apart from leaving a small bequest and the house to his wife, he'd bequeathed everything to Lizzie, with the proviso that she paid the monthly allowance that his wife was accustomed to receiving for her expenses and all the bills on the house, just as Aunt Miriam had said.

'As you will see when you come to the accounts, the business isn't doing as well as it was before the war, despite the Government contracts – however, there is still a reasonable profit and perhaps you can improve that, Mrs Winters,' the lawyer said, rounding up.

'I should like to double the amount Aunt Miriam

is paid,' Lizzie said, 'and that is the only way I will accept the bequest.'

The lawyer beamed at her. 'Well said, Mrs Winters . . . I am certain the business will stand the increase.'

'Oh, Lizzie, I don't need it,' Aunt Miriam murmured and dabbed at her eyes. 'But since you insist – I shall give my niece a hundred pounds when she gets married. I am sure Bert would have done so had I asked.'

'Of course you must give her whatever you want, and if you need more from the business you have only to ask.'

'Then all I need to do is to give you this letter from Mr Oliver, Mrs Winters.'

The solicitor wound up the last few items and took his leave.

Later, at her workshops, Ed congratulated her on her new status, confiding that he thought they could double Oliver's profits if Lizzie brought her magic touch to bear.

'I always thought the business could do better and Oliver let things go recently,' he said. 'It will need some hard work to get it back on track, but we can do it, Lizzie.'

'Yes, together,' she agreed. 'I want to give you a quarter share of the profits from Oliver's, Ed. Once we've paid Aunt Miriam, naturally. You'll retain your share in Lizzie Larch as well, but I'll be trusting you to manage the workshops here for us, Ed.'

'You don't have to do that,' Ed said gruffly. 'I've already got my wage – and my share of *Lizzie Larch Hats . . .*'

'But I want you to have this as well. I could never have managed without you. I'm going to look for another cutter, and he will help you out here. Once we find him, he can do the Government work and you can continue to cut some of my shapes – in the meantime I'll be doing most of the cutting and Tilly will trim the Lizzie Larch hats. I shall want more staff in the future, but we'll take it slowly for a start,' Lizzie said. 'If things go well for Beth, I want her to come back to work for me . . . for herself really, because I want to give her a quarter share of the profits from the workshops here too.'

'You're a generous woman, Lizzie.'

'I've been lucky and I have good friends,' Lizzie said. 'I don't intend to give Beth her share just yet, because the way things stand at the moment Bernie would take it away from her. I'll put her share of the profits away, and one day, if and when she needs it . . .'

'Very sensible,' Ed agreed. 'If Bernie Wright got his hands on her shares, he'd make your life a misery.'

'There will be nothing in writing yet,' Lizzie said. 'Beth needs to leave him, but it isn't easy for her . . .'

'She came to the funeral but Bernie didn't . . . I thought he might come to show respect.'

'I doubt he had the guts to look me in the face,' Lizzie said. 'Beth suspects he's up to some sort of mischief, Ed. She didn't know more, but she was sure he was planning something evil . . .'

'I just hope she's careful, because I wouldn't put anything past that man after what I've been told . . .' he lowered his voice. 'He's a bad apple, Lizzie, and no mistake . . .'

Lizzie opened the letter from Harry's uncle when she was alone. The first page dealt with various business items, but on the second a paragraph caught her eye.

I thought you should know that Bernie Wright has a grudge against you, Lizzie. He's told me a lot of tales about you and like a fool I believed them – but I realized recently it's to do with the deal he wanted me to sign just before you married Harry. He wanted me to sell him the workshops and I thought I might; business was just turning over and I was getting a bit tired so I said yes, but then you came along and I saw that everything could be better, so I refused his offer.

He didn't like it and we fell out. I thought no more about it, but I learned a few weeks ago that back then there was a plan to clear the area and my property was the key to a big deal going through. Wright had a lot of money involved and when I said no it all ground to a halt. It sounds stupid, but he might have held a grudge over that old deal, so be careful of him – and don't sell to him whatever he offers . . .

I'm not sure how true this is, Lizzie, but I've heard that Bernie's mother used to shut him in the cellar when he was a lad, and I know he hated her. When she died he got drunk and told me he was glad, and he called her an old bitch, and a lot of other names. I'm not sure what kind of a man does that, but I think you should stay clear of him . . . and forgive me if you can for trying to spoil your business. I was angry and hurt, but I would never have harmed you physically . . . I always believed in you, Lizzie, and I know you'll succeed. I only wish I'd treated you better – and Harry's daughter . . . forgive me.

Lizzie stared at the letter in disbelief. She'd wondered why Beth's husband should hate her so much, thinking that his jealousy would surely not drive him to try and harm her, but now she saw that so much more was involved. Bernie's plans for the area had been thwarted because of her, and then Beth had moved in with her and turned Bernie down, because Lizzie needed her. He must have been feeding on his hatred of her all this time – but what sort of a man would want to hurt a woman he didn't even know, even if she had got in his way?

A very vindictive one. The sort who could insult his dead mother and inflict pain on a young woman he'd professed to love! It all made a horrible kind of sense that a man like that might be capable of anything . . .

Beth wasn't safe in that house. The sooner she made up her mind to leave, the better . . .

Beth looked around the house she'd been brought to as a bride. She'd done her best to improve it, but it would always be dull and dark – a mausoleum to the past in her opinion, with its photographs from Victorian days onwards, all of the women in Bernie's family and one of a Victorian man with a white beard wearing a dark suit.

She wouldn't be sorry to leave when the time came. Beth had so wanted to tell Lizzie what she'd overheard her husband telling that man in his study. She hadn't been able to at the funeral, and it wouldn't have done much good if she had; she'd already decided that Lizzie couldn't help – and telling her father was a big step. She knew that he would demand that she leave Bernie and come home immediately. In her heart it was just what she wanted but she feared what her father might do next.

He would surely go to the police and tell them the whole story. Yet perhaps he might doubt that she'd heard properly and the police would probably say it was circumstantial evidence unless she gave them the notebooks and the money. Beth wasn't too sure what they proved, but the police might have more idea. Perhaps they even suspected Bernie's nefarious dealings but just lacked the proof.

She just needed the courage to go to her father and tell him all she knew. Beth believed Bernie meant to have Lizzie murdered. She had to stop him, but once she left this house she couldn't return – and supposing her father didn't believe her? Surely he would?

Beth glanced at the clock. It was too late to go this evening, because Bernie would be home at any minute now . . .

Beth was just thinking that if she didn't take Bernie's supper out of the oven soon it would be ruined. It was well past the time he normally got home and she'd begun to wonder what was wrong, because although he sometimes went out after supper and didn't always come back until the next day, he never missed his meal in the evening.

She bent to look in the oven and decided to take the pie out, because it was already looking a bit too brown and she thought it would be dry and horrible if she left it any longer. She removed the dish from the shelf and placed it on the pine table and then moved the greens off the heat. If Bernie didn't come soon he would be getting bread and cheese for his supper . . .

Hearing the front doorbell ring, Beth hurried to answer it. Surely Bernie hadn't forgotten his key? She opened the door and stared as she saw her father and mother standing there looking anxious.

'What's wrong?' she asked and stepped back, allowing them to come into the hall.

'We've just heard there's a fire at the factory,' her father said. 'I've been told there was a small explosion and it happened where they store the nitro-glycerine. It set off a chain reaction and then the whole building went up in flames. They've got several fire engines out there now . . .'

'Some people have been taken to the hospital,' Beth's mother said. 'As soon as your father heard the news we came round – I'll look after the twins, love. You'll want to find out more, and if Bernie's been hurt you'll need to get to the hospital. Your father will take you.'

'Yes, of course,' Beth said, because it was expected of her and how could she tell her father that she didn't care about Bernie, would be relieved if he didn't come home for a while?

'We'll go to the police station near the factory,' her father said as she took a coat from the hall stand. 'They will have some idea of where the casualties have been taken – and then we'll see . . .'

'Yes, Dad, thank you,' Beth said. She felt emotional because her parents had come to her at once. 'I'm glad you came round. I was just beginning to wonder where he was . . .'

Her father looked at her oddly. He must wonder at her calm manner, but how could she explain now that she'd been on the verge of leaving Bernie? It would be wrong at such a time, and Beth felt concern for the others who had been caught up in the accident at the factory. She'd known girls in the office when she worked there, and been friendly with those who worked at their benches handling dangerous materials day after day; the chemicals turned their skin yellow and they all knew there was a risk of explosion and fire, and yet they stuck to their duty, because the country was at war and needed them. Beth prayed that those brave girls had escaped harm.

'I'm very sorry, Mrs Wright,' the hospital matron said when they finally arrived at the ward they'd been directed to. 'Your husband was alive when he was brought in, but his injuries were such that he died before we could help him.'

Beth gasped, feeling a shaft of guilt strike her. She'd thought more than once that she wanted to be free of Bernie's tyranny, but this was too horrible.

'What about the others? I understand there were three young women caught in the blast?'

'Yes, they've all been brought here to us and we have them in intensive care. It seems your husband pushed them out of the fire in front of him and went back in to the affected area to search for others that might have been trapped by the flames

301

. . . people are calling him a hero for getting the women out . . .'

'Oh . . .' Beth wanted to laugh wildly. Her husband a hero! If only they knew the truth!

'It was fortunate that the day shift had mostly left. Your husband was one of the last to leave, and no one knows why he was in that part of the factory – but he undoubtedly saved lives by his swift actions.'

'Do you want to see him, Beth?' her father asked.

She shook her head. 'No, not yet. I'll say goodbye when they bring him back to – to the funeral parlour.' She couldn't have him in the house. She wouldn't, whatever people thought.

'I'll take you back then,' her father said 'Your mother will stay with you tonight – unless you'd rather come home with us?'

'I'd rather do that, if it's all right?'

'Yes, of course it is. We should all stick together at a time like this . . .'

Beth lay awake long after her children were tucked up in bed and her parents had said goodnight. Both her father and mother had given her some odd looks, as if they expected her to weep or have hysterics. Beth felt like laughing hysterically, because the whole situation was so farcical. Everyone thought her nice kind husband was a hero and the truth was that he was a cheat and a liar and worse . . .

Beth couldn't mourn the man who'd raped and

humiliated her and made her children's lives a misery: Matt was so afraid that he'd screamed whenever Bernie bent over him. Yet she couldn't celebrate her release either, because a man had died and three innocent girls had been injured. Beth felt numb and uncertain of the future, because although Bernie couldn't hurt her anymore, she was going to carry the memory of what he'd done for a long time.

CHAPTER 21

'Oh, Beth,' Lizzie said when Beth went to her the next day, and they embraced. 'You shouldn't feel guilty, love – none of this is your fault.'

'I know, but he did try to save those girls . . . how can I tell anyone what he was really like, Lizzie?'

'You can't for the moment,' Lizzie agreed.

'Yes, I know,' Beth agreed. 'What should I do, Lizzie? Everyone is talking as though Bernie is a hero, but he was a nasty bully – and I wish I'd never trusted him. My marriage was the worst thing I've ever done. He was a bully and a crook . . .'

'Will you attend his funeral?'

'I don't see how I can avoid it; I'm his wife . . .'

'If you go I'll be with you,' Lizzie said and hesitated. 'Why don't you let Ed give those things you found to your father? I think he would be upset if he knew you'd hidden it all from him. Ed knows more than we realize, but he won't tell me details. Shall I ask him to talk to your father?'

'I think I'll tell him this evening and if he believes me he can ask Ed for the books and money and decide what he thinks is the best thing to do.' Beth drew a shaky breath. 'I'm sure Bernie has asked someone to kill you – the police ought to know that . . .'

'You don't know who it was?' Beth shook her head. 'Don't worry. I'll be careful – besides, why would they bother now Bernie's dead? If he paid them, they've got the money for nothing, and if he didn't they wouldn't get paid.'

Beth sighed with relief, 'Do you really think it's all right?

'Yes, I think so.' Lizzie was thoughtful. 'I guessed he was behind those other attacks and I was in danger then but they're both gone now.'

'It's all horrid,' Beth shuddered. 'To think I married a man mixed up with such dirty things; it makes me feel sick and . . . unclean.'

'You couldn't have known,' Lizzie said and gave her arm a squeeze. 'We all make mistakes, love. Yours was in trusting a man who wasn't worthy of your trust.'

Beth grimaced. 'I don't seem to have much luck in men, do I?' She shook her head. 'It was my own fault. I thought marriage to Bernie was the easy way out and I should've known better.'

'Well, make a clean breast of it to your father and let him decide, Beth. Your parents wanted you to marry Bernie; they encouraged you and it's right that your father at least should know the truth. I'll come round and be with you if you like?'

'No, it's all right,' Beth said and raised her head.

'I can tell him – after all Bernie is dead and Dad can't go charging round there after him now . . .'

'The filthy pig!' Beth's father exploded with fury as she haltingly reached the part in her story where her husband had raped and abused her. It wasn't easy confessing such awful things to her father but she'd had to tell him everything so he understood. 'If you'd told me I'd have killed him.'

'And where would that have left Mum and all of us?' Beth smiled at him mistily because he'd believed her immediately and she'd been afraid he might think she was making it up. 'I didn't want you to hang for Bernie, Dad. I wanted to tell you and Mum so many times, but I couldn't – and it isn't the worst of it.'

Her father's expression grew grimmer by the second as she continued her story of corruption and brutality.

'I'm almost certain it was Lizzie he was planning to kill and that he had her premises attacked and that awful man shadowing her; she was attacked but a young soldier on leave stopped her being badly hurt . . .'

'He might have succeeded in having Lizzie killed. It's a pity you didn't let me go to the police, Beth . . .'

'Yes, I know,' Beth said a little sob in her throat. 'You and Mum were so keen on Bernie and I thought you might not believe me.'

'And you were frightened of him, of course,' her

father nodded. 'I'm to blame as much as you, Beth. If you'd known you could rely on me, you would've come to me at the start – but I haven't always been fair to you. When I heard that you were pregnant I was so angry with you for letting me down. You know I love you, Beth. One shouldn't have favourites, but you were mine – and that's why it hurt because my precious little girl had stopped being a little girl and become a woman overnight . . .'

'Oh Dad,' Beth gave a cry of relief as he took her into his arms and held her close for a moment. 'I'm so sorry. I never meant to let you down, but I loved Mark and . . .'

'Shush now. It's over and I've forgiven you – how could I not forgive when you've given me those beautiful grandchildren?'

Beth gulped and let him wipe the tears from her cheeks. 'Thank you – so you'll talk to Ed then?'

'Yes, and we'll look at the notebooks and then we'll take them and the money to the police. You know they will confiscate it if it's from unlawful earnings?'

'I don't want a penny of it, Dad. I don't want anything of Bernie's – not his house or his money.'

'Well, we'll see what the law has to say about things when they've investigated. You may be entitled to something as his wife.'

'If I am I'll give it to charity.' Beth's chin went in the air. 'I don't need dirty money.'

Her father smiled and nodded his head approvingly. 'I'm proud of you, Beth. Leave it to me now – and the funeral. You won't need to attend. I'll go to represent you. I'll tell people you're not up to it – and when the scandal breaks, they'll know why you didn't go.'

'People will think I knew what he was when we married – and perhaps I should have guessed about the black market racket he was involved in.'

'I was fooled and so were most. Folk won't believe it for the start, but I'll make sure they don't blacken your name . . . You're my daughter, Beth, and if you want you can stay here with your mum and me. She'll look after the twins for you, at least some of the time.'

'Lizzie told me I can live with her and work for her again – and she's giving me a quarter share in Oliver's workshops. I told her it was too much, but she insisted she wanted to do it and I'm grateful. I'll do part-time; it will give me more time with the children, but I'll still get the pleasure of going to work and seeing Lizzie often. Now that she's got two workshops to look after, she will be busier than ever.'

'What will happen when her husband comes home?' Beth's father asked. 'It's all right you living there while he's away but he won't want you and the twins there when he gets back.'

Beth frowned. 'I'm not sure, Dad, but I'll have a bit of money coming in by then and perhaps I'll find a house of my own. Who knows what might happen.'

'It's a pity you didn't marry Tony,' her father

said. 'He's got that nice little shop of his with its own flat – but I heard he was going to marry the girl that looks after it for him . . .'

'Yes, well, I expect they've grown close,' Beth said and swallowed the pain her father had unknowingly inflicted. 'Besides, Tony made it clear that he didn't want me after I had the twins . . . he's even less likely to once he hears what kind of a man I married . . .'

Her father stared at her hard. 'I'm sorry, Beth. I didn't know you still cared for Tony.'

'I don't,' she said and blinked hard. 'Of course I don't. I doubt if I could ever love or trust any man as a husband again.'

He touched her face gently, sympathy in his own. 'If Bernie wasn't dead, I'd strangle him with my bare hands . . . I'm sorry I didn't look after you better, love.'

Beth sniffed and swiped her hand over her eyes. 'Forget it, Dad. I'm not a child. I should've known better than to trust that worm . . .'

Her father nodded, then, 'Well, I'm going to have a chat with Ed and then I expect we shall go the police with the evidence, so you're going to have to be a big girl, Beth, because it isn't going to be pleasant for a while for any of us. You'd better tell your mother, at least some of it, but spare her the sordid details, because it would upset her too much. Just let her know what to expect, because it isn't something we can keep a secret . . .'

*　　*　　*

309

Beth's mother wept when she retold the story she'd told her father, leaving out a few of the details she hadn't spared him, as he'd suggested. She groped for her handkerchief and wiped her face, and then got up and embraced Beth.

'I'm so sorry, love. I should have thought more, because I suspected he was dabbling in the black market, but I was so worried about Mary and I thought you were lucky to get a chance for a new life – if I'd only known about the other stuff . . .'

'You couldn't have known, Mum, no one did,' Beth said. 'I didn't want to tell you any of it, but you have to know. Dad says we can't keep this quiet . . .'

'No, we can't,' her mother agreed. 'Nor should we try. You were blameless, Beth. Your husband was a scoundrel and I'm not going to pretend he was a hero just because he pushed those girls out of the fire.'

'I can't pretend to mourn him or to think he was a hero either.'

'Nor should you! To think of all the misery, he caused you, as well as Lizzie – and we all blamed Harry's uncle for what happened to her. Well, it just shows you can't judge a man by appearances. Who would have guessed what he was really capable of?'

'We knew he must buy from the black market, Mum,' Beth said. 'I suppose we should've been warned.'

'Yes, but a lot of people buy an extra bit of sugar

or dried fruit if they can,' her mother reasoned. 'They aren't all bad, Beth.'

That was true and Beth didn't want to argue the point. She just wanted to forget her marriage had ever happened, but the police were going to want to question her, and if it all came out in the papers she'd be questioned by reporters and photographed in the street as the wife of the villain Bernie Wright.

Beth cringed at the thought, because she felt humiliated enough as it was and she didn't want people thinking she'd condoned Bernie's activities – but she didn't want them to pity her either.

She was on thorns until her father returned looking grim. The news he brought was worrying, because the police had not only believed her story but told her father that they'd been investigating Bernie for some time. They'd taken the notebooks and the money, listened to his story and told him that someone would come to interview Beth in the morning.

'They don't want you to go down the station, Beth. You're not under suspicion, love, but they will ask you to confirm everything I've told them – and then we shall have to wait and see . . .'

CHAPTER 22

'I've been told not to leave London, as the police might want to interview me again,' Beth said to Lizzie the next afternoon when she arrived at the workshops after her visit to the police station. 'They made me feel as if I'd done something wrong, though the Inspector did say that I'd acted properly in handing important evidence to the police.'

'Oh, that's just their way, Beth. It isn't pleasant, but I suppose they have to be suspicious of everyone; it's their job.'

'If I'd been involved with Bernie's nasty little rackets I wouldn't have handed over the money I found,' Beth said bitterly. 'I suppose I have to be thankful that they didn't come at one in the morning with a warrant to search the house.'

'If the incident at the factory hadn't happened, it might very well have been their next step.'

'Yes . . .' Beth shuddered. 'I can still hardly believe what sort of man I married, Lizzie . . .'

'You didn't know what he was,' Lizzie said but Beth still looked upset.

'I didn't know some of it, but I did know he was

into the black market,' she said at last. 'It should've told me that he wasn't honest . . . I ought never to have married him . . .' Beth choked back a sob.

'Oh, Beth love,' Lizzie comforted as best she could. 'Try not to dwell on things, because there's nothing you can do now . . .'

'I know . . .' Beth flicked the tears away with the back of her hand and picked up a sketchbook lying on the desk. 'You've been busy I see . . .'

'These are designs for my winter collection . . .' Lizzie said. 'I draw whatever I feel like and then Ed helps me work out if they are possible. I miss him being here. If I could find someone else to look after Oliver's place, I would rather have Ed working with me.'

'Couldn't you just sell Oliver's?'

'That wouldn't be fair to Aunt Miriam. The workshop was left to me for a reason, because he wanted it to continue and grow – besides, one day I may need it.'

'You mean if your designs become so popular that you can't manage all the production here?'

'Something like that,' Lizzie agreed, and then hesitated. 'I suppose basic hats will always be wanted, but I want to concentrate on designer hats – so I'll just let Oliver's go on with the Government contracts and have the more expensive hats here. And whatever I do, I want you to be a part of it, Beth.'

'Thank goodness for you, Lizzie. I was feeling as if I wanted to tear my hair out when I came round, but I feel better now.'

'It isn't going to be easy for you, love. Once the story gets out about Bernie, people will gossip – and you know what vicious tongues some of them have.'

'Yes, I do, and I know what happened to your business when people saw the insults painted on your premises and Bert Oliver was spreading lies about you.'

'Some of that was down to Bernie, though Harry's uncle did try to ruin my business.' Lizzie sighed and then brightened. 'Well, that's over now. We've got the future to look forward to . . .'

'How are you, love?' Lizzie asked when Beth entered her office, after a further meeting with the police a week or so later. 'Has anything else happened?'

'I've been warned not to say anything about Bernie or what he is suspected of having done. The police are investigating his affairs and they've uncovered a couple of houses that were being used for prostitution and gambling. Both have been closed down and the property confiscated by the Crown'

'Oh, Beth, how awful. I mean the black market is one thing . . . but this other is nasty . . .'

'It makes me feel dirty . . . to think that money paid for the clothes we wore and the food we ate . . .'

'Will they confiscate everything – what about Bernie's house? Does that belong to you, Beth?'

'It came to Bernie through his father and since there's nothing known about him it seems I could inherit the house – if I want it . . .'

'Surely you can sell it? The money would be useful, Beth.'

'That is what my mother says, but I'm not sure I want anything that belonged to Bernie, Lizzie.'

'Well, that's up to you, but I think he owes you – even if you put the money away for the twins.'

'I suppose I could do that,' Beth said. 'Yet it goes against the grain somehow . . .'

'You deserve something for what he did to you . . .'

'I suppose so . . .' Beth said. 'Sometimes I get so angry about it all – but that's a good thing. It stops me feeling sorry for myself.'

'I think we all feel a bit sorry for ourselves some-times,' Lizzie said and laughed softly. 'What with rationing on almost everything, the awful news from the war in the papers – and everyone living in dread of a telegram, we aren't exactly having a good time, any of us. Even though the Luftwaffe have stopped bombing the hell out of us every night, we still get warnings and the occasional raid, if not in London on the coast somewhere. The threat is still there all the time . . .'

'I suppose I have to think myself lucky we're all alive and have got a roof over our heads,' Beth said. 'Would you mind if I moved in with you again soon, Lizzie? I won't live at Bernie's and don't want to live with my parents. I've been waiting until this business with the police blows over, but I think they're going to bury it in their archives.'

'Who told you that?'

'The Inspector,' Beth said. 'He says that they've gone as far as they can in the circumstances, but since Bernie is dead there's no point in bringing a case against him.'

'So that's the end of it.'

Beth frowned. 'Do you recall that man they fished out of the river several weeks ago – had his head bashed in?'

'Yes . . .' Lizzie frowned, 'Why?'

'Inspector Groves told me believes Bernie killed him. A witness has claimed he saw it happen but was too frightened to tell them at the time . . .'

'Bernie killed him?' Lizzie felt a cloud of doubt lift; she hadn't been responsible for a man's execution as she'd feared when she'd asked Jack to help her get rid of her shadow. 'Are you sure?'

'So the Inspector said, and I suppose he knows. He told me I wasn't to speak of it – but you're not going to tell anyone, are you?'

'Of course not.' Lizzie felt relief flood through her. 'If Bernie hadn't died in the fire he might have been tried for murder. I'm glad that didn't happen, love. It's so much better this way.'

'Yes, it is,' Beth nodded. 'It has all been hanging over me like a dark cloud these past weeks, but now it's lifting. I think we have something to look forward to at last, Lizzie.'

'Yes, thank goodness,' Lizzie gave her a hug.

'We'll give the children a lovely christening party next weekend and forget all about this nastiness as much as we can . . .'

It was cold in church, rain hitting the stained glass windows, but Lizzie was determined the raw early November weather wasn't going to spoil things for any of them. All three children objected noisily to the ceremony and Matt screamed his way through it, though Jenny and Betty were soon all smiles again.

Soon they were back at the house, enjoying the hot vegetable soup, sausage rolls and cheese pastries that Hatty had provided. She'd managed a large and delicious sponge filled with strawberry jam and fresh cream – that Lizzie had somehow charmed out of their milkman for the occasion – corned beef sandwiches and buns for the kids. Mr Court had supplied them with some oranges and apples, and there was a big apple crumble with custard to finish the treat.

It was all washed down with cups of tea and a few glasses of wine – wine that Sebastian had bought before he left and had remained untouched in the pantry. Lizzie had fetched it out, deciding the grown-ups needed a treat as much as the children, and watching Beth's twins, Betty and Tilly's little girl playing together was a delight in itself.

Tilly put a hand to her aching back and smiled. 'It was good of you to ask us, Lizzie. Sally doesn't get cake or fruit very often . . .'

'Mr Court supplied the fruit from his stall, but Hatty chipped in her own rations to make the cakes for the children.' She smiled as Tilly sighed. 'Back aching? I know mine was constant when I was at your stage.'

'Just over two months to go . . .'

'I expect you'll be glad when it's over. Having babies isn't much fun . . .' She looked lovingly at Betty. 'But children are their own reward . . .'

'Yes, I know, and I can't wait to hold my baby. I'm all right really. I like working for you – I can come back for a few hours when I'm over it, can't I?'

'You know I'll always be glad of your skill . . .'

'Oh, look at Sally! That's the third bun she's had . . .'

Lizzie smiled as Tilly went off to stop her little girl stuffing the cake into her mouth all at once. Her gaze travelled round the room; all her friends were here, all the people she cared about except one . . .

Even in the midst of the chatter and laughter, Lizzie knew a pang of loneliness. She was happy with her friends and the people she thought of as her family, but where was Sebastian. Without him, her life could never be complete . . .

CHAPTER 23

Beth kept her cheerful face in place when she was serving customers and talking to Lizzie. It was better living with her and Hatty, because her parents treated her as if she were made of fine china and might break. Especially her mother, who blamed herself for Beth's unhappy marriage.

Beth could only feel relieved that it was over and try to forget the past. Unlike Lizzie, she didn't suffer from nightmares, but sometimes the thought of Bernie, what he had been and what he'd done to her, caught her out and made her shudder.

She'd been to the doctor, explaining in confidence that she believed her husband had been with prostitutes, and asked him to make sure she didn't have a venereal disease. He'd done some tests and reassured her that she was perfectly healthy, but Beth couldn't help feeling unclean, even though she'd scrubbed the memory of his touch from her body. Bernie had sapped her confidence and made her feel unworthy, but she knew she had to fight those feelings, because her children depended on her and she had to be a good mother. She mustn't

319

let Bernie's shadow spoil her life, if not for her own sake for that of Matt and Jenny.

Now that the news had broken, there was a lot of gossip concerning Bernie's secret life. People were shocked that a man who had seemed so respectable had owned and run brothels. It wasn't easy to accept the odd looks she got from women in the market when she went shopping, and more than once she heard herself described as being the wife of *that* Bernie Winters . . . the one that had died in the factory fire and had been involved with houses of ill repute . . .

However, it wasn't until the beginning of December that Beth was confronted by a woman in the street who demanded to know how she could live with herself, carrying on as if nothing had happened.

'What do you mean?' Beth asked, startled and shocked by the woman's belligerence. 'Why shouldn't I?'

'Keeping a brothel that's what I heard . . . and you living off the proceeds. You should be ashamed of yourself.'

'How was I supposed to know what he was doing?' Beth demanded hotly. 'And the police have confiscated all of the houses so I shan't get a penny and I wouldn't take it if I was offered it . . .'

The woman looked at her in disbelief and stalked off, leaving Beth feeling shaken. There had been real malice in the woman's voice and her eyes were hard with hatred. Beth was on the verge of tears and knew she needed to sit down. A strong cup of coffee was in order. She walked blindly into the nearest café and sat down, ordering from the waitress when she came over.

'I'd 'ave the tea, love,' she said. 'The coffee is awful.'

Beth nodded her head. She didn't feel like talking and when someone came up to her table and asked if he could sit down she looked up with the words of denial on her lips, but there, looking much as he always had but stronger and older, was Tony.

'Tony . . . what are you doing here?' she breathed his name, unexpected emotion blinding her eyes as she saw him wearing his uniform. 'Yes, of course, if you wish.'

'I'm on leave,' he said, his gaze narrowing in concern. 'What's wrong, Beth? Has something upset you?'

'Yes . . . a woman in the market. She was quite unpleasant . . . about Bernie . . .'

'Your late husband?' Tony sat down and looked at her. 'I've seen your father. He told me all about it, Beth. I'm really sorry for all you've been through. I'm not just saying that, love. You didn't deserve it after everything else.'

She hadn't expected him to show such sympathy and understanding, but he seemed different, older perhaps? Beth blinked back her tears as the waitress arrived with what looked more like dishwater than tea. Tony gave the girl sixpence from his pocket to pay for the tea and then stood up and took hold of Beth's arm.

'Come on, I'll buy you a proper drink in the pub. It looks as if you could do with a sherry.'

'If they've got any,' Beth said and gave him a wobbly smile. 'Thanks, Tony. I could do with some company.'

'I've got broad shoulders,' he said and grinned at her. 'Come and tell me all about it . . .'

Beth liked the feel of his strong arm about his waist. Tony had grown up, become stronger and more decisive since they'd courted. It was clearly the influence of the Army and the things he'd seen. She rather liked him as he was now and found herself thinking regretfully of what might have been.

When they were seated at the table in the pub with their drinks in front of them, she looked at him thoughtfully. 'Dad said you're engaged to be married. Is it to the girl who works in your shop?'

'Yes. Vera has looked after everything while I've been away, kept it ticking over, though it isn't exactly a goldmine. I might have done better to wait for a while, until the war was over.'

'Do you think it ever will be?'

'In the end we shall beat them,' he said and there was a hint of steel in his eyes, which she found oddly reassuring. 'I know things look black most of the time, but our boys are determined – whatever they do we shan't break. We'll beat them in the end – but we need the Yanks. Once they're in, the numbers will be on our side.'

'If it ever happens.'

'It will. I'm sure it will one day,' he said, 'but

tell me what is upsetting you, Beth – what did that old harridan say to you?'

Beth explained and Tony's brow furrowed. 'She had no right to attack you for what Bernie did. It's not your fault . . . Bernie's ill-gotten gains will be dealt with by the authorities. 'Did he have any cash hidden away that you know of?'

'What I found, Dad took to the police at the start.'

'Then your conscience is clear.'

'I suppose there's the house,' Beth said. 'I've been told it is mine, Tony. It belonged to Bernie's family and there's no one else to inherit – but I don't want it. I don't want anything of his . . .'

'You should sell it and put the money away for the kids, unless you need it?'

'I might, but I live with Lizzie and I have a share in Oliver's old business, so I earn enough to keep them. It isn't a lot, but it makes the difference between having some savings and not knowing where the next penny is coming from.'

'Yes, your father said you were an independent woman. I'm glad you've come through this so well, Beth. I'm proud of you for standing up to that monster – and I'm glad you're happy.'

'I wouldn't say I was happy,' Beth told him. 'I've got the children, my parents and friends . . . but . . .' she left the rest unsaid, because there was nothing she could say. It was better to end this now. 'Thanks for the drink and for cheering me up and setting me straight. I hope you have a good life, Tony – and I'm pleased you've found someone to love.'

'Beth . . .' Tony hesitated for a moment, seemed as if he wanted to speak and then changed his mind. 'Yes. Vera is a lovely girl and we're getting married at Christmas. Good luck, Beth . . .'

Beth nodded, feeling wistful as she got up and walked away, because if she hadn't she would have let her feelings show too much. Tony had wanted her to help him with his shop when they'd been courting before the war. If only she'd agreed to give up her job when he'd wanted her to. Perhaps then she would never have felt the hurt and pain the last couple of years had brought her – but of course then she wouldn't have had the twins and she wouldn't change them for the world.

Lifting her head, Beth made sure she'd got her shopping and left the pub. It had cheered her up talking to Tony. Before he'd joined the Army, he'd been young and a bit on the selfish side, but now he was a man and she liked what she'd seen of him. Vera was a lucky girl. Beth knew that if she had another chance with him she would take it – even though the memory of what Bernie had done still sickened her.

Fortunately, he hadn't broken her. Perhaps if she'd been made differently he would have succeeded in breaking her spirit, but it was only bruised. Beth had been living under a cloud since her marriage, but now she saw the clouds could be blown away. It was up to her to get on with her life and that was just what she intended to do . . .

CHAPTER 24

It was ten days before Christmas and Lizzie was at home with Beth. They were putting the finishing touches to various presents they were making for the children. Despite the doom and gloom that the war continued to cast, they had decided to make this a good Christmas for the little ones. In early December the Japanese air force had attacked Pearl Harbour, and because of it, the Americans had now joined the war effort. Everyone said that it was sure to make the difference and things would get easier now they were in. However, the news was increasingly bad from Asia and in other parts of the world. Churchill had decreed that the collection of scrap metal must intensify and everyone was asked to give what they could spare. Life was hard in Britain and it was impossible to buy new toys for the children, so they'd decided to make what they could themselves. And they were having Beth's family and Aunt Miriam to Christmas dinner, everyone contributing what they could to the meal. Hatty was spending Christmas with her daughter-in-law, even though she'd told Lizzie she'd miss being with them all.

Aunt Miriam was now working part-time for Lizzie three days a week in her showroom. She'd also joined an afternoon tea dance club for older ladies and went dancing once a week on a Thursday afternoon. She looked younger and happier and Lizzie wondered if she might have met a gentleman at the tea dances, though as yet she hadn't mentioned anyone.

'I've finished Jenny's party dress,' Beth said and put down her sewing. 'I think I'll put the kettle on . . .' A ring at the door interrupted her and she sighed. 'Who can that be at this hour?'

'No idea – perhaps Hatty forgot her key?'

Beth was on her feet. 'I'll go . . .'

Hatty had gone visiting with one of her daughters-in-law and wasn't expected back until later. Lizzie snipped her cotton and held the dress she'd made for Aunt Miriam's Christmas gift up to look at it. She'd sewn tape to the hem to make it hang better, as the material available wasn't as good quality as she would've liked, but Miriam would be pleased.

'Lizzie . . .' Beth had returned to the sitting room looking strange. 'There's a man at the door. He wants to speak to you – says he has a message for you; he wouldn't give it to me . . .'

Lizzie felt a chill at her nape. She rose and went through to the hall. Outside the door, a man wearing a raincoat and a trilby pulled low over his forehead reminded her of the man who had once threatened her and she hesitated, half afraid of his

326

intentions. But as she reached him, he spoke and she was reassured.

'I'm Jack,' he said. 'I've got news for you, Mrs Winters and it isn't good.'

'Won't you come in?' Lizzie asked, beginning to feel shaky at the mention of that name. Sebastian had told her to go to Jack if she needed help, but only in an emergency. Why had he come now? She felt frightened as she saw the serious expression on his face.

'What is it . . . what's wrong?'

He stepped into the hall but avoided moving into the light. 'Sebastian made me promise that I would tell you myself if the news was bad. Something went wrong with his mission and he disappeared – about three months ago. We hoped he might turn up somewhere but he hasn't. I can't offer you proof that he's dead, but neither can I offer you hope that he's alive . . .'

'I see . . .' Lizzie swayed, reaching out for the wall. Three months back was about the time she'd had that dream, the strong premonition that Sebastian was hurt and calling for her. A firm hand took hold of her arm and for a moment she looked into a pale face with piercing grey eyes. 'But you don't know for sure either way?'

'I know that it isn't like him to break contact for this long,' he said. 'I can't tell you anymore and I must ask you not to talk about what I have told you – but your husband is a brave man.'

'I know,' Lizzie said and the silent tears were streaming down her face.

'You have a friend here with you?'

'Yes . . .'

He nodded, went out and closed the door behind him. She wanted to scream at him to stop, to demand to know all the details he hadn't told her, but she didn't. She felt numbed, drained of emotion, empty.

Lizzie sank to her knees, covering her face with her hands. It couldn't be true – Sebastian dead? No, she wouldn't believe it, didn't want to believe that she would never see him again. The tears were slipping down her cheeks as the numbness began to wear off and she felt the pain strike at her heart, and a cry of despair left her lips.

'Lizzie . . . Lizzie love, what is it?' Beth was suddenly there with her arms about her, holding her as she wept, sobbing wildly now as the grief poured out of her.

'He said Sebastian is missing presumed dead . . .'

'Oh, Lizzie . . .' Beth's lips were on her hair, her arms tight around her as they rocked together in grief. 'No, it's not fair. You've suffered enough; it can't happen . . . not again . . .'

Lizzie didn't know how long they stayed there on their knees, Beth holding her, sharing her grief, doing what she could to comfort her. In the end her grief wore itself out and she stood up, pulling her friend to her feet. She found a handkerchief and wiped the tears from her cheeks.

'I'm not going to accept it,' she said. 'I know every woman who gets this sort of message refuses to believe it at first, but I can't . . . I can't. . . .'

'I felt like that when Mark went missing,' Beth said, 'but his ship was lost at sea and after a few months I knew he really was gone and I had to accept it – but perhaps you'll be luckier . . .' She frowned and looked puzzled. 'Why did he come to the house instead of sending a telegram?'

'He told me that he'd promised Sebastian that he would tell me if anything happened. Apparently, Sebastian has disappeared.'

They were back in the kitchen now. Lizzie put the kettle on automatically. A cup of tea wouldn't change things, but it was the first thing that came to mind when you'd had a shock. She knew that she was probably letting herself hope for no good reason, but something inside her just wouldn't let go.

Beth folded up the piece of sewing she'd finished and then looked at Lizzie doubtfully. 'Will you go on with the Christmas party now?'

'Of course,' Lizzie said. 'I can't let everyone down, Beth. Aunt Miriam is looking forward to it and your mum and the children. I'll get through it and I'll get through the days and months ahead – until I know for certain that Sebastian isn't coming back to me.'

'Oh, Lizzie love . . .' Beth looked at her sadly. 'I wish I could take the pain away from you or even share it . . .'

'Just having you here helps.' Lizzie smiled at her. 'You mean so much to me, Beth . . . you and the children.'

'We're like sisters, only closer than most,' Beth said. 'You were there for me when I discovered I was carrying Mark's babies . . . even my parents didn't want to know, but you stood by me. We've come through a lot these past few years. We'll get through this together . . .'

Lizzie nodded, leaving Beth to get on with her sewing while she went up to look at the sleeping children. They were all asleep: Matt with his covers thrown off, Jenny tucked up like a little dormouse – and Betty was curled up on her side, her eyelashes shadowed against her cheek and her tiny fists curled. Lizzie felt a pang of love. Her child was so innocent and lovely . . . and so precious . . . and the sight of her lying there made Lizzie ache with longing and loss, because her darling daughter had lost the man she'd begun to know as Daddy . . .

'He'll come back to us, my darling,' she whispered and stroked Betty's head with the tips of her fingers. 'I know he isn't dead . . . he can't be . . .'

CHAPTER 25

Somehow Lizzie got through that Christmas with a smile on her face for the sake of the children. She and Beth had decorated the parlour and it looked wonderful with a tree and all the trimmings. The children had lots of presents and everyone joined in the fun, determined to make the best of what they had despite the war and all the hardships it brought.

In the first few months of 1942 the news from the Front seemed to get worse and worse and everyone looked at each other fearfully. Life was hard in Britain, but the people were tough and they were learning to go without or mend and make do. Women were told to wear shorter skirts to save on material and Lizzie lived with the daily expectation that she would be told hats were to be rationed, but it didn't happen.

For Beth and Lizzie life went on much as before, despite the lengthening queues and the cuts in electricity and the shortage of coal and sometimes even logs. As the year wore on the fear was that the Allies were losing the war in the desert and everyone read the gloomy reports and wondered if anything would stop the German onslaught.

'What will happen if the Germans come?' Aunt Miriam asked fearfully when she was nursing Betty on her second birthday. September was still nice and warm but with the prospect of winter to come the shortages were beginning to bite and it was hard to keep cheerful, but Lizzie did her best to keep from showing her heartache as month after month passed and she heard nothing more of Sebastian.

'They won't come,' she reassured Aunt Miriam now. 'Our soldiers are doing all they can, and we're bombing them too. I know everything seems gloomy, but the Americans are helping. It will get better soon, I'm sure.'

'Well, if you say so, Lizzie. I couldn't bear to think of this little one being hurt . . .'

'None of us want that, but I try to believe that everything will be all right.'

'You're so brave, Lizzie. You haven't heard a word from Sebastian, have you?'

'No . . .' Lizzie blinked and turned away. It was so hard to keep believing when she had no word from him. As yet nothing official had come and she was praying that somewhere he was still alive.

It was just before Christmas 1942 when Lizzie had a letter from Whitehall. Her hands shook as she opened it and discovered that it had been signed by someone from the Prime Minister's office.

Dear Mrs Winters

I am sorry to have to inform you that your husband has been missing for some months. He was on official business for the Army, arranging the logistics of vital supplies and something happened. As yet we are unable to tell you more, though we believe he may have been caught up in a German raid and been killed. You will of course be informed if we have more news, but for the moment you should consider him missing believed killed on active service.

There was a paragraph saying how sorry they were and what useful work Sebastian had been doing and it was signed by someone whose handwriting she couldn't read.

Lizzie stared at the page as the lines blurred and the words ran into a meaningless jumble. Someone had thought enough of Sebastian to write to her and it looked as if the official view was now that he was dead. The visit from Jack had been unofficial, but this was a blow to her heart.

For a few minutes Lizzie felt as if her life had been torn apart, but then she suddenly rejected what had been written. No, Sebastian's life couldn't end in a few formal lines of regret and sympathy. He was too vital, too strong, too important to just disappear like that. Lizzie's head went up. She screwed the letter into a ball and tossed it into the fire. She wouldn't believe this lie.

Sebastian was alive. She'd endured a year of not knowing where he was and she would go on for as long as it took, but something inside her was sure that he would return.

'You have to be alive,' she said aloud to the empty room. 'I won't let you be dead, Sebastian. I refuse to let you go. You've got to come back to me. I want you, need you . . .'

But even as she said the words, the tears were trickling down her cheeks.

'Please come back, my darling . . . please don't leave me . . .'

'Good!' Beth looked up from the newspaper she'd been reading. 'It says here that the Ruhr in Germany has been getting a pounding from our boys and Berlin has been bombed again. Serves them right for what happened at the Tube station the other week . . .'

Lizzie nodded, understanding why Beth felt so bitter. It was April 1943 and they'd been at war for almost four years now and were used to disasters; children killed when a school was hit on the south coast, factories destroyed and thousands of men dying, but the recent Tube incident had upset Beth more than most. There had been a daylight air raid warning and people had hurried into the Tube station at Bethnal Green. A woman carrying a baby had tripped and tumbled and people who were rushing to get to safety fell over her. Several people had been crushed in the freak accident, including Beth's friend Janet Redd, a girl she'd known at school.

'Yes, that was awful, and I agree it does make you feel that way about getting back at the Germans for all they've done; the Blitz of London, Birmingham, Coventry, Liverpool and other cities . . .'

The two woman looked at each other, because although there were encouraging signs that the Allies were at last making progress in various parts of the world, tragedies kept on happening and everything was still pretty gloomy.

'It says here that clothes rationing may be tightened again,' Beth said. 'Only three pairs of new shoes allowed a year now. If they cut it much further, we'll all be walking around with only rags to our backs – have you heard whether they're going to ration hats?'

'No, nothing has been mentioned yet,' Lizzie said and smiled. Beth was in one of her grumpy moods. Matt had been fretful again and his cries had woken both Lizzie and Beth in the night. He'd got out of his bed and gone to rouse his mother, demanding a drink of orange squash, which was the reason she was tired. At nearly three, the twins were becoming a handful, Jenny almost as bad as her brother these days. Betty was quieter, but got frustrated when she couldn't keep up with the other two. 'I'm finding it difficult to buy new parts for the machines; it seems I need a permit to buy them . . .' She sighed, then brightened, 'Mind you,

Lizzie Larch Hats is doing well, and Oliver's has all the Government work they can manage. Hatty says if women couldn't have a new hat sometimes they would make more trouble for the Government than the Germans have dreamed of . . .'

'Everything is rules and regulations, but we're luckier than most,' Beth put the paper down as the doorbell rang. She got up and went through to the hall, leaving the door open so that Lizzie could hear as she answered it and invited whoever was there inside. 'You'd better come through to the kitchen . . .'

A young woman dressed in a grey coat and a jaunty red hat with a feather followed behind Beth. She looked ill at ease and seemed hesitant to say what she'd come to say.

'My name is Vera . . .' she began, looking from Lizzie to Beth. She'd taken off her gloves and was twisting them nervously. 'You'll probably think I've got a damned good cheek coming here . . .'

'Do I know you?' Beth asked and then, her voice rising indignantly, 'You're engaged to Tony. You were getting married – at Christmas in '41?'

'Yes, we were, but something happened and his leave was cancelled. I haven't seen him since that November and now . . .' Vera took a deep breath. 'Well, the truth is, I've met someone else. He's an American and we're getting married as soon as he gets permission from his commander . . . but I've come about Tony . . .'

'Spit it out then,' Beth said warily.

'Well, I know you used to go out with him and the thing is . . . he's been hurt bad and shipped back to England. He's in the hospital in Portsmouth and they contacted me to go and see him. I can't, because . . . I can't face him after I wrote and broke it off . . .'

She floundered to a finish, looking red in the cheeks and nervous. 'So you want me to visit in your stead?' Beth stared at her in disbelief. 'You rotten little cheat. Do you mean he doesn't know you've ditched him?'

'Well, I told you I wrote, but he didn't get the letter, because his CO thinks we're still engaged . . . I thought I'd tell him face to face, but now he's in hospital and I can't do it. Would you visit him and tell him . . .?'

'Of all the cowardly, disgusting things!' Beth glared at her. 'What he ever saw in you I don't know. Yes, I'll visit Tony, not because you've asked me, but because if I'd known he was hurt, I would've gone anyway.'

'You will?' Vera looked relieved. 'I'll probably be moving out of London soon, when my feller gets posted to his new billet I'll be going with him in married quarters . . . at least that's what I hope, so I shan't be able to look after the shop. I've brought the keys round for you . . .' She handed them to Beth, who gave her a disgusted look but accepted them. 'Thanks. I didn't know what to do when I got the letter asking me to visit – but then I thought of you . . . I know Tony still likes you . . .'

Beth led the way to the door, opened it without a word and then shut it behind Vera with a snap, her eyes dark and angry as she returned to the kitchen and Lizzie.

'Have you ever heard anything like that? I should think he's well rid of her – leaving him in the lurch when he really needs help.'

'When shall you go down, Beth?'

'Tomorrow,' Beth said. 'Tony and I go back a long way, Lizzie. He's still my friend and I need to tell him about Vera – see what he wants me to do about his shop. I can get an assistant to look after it for him, but someone will have to do the ordering and bank the takings. You can't leave it all to a new girl who hasn't done it before.'

'Well, you could do that yourself,' Lizzie suggested mildly. 'You spend three days at the workshop, but that still gives you time enough to look after Tony's business. You could oversee it, and there must be plenty of responsible people who would love an assistant's job – an older woman or man perhaps . . .'

'Yes, I'm sure there are,' Beth said, she'd already mentally stepped into Vera's shoes, but there was a more pressing issue on her mind. 'Vera said he was badly hurt . . . what do you think that means, Lizzie?'

'It could mean anything. She obviously hadn't bothered to inquire as to the nature of his injuries . . . would you like me to come with you to the hospital? Aunt Miriam would look after Betty and your mum would have the twins.'

'Oh, Lizzie, yes I would,' Beth said. 'I told you we met that day in the market? It was just after Bernie . . . and I was really down. Tony bought me a drink . . .' Beth was remembering. 'I thought he was going to marry Vera – but I do care for him. I suppose I always did in my way. I know he isn't interested in taking the twins on; he made that clear when I was still carrying them, but I care if he's all right – I care if he's in pain. I want to help him as much as I can.'

'Yes, that's natural,' Lizzie said. 'I understand how you feel, Beth. Perhaps Tony may have second thoughts if he comes through this – it might be a second chance for you, love.'

'I wish . . .' Beth shook her head. 'No, I won't start wishing for the moon. I'm just going to be there for Tony, visit him and help him when he comes out of the hospital . . .' She suddenly sat down, her face white. 'Oh, Lizzie. I don't think I could bear it if . . .'

'Just stop that,' Lizzie said sharply. 'Vera had been asked to visit. He must be alive and the doctors clearly think a visit from his fiancé would do him good – so just hang on to that and pray . . .'

'At least he's alive,' Beth said. 'I didn't think I would see him again. I thought he would be married and that was the end of it, but now . . .' Her throat caught with tears. 'I'm frightened,

Lizzie – supposing he doesn't want to see me instead of Vera?'

'I think he'll want to see you – but you may have to prepare yourself for seeing him if he's badly injured?'

'It's Tony, Lizzie, and no matter what he's like now, I have to help him to get his life back . . . just the way you've helped me since what happened with Bernie . . .'

Lizzie saw the fear in Beth's eyes. She'd been brave all the time they'd been on the train but now she was beginning to get anxious. Lizzie wasn't sure whether it was what she was going to see when she was taken to Tony's bedside or telling him about his ex-fiancé – or just generally feeling nervous.

'I'm going for a walk round the town,' Lizzie said. 'I'll be back in an hour. If they put you out of the ward before that I'll meet you in the canteen.'

'All right,' Beth said and walked up to the desk. She inquired about Tony's whereabouts, was asked a few questions and then returned to Lizzie. 'He's only allowed one visitor a day and I'm it. I'll see you later.'

'Yes,' Lizzie said and squeezed her waist. 'It will be all right, I promise.'

Beth nodded and walked off in the direction she'd been given. Lizzie went back to the hospital entrance and stood outside in the cool air. At least it was dry. She could walk into the town and have a look round but she would be back in plenty of time, because Beth was bound to be upset when she left Tony . . . but at least she knew that he was still alive.

Lizzie knew now that it was more than likely that Sebastian had been killed. Seventeen months had passed and she'd heard nothing from him. She was a fool to go on hoping, but Lizzie couldn't let go. Something inside her just refused to give up hoping.

Beth gave her name to the nurse in charge of the ward and was directed to the bed at the end of the ward. There were screens separating each bed and that made her heart catch, because she thought it might mean that the patients were dangerously ill.

'How is he today?' she asked.

'About the same,' the nurse said. 'You can have twenty minutes with him, but he is still very easily tired so you mustn't expect too much.'

Beth walked towards his bed, her heart pounding, because she wasn't sure of Tony's reaction when he saw she'd come instead of Vera. She paused outside the screens, took a deep breath and then went in. She felt her throat tightens she saw the white bandage around his head. The lower half of his face was unscathed, but there was a red line just beneath where the bandage finished. A cradle in the bed held the bedclothes off his legs;

one arm lay atop the sheets but Beth's stomach turned as she realized that the left arm of his pyjama top was empty. He'd lost an arm . . . For a moment the pain of it took her ability to speak, but then in another heartbeat she'd recovered. Whatever her pain and shock she had to be strong for Tony, because he would need her.

'Tony,' she said softly, because his eyes had remained shut even though she was sure he sensed someone was here. 'It's Beth . . . I wanted to see you . . .'

'Beth . . .' Tony opened his eyes and for a moment hope flared and she knew without a shadow of a doubt that he wanted to see her, even though the look had gone in an instant and he was frowning. 'It was good of you to come all the way down here – who told you?'

'Vera came to see me,' Beth said, because there was no point in pretending. 'I'm so sorry, I have to tell you . . . She has found someone else, Tony. She gave me the keys to the shop and, if I have your permission, I'll find an assistant and look after things myself until you come home.'

For a few moments Tony just stared at her, then inclined his head, a slight twist to his mouth. 'If you remember it was what I always wanted . . . for you to look after the shop and . . .' the words died on his lips but Beth knew that it was a reproach for her refusing his request when they'd been courting before the war. She'd been so young then, not ready to settle for being tied to a shop, but now she knew she would give anything to turn back the clock.

'Oh, Tony, please don't . . .' she begged because it hurt, especially when he was lying there so pale and still. 'I wish . . .'

'What do you wish, Beth?'

Tears caught the back of her throat and she couldn't speak for emotion, but then she sat on the edge of his bed and her hand reached for his; he seemed to resist at first but then took her hand in his own. 'I wish we could go back . . .'

'So do I,' he said fiercely. 'You don't know how much . . .'

Beth was close to tears. She knew she had to steady things down, for both their sakes.

'We can't change things, but I can look after the shop if you want? I work three days a week for Lizzie, but that gives me plenty of time to do your accounts, order your stock and make sure everything is running properly. If you'll trust me to choose a new assistant to serve in the shop?'

'I don't have much choice . . .' he said, a note of bitterness in his voice, but then shook his head. 'I'm sorry, I didn't mean that, Beth. If you have time . . .'

'I'll make time for you, though I can't promise to turn the business round immediately . . .'

'Well, you won't do any worse than I did,' he said flatly. 'I might have known Vera would run out on me the minute she found something better.'

'I'm sorry, Tony. I didn't like telling you, but you

had to know.' Beth pressed his hand, her throat tight with what might have been sympathy or even love, because seeing him was making her remember how much she'd cared for him. 'I didn't want to hurt you . . .'

'You haven't told me anything my mother hasn't already hinted at,' Tony said bitterly. 'She thought I was a fool to break up with you, Beth. Go round and tell Mum that you've taken over managing the shop. She thinks Vera has been helping herself to the till for months, so she'll be pleased.'

'Oh, Tony. I am so sorry.' Beth wanted to put her arms about him, hold him and take his pain away, both mental and physical, her eyes stinging with the tears she couldn't shed.

'Nothing for you to be sorry about.' He closed his eyes for a moment. 'They tell me I'm lucky. Most of my injuries are superficial. I'll be out of here in another month or so . . . and the loss of an arm is nothing. I'll have an Army pension and maybe a desk job somewhere – I might even get a false arm if I'm lucky. Some of the chaps were promised their prosthetic limbs ages ago and they're still waiting. Too many of us, I suppose – dumped on the scrapheap now that we can't fight . . .'

Beth was close to tears. He was so bitter and she couldn't blame him; he'd lost an arm in the service of his country and he'd lost the girl he'd loved because she'd gone off with another man and she couldn't even be bothered to tell him herself: little wonder that he was angry. Suddenly, she knew that it was important to her that he survived, came out of this as a whole man ready to live again and find happiness. She bent down to him, willing him to hold on to her, to her strength and her love. Yes, the love she'd once felt for his was still there, perhaps it had never gone away.

'You can fight, Tony,' she said fiercely. 'You can fight the way everyone is – by not letting them kick you when you're down. Maybe you will still have to do a desk job for a while, but if they give you a pension and demob you, you'll have the shop. It was what you always wanted, your ambition to have a newsagents and tobacconists like your grandfather . . .'

'I wanted the shop, but I imagined you looking after it and me working, bringing in a wage so that we could really get on – make something of our lives . . . have a nice house and a car.'

'Well, perhaps you can find some sort of a job. Not what you were doing but something else . . .'

'Don't humour me, Beth. I get it from my mother all the time when she visits – I don't want it from you too.'

'Please yourself,' Beth was suddenly angry, desperate to pull him out of his despondency. 'You always were damned hard to please, Tony. You can lie there and wallow in self-pity for months if you really want to – but you should work at getting out of that bed so someone who needs it more can get in. Yes, you've lost and arm but you're alive. Don't throw that gift away by moping here. The hospitals are overflowing and the nurses have more to do than look after you.'

Tony stared at her, his eyes opening in shock. Beth knew she'd taken the wind out of his sails, so good, let him get mad at her; it was better than feeling sorry for himself, even though he had the right. Suddenly, he gave a harsh laugh.

'You never did let me have my own way, did you, Beth? I was a bloody fool to let you go – I should have hung on to you tight.'

'Yes, why didn't you?'

'Pride, I suppose. Why did you let me go?'

'Pride, I suppose.' Beth smiled as she saw the beginning of hope in his eyes. Now he looked more like the old Tony – the man she'd loved, but there was something more mature, something new she liked there too. 'Well, do you want me to take care of the shop until you're ready to take over?'

'It would be a start,' Tony said and there was a definite gleam in his eyes now. 'How did you get in here? Sister said only relatives or my fiancé could visit . . .'

'Well, I was your fiancé once, so I lied,' Beth said. 'I wasn't going to come down here just to be turned away, was I?'

'No, not you,' Tony said and he was smiling the way she remembered so well. His hand gripped hers with renewed strength. 'So I've got to fight, have I? Fight to get on my feet and out of here

– fight to lead a normal life . . . and what do I get if I do all that?'

Beth leaned down so that her face was opposite his. She bent and brushed her lips over his softly, a naughty smile in her eyes. 'Well, we'll just have to see, won't we?'

'Donkey and carrot?' Tony asked, amused.

'I've got a big stick I can use instead,' Beth challenged and he held up his hand in mock protest.

'Don't think I'm quite up to that yet, Beth.'

'Your time is up,' a nurse said, coming round the screens. 'I'm sorry, but Sister is very strict about visiting times for our boys . . .'

'My fiancé had a long journey to get here – couldn't you let her stay a few more minutes, please?'

The nurse gave him a long hard look and then nodded, 'Well, you've certainly cheered him up, miss . . .'

'Beth – and thank you, nurse. I'll only be a few minutes more.'

'Ten minutes, because Sister will be here after that and she'll have my guts for her garters if she catches you still here . . .'

'She's all right, Nurse Joan,' Tony said as she left them alone. 'When can you come again, Beth? I know it's a lot to ask; you've got work and the twins . . .' He grabbed her hand. 'What I said to you about them when I first knew you were pregnant was rotten. I was jealous and angry and I wanted to hurt you. I'm sorry, Beth.'

347

'It's all right,' she said and squeezed his fingers gently. 'It was a long time ago, Tony and we've both grown up since then . . . You mustn't worry about the shop. I'll make sure things are up and running as quickly as I can – and I'll try to get down to you every weekend.'

'They might transfer me to London soon,' Tony said. 'You're right about them needing the bed for more seriously ill patients. Once I can manage to get out of bed by myself and go to the bathroom alone, they'll send me closer to home. Unless they send me to a rest home for a while, but I'd rather come home . . . to you.'

'I want that too, Tony. I'll come down again next week – and now I'd better go. I'll write to you in the week . . . Oh, I nearly forgot, I brought some grapes . . .'

'Thanks, the nurses will enjoy them,' Tony said. 'We all give our fruit and sweets to them, because they have to put up with so much from us when we first come in.'

'All right,' Beth said and bent to kiss him briefly. To her surprise he caught her behind the head with his good hand and kissed her firmly on the lips. She smiled when he released her. 'That's better . . . I expect to see you out of bed when I come next time.'

'Yes, doctor,' Tony said and sent her a mock scowl. 'Thanks for coming, Beth. I know it can't have been easy for you – but like Nurse Joan said, you've cheered me up.'

Beth touched his hand and then turned away and went round the screen. She deliberately didn't look back because her eyes were blurred with tears. Tony had cheered up because she'd reminded him of old times and brought him out of himself, but what kind of a future did he have to look forward to – what did any of the men in this ward and all the other wards have to look forward to?

This wretched, wretched war had robbed them of their health, their limbs and so many of their lives. Tears were trickling down her cheeks as she made her way to the canteen. It wasn't fair and it was going to be hard, but Beth was determined to make things better for Tony somehow.

'Miss . . .' a voice called to her and she stopped, seeing the Sister approaching. 'I'm glad I caught you. You've been visiting Sargent Tony Armstrong. How did he seem?'

'He was a bit down at first, but he cheered up a little when we talked.'

'Yes, that's what we'd hoped, Miss . . . I'm sorry I don't know your name?'

'It's Beth Court,' Beth said.

'You're Tony's fiancé?'

'Yes, I am.'

'And you're prepared to stand by him?' Sister asked

Beth raised her head, a gleam of determination in her eyes. 'Yes, of course.'

'Good. He has some way to go yet – one or perhaps two operations and then a period of convalescence, which we'll try to arrange in London so that he's nearer his family.'

'What operations?'

'There is some shrapnel in his leg . . . and we're not sure about his head wound yet, but the doctor will know more soon.'

'I see . . .' Beth took a deep breath, because getting Tony better might be even harder than she'd thought, but she would support him and pray for him and hope that was enough, because she wasn't going to give up on him. 'I'll be around whenever I'm needed.'

'Very well, Miss Court.' Sister nodded and walked off, leaving Beth to continue to the canteen.

Lizzie wasn't back yet so she ordered a cup of tea and sat down, but made no attempt to drink it. She hadn't let Tony see her shock and grief, but she knew he was still in pain and despite the fact that she'd made him smile, the anger and bitterness of war was still there inside him. She could only pray that somehow they could make a future together.

Lizzie looked at Beth as they sat on the train. She'd bought magazines for them both but neither of them felt like reading. Her hand reached for Beth's and held it tight.

'Was it very bad?'

'No, not really. I thought he might be worse than he is – but lots of men have lost limbs. Tony's alive – and he has his shop. He has a lot more than many other men who've been wounded.'

'Yes, but I know you. I know you're worried.'

'He was so bitter at first – then I managed to pull him out of it, but I'm afraid he'll slip back when I'm not there. We're hoping he will be transferred to London soon for rehabilitation, but it probably won't be for some weeks yet. He has a piece of shrapnel in his leg that has to come out and they're not sure about his head wound yet. He will be under supervision for a while . . .'

'At least he's alive,' Lizzie said. 'You said he wasn't scarred facially?'

'He looks much as he always did, though I think he'll have a scar on his forehead – but none of that matters . . . it's what he's like inside. What kind of a man he will be?'

'You're thinking of the way Bernie treated you?' Lizzie reached for her hand again. 'Don't, Beth, don't even think it. Tony wouldn't hurt you, believe me. He always loved you, even after you broke up.'

A little shudder went through Beth. 'I want to believe that, and I do love him – but I've heard women say their husbands are changed by the war . . . some of them become violent.'

'Tony might be angry and bitter, love, but not with you. Remember the way it was between you and don't let Bernie's cruelty overshadow your lives. You've been getting on so well, putting it behind you. Tony needs you, you can't let him down.'

Beth lifted her head and smiled. 'I know and I'm just being silly – I suppose it's reaction. It's not going to be easy – he's going to resent what happened to him.'

'Yes, of course he will,' Lizzie said, 'but in time he will accept it and you'll have a chance of a good life together. You're going to need to be strong for Tony, Beth – and forget Bernie. If you love him, Tony has to be your priority.' Lizzie hesitated, then, 'Why don't you take some time off and spend a few days with him? You could leave the twins with your mother. I'm sure Aunt Miriam would be glad to help too.'

'What about his shop?' Beth said. 'I can't just leave it closed or he'll lose everything.'

'I could find someone to look after it for you – and I'll order anything that's short for the moment. You can sort it out properly when you get back.'

'I suppose I could . . .' Beth looked at her, a gleam of excitement in her eyes. 'We could go to the shop tomorrow – and you know what sort of person we need in there . . .'

'Yes, I do,' Lizzie said. 'As a matter of fact, I might know the very person. Jean was telling me about her sister-in-law. Her husband is away in the Army; she has to work to provide enough money for her kids, but she hates working in a factory and she used to work in a shop like Tony's before the war started. I'll ask her if she can help out if you want . . .'

'She sounds just right,' Beth said. 'You don't mind if I take time off from the showroom?'

'We'll manage, although I'll miss you. But it's what you need to do for both of your sakes, Beth. Tony needs support to get him through this – and you need to be with him, to get to know him again. After all, it's a long time since you were going out together . . .'

'It seems like a lifetime,' Beth said and her throat caught on a sob. 'I wish none of it had happened, Lizzie. I wish I'd married him and worked in the shop when he asked me.'

'You can't wish the twins away?'

'No . . .' Beth shook her head. 'No, not them, I love them – but all the rest . . .'

'We'd all like to change things,' Lizzie said. 'I wish I'd gone to work for Sebastian when he first asked, and yet then I wouldn't have met Ed or had Betty. We both have memories, Beth. Some of them good, some of them bad – but they make us what we are, love.' She shook her head sadly. 'I just wish I had another chance to be happy . . .'

'Sebastian will come back to you if he's alive.'

'Yes, I know. Sometimes I'm so sure he is, so sure he's thinking about me – at other times I feel close to despair, but I have to carry on and wait . . . it's what we all have to do, Beth.'

CHAPTER 26

Lizzie looked up as the door of the office opened and a man in a grey suit entered. She frowned, because she didn't know him and wasn't expecting any salespeople or visitors.

'Your receptionist told me to come through,' he said and offered his hand to her. 'I'm Richard Forrest and I work for Black, Forrest and Grant the solicitors . . .'

'Is something wrong with my lease or have I broken Government regulations?'

'Nothing of the sort, Mrs Winters. Some time back we had an official letter informing us that your husband was missing presumed dead and naming you as his next of kin. I wrote at the time but you didn't reply. You hadn't been in touch with us so we thought you might not be aware of your husband's will naming you as his sole beneficiary . . .'

'No, I wasn't aware, though Sebastian told me he would make provision for me,' Lizzie said. 'I'm afraid I never received your letter, Mr Forrest. The reason I didn't think it necessary to contact anyone was that I don't believe my husband is dead.

He is missing, but as far as I've been told they haven't found proof of his death . . .' She caught her breath. 'Was your reason for visiting me important?'

'Yes, I believe so. Your husband owns quite a few properties, Mrs Winters. Some of them are let to the Government for the duration and the rent continues to be paid annually, as before, which is one of the reasons we needed to speak to you. Your husband had it paid into an account, which at the moment you could not access.'

'I have no wish to access it. Besides, surely we have to wait seven years before Sebastian is confirmed dead in law?'

'Yes, that's true, but your husband was a thoughtful man, Mrs Winters. He wrote it into his will that if after eighteen months he was still missing and nothing definite had been decided, you would be entitled to dispose of the property if you wished or to use the capital – I imagine he didn't want his business affairs to be a burden to you. I was instructed to contact you if it became necessary and ask for your instructions in the matter of his property.'

'I have no need of either the capital or the income for the time being . . .' She wanted to push him away, to stop him, because to hear him discussing Sebastian's property was like admitting he was dead. Yet she had to face up to it, and she had to do whatever was needed – for Sebastian's sake. He would expect her to look after things and not let them slide.

'I realize this must be painful for you – when you have a funeral and closure these things can be dealt with, but in this case we shall have to manage the property for your benefit until your husband returns or . . .'

'What about the other properties?' Lizzie asked quickly, because her throat was tight and it hurt too much to listen to him speak in that way of Sebastian.

'Yes, well, there is the lease on your husband's own house. He lent it to some American friends for as long as they required it and they are leaving for home next month – we need to know if you wish us to lease it to similar clients?'

'No, I don't think so,' Lizzie said. 'Do you have the keys?'

'Yes, of course. You could view it after the sixth of June if you wish?'

'Yes, I should like to see it,' Lizzie said. 'I'm not sure what I would wish to do with it if – if my husband did not return, but I have not yet given up hope, and I wouldn't dream of selling his home while there is hope.'

'Quite. So you wish it to remain empty for the moment?'

'Perhaps we might engage a part-time house-keeper to look after it – keep it aired, warm in winter and so forth?'

'Would you like me to see to it for you?'

'Yes please,' Lizzie said. 'Was there anything else?' She wanted this interview over and him gone, because this was too painful.

'Captain Winters made several investments that are due to end soon – would you wish me to reinvest in similar projects?'

'That I can't answer until I know more about them,' Lizzie said. 'I suggest we have a meeting after I visit the house – and then we'll decide what is best. However, no assets are to be sold or disposed of until my husband returns or . . .' she shook her head. 'If that is all for the moment . . .' She just wanted him to go, because it hurt too much to think about the future without hope of Sebastian ever returning.

'Yes, Mrs Winters. I must say you seem to have a clear head for business. I hadn't expected that, but I am glad to know that you've taken charge.'

'In my husband's absence I must look out for his affairs,' Lizzie said. 'Thank you for calling on me – I shall be in touch soon.'

'Yes, of course. I shall leave you my card.' He placed it on the desk, inclined his head and went out.

Lizzie sat down feeling as if all the air had been squeezed from her body. It seemed that everyone was accepting that Sebastian was dead – everyone but her. She blinked hard, determined not to let the tears fall. She wouldn't give up and she was angry that the solicitors had assumed he was dead, whereas she'd only been told he was missing. No one knew for sure and it wasn't right just to dismiss him like that.

'Sebastian,' she whispered. 'Please don't be dead,

please come back and prove them all wrong, my love. I want you . . . love you so much . . .'

Lizzie wasn't going to sit and feel sorry for herself. She got up, pulled on her suit jacket and set a hat on her head. Ed was expecting her to visit him at Oliver's workshops and that was just what she intended to do.

A smile touched her lips as she thought of her great friend and partner. She wasn't sure, but she suspected that Ed had recently met a young woman he rather liked. Her name was Anne and she was a buyer for a prestigious chain of fashion shops in London, Birmingham and Manchester. He hadn't said anything to Lizzie yet, but her name seemed to come up in his conversation quite often.

Walking to her bus stop, Lizzie's thoughts turned to Beth. She'd gone down to Portsmouth to be with Tony as he prepared to have the operation on his leg. When Beth had telephoned her the previous night, she'd said it looked as if his head wound was all right; the doctors were satisfied there was no shrapnel embedded in his skull and the amputation of his arm was no longer hurting him as much. Apparently, the doctors were talking about him being able to come to a hospital in London soon. It was wonderful news and Lizzie was pleased for her friend. Beth had sounded far more cheerful.

'Tony is really pleased that I came down for a few days. He knows I have to be back in London soon, because of the twins, but I've promised to get down as much as I can and he seems set on getting better and out of hospital as soon as possible.'

'You've given him faith and hope in the future,' Lizzie said. 'What about you, love – are you feeling better about things yourself?'

'Yes, I am. I was silly to worry, Lizzie. Tony isn't a bit like Bernie and I like it when he kisses me. I think it's going to be all right . . .'

'Well, just keep strong and it will,' Lizzie had told her. She had to do the same thing herself, because it was hard having to face up to the fact that the solicitors might be right. What use would she have for a shop in the West End and a big house if she couldn't have the man she loved?

'We've employed two new seamstresses and a cutter,' Ed said when they talked in the office over coffee later that morning. 'The government has renewed the contracts for the berets and caps we've been making, and we've just started producing the new line of straw hats you designed for the summer.' He looked pleased to be running the workshops, as if he'd always felt he belonged at the helm. 'But I'll be glad when we can do more of your hats and less of the bread and butter stuff, Lizzie.'

'I was afraid they would want us to continue with the military stuff,' Lizzie said. 'I would rather have turned my full production over to stylish hats again, because the orders are coming in so fast recently that we can't keep up. I think women are so fed up with the Utility fashions that they cheer themselves up with a new hat, and who can blame them with the way things are going? But I suppose we can't refuse the Government work.'

'It's necessary for the moment, Lizzie. Brenda can do it with her eyes shut – and now we have the new staff, I can come back to you two days a week.'

'That is good news,' Lizzie said. 'I do miss working with you, Ed – especially when Beth is away too.'

He nodded and looked pleased, then, 'How is that young man of hers?'

'He has his operation today. If all goes well, Beth should be back at work on Monday. She'll go down again on Thursday and stop until Sunday evening. Her mother doesn't mind – and Aunt Miriam has the kids half the time anyway.'

'I'm glad Beth has another chance to be happy,' Ed said and there was a slightly wistful expression in his eyes. 'Oh, I might be going away for the weekend, Lizzie. I've promised to take a friend to the sea for a couple of days.'

'Lovely. Someone I know?'

'Yes, you've met Anne. She's a widow and she has to support herself and her teenage son . . .'

'Well, have a wonderful time . . .'

'I think we shall,' Ed smiled. 'Something on your mind?'

'You know me so well . . .' Lizzie smothered a

sigh. 'I had a visit from Sebastian's lawyers today. They wanted to know if I required them to re-let his house once the present tenants return to America.'

'And shall you?'

'I don't know what to do,' Lizzie confessed. 'I've only been to the house once – it is beautiful. The gardens were lovely before the war, but I don't know if they still look the same. I intend to take a look around soon.'

'Would you like me to come with you?'

'I'm not sure,' Lizzie said. 'I'm glad of your company often, Ed – but I think perhaps not . . . I want to be alone . . . to sense if he's still there . . .' she gave a self-conscious laugh. 'That sounds ridiculous I know, especially after there have been tenants there for months . . .'

'No, it isn't ridiculous. I completely understand how you feel,' Ed said, 'but if you change your mind – you know I'm always here for you, Lizzie.' He touched her hand briefly.

'Thank you. I might come and find you afterwards,' Lizzie told him. 'I shall need a friend, I think.'

'Sebastian Winters is a brave and resourceful man,' Ed said. 'He's the kind of man who knows how to survive. Something happened and he disappeared – but he might have had a good reason for simply vanishing into thin air.'

'Oh Ed, thank you,' Lizzie said her throat tight with emotion. 'It's what I've been telling myself

– but that solicitor seemed to think it was all cut and dried.'

'I know this much. If Sebastian is alive, he is thinking of you and doing his best to come back to you and Betty.'

Lizzie entered uncertainly and stood in what was obviously Sebastian's bedroom and looked around her. She felt a little as if she were intruding on his privacy, and yet he would have probably hoped she would live here with him after the war. They hadn't decided, leaving it until the time came, but it was his home after all. The room was simply furnished but everything was of good quality; the bed was huge and covered with a black and gold bedspread, which matched the curtains. She thought it was a very masculine room and smiled as she thought of the changes she would make if she ever came here to live: this was the room of a very private man and there were no photographs, nothing personal, apart from a few books in a mahogany bookcase – more like a house that was rented out rather than a home.

She walked over to the bookcase and picked up the first much-used tome; it was a work of Shakespeare and next to it was a French volume by an author Lizzie had never come across before – and next to that were three books written in what she thought was German. She frowned as she saw that one of them had the name of Adolf Hitler on the front and the title was 'Mein Kampf'

362

. . . she dropped it as if she'd been burned, feeling slightly sick.

What was a book like that doing in Sebastian's bedroom?

She bent down and picked it up, replacing it on the shelf beside the others and taking a deep breath. It was silly to react so violently. Sebastian wasn't a traitor just because he had a copy of that hateful book on his shelves . . . no doubt other people had bought them to try to understand the mind of the man who had brought the whole world to war. Yet it reminded her that she knew so little about the man she'd married.

Lizzie felt calmer after she left the bedroom. She'd looked round and seen all she wanted to and it had convinced her that she would never want to live here on her own. Perhaps if Sebastian came home . . . but as the months passed and there was no word even she was beginning to doubt.

What was he doing that he couldn't send a message to her? A little shiver ran down Lizzie's spine as she locked the house and walked away. Whatever it was, it had to be dangerous . . . something very secret, so much so that he couldn't even tell the people he was supposed to trust . . .

CHAPTER 27

'It looks good,' Tony said as he limped up the stairs to the flat above the shop. 'You've improved the way the shop is set out and it's much better up here . . . you've even got the bed made up . . .'

'I wanted it to look nice for when you came home,' Beth said and took his hand. 'I know this is just a visit and you have to go back for more rehab treatment – but I wanted you to have your own home waiting . . .'

'Thank you, because I was dreading going to my parents' house. Mum thinks I can't do anything for myself. I think she would come to the toilet with me if I let her.' He looked at Beth, his eyes steady and fearless. 'I've come through the war, love, and a hell of a lot better than many of my friends – and now I want to think of the future. Life is what we make it and I don't want pity from anyone – even my mother . . .'

'Your mother loves you and she wants to make things better for you, Tony.'

'She can't change what happened, none of us can,' Tony said and frowned. 'I can't do everything,

364

but I can manage to dress myself and shave – and I wear shoes that don't need lacing. It all takes longer and it looks awkward, but I can do most of it. I can manage; I can face life even if I have lost an arm, but I can do without being fussed over.'

'Yes, I know,' Beth said. 'That's why I thought if you had your own place . . .'

'It's just what I need, somewhere I can get away from well-meaning people.'

'Does that include me?'

'You know it doesn't,' he said and put a hand on her arm. 'Come here, Beth. I want to kiss you . . .' She moved closer and he put his arm about her, holding her firmly. His head bent and his mouth moved over hers, kissing her in a way that left no doubt about his feelings for her. 'I want to marry you, Beth – I want to look after you and the twins, for things to be as they should have been long ago. Will you let me?'

'Are you sure that's what you want, Tony? I know you've been through a rough time, but you don't have to feel grateful or . . .'

'Don't be daft,' he murmured, bending his head to caress her lips with his. 'I love you and I want you – that's if you can bear it after what Bernie did to you?'

'You're not him,' Beth said, lifting her head proudly, 'and I always regretted that we quarrelled. I care about you a lot . . . and yes, I can bear it because I'm not going to let that man ruin my life. You'll have to be a little patient, but remember that I love you and I want you . . .' She smiled up at him. 'Kiss me again, Tony, because it was lovely . . .'

'Yes, it always was good and I was a damned fool to think that anyone else would do. Sex for the sake of it is okay, but it doesn't really mean anything unless it's the right person.' He laughed softly, drawing her close. 'I never stopped loving you' Tony said fiercely. 'I wish I'd made sure of you, years ago . . .'

'So do I . . .' she said and tears were on her cheeks. 'I wish it so much . . .'

'Why are you crying?' Tony asked, smoothing away her tears with his fingertips. 'You're not thinking of him – the twin's father?'

'Mark was a young girl's love, exciting and an adventure, but it would never have lasted, because we were from different worlds – and now I've come full circle and I'm back where I belong . . .'

'I'm glad,' he said and bent his head to kiss her softly. 'So when will you marry me, my darling Beth?'

'Just as soon as you're ready,' she whispered against his ear. 'I can't wait . . .'

'I can't believe it's my wedding day,' Beth said to Lizzie as she handed her the beautiful hat she'd made for her. The wedding was to take place at the Registry Office that gorgeous hot day in August, and Beth was wearing a pale blue suit that had been designed by Lizzie and made in her workshops, as was the gorgeous creation in white satin and tulle she had just placed on her head. Her pale hair had been freshly cut, washed and styled, and everything she was wearing was new. Lizzie, Aunt Miriam and Beth's mum had pooled what clothing coupons they had so that Beth could get married in something smart. 'I never thought I would marry again . . .'

'You are happy, aren't you, love? You're not doing this just for Tony?'

'No, I'm doing it for me,' Beth said. 'It's what I want, Lizzie. We're going to live in the flat over the shop until we can find a decent house. It isn't ideal but it's all we can manage . . .'

'No, it isn't,' Lizzie said, 'because I'm offering you this house at fifteen shillings a week, Beth – if you'd like it?'

'But you can't do that,' Beth said. 'You've already given us a lovely wedding gift. This is your home – where will you live?'

'I'm going to move in with Aunt Miriam for now,' Lizzie said and smiled at her friend's shocked look. 'Yes, I know you're lost for words, but it's what I want to do, Beth. This is your home and it is just right for you and your family. I'll be fine with Aunt Miriam for the time being. She has a big house and she asked me if she should sell it, because she's leaving it to me and then Betty – so I decided we might as well live there together for a while at least. Hatty is going to be leaving me soon, because one of her daughters-in-law wants her to move to the country with her – so it makes sense to move in with Miriam. She adores Betty and will love having her when I'm at work.'

'But will you be happy at Aunt Miriam's place? It's a bit old-fashioned and dark. Why don't you move into Sebastian's house? I remember it was beautiful, what little we saw of the house when we went to that party years ago. You haven't let it to tenants, have you?'

'No, and I'm not going to,' Lizzie said. 'I'm keeping it for Sebastian until . . . one day in the future I might sell if I can't manage it, but not for a long time yet. I'm not sure I want to live there, and I definitely don't want to live there alone. Aunt Miriam's house is all right; it has a big garden and it's not far from my work . . .'

'But don't you want a shop in the West End? I mean you've sort of got one . . . haven't you? Sebastian's old shop . . .'

'Yes, Sebastian wanted me to have everything if he didn't come back. I've been to look round, but it is being very well managed for me,' Lizzie said and shook her head. 'One day I'll have to face up to it, Beth, but I can't just take over Sebastian's life, even if his will gives me the right.'

'You might marry again . . .'

'I suppose one day – if I know for sure that he's never coming back and I fall in love again,' Lizzie shrugged carelessly. 'For the moment I can't even think about it. All I know is that I'm waiting for something . . .' She was waiting for Sebastian to come back, even though common sense told her he was lost to her, but she couldn't give up, because then she and Betty would be alone.

Beth moved to hug her. 'Lizzie, I've found happiness again. I didn't think I could after what happened with Bernie. It was the shame of the way he used me, I suppose, and I wondered if I'd ever want to be touched again . . . but when Tony kissed me it was so sweet and lovely I knew everything would be all right . . .'

'I'm so glad for you,' Lizzie said, tears stinging her eyes. 'I knew you'd suffered at that monster's hands and I was afraid you might not recover from it – now I can feel really happy for you.'

'Everything is just perfect,' Beth told her. 'Are you sure about offering us the house, Lizzie? Tony told me he wanted to find one like it for us and the children, because we're hoping to have a big family. At least another two . . . he'll be so excited when I tell him. He's proud and he may want to buy it from you one day. We can move in here after we get back from honeymoon, if that's all right – and then he can let the flat over the shop and that will pay our rent here. But I'm sure you could get more for it . . .'

'I want you to have it and you can tell Tony that he can buy it when he's ready. Honestly, Beth, you'll be doing me a favour.'

'Oh, Lizzie, I'm going to miss you, love.'

'I'll miss you too – but you'll have Tony and life will be so much happier for you.'

'Yes, you're right. Tony is getting so much better. He asked me to thank you for finding out about that place where he can get his new arm done privately rather than waiting for the military hospital to call him in.'

'I heard about it from one of my customers whose daughter had to have her leg amputated because of blood poisoning,' Lizzie said. 'It will make him feel more independent when he learns to use it.'

'Beth, are you ready love?' The bedroom door opened and Beth's mother entered, wearing a heather tweed suit she'd bought before the war with a new pale lilac hat that Lizzie had made to compliment it. 'The cars are ready to leave, dearest. You don't want to be late.'

'No, I don't,' Beth said and laughed because she was excited and happy. 'Lizzie says we can rent this house for three pounds a month if we want to – aren't we lucky?'

'Yes, you are lucky to have such a kind and generous friend,' her mother said and looked at Lizzie with surprise but also pleasure. 'That is very generous of you, Lizzie.'

'I'm moving in with Aunt Miriam for a while. She wants to have us there and she ought to have her turn looking after Betty. She adores her, but Bert wouldn't allow it much when he was angry with me,' Lizzie replied. 'I don't want to live here alone and I'd need a housekeeper and someone to care for Betty – of course Sebastian has a beautiful house if I want it . . .'

'I understand it's very large,' Mrs Court said. 'You wouldn't want to live there alone, Lizzie – and it's so far from all your friends.'

'Yes, that is the trouble,' Lizzie said. 'I'm getting more used to it, because I go over every so often and make sure the heating is working and everything is as it should be . . . though of course I have someone who looks after it for me. She cleans twice a week and checks it most days . . .'

'It's not like someone living there. Perhaps you should let or sell it . . .' Beth's mother glanced at her watch. 'We must go down. The cars are already here and your father is getting impatient, Beth . . .'

Beth looked out of the hotel window. Tony had brought her to a small resort on the Devon coast and their hotel was at the top of a winding hill, which the taxi had struggled up earlier in the evening. The stars were out in force, because it was a clear night and they seemed to be reflected a thousand times in the silver sheen of the sea as the waves moved restlessly to and fro, breaking on a spur of black rock that jutted out from the cliffs.

'It's so peaceful here. You could almost forget that there's still a war going on,' she said as Tony came to stand behind her, his arm going around her and holding her close to his body. She could smell the fresh smell of soap on his skin and feel his arousal through the thin material of her night-gown and felt a tingle of pleasure. She'd half been dreading the night, fearing that her experiences at Bernie's hands would leave her cold, but Tony's kisses had melted the ice inside her and she knew that she was ready to love again and to be happy. After all, she'd known the pleasures of physical love once before with Mark – and Tony had been her first innocent love; her fighting spirit was back and she was determined that nothing would stop her taking the happiness that had come her way. She had seven days to relax and think of nothing but making love, walking along the cliffs, and eating leisurely meals that someone else had cooked. 'We're so lucky, Tony. You've come through the war and we have a good life ahead of us.'

'Yes, my darling, we are lucky to have each other,' he said and kissed the sensitive spot at the nape of her neck. 'I thought I'd missed my chance with you and at first I didn't care if I lived or died – but after I saw you again in that café I knew I still wanted you, loved you – and I'd made up my mind to tell Vera, but she was so excited about the wedding that I couldn't. You have no idea how relieved I was when you told me she'd found someone else.'

'I felt so awful about telling you,' Beth said and turned in his arms. 'I thought you were upset over it?'

'I just hated it that I'd lost an arm and I didn't think I could ask you to marry a cripple – and then you told me you were going to look after the shop and you kissed me . . . and then I knew it was worth trying to get better . . .'

'And do you still think so?' Beth whispered and laughed as he pulled her hard against him, and she pressed closer, seeing the answering fire in his eyes.

'Get to bed, you wicked woman, and I'll show you,' Tony said fiercely. 'You're mine now, Beth, and I don't ever intend to let you go.'

'That's good, because I don't want to go anywhere without you . . .'

CHAPTER 28

'Well, I think I'll go up,' Hatty said and yawned. 'It has been a long day and my daughter-in-law is calling for me early in the morning. She's taking me to see the cottage they've found for me. Apparently, it's just across a narrow lane from where she and my eldest son are going to live now that he's been invalided out of the Army with that weak chest of his. The doctors told him he needs country air and he's going to join a country practice of lawyers. John is an intelligent man and he made a good officer. It was a pity his Army career had to be cut short, but he says he's more of a liability than an asset these days, with that cough of his.'

'When do you think you will leave?' Lizzie asked. She was going to miss Hatty who had been more than a housekeeper these past months.

'In about two weeks, I should think,' Hatty said. 'It will need some restoration and there's the furniture. I have a few bits in store, but we'll need more.'

'Well, I shall move into Aunt Miriam's house in a few days, but you must feel free to stay on here until Beth and her husband return.'

'I can stay with my daughter until I'm ready to move,' Hatty said and sighed. 'I've enjoyed working with you, Lizzie, and I shall miss you, and especially Betty, because she's such a sweetheart and I've loved her – but my place is with my daughter-in-law. She has three children and with John likely to have bouts of sickness, she will need help.'

'Yes, of course. I perfectly understand,' Lizzie said, 'but we'll miss you.'

Hatty smiled, picked up her mug of cocoa and left the kitchen. Lizzie sat down at the table and sipped her own hot drink. Life moved on and things changed. Hatty leaving was another setback, because she would miss her. She was going to miss Beth too, but she would see her at the workshops three mornings a week. It wouldn't be the same though. Beth was happy now and her husband and family would come first. With Hatty leaving her as well, Lizzie was aware that she would find a large hole in her personal life. She had the workshops and her friends there and she had more money than she'd ever imagined having . . . even a stylish shop in the West End, where her own hats were selling to customers who paid highly for the privilege. Yet it wasn't enough. Her dreams had all come true, but without love – without that one special person in her life – it wasn't enough . . . not nearly enough. Lizzie needed her husband and Betty needed a father . . .

Lizzie finished her cocoa and put the mug into hot soapy water to wash. She was thoughtful as she went upstairs to look in at her beloved daughter sleeping peacefully. She was so lucky to have her darling little Betty. It was wicked of her to feel lonely and sorry for herself when she had her daughter – or to feel sometimes that life was hardly worth the effort.

Betty was hers to love. The child had no father and only an elderly great-aunt to love her if her mother wasn't around. Lizzie must make the best of life for her daughter's sake. Betty would go to a good school; she would have pretty clothes and a chance to make something of her life and Lizzie would do her best to keep her safe from harm.

She decided that she would visit Sebastian's house again the next day. It was a Sunday and the housekeeper didn't visit then. If it was nice she could have a picnic in the garden with Betty – and perhaps she could make up her mind to sell the house.

It was a long time since she'd been told Sebastian was missing without trace, and she knew it was foolish to go on hoping he would turn up. If he were alive someone would know – she would have heard by now. Surely he would have found a way to get in touch with her?

Beth was right, Lizzie was still a young woman, even though she felt much older than her years. She had to let go of the past and then perhaps she might find someone she could love again.

★   ★   ★

Lizzie had spread rugs in the garden and unpacked the picnic basket. She'd brought cheese rolls, apples, ripe tomatoes and some small sweet almond cakes she'd made. Betty loved them and crumbled them all over her as she looked around in excitement at the strange new place she'd been brought to. Clutching her cake in one hand, she was up on her chubby legs and toddling from one new thing to another. She would be three in September and chattered away when she felt like it, but she wasn't a noisy child, not like Beth's twins!

Sebastian's roses were in bud and beginning to scent the air, and the grass had daisies growing, their yellow hearts open to the sun. The lawn needed a cut, Lizzie thought, wondering if she had the energy to find the mower and push it over at least part of the lawn. Alfie Jackson, the new housekeeper's teenage son, was supposed to cut the lawns and tend the garden at the weekends, but he obviously hadn't been for a week or two. She would have to discover why and perhaps get another gardener.

Betty had sat down on a patch of grass warmed by the sun. A hungry robin was taking advantage of the crumbs she had scattered, hopping closer and closer to where she sat and gobbling up the delicious morsels. Lizzie smiled as she saw her daughter watching the tiny bird with its bright red breast. Betty was obviously enjoying her visit to this beautiful garden, and Lizzie remembered her first time here, when she and Beth had come to display their stylish hats at one of Sebastian's parties in the hope of getting Lizzie's name known as a designer. It seemed such a long time ago since she was that young girl . . .

Lizzie had felt out of place amongst so many fashionable people and she'd wandered further into the garden, across the little bridge over the large pool. She'd sat on the bench and watched from a distance until someone came to fetch her and after that she'd enjoyed herself, mixing with the guests and talking about her hats.

Betty was up on her feet, running after the robin that had flown further into the garden – towards the pool. Lizzie rose quickly and ran after her daughter, afraid that she might fall in.

Reaching her darling Betty, she took her tightly by the hand and walked her over the bridge to the bench. Lizzie wondered what it would be like to live here, to have a house filled with children running in and out – and to have time to play with them and watch them grow. She hadn't had enough time to be with Betty – not as much as she ought, but sitting here enjoying the peace and quiet, she decided that she was going to spend more time with her in future. Hearing her daughter laugh as she saw the robin descend on their picnic basket and help itself to a large piece of cake, Lizzie thought what a wonderful sound it was. Betty was happy here . . .

Taking Betty safely back away from the pool, Lizzie gathered up the debris and scattered more crumbs for the birds. As she walked away, Betty scampering in front of her, occasionally sitting down suddenly on her bottom or taking a tumble only to get up again and laugh; Lizzie realized that she too was happy, more relaxed than she'd been in a long time.

She went into the kitchen and put the basket on the scrubbed pine table. It was cool despite the heat of the day, spacious and well equipped, much bigger than her kitchen at home. Perhaps she would be foolish to think of closing up such a lovely house. She had intended this to be her last visit, and only to the gardens, but now she decided to have another look round.

She walked through the downstairs rooms, noticing that everything was beautifully cleaned and smelled of polish; the curtains had been drawn back to let in the light, which was a little strange – unless Mrs Jackson thought the house could do with some sunlight to warm it. Actually, it made everything seem warmer and nicer, Lizzie realized. She'd only seen the downstairs rooms shrouded in dust covers, though she vaguely remembered it as it had been on the day of the party. Suddenly, she started pulling the covers off tables, chairs and settees, bringing it all back to life. The dark shapes became beautiful objects again, what had seemed a mausoleum became a home once more; antique chairs and cabinets, and comfortable squashy chairs to relax in by the fireplace.

A house could only be what its owners made of

it, Lizzie thought. She left the dust covers lying on the floor for the moment and went upstairs. She hadn't explored many rooms up here, because the book she'd found in Sebastian's rooms had upset her, but now she started exploring the bedrooms one by one, discovering large sunny rooms – including one that might have been a child's room. It had a large rocking horse, a doll's house, two pretty dolls with china faces sitting in a Victorian-style chair and a teddy bear sitting on the bed.

Betty gave a squeal of delight, ran ahead of her mother and bounced onto the bed, grabbing the soft toy and chattering to herself as she nursed it. It was the first teddy bear she'd seen to Lizzie's knowledge and it was clear that she loved it as she crooned and held it to her face.

Lizzie laughed, because the toys here were old but still in wonderful condition. It was impossible to buy anything comparable now and Betty had very few toys at home. Suddenly, feeling a surge of joy such as she hadn't felt for years, Lizzie picked her daughter up and put her on the back of the rocking horse, setting it in motion. Betty shrieked with glee, bouncing up and down in her excitement.

'Mumma . . . go faster . . .' she pleaded and screamed in delight as Lizzie rocked her faster. Betty clung on and refused to be parted from her new toy, complaining when Lizzie tried to lift her off, clearly not ready to abandon her treat.

Judging her to be safe enough, Lizzie left her to

play while she explored one or two of the other rooms. There was a beautiful room decorated in colours of soft rose and cream, with painted and gilded furniture and a shaped dressing table with glass pots with gold-plated tops. It was obviously the room of a woman who had been spoiled – perhaps Sebastian's mother, if this had been his family home.

Once again, Lizzie realized that she knew so little of her husband's former life. She went next to the room she knew was his and opened the door, looking about her at the furniture and the huge bed; she'd never seen such a lavish one and it made her smile to think of Sebastian there. She wandered about, feeling both pain and pleasure as she touched his things and wondered if she could really smell the scent of his cologne, and then she heard a shriek from down the hall. That was Betty! Lizzie ran from the room back to the child's bedroom where she'd left her daughter. A man was bending over the child on the rocking horse, making it move faster and faster, and she realized that Betty had been screaming in pleasure.

'Who are you? What do you want here?' she demanded fiercely, heart racing with alarm.

Lizzie moved forward as the man turned and looked at her and then gasped as she saw his face, because she knew him and yet she didn't . . . the scar that ran from the corner of his left eye to his chin was red and livid, and his hair at the sides was almost completely grey. He had aged far more than he should in the months that they had been apart, and yet it was him.

'Sebastian . . .' she said in a hoarse whisper, her body beginning to tremble with shock and disbelief as she moved towards him. 'I thought when she screamed . . .'

'Lizzie darling . . .' Sebastian opened his arms and she moved into them, feeling as if she were dreaming. 'My dearest love . . .'

'Is it really you?'

'Yes, it's me. I'm real, not a ghost . . .'

'When I saw you I was afraid because I didn't know it was you . . .' she felt choked with emotion, too stunned to go on and hardly able to believe her own eyes.

His arms closed about her and he bent his head, kissing her hungrily. 'Lizzie, I've missed you so much. You have no idea . . .'

Tears wet her cheeks as she gazed up into his beloved face. 'You've been away so long and you didn't write . . . I was told you were missing believed dead. All this time I've been left wondering . . .'

'Nineteen months and twenty-five days since I left you,' he said in a voice hoarse with emotion. 'I've counted it to the minute and it's been like a lifetime. I couldn't write, Lizzie. If I'd done anything that could betray my cover it might have killed others – people who relied on me . . .'

'You've been doing dangerous work for the Government, haven't you?'

'Yes, things I couldn't tell you and still can't – but that doesn't matter now.' He glanced down. Betty was pulling at his sleeve, wanting him to rock the horse again for her. 'She's so beautiful, our little girl . . .'

'Yes, she is,' Lizzie said, 'and the sweetest little angel you've ever known. She's quiet at the moment but sometimes she chatters away for hours . . .'

'She's like her mother then . . .' His eyes were on her face, smiling as he said, 'Betty loves the horse, just as I did when I was a child – and my sister. We shared this room until we were seven and then I went away to boarding school . . .'

'You didn't tell me you had a sister?'

'There are a lot of things I haven't told you, Lizzie.' His eyes were just as blue and just as bright, even though he'd changed so much. 'Some of them I couldn't speak of – talking about Sarah was one of them. You see she died of diphtheria that summer, the summer I went away to boarding school – and I never saw her again. For a moment when I saw Betty I thought . . .'

'You thought your sister had come back?'

'Yes, just for a moment,' Sebastian looked so sad that Lizzie's heart caught. 'I never came to this room after she died. Mother gave me another when I returned home for her funeral and then I went back to school – and later on to higher education in Germany . . .'

'In Germany?'

'Yes; before the Nazis really got going there were

some excellent schools for young men like me. Now, I wouldn't be allowed there.' Sebastian smiled oddly. 'My grandparents were Austrian Jews, Lizzie. My father married an Englishwoman and came to live here. He always wanted his parents to come and live with us – but they wouldn't leave Austria. They believed they were safe there even when my father warned them years before it all started that Hitler would destroy all the Jews if he could . . .'

'What happened to them?' Lizzie asked in a hoarse whisper, because she'd read some of the horror stories in the newspapers about the way Jews had been treated.

'They died before the war started,' Sebastian said, a nerve flicking in his cheek. 'They were very old, Grandfather ninety-three and Grandmother eighty-nine. I think they never got over my parents' deaths . . . *they* were killed in 1936 on a visit to Austria. It was supposed to be a car accident, but I learned later that the brakes of their car had been tampered with. My father was an academic and he had been speaking out against the rise of fascism . . .'

'Oh, Sebastian, no . . .' Lizzie's throat caught with tears. She looked at him, because he was like a stranger, someone she didn't know – had never met before, and yet if anything she felt closer to him than ever before. The man who was always teasing her, always setting her a challenge wasn't here; this man went deeper and had many scars that he'd kept hidden for years. He was a man she knew she could always trust, and share her thoughts with. 'I'm so sorry.'

'Don't be. It no longer hurts me.'

'How long have you been here today?' her eyes were pricking.

'I've only just arrived,' Sebastian said. 'I went to your house but you weren't there. Miriam Oliver told me you might have come here – and then I saw the dust covers had been removed and heard Betty up here . . .'

'We've had a picnic in the garden. I suddenly had a fancy to see the rooms without dust covers and then we found this room – I didn't know it was off limits. I'll take her out of here.'

'Why? These things were made for children. If she enjoys them that is a good thing.'

'You don't mind her touching Sarah's things?'

Sebastian shook his head. 'No, that has all gone now. I was happy to see our daughter playing here, Lizzie.'

'I'm glad . . .' Lizzie faltered, her throat tight. She was a little nervous of this stranger, even though when he'd kissed her it had seemed he was the same – her Sebastian, but their greeting had been instinctive. She could see that he had changed, suffered. Was he still there inside? She could only pray that whatever he'd suffered hadn't fundamentally changed the man she loved. 'When did you get back?'

'A couple of days ago. I've had hours of

interrogation and debriefing, because I wasn't able to make contact for a long time – that's why they sent you that letter. It was thought I was probably dead, but I had to keep moving and the information I was gathering was sent in by various operators . . . I couldn't let anyone know it was me, because there was a traitor in the group and until I could expose him he would have betrayed me and others to the Germans . . .'

'Should you be telling me this?'

'No, probably not, but I want you to understand, to realize why I couldn't let you know I was still alive. I always intended to come back to you – but I had a job to do and I couldn't come back until it was finished – besides, it's over for me, Lizzie. I can't go back out there. Too many people want me dead because of things I did . . .'

'Were you in a lot of danger?' she asked, sensing what it was costing him to talk about his experiences.

'I worked at the German headquarters using a false identity for a time after I left the group . . .'

'You worked for the Germans? Sebastian . . . you couldn't have changed sides?' Lizzie went cold all over as she remembered the books she'd seen on his shelf.

'No, my darling, I had to make them think I was one of them; it was the only way to get close to certain people and obtain the information we needed. I was sent out there for that purpose, because my German was so good. Some of the group may have thought I'd changed sides for a while, but one person knew what I was doing all the time, even though he couldn't tell London for fear the traitor got wind of it . . . you see we didn't know for sure who he was until he made a fatal mistake, but he won't betray the group again.' A bitter smile twisted his mouth. 'Believe me, no one hates the Nazis more than I do, Lizzie.'

'Then why . . . why did you read that awful book upstairs?'

'You mean Hitler's book?' He nodded and then laughed. 'Did you think I'd gone over, Lizzie? No, my love. In my opinion it's always good to know the mind of your enemy; in his own way Hitler is clever, but twisted and evil, perhaps mad.'

'No, I knew you couldn't have, but at first I couldn't understand why you would have such a thing. Did you get the information you wanted?' Lizzie was desperate to understand, because it hurt that he'd let her suffer so long. 'Was what you did very important?'

'Yes, it was very important, and I got what we needed in the end. There was a lot more to what I did, Lizzie – things I could never tell you, even if I wasn't bound by the secrets act . . . believe me, I'm not proud of them, but they had to be done.'

'You were a soldier even if you didn't wear a uniform,' she said. 'I expect most of you did things you didn't want to . . .'

'Yes, I'm sure we all have . . .'

'And they won't send you out there again?'

'I doubt I'd be much use to them now – there's a

price on my head and certain members of the German Gestapo would like to get their hands on me.'

'Oh Sebastian . . .' Lizzie shivered. 'Is that why you look so . . . tired?'

'I think you mean old,' he said wryly. 'It has been a hard few months, Lizzie. I'm hoping they'll give me a desk – or let me train . . . people like me . . .' He hesitated, then, 'This is classified information, but I know it will go no further – the Germans are developing deadly new weapons. I was able to bring details of various sites back with me, but if they're not stopped it could prolong the war.'

Lizzie was shocked that he'd told her something that was obviously top secret. He was trusting her to keep his secrets and it humbled her, brought tears to her eyes as she said, 'Things had seemed to be getting a bit better recently . . .'

'Yes, I know, but the war isn't over yet, my darling. I wish I could say it was, but I'm afraid there's a long way to go . . .' He reached out and took her hands. 'That's all I can ever tell you, my darling – is it enough to help you forgive me for causing you so much pain?'

Lizzie swallowed hard and then smiled and gripped his hands tight. 'Yes, of course. I'm honoured you told me so much, and you know I shan't tell anyone – but I'm glad I understand a little bit of what you went through, Sebastian . . .'

'I hate that there has to be any secrets between us, but there are still people in the field who could be in danger if I said too much to anyone . . .' He smiled, bent his head and kissed her. 'Have you forgiven me?'

'Yes, if there was anything to forgive . . .' Tears trickled down her cheeks, but they were tears of happiness. She could scarcely believe that he was here with her, alive and her own darling Sebastian, just as she longed so often. 'It's so good to have you here, Sebastian. Would you like something to eat – and a hot drink . . .?'

'Yes, please.' He smiled as she lifted Betty from the horse. 'Did you say you'd had a picnic? I would love a proper cup of English tea . . . but I must wash my hands . . .'

'I've got fresh milk in the refrigerator. I'll go down and put the kettle on . . .'

In the kitchen Lizzie went through the motions of boiling water, rinsing the teapot and setting out the cups and saucers. She settled Betty in the high chair that she now knew had been used by Sebastian's sister and gave her some orange squash and another bun, which she proceeded to crumble all over the tray in front of her.

'Will you have to go away again soon?' she asked when Sebastian came back from the bathroom.

'I still have some important people to talk to, but then I'll get a good long leave before they relocate me . . .'

'Important people?' she asked uncertainly.

'The very highest,' he said and grinned at her. 'Winnie wants to see me next weekend. He's going down to Chequers and he's asked me to bring you and Betty . . . you'll have tea with his wife, Lizzie. Apparently, she's a fan of your hats . . .'

'No!' Lizzie stared at him in utter disbelief. 'You don't mean it – me having tea with Mrs Churchill . . .'

'Well, why not? This is England, after all . . . and believe me, Lizzie, there's no other place like it in the world . . .'

'Oh Sebastian . . .' Tears started to her eyes, because he was still the man she remembered and loved. 'I've been so afraid . . . afraid that you were dead and I would never see you again.'

'Lizzie, my love.' Sebastian put down his cup and got up, coming round the kitchen table to take her into his arms. The next moment she was sobbing into his shoulder; she just couldn't hold the tears back, as all the grief and fear of the past few years came pouring out of her.

'I thought I might never see you again. I was so lonely . . . so empty without you. Nothing seemed to matter much. If it hadn't been for Betty . . .' She looked up at him tearfully. 'I want us to have lots of children, Sebastian. I want us to be together and . . .'

Whatever else Lizzie had to say was lost as he kissed her. Such a sweet passionate kiss that her body felt as if it were dissolving with pleasure, melting into him. All the doubts she had, all the soul-searching she'd done, didn't seem to matter now that she was back in his arms. Maybe she didn't truly know the man she'd married, but he was still there, the man she'd fallen in love with – and she had years to discover all the rest.

Lizzie didn't go home that night. They slept in the room that had once belonged to Sebastian's mother, Betty in a big cot Sebastian had fetched from somewhere. She slept soundly after a day of playing with so many toys she didn't know which one to pick next, and since she'd cried when Lizzie had tried to part her from the teddy, it was tucked up in the cot with her.

Lizzie lay in her husband's arms after they'd made love over and over again. Neither of them wanted to sleep, because it was too good to be together, to touch and kiss and discover each other's bodies all over again. They had had such a short time together when they were first married that it was like another honeymoon, but perhaps even better. Having experienced a long parting, Lizzie wanted to hold him forever in her arms and so when she woke to find the bed cold beside her, she felt bereft and wondered for a moment if it was all a dream – but she wasn't in her own bed.

As she rose to pull on a dressing gown that smelled faintly of roses and which had also belonged to Sebastian's mother, she smelled bacon frying and ventured downstairs to the kitchen. Sebastian had Betty in the beautiful old-fashioned high chair and she was sucking a tiny piece of bacon and clearly enjoying the taste. Besides the frying bacon, tomatoes and eggs, there was already a rack of toast and some marmalade in a dish.

'Where did all this come from?'

'They gave me a new ration book so I went out and blew the lot on provisions,' Sebastian said and smiled. 'I was going to bring a tray up in a few minutes, but Betty wanted a piece of bacon.'

'She does like it,' Lizzie said and saw how happily her daughter was chomping away. 'I mostly give her egg because it's easier for her, and we don't get much bacon now . . . you don't mind it then?'

Sebastian looked puzzled and then laughed. 'Because my grandparents were Jews? No, my mother was a good Christian and brought me up to be the same. My father wasn't any religion really. I think he actually questioned the existence of a god, but he believed in allowing everyone to follow their own faiths. I might incline to his way of thinking these days – but to all intents and purposes I'm C of E, just like you . . .'

'Good, because that's what I want our children to be . . .'

'Our children, Lizzie?'

She laughed as his brows rose. 'Well, I'm hoping there will be a few – as I told you yesterday.'

'And what about your ambition to design beautiful hats?'

'Do you recall telling me once that all you required of me was to design lovely creations you could sell, that I could have others to look after everything else . . .'

'I do vaguely remember,' he said, his eyes intent on her face, 'and would you be happy with that, Lizzie?'

'I think I might, most of the time – though I might want to make a few special ones myself, and to visit the workshops occasionally, but I'll be content to be a wife and mother – if it's what you want too?'

'You know the answer to that,' Sebastian smiled as he set a plate of sizzling bacon in front of her. 'I've always seen you here in my home as my lover and my wife, the mother of my children – but I want you to have your dreams, Lizzie.'

'My dreams have all come true,' Lizzie said. 'I'd like you to look after the business side of things and let me design and make beautiful hats – but to do it here, in my own home with my family about me . . .'

'We can have housekeepers and nannies, and people working in the shops and the workshops,' Sebastian said. 'You've had to work hard and I know things were difficult for you for a long time – now I want to take care of you. I want to give you the earth . . . to spoil you and Betty . . .'

'She is already in seventh heaven,' Lizzie smiled up at him. 'I was going to move in with Aunt Miriam – but now, if you don't mind, I'll offer her the chance to come here . . .'

'We have plenty of room,' Sebastian said. 'It's a long time since this house really felt like home. I filled it with people and gave big parties, but I hated being here alone. When I got up this morning and saw you in my bed, and Betty putting her arms out to me to be picked up, I suddenly realized what was missing all those years.'

'We'll make it a home together, Sebastian.'

'I was a fool to stay here alone with my ghosts for so long . . .'

'We both have ghosts to chase away,' Lizzie said and moved close enough to kiss him. 'You know most of mine, but I didn't know about yours until you told me yesterday – and I'm glad you have.'

'Bring Aunt Miriam here if you want – Beth and her twins too if you like. The sooner this big house has a family to fill it the better . . .'

'Beth is married to her old love, but I'll ask her to visit often, because Betty loves the twins and Beth's like a sister to me.'

'Then she's my sister too, because I want to share everything with you – if you'll let me?'

'Yes, my darling. We'll fill the house with love and laughter and people,' Lizzie said and looked up at him, her love flowing out to surround him and draw him into their own special place. 'And the more of them that are children, the better . . .'

'Amen to that,' Sebastian said and from a room somewhere above them it seemed to Lizzie that for a moment she heard the sound of childish laughter and a rocking horse.